SKINHEADS

John King is the author of six previous novels:
The Football Factory, *Headhunters*, *England Away*, *Human
Punk*, *White Trash* and *The Prison House*. *The Football
Factory* was made into a hit film in 2004. He lives in
London.

JOHN KING

Skinheads

JONATHAN CAPE
LONDON

Published by Jonathan Cape 2008

2 4 6 8 10 9 7 5 3 1

First published in Great Britain in 2008 by
Jonathan Cape
Randon House, 20 Vauxhall Bridge Road,
London SWIV 2SA

www.rbooks.co.uk

Addresses for companies within The Random House Group Limited
can be found at:
www.randomhouse.co.uk/offices.htm

The Random House Group Limited Reg. No. 954009

A CIP catalogue record for this book is available from the British Library

ISBN 9780224064477

The Random House Group Limited supports The Forest Stewardship
Council (FSC), the leading international forest certification organisation. All
our titles that are printed on Greenpeace approved FSC certified paper carry
the FSC logo. Our paper procurement policy can be found at
www.rbooks.co.uk/environment

Mixed Sources
Product group from well-managed
forests and other controlled sources
www.fsc.org Cert no. TT-COC-2139
© 1996 Forest Stewardship Council

Typeset in Bembo by Palimpsest Book Production Limited,
Grangemouth, Stirlingshire
Printed in the UK by
CPI Mackays, Chatham ME5 8TD

For Mike King
A free spirit

ESTUARY ENGLISH

Original Skin

TERRY ENGLISH STRETCHED AND yawned and focused on the rain chipping at his living-room window, eyes following a silver thread as it shunted sideways, chugging against the flow, eventually forced to stop, an inky teardrop swelling, frustration growing, turning to anger, finally exploding and charging on – twice as strong. He reached for his mug and finished the last mouthful of coffee, leant his head into the couch and wished he was back in bed. He was knackered. Cream crackered. His thinking slow, body aching. Lightning fizzed outside and April's face sparked, her hair soaked and make-up smudged, ears dripping skinny pearls. He counted the seconds, waiting for the thunder to explode, heard a shotgun empty both barrels, three miles away.

Every time it rained he said the words April Showers, and he whispered them now, and while it wasn't very funny, not exactly Judge Dread class, his wife always smiled and answered May Flowers. She never let him down, and he heard the murmur of her voice, smelt perfume and nail varnish, the damp of her clothes. They both loved the rain, the ragged storms tearing across the rooftops, sheets of music skidding off slates. He turned and stared at her photo, trimmed inside a black frame, felt the years bubbling, squeezed his right fist so tight the tattoo on his forearm stretched, a Union Jack ready to burst. His face clouded, but April pouted and teased, blonde feather-cut catching the white light of summer, pure blue eyes full of love. Everything was possible. They loved the sun as well as the rain, and it was a good job. This was England. You never knew what was coming next.

April blew a kiss and Terry frowned: medicine playing tricks.

He stood up, broke the spell, went over to the back door and looked out across a soggy lawn to the field beyond, the land hidden from the dual carriageway by a thick wall of trees, ferns and brambles, an overgrown hedge of hawthorn and purple wire on his right, two tinker ditches beyond, houses filling the other two sides. He searched for Bob and Molly, and found them in their shed, looking out from under a rusty boot-boy roof, watching the rain feed heavy meadow grass. Bob was the older of the two horses, past his prime and with dashes of white in his black Crombie coat, but strong and distinguished, a healthy presence. Molly was younger, smaller and more nimble, and Terry smiled as she glanced at Bob, when he wasn't looking, as if she was watching out for the big lump, at the same time letting him think he was in charge. That's how he imagined it, anyway. He loved watching the horses, his normal smile quickly returning. The people in the houses were brand new, the horses safe, fed with sugar and carrots and all sorts. It was a good place to live. He was a lucky man.

Terry had done well for himself. The mortgage on his three-bed semi was paid off, he ran his own firm, and had money in the bank. Mind you, he'd earnt every penny, was an old-firm grafter, even if he was happiest sitting in the boozer with his pals, a pint in his hand and a classic ska tune on the jukebox, looking forward to the football, playing pool and having a laugh with the boys. He was the first to identify April as the brains behind his success. He owed his comfort to her. She was the one with the ambition, and had pushed him, but having a few bob had never changed either one of them. His interests were the same as when he was a teenager, and it was hard to believe he was going to turn fifty soon. He told himself he didn't care. Had more important things on his mind. And he had seen enough boring teenagers and snappy pensioners over the years to know it was how you lived and conducted yourself that mattered. A boy of fifteen could be ten times more clued-up than blokes in their seventies, while an eighty-year-old woman could have more sauce than ten sixteen-year-old girls put together.

Life was what you made it, and he had always made himself see the best in people.

He closed his eyes, ready to nod off on his feet, knew he had to show his face at work, make sure everything was ticking over. He'd had yesterday off and being the boss meant he had responsibilities. The sickness would pass, and he sighed and wondered about his son Laurel, hoped he would turn out okay. He had left the house early and Terry wondered where he was, what he was doing. With his two daughters in their twenties and settled down, it was Laurel he worried about. He was only fifteen and boys his age could get into some serious trouble. Terry knew that from experience and was glad life was easier these days, that the aggravation and anger of his youth had faded, but he still worried. It was only natural. It was hard for the boy not having his mum around.

The phone rang.

– 456 *is* my number.

– Terry, you fat cunt, get out of bed.

It was his old mate Hawkins, working for him after twenty years driving coaches, long hours ferrying mobs of pensioners down to Bognor and Selsey Bill, Dave Harris and his squad into Leeds and Leicester. Hawkins was glad to be behind the wheel of a minicab, and kept the rest of the firm amused with stories of him and the boss in their youth, tales that got so tall and fat that after a while Terry didn't recognise himself, dismissed them as fiction. But everyone enjoyed some social history, especially the younger lads, glad to know they were part of a tradition.

– You up yet?

– Course I'm up.

– Bet you're standing there having a wank.

– Not me.

– Staring out the back window thinking of Angie, doing the old knuckle shuffle.

Terry looked over his shoulder, worried he was going to find his friend's ugly mug pressed against the glass.

– Now why would I being doing that?

– Come on, mate, she's fucking gagging for it.

– Do me a favour, will you.

– You must be fucking blind. She fancies you something rotten. Poor girl doesn't know what she's letting herself in for, though, does she?

Terry saw April jumping back as she undid his Sta-Press for the first time. Later she would hum 'Big Nine' when she was in the mood, emphasising the complex lyrics. He loved April and he loved Judge Dread, but Hawkins had sex on the brain. He was fresh back from Thailand and had been spending too much time with The General.

– I'm old enough to be her dad.

– What's the age difference? Fifteen years?

– Something like that.

– Fifteen years. She's thirty-four.

– There's nothing there.

– Drop some Viagra and there will be.

Hawkins rambled on and Terry drifted. He yawned and the bloke got to the point.

– I'll be in The Rising Sun at half-three, four o'clock. Got to see this geezer about those shirts I brought back from Thailand. You fancy an early start?

Terry perked up.

– Let me know when you're on the way and I'll knock off early.

– All right. Better go, I've got a fare.

There was a pause.

– Dear oh dear, look at the lungs on that.

The line went dead.

Terry grabbed his mug and washed it up, wished he'd had some proper breakfast. His doctor had him on yogurt and fresh fruit, organic muesli and orange juice, all sorts of health food he was trying to like, but what he really needed was a fry-up. It was the one thing he could cook, and he did it in style. He went back over to the window, the rain easing a little, saw Bob and Molly strolling out towards the middle of the field.

Pulling his Crombie on, Terry stopped in front of the

mirror in the hall and smiled. He dressed smart and moved with the times, always wore a neatly ironed Ben Sherman shirt and Levi jeans, his hair shaved in a number two crop, the main difference from his youth the air-ware soles of the Timberlands he sometimes wore to work. Even those matched the DM model. They said everything was different these days, but nothing had really changed. The skinhead style had gone mainstream years ago, even if the kids traded under different names. His cherry-red Doctor Martens were upstairs, polished and ready for action, and to this day he never went to football in anything else. DMs and a black Harrington. The combination had never been bettered. He saved his brogues and tonic suit for special occasions, proper skinhead nights. And he was a skinhead all right. One of the originals.

He left the house and climbed in his Merc, slipped a CD in, eased off the drive to the sound of 'Gun You Down' by The Ethiopians. He was soon on the road linking Uxbridge and Slough, through George Green, the Five Rivers on his right, flying an Indian flag and advertising lager, curry and satellite football, The George on his left with its St George's Cross and the same essentials, plus a Sunday roast for £5.99. He spotted Major Tom in the allotments and slowed down, not sure if it was because of the speed cameras or the Major, passed the site of the Drill Hall where he had trained as a young man, demolished and replaced by flats, and those weekends away with the TA had given him the chance to do the sort of things you couldn't do on your own, wouldn't even think of trying. Salisbury Plain and Brecon Becons were the two places he remembered best, camping out and seeing the stars like he'd never seen them before.

Terry thought about his father and that magical night in Salt Park, eased the memory away as he crossed the canal and railway bridges, was soon in the small roads near the high street, parking under the Estuary Cars sign, waiting for 'Harry May' by The Business to finish, pumping himself up for the day. It was the only Oi song he listened to, passed on by his nutty nephew, an aggro-merchant gem in the Slade tradition. He grinned. 'Gun You Down' meets 'Harry May'. Two versions of the skinhead world.

– Morning, he announced, entering the office.

He was glad to be back, enjoyed company, quickly bored on his own. Life was all about staying positive, dodging the horror.

– Hello, Mr English, Angie beamed. How are you feeling?

He smelt coffee, heard a radio mumbling in the kitchen, the radiator tapping out messages as it circulated a musty brand of heat.

– Tired. Must've been one of those twenty-four-hour flus.

– You keep getting them, don't you?

Angie was in charge of the office and, Terry knew, more or less ran the firm. She was sharp and efficient, and though cheerful enough she was tough when she had to be and could handle the drivers. The boys didn't take the piss with Angie around. She was also gorgeous, proper stunning, and easily fitted in with the company's strict dress code. With her shiny black hair cut in a mod-girl style, she really looked the part.

– Did you watch that programme last night? she asked.

Terry had seen it advertised. Called *Skinheads And Swastikas*, it dealt with far-right groups in Eastern Europe, shaven-headed youths in green flight-jackets, *sieg-heiling* for the cameras. He knew it would be the same old bollocks, the chance for the ponces in the media to boost their egos and pocket some easy cash. They didn't have a clue what being a skinhead was about, and didn't want to know either. But he refused to get angry, shut all that shit out.

– I went to bed early, he said. Any good?

Angie's eyes flared and her mouth bent out of shape.

– It was rubbish. Who pays people to make stuff like that? She handed him a video.

– I recorded it for you. I thought you would miss it, being ill and that.

It was nice of her to go to the trouble, but Terry wasn't interested, had seen it all before. He took the cassette and put it on his desk. He sat down, looked at the mess of letters,

8

papers, sweet wrappers and an empty milk carton. He drummed his fingers on a patch of clear wood. He thought for a minute, opened a drawer and took out a packet of biscuits, popped a chocolate digestive in his mouth, held them up in the air. Angie smiled and shook her head, began talking into the radio.

– He asked for you, Ray. He's going to The Moon Over Water.

Terry began tidying his desk, but was soon sitting back and wondering what to do, rocking on his chair. Everything was running smoothly enough.

– I thought Carol was coming in this morning? he said, at last, when Angie was off the phone.

– No, she couldn't make it today.

– She all right?

– She's fine, thanks to you.

Angie was really smiling at him. Terry wished he hadn't asked.

Carol's husband Steve had worked for Estuary Cars before his death, and his widow had fallen on hard times. She was also Angie's cousin, so when Terry found out he gave her enough to pay off her debts and put something in the bank, offered her a job. She had a child to look after and accepted his help. Angie made a big fuss about it, but really he felt bad he hadn't known what was going on. It was easy to forget how important money was when you were flush.

The phone chirped.

– Estuary Cars, Angie sang.

Terry looked at the clock and checked his watch. There was fuck-all for him to do. He had to be honest. He waited for Angie to finish talking, but knew the answer to the question he asked.

– Have you seen Laurel today?

Angie smirked at the name, then remembered herself.

– Lol hasn't been in here, and I haven't heard from him.

Terry didn't like the name Lol, but kept quiet. It made him think of a hippie lolling around all day, skiving when he should be at work. Named after the legendary Laurel

Aitken, Terry was the only one who didn't call him Lol. He wanted the boy to come in and do some work, get a feel for the place, maybe work his way into the firm when he left school, even take it over one day. He was on his half-term, and it was also a chance for him to earn some cash.

Angie saw the disappoitment in his face.

– He's only young, she ventured. He's probably out with his mates.

– I suppose so. I thought it would be good experience, that's all. Put some money in his pocket.

– Think what you were like at his age.

Terry laughed.

– That's the problem. I was always out and about, but I don't want him getting up to the things we used to. I would've jumped at the chance to earn some easy money. I was always ready to work.

The radiator laughed.

– Do you want a cup of tea? Angie asked.

– I'll make it, Terry said, jumping up.

He went in the kitchen and found Gary sitting at the table with a can of Coke and a sandwich, studying a topless blonde bird in the paper.

– How you feeling? his driver asked.

– Still got a pulse.

Gary laughed, not sure if his boss was joking. Terry was famed for his good nature, so he relaxed.

– Did you see that documentary last night?

– No, but Angie copied it for me.

Gary grinned.

– It's one of the worst ones yet. A load of fucking shit.

Terry wouldn't watch it. He had better things to do.

– You know what, Gary said. It's worse than McIntyre.

– Nothing can be that bad.

– Straight up. Worse than that cunt McIntyre.

Terry was feeling rough. He was starving as well. The memory of last night's rogan josh stirred his taste buds. He was a big man and needed feeding, couldn't survive on rabbit food. Chappati Express never delivered a dodgy meal, so it had to be his treatment.

He made two mugs of tea and took them back into the front. The office was small and cramped, the fresh smell replacing old coffee.

– I'm going to go and have some breakfast, he announced, once he'd guzzled his PG Tips.

Angie glanced at the clock.

– It's half-eleven.

– I didn't have anything this morning. Not real food, anyway. I can't wait till dinner time. Do you want something?

– No thanks.

– You sure?

– No, I'm fine. Where are you going?

Terry mulled this over in his head. The cafe round the corner did a fine fry-up, but he'd been in there the day before yesterday and the memory of that curry was suddenly pushing him towards something more spicy than brown sauce.

– I might have a *ke*-bab.

– For breakfast?

– He frowned and Angie smiled sweetly.

– You want me to bring you a kebab back?

– I've made sandwiches.

– You sure?

– Cheese and pickle. They'll do me.

– All right, I'll be back in an hour or so.

Angie answered another call.

– Estuary Cars.

Terry left the office, dodging the oil where so many of the boys paused, engines leaking, a soggy newspaper splashed across the kerb, information melting as the print seeped into the gutter. Gary followed him out and was soon pulling away in his Mondeo, Terry heading off in the opposite direction on foot, not sure now if he wanted a kebab. He looked at the sky and saw more dark clouds blowing in, knew that you couldn't beat the Full English when it was cold and raining. He passed the top of the street where his working-day cafe waited. He was a man pulled in many different directions, the thought of that rogan josh fighting with the promise of a large donner and chips. He was spoilt for choice, glad he lived in a democracy. He had to make a decision and headed for the cafe, knew it was the right choice as he stepped inside and heard thunder crack.

Sitting by the window, waiting for his food to arrive, Terry stared into the street in the age-old tradition, sipping a fresh mug of tea. He trailed people outside, heads down and bodies soaked, two blonde shop assistants screaming as they splashed past, laughing through red lipstick. He saw April, older and wrapped in a blue towel, fresh out of the bath, dropping it on the carpet, parading naked in front of him. She was beautiful as a teenager and improved with age. It had been love at first sight, and the passion never faded. Terry and April – for ever together. They were good for each other. Everyone said so. She had been dead for nearly ten years now, and despite the promises it didn't get any easier. He felt so sad, empty inside, and this wasn't normal, not like him, and he fought back, thought of the fry-up instead, his mouth watering. Lightning lit up the street and he waited for the thunder, counting seconds once more.

Rage and Love

THE LIGHTS CLICKED GREEN and Ray tried to slip into first, the gearstick refusing to connect, and he tried again, had two more goes before pushing harder, doing his best to stay calm, finally slamming it forward one, two, three, four times. His forehead scrunched up and his face turned red. He remembered the old boy in the back seat, and gritted his teeth as he fought the urge to nut the wheel, blood and oil swilling, pulse banging, wasps screaming in his ears.

Singer's old man dealt with most of the Estuary cars, and did a good job at a decent price, but the last thing Ray needed was the expense of a new gearbox, never mind time off the road. He had two beautiful daughters and a stroppy wife to support, as well as the rent on his room at Handsome Mansions. It wasn't right. He worked hard, put in the hours like no one else on the firm, but was only ever getting by. The moan of machines passing in the outside lane increased the pressure in his head, a raw nagging that made him want to damage something, or someone, a too-loud horn making him look in the rear-view mirror. It was no gentle tap either, the insult lasting three or four seconds. The rain had stopped. His stare pierced the mucky windscreen of the Nissan behind. He began to relax.

Two men were busy mouthing insults and shaking their heads, thin lips peeled back, sneering, thinking Ray had stalled. He didn't like people who sneered. He had dealt out a few slaps in his time, kicked some teeth in as well, but he never sneered. There was something sick about a sneer. It showed more than anger, more than hatred. It was nonce-like. When they hit the horn again, a smile jogged across his features, anger shunting in a worthwhile direction. He felt warm, like he'd just stuffed his face with one of his uncle's famous fry-ups, all that heavy food that cheered you up when you had a hangover or were just fucked off with life.

Making sure he was in neutral, Ray turned the engine off and climbed out, unrolling his six-foot-four frame, the hyenas in the Nissan silent suddenly as seventeen stone of skinhead muscle marched their way. The driver saw a huge skull shaved to stubble, liquid blue eyes shining inside marble sockets, plates shifting as Frankenstein's monster blocked out the sun. The div had been watching too much TV, imagined a Neanderthal dragging his rocky fists across pikey scrubland. Nissan Man raised both hands in surrender, while his passenger turned his head away.

Ray's brain was chasing his rage, steaming to catch up and pull it back, but this was nothing new. Known as Nutty Ray in his youth, and sometimes just plain Oi The Nutter, he was a family man these days, even if he had been living apart from his wife for the last four months. He was a dedicated father who worked hard, lifted weights, deserved a drink on the weekend. During the week he had a sociable pint, but stayed sober for his job. He had a high IQ and his teachers had said he was university material, but he was never interested in formal education, preferring the people's poetry of Jimmy Pursey to the purple pose of Byron and Shelley. Because Ray was smart he was always asking questions, never receiving answers. This made him angry. He had always read, from his nights working at the airport as a teenager, but since moving into Handsome Mansions he was going through two or three books a week, a powerful dose of history and politics that was winding him up worse than ever. Inside, Ray was raging. Outside, he stayed calm. He hated that old Nutter tag and was glad he had stamped it out. It was long forgotten.

Ray was a proud man. Proud of his family, his culture and his country. He didn't like people taking liberties. He showed respect and expected it in return. He was a man of principle. He was a skinhead. Proud to be a skin.

Reaching the Nissan, he palmed the window, leaving a massive imprint on the grease, threatening to smash the glass with a drawn-back fist when the driver was slow opening up. The scum inside were in their late twenties and should've been able to back up their sneers, but their arses had gone and, with the window lowered, he leant down and pushed his head inside.

– What's your fucking problem?

– Nothing, mate.

– I'm not your fucking mate.

– It was an accident.

– What do you mean, an accident?

– It was a mistake.

– Too right it was a mistake, you fucking cunt.

Ray stared into the driver's face and saw the weakness of a small-time bully, pale skin cut with hamburger stains, the skid marks of a sneak. He smelt sweat and grime and a druggy sort of slime. He looked past the driver at his pal, a skinny fucker in a Nike baseball cap. A corporate cocksucker. Cheap-logo man.

– What about you?

A soggy head turned.

– We didn't mean it. Honest.

– Get out of the car. Both of you.

– Look. We're sorry.

– We're sorry. We really are sorry.

They'd thought that because there was two of them and one of him they could take the piss. Ray was seriously tempted to give them a slap, but held back. It wasn't going to end with a slap and he was surrounded by people slowing down and having a good look, and there were cameras by the lights. He shook his head, back in control, turned and walked to his car. He turned the key and slipped easily into first, smoothly pulling away as the lights, which had turned red, then moved back to green.

He picked up speed and rolled his shoulders. His wife did a good massage, but he couldn't ask her at the moment. Liz was sick of him and he was staying with his mate

Handsome. Enjoying it, too. He had time to think straight and was near enough to his daughters that he could easily see them. Liz was still talking to him, which was something, and had said he could go round later for some tea. She wanted him to calm down, that's all, stop ranting and raving. He was doing his best, trying really hard. He heard the rustle of his passenger in the back seat.

– Sorry about that, Ray said.

– People are impatient. They don't want to hang around.

– Yeah, they are. No manners.

– Running around changing things when they don't need changing, causing more problems than they solve.

Ray nodded. It was daft getting wound up, but you couldn't let people sneer at you like that. He laughed. It was true what the old boy said.

– Change for change's sake.

He had picked this bloke up before, and was taking him to The Moon Over Water. He was the one who had got Ray reading up on the history of the European Union, one recommendation setting off a chain reaction. Ray had been shocked, naturally hating the betrayal of Britain by the political establishment, but only recently discovering how deep and far back it all went.

– If you say anything, they say you're out of touch, old-fashioned, stuck in the past.

– It's all a con, Ray said.

– I don't mind the internet and mobile phones and the naked birds on Babecast and those other satellite channels, that's great, just wish I could afford to join in a bit more, but you don't have to change every single thing. That's capitalism gone mad.

Mike was in his seventies, and went into the town centre a couple of times a week to meet his pals Gerry and Del. They sat at Table 29 and drew a range of dinner-time drinkers, Mike annoyed that he could only manage three or four pints these days. The buses didn't bother turning up where he lived, a private firm taking over from London Country, the fare not much less than a cab.

– I see Blair's in the clear again, Mike said.

– Teflon Tony, nothing sticks.

– Except Peter Mandelson. Can't get rid of the bastard.

– He's got that plum job in Europe.

– The politicians nobody wants get shipped over to Brussels.

– Chris Patten, Neil Kinnock, Leon Brittan – Tory or Labour, it makes no difference.

– Bloody rubbish, the lot of them. All earning fortunes. The socialists soon lose their values, don't they?

– Same as those so-called Tory patriots.

– True enough. Bunch of wankers.

Ray had learnt how the EU wanted to break up Britain and destroy England, turn it into regions. This desire went back beyond Adolf Hitler to Napoleon, some believing as far as the Holy Roman Empire. War had failed to create a European state, so now the power-brokers were using the short-term nature of human memory, working over decades, the media silent as it guarded its interests.

– Blair wants to be President of Europe, Mike continued. I hate every one of them. Ted Heath should have been shot as a traitor.

– Tony Benn's all right. Listen to him talk on Europe, but he hardly gets the chance. The media censor anyone who doesn't agree. Give everyone cheap credit and they don't bother protesting. To think we fought a war so we wouldn't end up in a dictatorship and this is what we get. It's unbelievable.

Ray guessed there were ordinary men and women who genuinely wanted a United States of Europe, who were actually excited at the thought of a single federal government, but he had never met any of them. The majority didn't know what was going on. You had to go out of your way and dig deep to see what was happening, that a dictatorship was almost formed.

– All it needs is one brave man, Mike laughed. He could pack himself with explosives and blow up the European Parliament.

The professionals Ray heard on the radio were arrogant

and dismissive, callers who thought differently cut off before they could have a proper say. The TV debates were led by media whores who had never had an original thought in their lives, sneering as lone voices in hand-picked audiences questioned the sense in handing sovereignty over to an unelected, foreign, centralised bureaucracy and then hoping for the best. A combination of university brainwashing and careerism ruled, the press no better, the liberal Left full of themselves, the Right full of shit.

– I was in Palestine after the war. I can see why those suicide bombers do what they do. The Palestinians were driven off their land and terrorised. I don't believe in killing innocent people, but if you're a Palestinian maybe you don't have a choice. It's the young ones doing it as well. That's going to happen in England one day if we end up part of the USE.

The television and radio were full of posh cunts and their snivelling lackeys, making fun of everything to do with England and being British. Prejudice was fine as long as it was aimed at ordinary white people. Ray felt his hands grip the steering wheel. It had been the same all his life, but the noose was getting tighter.

– One brave man, that's all. Those suicide bombers aren't cowards. They might be wrong killing civilians, but you have to be brave to die for a cause, to have that sort of belief.

Ray didn't agree with the suicide attacks on the British and Americans in Iraq and Afghanistan, but he understood the logic.

– How about you? Ray asked, grinning. Why don't you volunteer?

– I haven't got long left. I'm an old man.

– That's what I mean. You'll go out with a bang. Your family would be proud of you. You'd be a hero.

Mike thought about this for a while. Ray glanced at his face and saw he didn't fancy the idea, preferred a drink in the pub with his mates.

– They might put a statue of you up on that block in Trafalgar Square.

– Do you think so?

– No, probably not. They're turning it into a piazza or something, for the tourists and yuppies. Ken Livingstone doesn't want the pigeons either, doesn't want them shitting in the cappuccinos. There's another one needs shooting. He doesn't fancy St George's Day, but gives every minority going thousands to celebrate their festivals.

– It could only happen in England. Seriously, suicide is wrong. If you're a Muslim you become a martyr and go to heaven and can chase all the women you weren't allowed to touch when you were alive, but if you're a Christian you go to hell. Or it is purgatory?

– Convert to Islam.

Mike shook his head.

– I couldn't kill innocent people.

Ray nodded.

–You would be in the middle of the European Parliament, and everyone would be fair game. There aren't going to be any passers-by. They wouldn't suspect an older man. Your mate Del knows about explosives, doesn't he?

– He blew up a castle once.

– And Gerry goes over to Amsterdam to see his son.

–You've got a good memory.

Mike looked worried.

–Well, get Del to layer you with explosives, and ask Gerry to take you to Brussels on his way to Amsterdam, stroll into their Parliament and flick the switch. Bosh. Job done.

Mike didn't like the sound of this, but played along.

– I could do it by remote control, use mobile phones. Give the number to my wife. She'd enjoy that.

– She'd have to set it off at exactly the right moment.

– She'd probably do it too early, so excited she wouldn't be able to wait. I'd end up blowing up the pub, just as I was having a farewell pint.

– All you need is someone who has nothing left to live for, Ray went on. It wouldn't even be that brave. Just going out in style.

– Charming.

– I was thinking of someone with a fatal disease.

– It sounds good, in theory, but it would be wrong.

That was the British for you, too fucking decent.

– Tell you what, Mike said, perking up. I'll ask round the pub. People come in and out all day, there's bound to be someone. I'll put a notice up.

Ray pulled over and Mike got out, grinning as he paid, the Estuary driver watching as he turned and headed for the pub, straightening his back and growing a good six inches, new-found energy in his step as he neared the doors. Ray heard Angie on the radio, asking who was nearest Tesco's. He grabbed the fare, back in the flow of traffic as he took the details.

– Is my uncle in the office? he asked.

– He went for something to eat.

– The Full English?

– Wouldn't be surprised.

They both laughed.

Ray circled the roundabout and passed the bus station, put his foot down and was soon pulling over, left indicator tapping as the cars behind flashed right. He heard a horn and mounted the pavement, jumped out, this time to open the boot for a woman struggling with a trolley full of plastic bags and two small boys. It was a silly place to wait, outside the car park, on the main road, with all those fumes, specially with kids. He didn't know why she couldn't grab a taxi in front of the supermarket like everyone else. Mind you, it was easier for him stopping here. He loaded the shopping quickly, arranging it neatly in the boot, and was soon on the move, coming back on himself as he circled the smaller roundabout and retraced his journey along Wellington Street, heading towards Manor Park. He concentrated on his driving as the woman fussed over her children, eventually stopping at the lights by the Nag's Head, earwigging their conversation, glancing down Shaggy Calf Lane, remembering that rockabilly bird who used to live down there. He wouldn't mind bumping into her again, the dirty old cow.

– We'll start making the cake as soon as we get in, the woman was saying.

– Can I help? one of the boys asked.

– And me?

– We'll do it together, then make the jelly and sandwiches. We'll have everything ready for when Barry comes to see us. He's going to be twenty-one. It's a special birthday. He'll be ever so happy. It'll be a big surprise.

The children started singing 'Happy Birthday'.

When the lights changed Ray turned left, the woman explaining things to her boys, keeping them busy with ingredients, and they concentrated, asking endless questions, two little herberts in old sweatshirts and freshly cropped hair. It was nice they were going to the bother, and he started thinking how someone should organise a surprise party for his uncle. It was hard to believe Tel was going to be fifty, a shock really, but he was in decent nick, had always been chunky, and behaved a good ten or fifteen years younger. It must the genes. The amount he drank. The non-stop diet of fry-ups and curries and kebabs, the chips and chinkies. It *had* to be in the genes. Ray was pushing forty himself and had never been fitter. Mentally, he was waiting for age to mellow him out. The sooner the better. His uncle had always been easygoing. He could do with some of that. His uncle had it sussed, stayed calm under pressure. The boys respected him. It had always been the same. Terry English was a gent.

One of the kids stood up between the seats.

– Be careful, Ray warned. If I have to stop suddenly you'll go flying.

– I don't care.

Ray smiled. The kid reminded him of someone.

– You will if you go flying and smack your head on the dashboard.

– How fast can you go? the boy asked.

– In this thing? Ray laughed. Not very fast.

– I bet you can.

– Not as fast as if I had a new car.

– Why don't you get one then?

– Maybe I will one day.

21

– I'm going to have a fast car when I'm old enough. I can't wait to be grown up.

– You stay a child as long as you can, mate. Best years of your life. Go on, sit down now.

The boy did as he was told and Ray stopped for a learner busy with a three-point turn. It was a stupid place to do it, but he felt sorry for the driver, a middle-aged woman wrapped tight in a bright sari, her face dark with worry. She stalled and he smiled, waited while she composed herself.

Ray remembered Terry strolling into the pub with Hawkins and a load of other geezers when he was a boy, and he had swelled up with pride when they stood with him and his friends at the bar. Terry didn't have a bad bone in his body, but was no mug, teased his nephew when he turned skinhead, saying he was more of a punk listening to those Oi bands, decked out in his green flight-jacket and black DMs, his head shaved down to the skull. It was a new version of the skinhead look, while the music was a million miles away from the reggae of the original skins, but he knew his uncle was pleased, glad he wasn't a greaser or a disco ponce. The punk joke was still running as well, and Ray eventually fought back, said that if he was a punk then Terry was a mod. They were both claiming the skinhead soundtrack.

His passengers were talking about the surprise party again and Ray thought of his own family, his house, was looking forward to seeing his girls, the learner moving off, Ray continuing on his way.

Standards

FORCED INTO THE NEAREST pub by another flash of rain, Terry nursed a pint of Timothy Taylor and waited for the downpour to stop. The Full English had cheered him up, the landlord's favourite the perfect afters. All he needed to polish things off was a pool table. He loved the game and played most days, knew every surface within a ten-mile radius, the nearest one a good ten minutes away. He had been playing since he was a boy and not many people beat him, but he wasn't bothered about winning, just liked staying on. It was the best way he knew to relax – measuring the angles, guessing the possibilities, planning ahead – and he soaked up the colour of the balls and the smell of the baize and the weight of the cue and the cracking sound it made when it connected with the white, the echo as the white smashed into a spot, stripe or the black, the feel of the chalk on his fingers and the touch of wood in his palm. The rest of the world disappeared and he was suddenly decisive, distractions narrowed down, the only things in his mind the next shot and where the white would settle.

At school he had lacked concentration and had left without any certificates. The teachers thought he was thick, and he half-believed them. His old man was disappointed, wanted his son to step forward and better himself, but never said as much, it was something Terry sensed, so the boy smiled to hide his embarrassment, lowered his head and went out with his mates. He wasn't afraid of hard work, but couldn't seem to plan ahead. April reckoned he was low on self-confidence, that he had to believe in himself more, called him a romantic, and yet he knew he could be tough, was able to make a

23

decision when something really important was at stake. Pool was a way to focus, and it became a habit, his skill coming in handy over the years, and it had even changed his life.

He put his glass down and stared at the beer.

The lease on the office was nearly up and he didn't know if he should renew it or move out, find somewhere better. He had more drivers on the books than ever before and the place was too small and needed decorating. He had to decide what to do, but was fed up, had even thought about selling the firm, yet felt he owed it to the lads to stay in charge. He couldn't see a new owner putting up with the likes of Hawkins. Too many of his drivers wouldn't last ten minutes under a new boss. These men made their own rules. He needed a change, was restless, and this was unusual, as he was a man of habit.

He wouldn't think about it now. He reached for his pint.

The pub was quiet, but would fill up when people started knocking off at one for their dinner break. Loners sat back reading papers and sipping their drinks, horses prancing across the TV screen, three white-haired Micks concentrating on their Murphys, patted-down quiffs matching the heads of their stout, a couple of young Slavs on lager. Terry didn't come in this pub very often. It was only the lack of a pool table really, as it was a decent boozer and was used by a lot of the latest wave of Poles. He bided his time, the horses galloping now, jockeys leaning over their necks, chubby men and women cheering from behind a white fence. Diana Ross led The Supremes through 'Someday We'll Be Together', off in the distance, making his eyes tingle. It was one of April's favourites. She loved her Motown and used to sing it to him pissed, in the pub or back at the flat with a bag of chips, a couple of cans and a warm stylus. It was sad enough back then, a choker now. He looked for the jukebox, found nothing, realised it was the barmaid's choice.

Two men came in, shaking themselves dry, Terry recognising Big Frank and Steve The Crisp from work. The ready-salted ordered, Steve said something to Kowalski, who leant forward, laughing into his chest. The barmaid smiled and flicked silver eyelashes. Frank was a lump, massive, even taller and wider than Ray but a bit less excitable. Something like that. Terry grinned. Sane was the word he was looking for. Steve was a live wire, bouncing foot to foot, fair hair just visible, a scar on the left side of his face from a slashing against Anderlecht. Frank and Steve were in their early thirties, good boys, and when they spotted their boss grinning over, nursing a pint, they collected their drinks and headed his way, Steve clutching a paper in his spare hand, dropping it on the table. They sat down.

Both men had their hair cut close to the skull, in accordance with Estuary regulations, as Terry was strict about appearance. Real skinheads had standards and Estuary Cars was a proper skinhead firm. No doubt about that. He was no tyrant, tried to be flexible, but no hairies were allowed on the payroll. No grease or crusties. Not even a smoothie. Anything between a number one and number four crop was fine. The Estuary commander also insisted on a Fred Perry or Ben Sherman shirt when the boys were on duty, preferring 501s or Sta-Press when it came to strides, liked to see a Harrington, accepted the flight-jackets of the Oi mob. Hoods were not tolerated. A Combie was more than welcome, though he accepted that looser clothing was easier when a bloke was driving. Ray was less tolerant, lived in his black MA1, a version of the green original. He always wore his steel-capped DMs and got angry at the older football chaps who chose Stone Island and Reeboks. Anything for a row. He had been like that since Southall. Ray was a nutter, and while Terry knew he could look after himself, he still worried about the bloke.

Ray was family, as close as any brother, but like a son as well, and Terry remembered him as a baby, the day he was born, and then his older sister's son became a bright-eyed boy, with a cheeky smile and an easygoing nature. His father turned out to be a tosser, had run off and left Viv with the two boys, Ray and his younger brother Ronnie. You couldn't tell why people turned out the way they did, if it was down

25

to Southall or his old man scarpering, but under the hard exterior Terry knew that Ray was a diamond. He saw the baby, that wide-eyed boy with everything to live for, and again he felt the sadness rise up.

The whole firm was like an extended family and that was the thing that kept Terry going into work. If it was just geezers off the street, strangers, his only aim to make money, he would have jacked it in years ago. He enjoyed the banter, the laugh and sense of belonging. They were his mates, and probably half of them had known him before they'd ever heard about Estuary Cars, a mixture of faces who grew up locally, football friends, mates of mates, pub pals and music cranks. He thought about all this, realised what it meant and felt warm inside.

Terry had near on forty drivers working for him, ranging from cocky youngsters in their early twenties to quiet characters in their fifties, a proper firm that had caused a stir last Christmas, the works do a choice between an all-you-can-eat buffet at the Canton Diner, or a drink-up. The second option won and Terry made sure everyone knew they had to be on their best behaviour. They were representing Estuary Cars. Reputation was essential. They were professionals, not a bunch of hooligans. It was a good night as well, the boys celebrating their Christian heritage in the usual pagan manner. Most were Chelsea, but Reading, QPR, Wycombe, Brentford and Glasgow Rangers were represented, the night exploding outside Fanny's, a dodgy lap-dancing club full of Latvian blondes, a coachload of ponces from fuck-knows-where stopping off for a sniff, spilling out as the first Estuary boys passed on their way to a late drink in The Rising Sun. When one of the gel-drippers mouthed off, an old-school clash between skins and plastic soulboys was inevitable.

Terry knew that as the boss it was his job to maintain order, but there were a good seventy-plus men getting ready to steam into each other, and when his half-hearted HOLD UP, IT'S CHRISTMAS failed, he felt he had to lead from the front. The London Pride had been going down a treat, and bollocks, it *was* Christmas. Pushing his way through the ranks he arrived as Ray's first punch connected with the bubbly nose of a full-size Robbie Williams lookalike, knocking the plank spark out. Frank slapped a spade in the air and the honey monsters legged it across the street, one turning and flashing a blade, his pals deciding to make a stand. Ray planted a DM bang in his nuts and the craft-work fanatic went down, the boot going in, the visitors cornered and battered as the firm made themselves busy, the Old Bill arriving inside a minute, waiting robocops cracking heads as the two sides quickly dispersed. The Estuary mob lost themselves in the nearby pubs and, thank fuck, nobody was nicked. Terry felt bad the next day. He wasn't a violent man, and if he didn't set an example the company had no chance. Next year they would have a Chinese.

Frank and Steve's burgers arrived with a smile and a flash of frilly black bra, the conversation slowing as they dug into the baps, ketchup swamping chips. Terry watched more people arrive, the painters and decorators and secretaries and shop girls and two salesmen in smart suits, friends of the men in overalls, shuffling mobile phones. The volume increased. Smoke filled the air. More horses pranced. He had nearly finished his pint and wasn't going to hang about. He could easy go on the piss, but it was too early and he had to get back to the office, make sure everything was okay. First he was going to have a game of pool. The need was there in his head, itching away.

– I'm going down The Rising Sun, he announced, polishing off the last of his Timothy Taylor.

– You'll drown, Frank laughed.

– They've got a pool table down there.

– You've won a few cups, haven't you? Steve asked.

– That was years ago. I play for fun.

– I can give you a lift, Frank said. But not for another half-hour.

– He's not joking, Steve joined in. You'll be drenched inside a minute.

Terry knew they were right. He might as well go back to the office. He was meeting Hawkins later and could play then.

– I'll walk back to the office. You want a drink before I go?

– No, thanks. We're working.

Terry stood up and looked out of the window at the front of the pub.

– There used to be a place round the corner from the office, Frank said, cutting into a stack of chips. They had tables in there.

– Pool tables?

– Yeah, pool.

Terry pushed his memory.

– What pub's that?

– It was a social club. It closed down years ago.

Terry thought hard. He had grown up in Wexham Park, before moving over to Uxbridge, knew the town centre well.

– Where was it?

– Don't know the name of the street. It's more of an alleyway, really. You come out of the office, do a right, then a left, and it's on your right, I think. The alley's not much more than the width of a car, and you can only get through the other end on foot. It might not even have a name.

Terry followed Frank's directions in his mind, guessing at the cut-through. There was nothing there. He must mean somewhere else.

– It was buried away, Frank continued, thinking back. Even when it was going you wouldn't know it was there if it wasn't for the flag outside. It's probably still boarded up.

Frank had to be muddled up.

– What was it called?

– Don't know. I was a kid when I went down there. It was started by a couple of Poles after the war. Them and some locals, I think. There was all sorts who used it. Poles, Sikhs, English, Irish. Everyone, really. It was a long time ago.

Terry shrugged. It didn't matter.

– It might still be there, Steve said.

– No. They haven't done anything with the building, but they would've cleared everything out, probably use it for storage or something. It was a mad place.

– Why did it close down?

– Don't know. This was the Eighties. It could be the blokes who started it got too old, or died off, or maybe the rent went up, or people lost interest. Don't have a clue. My grandad used to take me. He was from Cracow, settled here after the war. I was only small. He was dead by the time it shut, and my dad never went much. I wasn't going either. I don't remember a lot, to be honest.

– A soldier's hang-out, Steve said. Like the British Legion.

– It was more than just old soldiers. It was different. There was a Union Jack out front. I remember at Christmas them having a tree and a Father Christmas and sausage rolls for the kids. They had bingo as well. Once there was a fiddle player. I think they even had a hobby-horse one time. Either that or I'm going mad. It was over twenty years ago.

Frank was laughing. Then, lost in thought, he shook his head and had another bite of hamburger.

Terry made his move.

– Right, I'm off. Time to get my flippers on.

Terry stayed close to the walls, head down, was almost back at the office when the rain skipped a beat. He hurried across the street, walked in, found Angie stretching across her desk, reaching for the calendar and scribbling something below the black boots of Chelsea and England centre-half John Terry.

It was hard to see what she was writing, but he couldn't miss her bum sticking in the air. He was slow to react, the sickness making him groggy, eyes fixed as she reached further forward, stretching her jeans, and he jolted, realised she wasn't wearing any pants, then realised he was looked for the line, the 501s riding tighter between her legs, hinting at a crack. He smelt April and felt ashamed, even though he had done nothing wrong. He was frozen, eyes stuck as Psychobilly Paul came out of the kitchen and caught him inspecting his assistant's shapely arse.

Now Paul had often imagined bending Angie over her desk and giving her a good seeing-to, specially when she was out back cutting his hair, decked out in black skirt and fishnets, tits inches from his face, but he wasn't going to risk a black eye trying it on. She was hard as nails. Mind you, English was the governor, and Angie acted very differently when he was around. He'd also heard his boss was hung like a fucking horse, so maybe the bloke had a chance. He grinned knowingly as Terry turned to look his way. Paul winked and left the building. Terry hurried into the kitchen. Angie turned, saw a blank wall and frowned, sat back down and wondered about the radiators. She heard Paul's car start and relaxed.

Terry filled the kettle and turned it on, sat down and waited for the water to boil. Old newspapers were stacked high on the table, mugs piled up in the rack next to the sink. He was embarrassed. Paul shouldn't be winking at him like that, getting the wrong idea. That's what happened when you made an exception and let a psychobilly onto the firm. If Angie had turned round she would've thought he was a right old perv. He wasn't one of these sad old gits who thought a young, fit bird was going to fancy his beer gut. No chance. Angie was vital to the running of the firm. Estuary Cars would fall apart without her. If she thought she was being harassed and walked away, they would be in serious trouble.

When the kettle boiled he went to the door, leant his head out and saw Angie sitting at the switchboard, flicking through an issue of *Scootering*, purple nails turning the pages.

– Do you want a cup of tea?

She almost did a backflip.

– Fucking hell, she shouted, jumping in her chair and nearly spilling over, swivelling and shaking her head, right hand over her heart.

Terry waited for her to calm down.

– Sorry. I didn't know you were in there, just that Paul had left. I thought I was on my own. I almost wet myself.

She blushed. Maybe because she swore. He didn't mind, was glad she hadn't heard him come in.

– Do you want some tea, then?

Angie nodded, her face still red, and he went back into the kitchen and made two mugs, brought them into the office and carefully placed one on her desk, sat in his chair. He felt bad about Paul, didn't want anyone getting the wrong idea. He would have a word with him. Or maybe it would be best to let it go. He blew on his tea and watched Angie as she answered a call, searching for the Estuary driver nearest Burnham station. She really was stunning when he stopped to think about it, and very polite and friendly. She had a sense of humour as well, a smile that could put you on the back foot, as it was hard to work out what she was thinking. It was good she was tough with the drivers. It would be chaos otherwise.

– Did you enjoy you kebab? she asked, smirking.

At least it looked like a smirk. Terry guessed he was imagining things.

– I had a fry-up in the end.

– The Full English?

She was laughing now.

– How did you know?

She remembered herself.

– Lucky guess, I suppose.

Terry nodded. He loved his fry-ups, it couldn't be denied. He grinned.

– Everything okay here? he asked.

– Usual Friday. It's picking up. It'll be busy tonight.

He nodded and sipped his tea, reached into his drawer and took out the letter from the landlord. He looked at it for a while, then put it back. He felt tired suddenly, muscles aching. It would pass.

– Did you find out about Symarip? Angie asked.

Club Ska were putting on Symarip, the skinhead legends responsible for 'Skinhead Moonstomp', and Angie had mentioned it to Terry after seeing an advert. He had forgotten all about it, reached inside his jacket, took out and opened his wallet, passed over two tickets. She reached for her purse, but he waved it away.

– Perk of the job, he laughed.

Angie argued for a minute, finally put the tickets in her bag.

31

She answered a call, passed the details to one of the drivers, and Terry took the chance to go for a piss. He went out back and stood over the bowl, eyes closed, April hovering nearby. Poor April. The first six months had been the worst. He had kept going for the children, but wished he could die as well, and eventually it became easier to block the memories out. Yet he still missed her, and now she was close again, watching over him. She had returned with his sickness. And soon he would be fifty. He was being sucked backwards, wasn't himself, the medicine weakening his defences. He finished and washed his hands, reached for the door, stumbled against the wall and thought he was going to fall. He steadied himself, waited for the pressure to pass. He swore and wondered where all this was coming from, fought hard to push himself forward.

Sitting at his desk he read a letter from a computer that was trying to sell him insurance, folded it in half and tore it into tiny pieces. He felt fine now. Maybe he should have had another day off, listened to his doctor. He was bored. After a while he looked up.

– Do you want a biscuit? he asked, reaching into his drawer.

– No, thanks. Got to watch my figure.

There was a pause. Terry didn't think she did, but he wasn't going to say anything. He munched away, checked his watch. It was nearly three. Kick-off time.

– If you don't need me here, he said, making one of those managerial decisions that showed true leadership, I'm going to nip down the Rising Sun and have a business meeting with Mr Hawkins.

He stood up.

– Mr English?

– Yes, Angie?

– Are you feeling okay?

Terry stared as his office manager.

– How do you mean?

– Well, you've had that bug a few times now, and flu, and you can't shake it off. You don't look too well. You're not

32

your normal self. Do you think you should be going out drinking?

It was true, he had felt rough earlier, but knew what he was doing. A drink was just what he needed most. It was all about morale. If you let your spirits fall you didn't stand a chance.

– I'll only have a couple. I'm fine. Honest.

Angie didn't look convinced, but he was sweet as a nut, the thought of a few light ales with his old mucker Hawkins the best medicine he could have, and he was thirsty, that pint of Timothy Taylor giving him the taste. He was looking forward to a game of pool as well, and there was usually someone in the pub willing to oblige. If not, he would play himself. Hawkins didn't want to know, said he was fed up being beaten, but first Terry was going to wash these mugs. He picked them up and headed for the kitchen, determined to do his bit.

Parrot Fashion

DOING A STEADY TWENTY miles an hour in the inside lane, stuck behind a lorry that was spewing muck over his bonnet, Ray was fuming. He loved Fridays, at least when he had the weekend off, but getting through today was murder. He wanted to overtake, glanced right, searching for a gap in the traffic, a blonde bird in an Audi smiling back. He frowned and her smile spread. She identified a moody bodybuilder, while he saw glamour-model hair that was fluffed and tinted and pretty boring for a skinhead raised on punkettes, skin-girls and 2-Tone sorts. A Cadillac drew his attention and he followed the car as it passed in the opposite direction, a black dog sitting in the back, nose pressed against the window. Hawkins was right behind in his Mondeo, and Ray waved, but the bloke wasn't looking his way, the blonde porn star blowing a kiss, red lipstick glistening as the tip of her tongue flickered. She had a pretty enough face and reminded him of Jordan, but without the inflatables. He preferred a punkier look, but she wasn't bad.

He didn't respond, was too busy braking to avoid the lorry which was doing a sudden left, indicator knocking late, the skin-flick girl shooting ahead, lost in the traffic. He was forced to stop, the driver in front taking ages to squeeze into a narrow opening, and he gritted his teeth, clenched his fists and squeezed the steering wheel, waited as patiently as he could, counting down, the lorry moving away so he could continue, working through the gears, daring them to jam and let him down.

– There's these three cowboys . . . his passenger sniggered.

Ray sighed. Trust him to end the week with a fucking

comedian. He didn't mind a joke now and then, but hated epics, the long-winded stories that went nowhere. His fare had launched two jokes already, and while these had been fairly short, he had a feeling it was going to be third time unlucky. The light he was approaching turned red. He was forced to stop.

– There's these three cowboys . . .

Ray thought about the blonde, wondered if she really was a porn star. He had little time for dirty films. Never had. He wouldn't want one his daughters on the other side of the lens and didn't expect anyone else to have to go that way either. It was the same with prostitutes. He felt sorry for them. Working for some lowlife pimp, some guttersnipe drug-dealer. Mind you, he was probably being unfair on the bird in the Audi, assuming she was a tart just because she had a dodgy tan and divvy haircut.

The light changed and Ray continued, waiting for first gear to mug him off, his fare starting over. This dickhead was getting on his nerves. He needed a slap. But Ray had to be professional, for the sake of his uncle and Estuary Cars and his job, and anyway, there wasn't long to go and he would be off till Monday. He saw an ice-cold pint of lager, bubbles rising, sitting on a bar, waiting.

– There's these three cowboys, right, and they're heading west, on their way to California to join the gold rush, and they decide to take a short cut through these ancient Indian burial grounds. They know it's not allowed, but think, well, nobody's going to notice us out here in the middle of nowhere. They don't think too much about it, but they're spotted by the local tribe, who take them prisoner, march these cowboys into the nearest village and tie them to these three posts.

The joker paused. Maybe he wanted a response from the audience. Ray ignored him. Cowboys by name, cowboys by nature. No respect for someone else's culture. What was funny about that? He imagined George Bush, Dick Cheney and that other cunt, the geezer with the German name.

– Anyway, all the braves in the village gather round and

there must be two hundred of the fuckers. Now, the old Indians aren't too happy with these cowboys. In fact, they're doing their nut. The chief puts his pipe down and walks forward, tells the cowboys they've been caught on sacred land and have disturbed the ancestors, that they need to be punished. It's the law of the land and you have to obey the law, doesn't matter who you are. This is serious.

Ray saw the Audi ahead, waiting at another set of lights, pulled up next to the blonde, nodded back as her mouth cracked. Puffed lips split nicely and he wondered if they'd been injected, a passing idea as he saw her sucking on his cock. He'd been away from home for a long time, and Liz didn't want to know. She had turned her back on him, but so far he had stayed faithful. There was only so much a man could take though.

– Anyway, the chief goes up to the first cowboy and says, 'White man, you have two choices ... death – or bochehemie.'

Ray forgot about the blow job. She was fit enough, but there was something wrong about her, driving around this part of Slough in a flash motor, smothered in make-up. The Europeans were pedalling all sorts of perversions and a smile creased his face as he toyed with the idea of asking her what her views were on the EU, how she felt about the unBritish activities being pumped into the porn industry by the deviants in Brussels.

– Well, the cowboy doesn't want to die, so he chooses bochehemie. The chief raises his spear in the air, looks at the braves, and shouts 'BOCHEHEMIE.' The braves untie the first cowboy and take him to the edge of the village and get stuck in. Every one of them had a turn bumming the cowboy, and by the evening there's not much left of his arse. They leave him bleeding in the dust and go back into the village. Somehow the cowboy manages to crawl off into the desert. The other two have seen the whole thing and they're shitting it.

Ray pulled away, forgetting the blonde. He wouldn't wish that on Bush, Cheney or anyone. He was glad the Taliban had been caned, pleased Saddam was removed from power, hated the posh-boy wankers in Al-Qaeda, but the Yanks had fucked it up, done it on the cheap. They had no respect and had used the situation to spread their free-economy, globalisation, corporate poison.

– By this time the word has spread and the braves from two nearby villages have turned up. There's five hundred of the dirty bastards eyeing up the two cowboys who are left. The chief goes up to the second one and says, 'You have two choices, white man . . . death – or bochehemie.' Well, the second cowboy has seen what happened to his mate, but he doesn't want to die, so he goes for bochehemie.

– The chief is shaking with excitement as he raises his spear in the air and screams 'BOCHEHEMIE.' The Indians are frothing at the mouth by now and the second cowboy is taken to the edge of the village and the braves pile in. It's fucking horrible, lasts two days, and by the end of it he's hardly alive. When they've all had a go the braves wander back into the village and leave the cowboy in the dust. After a while he wakes up and manages to drag himself away.

The Estuary driver saw their destination and indicated left, put his foot down.

– Word spreads even further and the whole Indian nation turns up. There's ten thousand warriors in war paint crowding around the last cowboy, who's just seen his two mates raped and nearly killed, and doesn't want the same thing happening to him. He's shaking in his boots, wishing they'd never left home.

Ray pulled up outside the man's house. His passenger didn't seem to notice.

– The chief walks up to the third cowboy and says, 'You have two choices, white man . . . death – or bochehemie.' The cowboy looks at the ten thousand Indians crowding round him, hard-ons bulging through the front of their trousers, and he says, 'There's no way I'm going through all that, I fucking hate queers, I'll take death.' The chief holds his spear in the air and turns to the massed ranks of braves and shouts . . . 'DEATH – BY BOCHEHEMIE!'

The man roared with laughter, slapping the seat. Ray felt sick. All that talk about poofs and rape made him want to drag the bloke out into the street and kick the fuck out of him. Who did he think he was, telling a stranger a joke like that?

The door of the house opened and a woman and two children waved. The comedian didn't notice Ray's silence, paid and carried his bag up the path, was hugged and kissed and welcomed back in the family home. At least the Bochehemie man had given Ray a decent tip.

He headed back into town, his mind on everyday matters as the radio whispered in the background.

His Estuary radio crackled and he heard Angie.

– I've got a Mrs Pepper waiting outside the Harrow View in Langley.

– Where's she going? he asked.

– West Drayton.

– I'll get her. Did you say Pepper? Like salt and pepper?

– That's right. Mrs Pepper. On the bench. Outside the Harrow View. Her and her friend.

The radio clicked. Angie was in a right mood. She was a hard mod, one woman he would not want to cross. Ray wondered if she was easy to live with, if her tough exterior was something she saved for work, or if she was like that all the time, and he thought about Liz and what it must be like for her when he was in a strop, raging about the world, and a year back he had lost the ability to keep his frustration out of the house. He didn't know why. The children were growing up and he was pushing forty, and he wondered if that was part of the problem, if anniversaries and birthdays and the memories they carried had some secret power, an energy that came back to haunt you like a disease. The future seemed bland and gutless and ignorant. The past handed on lessons, showed what worked and what didn't, but an addiction to profit meant everything had to be destroyed and rebuilt, repackaged as if it was an advance.

Driving all day gave Ray too much time to think. The

38

radio wound him up. He didn't see why Liz wanted him to turn into a brain-dead tosser who had no opinion. He worked and did nothing about the destruction of his country. Events repeated themselves. He saw it clearly, but was powerless, punched the dashboard and launched into a long and detailed series of insults aimed at his usual targets. He was a good old boy tied to a post, shafted by chiefs and their lackeys. He turned and saw an elderly couple in a VW watching him, surprised by the shock on their faces. He smiled and tried to show he wasn't dangerous, but the woman said something to her husband and he put his foot down.

Ray continued, inside ten minutes approaching the pub, entered the shopping-area car park, ducked into an empty space and slammed into reverse, backed out fast, found first and pulled up next to the woman sitting on the bench, an argument going on outside the pub, a gypo and a bonehead shouting at each other. Just what he needed. He rolled out of the car and walked over.

– Mrs Pepper?

– Yes, dear?

– I'm your taxi.

She had a bundle next to her, wrapped inside a multi-coloured blanket, a brown belt holding it all together. He looked around for her friend.

– You alone?

– Just me and Peter.

Ray nodded.

– Shall we get him and go home?

He looked around, realised the old girl was on her lonesome. She was frail and muddled. There was no Peter. He felt sorry for her, thought about ghosts and memories, had heard folic acid was good for the brain. He reached for her bag, but she wanted to carry it herself. It was either shopping or washing, so maybe she didn't want to break any eggs or show off her drawers. He opened the back door and she pushed it inside, was a lot stronger than she looked. He waited until she was safely in as well and eased the door shut.

– Whereabouts in West Drayton do you want to go? he asked, back behind the wheel.

– If you get on the Cowley Road I'll give you directions once we're past The Packet Boat.

– All right, darling. I know where you mean.

Ray pulled out of the car park and headed towards Uxbridge. It took him a while to cross the road and pass through the mini-roundabout, but he was soon ducking under the train tracks and passing the station, over the canal with the dump on his left, accelerating away now as he levelled out on a long stretch of empty road, racing towards Iver, and he felt better, guessing what it must be like to be a trucker in America or Australia, with so much land and space and freedom, driving for days and never reaching your destination, the only sounds on the radio redneck hillbilly and small-town punk. He loved the occasional long-distance jobs, when the motorway was clear and he sailed along. It was the traffic that made minicabbing difficult. He didn't mind nights. The roads were quieter, though you had the drunks and nutters to deal with, sitting around outside pubs and clubs, meeting mouthy cunts, but he enjoyed the challenge, didn't mind a bit of confrontation. Nights could muck your days up. It just depended what time he knocked off.

He glanced in his rear-view mirror to see how Mrs Pepper was and nearly had a heart attack, swerved but stayed in control of the car, slowed down, chest pounding as he shifted his eyes back to the mirror, looked again at the huge parrot sitting in the back seat, a monster skull inches from the back of his head. The parrot stared back. It didn't blink. It was eyeballing him. He looked away.

– Is that a parrot? Ray asked, once he'd calmed down.

The bird seemed to sneer when he said this, thinking, 'Of course I'm a parrot, you fucking idiot.'

– He doesn't like it in his cage, Mrs Pepper explained. I only put him in when he's outdoors, so he doesn't fly off by accident. He gets angry at you, so I put a poncho over him. I never know how he's going to behave. It reminds him of home, see, and it means people don't stare at him.

He doesn't like it when people stare at him. The parrot twitched and Ray saw its beak quiver.

He concentrated on the road, sneaking a look every few seconds. The parrot kept staring into the mirror, lids slowly lowering and opening.

– Blimey, was all Ray could conjure up.

His heart was thumping.

– He likes riding in cars, don't you?

Ray saw the parrot turn and look outside, the woman's hand stroking the back of his head, and the driver had to admit it was the biggest bird he had ever seen. It was more like a fucking eagle or something, done up in warpaint. That beak was huge, same as the jaws on a digger. One peck and you'd be a goner. Ripped to shreds if he went into a frenzy. The bird turned back to stare in the mirror, straight into Ray's eyes. Maybe he was another species.

– You sure that's a parrot?

– Oh yes. Peter is a parrot all right.

– Can he talk?

– He says a few words.

– He could get a job on the radio.

– He can't answer questions or anything like that. He is very intelligent, though. Sometimes I think he knows what people are thinking.

Ray hoped not.

– He wouldn't need to, would he? Just repeat a few one-liners.

Mrs Pepper smiled, humouring the boy taking her home.

– It isn't as easy as you'd think, you know, getting them to speak. It's mimicry. They say a parrot doesn't know what the words mean.

– It's the same on the radio. You stick him in a studio with a load of politicians and you wouldn't be able to tell the difference.

Ray imagined the parrot in a radio studio, shitting all over the carpet, chewing up the schedule.

– Peter understands what the words mean. He's very special

Ray jumped as the bird leant forward, his beak almost

41

touching the driver's neck. He wondered how Mrs Pepper kept him under control. He wouldn't want to sleep in the same house as Peter.

– Peter Parrot, he said out loud.

– No, just Peter.

Mrs Pepper thought about this for a minute.

– Or Peter Pepper, I suppose.

They drove on in silence, through Iver and towards Cowley. The world was full of cranks and fruitcakes, and that was what made life worth living.

Ray crossed the M25 and saw the traffic crawling, glad he wasn't down there, looking forward to the weekend. Chelsea were at Arsenal tomorrow and they were meeting in The Gaslight. It was a late kick-off and they would have a good drink before the game. His Uncle Terry and Hawkins had extra tickets for the Clock End. He made himself think about the trip to Finsbury Park. The drink tonight, warming up. Anything to take his mind off Peter and stop him looking in the mirror.

Once he had pulled up outside Mrs Pepper's house, he glanced over his shoulder and looked the parrot in the eye. Man to man.

– What do you think about the war in Iraq? he asked.

There was a pause. The parrot blinked.

– Bollocks, he said.

At least it sounded like that. Mrs Pepper didn't seem to hear. She paid the fare and gave Ray a pound tip. The parrot sat on her arm as she carried the cage in her free hand. His beak seemed even bigger from a distance, out of proportion to the rest of his body.

– Bollocks, Peter squawked, looking over. Wanker.

Ray watched them safely inside and turned around, sticking to the back roads as he headed to Slough, his confidence slowly returning as he picked up speed, feeling the warmth of the sun breaking through his windscreen, left it a while before calling the office.

Best of British

DEAD ON THREE, TERRY walked out of Estuary Cars, rubbing his hands as he stood in fresh sunlight, the sky clear at last, air sweet with the smell of evaporating water. Angie was minding his car keys, and would arrange for one of the lads to take the Merc home. It was the end of the week and he deserved a drink, couldn't afford another ban and wasn't going to leave twenty grand's worth of motor sitting around overnight. He walked towards the pub, lanes quiet, glass catching the yellow glow of the sun, dubbing it towards moonlight, and he took his usual short cut through the craters, thought of Frank and stopped at the end of a tiny short-cut street he'd used hundreds of times. This was the place the bloke meant, he was sure of it, but there was no club. Nothing at all. A grey wall flaked skin on his right, scabbed breeze blocks ribbed with cement, the pavement sinking arches into crumbling tarmac. To his left the wall was whiter, pale and smooth, and he shook his head, squinting now as he spied wrinkles, three wooden boards painted to blend in with the plaster. He looked up, found a few inches of glass above the panels, and above that there was a flag-pole. It was incredible. He had never noticed any of this, walking the streets and not seeing what was around him, blocking out more than memories.

Terry moved forward, felt a chill in his lungs, the sun squeezed away. He thought about hurrying to the pub, reminding himself that the past was best left alone, but another part of him was excited. He followed the wall, reached a thick gate, the padlock chunky and the chain rusty, easy enough to break. He pushed the slab open and stood at the

43

end of a narrow passage, water dripping drops from a gutter, more cheerful than tearful. He closed the gate. A high wall hid the building beyond, broken glass lining the top, a rich smell of coriander floating around. He crossed more cracked concrete, moss making him slip, the shell of a can snapping as he steadied himself. He squeezed past a boiler, cobwebs wrapping around his face, easily brushed off. Up ahead wooden crates were stacked under a small lean-to, the edges of the roof pimpled with mildew, a hill of spirit bottles spilling out, tumbling towards hundreds of beer bottles. Terry stopped and wondered what he was doing. The only sound was the faint drip of water. The gate shut out the rest of the world. This had to be the most forgotten place in England. Nobody would think to break in here. The vandals and graffiti merchants didn't want to know. He shivered. The coriander became stronger.

Terry continued to the end of the passage, reached a door and turned the knob. It was unlocked. He stepped inside, a whiff of ammonia waiting, signs for Ladies and Gents on doors to one side, another door at the end of a short corridor, painted black. He stopped and listened, imagined he was entering a tomb, wanted to turn and run away like a worried child. He heard footsteps and moved back, felt them hollow out and fade, a distant cough and whisper following, and he wished it was someone passing in the street, but didn't think the noise would carry that far. He wasn't scared now. It wasn't a tomb, just an empty building, closed down and boarded up, its memorial a taste of fermenting piss and endless empties. He was suddenly sad, thought of his parents, dead and buried, their lives unrecorded. They had stories, more important and special stories than most people alive today, and he didn't know them, had been too young and selfish to stop and find out. Mind you, his old man didn't give much away, his mum was different. He imagined her shushing him, telling him to try and understand his dad, clicking her shoes as she walked across this vinyl floor, and he snapped awake and walked on, moving fast, opened the black door, stopped and stared and shaded his eyes.

Sheets of light cut across the room and dazzled him, a flashbulb effect as if he was being snapped in an old black-and-white film. He looked away, to his left, guessed the outline of a bar, the light stuck in his eyes making it appear white, and he blinked quickly, trying to see properly, realised this whiteness was dust. He saw a face and jumped, the cheeks and forehead merging, and he felt stupid as he realised it was his reflection in a long glass mirror, tried to laugh at himself, couldn't, his imagination insisting the figure had combed-back hair and black bullet eyes. His lungs tightened and he didn't look at the mirror again. There was no such thing as ghosts. He knew it was a trick of the shade and light.

He took his time, everything coming into focus as his eyes adjusted, marching into the present, time sheared and stitched together. It was mental. Frank assumed everything had been cleared out, but the place had been boarded up and seemed like it had been left untouched. The street outside was rotting, but this place was dozing, the walls covered in framed photos, two pool tables waiting across from the bar, beyond the bulk of the club's tables and chairs, a raised level skirting the room by a foot, a banister separating its wood from the lower-level carpet, a pinball machine wedged in a corner. The front door was protected by an inner porch, and this was fitted with patches of stained glass. It was a treasure chest, and Terry moved around, looking more closely at the photos, the light from the top of the windows adjusting itself. He saw Winston Churchill inspecting a row of soldiers, the Queen as a young and also as a middle-aged woman, a painting of a Spitfire chopping its way across the sky, and there were other faces he didn't know, several group pictures, an Indian regiment, full of Sikhs, and others which he guessed were Poles, a Caribbean mix of blacks and browns. There were English soldiers sitting on a German tank. Another marked Irish Guards. A portrait showed an officer, the name on the frame telling Terry that it was General Sikorski. He stood back and looked at Sikorski. He wondered why all these special photographs had been left behind. It didn't make sense.

He ran his finger through the dust on the bar, found quality wood which was varnished and in near-perfect condition. The shelves were empty, pumps selling Directors, Harp, Guinness. Terry looked at himself in the mirror, watched the light behind him strutting, a smart special effect that made him relax and feel at home. The club had a warm atmosphere. He wished he could peer through the years and glimpse the people who had socialised here, but at least had an idea from the pictures on the wall. He drew a stick man in the dust and turned, walked through the tables, stopped at one where an empty mug rested, next to a small ashtray with the stub of a single cigar poking out. He stared at it for a long time. The last man out drank a cup of coffee and smoked a cigar before he walked away. Maybe he thought he would come back. Maybe he knew it was all over and made a clean break. Terry would probably never know. Perhaps the bloke died suddenly. Why leave all the photos behind?

The pool tables had been covered with plywood, the surfaces clean and in good nick, and they were proper tables made from more good wood, the balls racked and waiting. He tried to imagine the men who played here thirty, forty, fifty years before. He went to the rack and took a cue, found unused chalk stacked in a neat pyramid, several worn-down pieces in a line, and he took one of these, chalked up, went over to the first table he had uncovered. Whoever closed the place up, maybe ran it, was neat and tidy and had left everything in order. Terry liked that. The man had concentration and self-respect. He looked for the white ball, couldn't see it at first, spotted two of them together on the floor, near the table with the mug and cigar stub. He walked over and picked them up, returned and placed one on the table. He lifted his cue, stopped and thought, put it back in the rack and replaced the wood. He put the white balls next to the chalk, making sure they wouldn't roll away.

There was a padded bench filling one wall, where people could sit and watch the pool players, and he sat down, absorbing the club, feeling more and more easy. He tried to hear the voices, smell the cigar smoke, taste the beer and spirits, but nothing reached him. There was a mustiness about the place, but it wasn't too bad, considering.

A bundle caught his eye and he went over to the chair where it sat, undid the rope holding it together, unrolled a full-size Union Jack. It had to be the flag that had hung on the flagpole outside. Terry stretched it across the pool tables for a proper look. The colours dazzled him and he remembered what a good-looking flag the Union Jack was. He stood for a long time, noticed slot machines, more pictures near the main door, the frosted glass in front of the boards, reaching halfway up the window, clear glass at the top where the light entered. He thought about the white balls, imagined the coffee-drinker leaving them on the table next to his mug, and then one day they moved, rolled away and bounced and didn't move again.

He didn't need to play pool. Not yet. He knew that he had struck lucky.

Terry checked his watch and realised he was late. He had been in here for ages. His phone rang. It was Hawkins. He ignored the call, stood up and walked out, closing everything carefully behind him, making sure the padlock on the outside gate looked as if it was secure.

He hurried towards the Rising Sun, felt lively, full of energy, entered the pub and saw Hawkins at one of the front tables, near the end of his pint.

– You're late. What's wrong with your phone?

Hawkins didn't like to drink alone.

– Where have you been?

– I got held up. Come on, stop moaning. Same again?

Terry went to the bar and ordered a pint of London Pride and a Carling top for the girl, saw the pool table was empty. He would have a game in a minute. He took the drinks and sat down. Hawkins reached for his lager and Terry took a long, slow gulp of his bitter. Lovely. The weekend started here and he was back on form, felt like he had just been eased into a dream, the rare sort that sets you up for the day, makes you feel invincible.

– This weather is doing my fucking head in, Hawkins

47

started. Ten days ago I'm walking around in a pair of shorts and the only decision I've got to make is whether to get myself a lager or a blow job first, both of them near enough the same price. In the end you just think fuck this, I'll have both at the same time. The sun's shining and it's a hundred degrees out, and I could be sitting on a stool right now with a dirty little Thai bird on each knee, rubbing my balls, girls who'll do anything for the price of a kebab. But no, that's too nice. Instead I'm stuck in here, drinking with a fat bastard in a pub full of geezers.

Hawkins had heard about Pattaya from some of the boys at football, and was still recovering from his first visit, swearing he would be going back soon. Terry was bored hearing about it, but let him ramble on.

– The gooks love it, see. It's all about size. If you went over there, fuck me, they'd make you a god. Build a shrine. Terry English, Lord of the Knobs.

Terry shook his head sadly.

– The Thais are used to their own blokes, Hawkins continued, serious as he leant forward. But Thais are small, short and lightweight, so they must have small willies as well. When an Englishman goes over there they're dealing with twice the volume. It's heaven for those girls. Same goes for the Vietnamese, Cambodians, all of them. They can't get enough of the white man, and specially the English. We're doing them a favour.

– They're poor people, Terry pointed out. They do it for money. Why would some young Thai girl want to have it off with an old codger like you?

– No, they love it. You haven't been there. You don't know what it's like. It's not the same as over here.

– Why don't you go live there, then?

– Fuck off, Hawkins spluttered. This is my home.

Hawkins tracked someone entering the pub, Terry turning to see who it was, saw a youth in a baseball cap, peak pulled low.

– I'll be back in a minute, Hawkins said, going over, sitting on a stool as they chatted at the bar.

– He's probably doing a Viagra deal, Singer laughed, appearing from the far end of the pub.

– He's trying to flog some shirts.

– Them and the Viagra. Did he tell you about Paul?

Terry shook his head. He saw Paul winking at him in the office, Angie bent over the desk, bum in the air. He should have a word with Paul about that, but what exactly would he say? Sometimes it was better to let things go. That way they were forgotten. Make a fuss and it became important.

– He's got this new bird, right, and she loves it, but he's having trouble keeping up. So he hears Hawkins is big on the Viagra, you know, goes over to Thailand on tour and wants to get his money's worth when he's over there, stocks up on the stuff. Paul's in the pub and Hawkins is listening to him moaning, and he gives him a couple of pills, says try one of these next time that tart of yours is in the mood.

Singer paused.

– Go on, Terry said.

– Well, Paul forgets about them till the next morning. He's not too sharp, old Paul. Nice bloke, but young for his age.

Singer was right, Paul winking like that. Did he know who paid his wages? The man who hired and fired, who kept him in a job?

– Paul's had his breakfast and has got half an hour before he leaves for work, remembers the Viagra and decides to try one, to see if it does what it says on the box. Anyway, things are quiet until he sets off, and then next thing he knows he's driving along and about to pick up his first fare of the day, almost at the address when he realises he's got the biggest hard-on he's had in his life.

Terry was shocked. Standards were vital in the minicab business. You couldn't have your employees driving around with erections. You'd scare the punters. It wasn't nice. Not nice at all. They'd get a reputation.

– He's outside this bird's house, and he can't exactly stroll up the garden path with this bulge in his jeans, so he sounds the horn. She comes out and she's a monster, and only goes and sits in the front next to him. So there he is with a hard-on, driving this bird, and all the time he's hoping she doesn't notice, but of course, she does, that's one of the first things she does, and worse than that, she only thinks it's for her. Keeps giving him looks, making comments and brushing against his arm. He finally gets rid of her, but it's a near thing. He's expecting her to jump him any second.

Terry was saddened by this lack of professionalism, but managed a half-smile.

– It goes on all day. He picks up grannies, old geezers, even an uphill gardener. The hours pass and he can't do anything with it, keeps phoning his bird, can't get hold of her. In the end he stops in a lay-by and lets the five-fingered widow loose, but even that doesn't help.

Terry wasn't pleased. He could see the front page of the local paper. ESTUARY DRIVER ARRESTED FOR WANKING IN MINICAB. That would be the end. Nobody would use the firm again. He would be asked for quotes, his name appearing near the headline. It would be a nightmare. Estuary Cars would be a laughing stock and he would be driven out of business. Maybe he could continue for a while, but his clients would be perverts and cranks, weirdoes coming out from under their rocks.

– Shows what a plum he is, Singer concluded, taking it just before he goes to work.

Terry held his head in his hands. There was a long silence. Singer sipped his pint, grinning at the display, putting it down to his boss's sense of humour. Terry sat like that for a long time. He didn't want to hear about the maniacs working for him, what they got up to in their spare time. He wanted an easy life.

– You fancy a game of pool? Singer asked at last, worried that the silence was going to go on forever.

Terry was miles away, running from the *Sun* and the *News Of The World*, from sleazy journalists who wanted to do spreads on minicab masturbation and the threat that rogue drivers presented to women late at night. Terry was running from them, dipping into that hidden club, hiding in the dark, doors sealed, vanishing into thin air.

– A game of pool?

Terry lifted his head. It took him a moment to realise what he was being asked.

– Come on then.

They walked down to the empty table. Terry remembered the Sikhs in the photo.

– Did you ever go to a social club round the corner from the office?

– The Union Jack Club?

– Could be. Frank told me about the place. It's all boarded up.

– They closed it down over twenty years ago. I used to go there with my grandad.

– That's what Frank said.

– I was only small.

– Why did it shut?

– Don't know. Don't have a clue.

Terry had the place fixed in his mind.

– Who used to go in there?

– Everyone, really. It was just a place we went. I was a kid. You don't think about things too much.

– Frank said that as well. We're all the same at that age, I suppose.

– They used to have a big party on VE Day, I remember that. Christmas as well. My grandad liked St George's Day. You could buy a pint for the price of a shilling, as long as it had King George's head on it.

– A lot of pubs did that.

Terry was going to add that the club was still there, but held back. He didn't know why.

Singer arranged the balls, while Terry ordered another pint of London Pride and a bottle of Magners, lager top for Hawkins. He watched Singer send the white skidding down the table, stepped forward and potted three stripes, missed a fourth, went and raided the jukebox as his opponent looked for a shot. It was one of those wall-mounted, CD-flipping efforts, but better than nothing. Terry put in a pound and punched the best buttons. The younger man was a decent enough pool player and would catch up. Desmond Dekker's vocals filled the pub, waking everyone up with 'Israelites', the volume cranked up nice and loud. Terry smiled and drank a third of his pint, Hawkins heading down the pub, mouthing the chorus. The boys were settling in for the afternoon session. This was what it was all about.

Class of '69 – Part 1

FOR TERRY ENGLISH BEING a skinhead is all about the boss sounds coming out of Jamaica – the pumped-up beat and stripped-down vocals of reggae music – and it's 'The Israelites' by Desmond Dekker and The Aces that sets him off – him and thousands of others – and soon he's finding out about Prince Buster and Laurel Aitken – Jimmy Cliff and Clancy Eccles – Dave Barker and Ansell Collins – the Trojan and Pama and Torpedo labels – 'Skinhead Moonstomp' by Symarip – The Shed clapping along to 'Liquidator' by Harry Johnson and his All-Stars – and being a skinhead is about hearing 'It Mek' and 'Monkey Spanner' and 'Double Barrel' and John Jones coming out of those massive speakers built by rude-boy Alfonso – with some help from his barmy Uncle Sam in White City – Rob the Mod selecting 'Skinhead Train' as Alfonso and Terry and the rest of the young ones stand around watching needle dig into vinyl – and for Terry being a skinhead is about getting out of the house – knocking about with his mates – sitting in a cafe with a hot mug of tea – standing on a street corner – and best of all it's being down the youth club – where he can show off his Brutus – his best mate Alan leaning against the wall – he's a proper Jack the Lad – they're very different – like chalk and cheese – his mum says – with Terry it's all about the music – while for Alan – being a skinhead is about the aggro – and the skinhead look is hard – but classy – with a big splash of colour – direct from the Colonies – and Terry and his mates cut their hair short – parade in cherry-red Doctor Martens and Harringtons – black and white and blue jackets – Terry hitches his jeans up Prince Buster style – that's far enough

– the older skinheads dress better – more money – you see
– and one day he'll have a Fred Perry cardigan and a Ben
Sherman shirt – a pair of shrink-to-fit Levi 501s – a sheepskin as well – but all he really needs now is the buster and
the boots – and the look is a laugh really – plays second
fiddle to the records – those are the essentials for Terry –
and he's learning about music from Rob – a proper herbert
– a mod who never turned soft – he never listens to that
weird psychedelic shit – that hippie noise – and Rob tells
him the records to look out for – earlier classics – explains
that you have to look back to move forward – Terry nods
– knows it's good advice – Rob says that's the biggest rule
in life – sort out the past to enjoy the present – and the
future – Terry hopes he remembers – will probably forget
– but it will be down there in his head – somewhere –
waiting to pop up – you never know – and there's some
people call reggae primitive – nigger music – jungle sounds
for coons and wogs – but the mods and the skinheads stand
up for the West Indian singers when they come to England
– and the sound of ska is special – he can't explain it – goes
to Woolies to buy his singles – skinhead reggae is right there
in the charts – and he always has his Tighten Up albums
playing – Volume 2 – going back to Volume 1 – and Rob
lends him Club Ska Classics – he listens to these in his room
– alone – his younger sister listening to The Beatles – and
Terry prefers The Who and The Kinks – The Rolling Stones
– London groups – The Small Faces – and none of the boys
he knows has money burning a hole in their pockets – that's
one reason the Trojan albums are good – they're cheap so
kids like him can afford them – but if you want other records
you have to go into London – to the reggae shops – and
he's been to Shepherd's Bush a couple of times – to Peckings
on Askew Road – Websters near the market – and he stands
there with his mates and listens – and sometimes he buys a
record when he's heard it played – there's a bloke in the
market chopping up roots with a machete – a woman sells
him a roti – he tries some jerk chicken – and they get a
bus to Notting Hill one time – it's richer there and he sees

54

hippies same as on the telly – Terry and Alan and the rest of them are clean and smart – they hate long hair – and he's never going to be a sponger living off the taxes of working men – like those hippies and students do – he'll stand on his own two feet – work hard and earn his place in the world – this is the skinhead way – they are the sons of their fathers – men who fought in the war – proud men – and he goes to Rayners Lane and South Harrow to buy records – he's been over to the East End a couple of times – but it's different there – Whitechapel and Aldgate – more Jewish – West London has the Caribbeans – but the East End is where you get the best Crombies and mohair – that's what they say – off the Jewish tailors – and walking around together – ten or fifteen-handed – they feel like the kings of the jungle – but really – there's always older skinheads around – West Ham in Whitechapel – QPR and Chelsea in Shepherd's Bush – and there are men who've read about these bovver boys – and the thing is a lot of skinheads are young – on their own they wouldn't have much chance – a schoolboy can't do much against a thirty-year-old – but when they stick together nobody's going to muck them about – there's strength in numbers – it's the power of the people – that's what the hippies say – and the older skinheads fight the greasers – and fight each other – football mobs – local gangs – and Terry is a friendly kid – stays out of trouble – Alan is the one – and it's a good life being a skinhead in the Summer of Love – his mum laughing and saying that if he had a quiff he'd look like James Dean – in his jeans and Harrington – when James Dean was in *Rebel Without A Cause* – and she says that's what all you boys are – rebels without a cause – what cause can there be after the war? – nothing gets near that – and have you ever heard of Rodney Harrington in *Peyton Place*? – he just smiles because Mum looks after him – treats him to his Brutus – he's so proud of this shirt – and she hugs him before he goes out – tells him to be careful – worries he'll get in trouble – like so many youngsters now – and his old man doesn't say much – probably thinks he's daft – maybe thinks he's thick – they

55

don't talk too much – and Dad is angry about the way the government is changing the money – planning to get rid of shillings and pence – it doesn't make sense – going metric – nobody wants it to happen – Dad says once you lose your currency you've had it – what did he fight a bloody war for? – it's all part of a plan to destroy Britain – he hardly ever gets angry – but he hates Ted Heath and the Conservatives – calls them traitors – and Terry is out and about and free – this is the modern era – the space age – and he's just one of hundreds of thousands of teenage yobs busy turning England into a skinhead nation – and everything about life is positive – he can't wait to wake up in the morning – England are champions of the world and Bobby Moore and Bobby Charlton are as well known as Winston Churchill – kicked fuck out of the Germans – in two wars – and the World Cup – and he's walking down the street – heading home – with his hands in his pockets – and the only thing missing in his life is a bird – he wants a skinhead girl who loves the same music as him – but he's no good around them – too shy – too romantic maybe – Alan is only interested in getting in their knickers – but Terry touches the scrap of paper in his pocket – a number and a name – and he thinks back to last week – in that amusement arcade with Alan and Jefferson – on Ealing Broadway – coming back from Shepherd's Bush – they're in the arcade – the place is packed – and the others say they're going over the road – see if they can get served in one of the pubs – Terry is shoving ha'pennies into the machine – watching the mountain of coppers grow – and he wants those coins – every now and then there's a clatter – he runs out – goes and changes a sixpence at the kiosk – hurries back – finds two skinhead girls at the next machine – and they're both good-looking – one with black hair cut more mod-style – the other blonde with a feather crop – and he hesitates – thinks about the coppers – holds a ha'penny over the slot and waits for the right moment – lets it go – watches it flip and flop like a Teddy Boy down the Crown – sees it slip in with the other coins – and he glances sideways

and the blonde is watching him – she looks away quick –
Terry doesn't know what to do – wonders if she fancies
him – no – she can't do – he keeps playing – feels both
girls watching him – he's nervous – turns and smiles – like
a stupid kid – and the blonde is so near he can smell her
perfume – and she has these brilliant blue eyes like he's never
seen – and he wants to say something clever but doesn't
have the words – goes back to the machine – the blonde
telling him to go on – you can get that lot – one more go
and we would have won – and he has two ha'pennies left
– the sharp little skinhead who rocks around in his brain
steps forward – makes Terry give her a coin – she thanks
him – you sure? – he sends his down the chute and sees it
slide harmlessly into the pile – he wanted to win in front
of this girl – impress her – pretends he doesn't care – watches
her lean against the machine – waiting for the moment –
and he sees how she presses forward against the glass – can't
miss her bum in the air – and she's wearing faded jeans –
filling her 501s – she has the curves all right – looks great
– and there's a crash as the coins come crashing down – her
mate screams and jumps up and down – the blonde turns
to Terry and grins – they want to give him half – but he
says no – and her mate goes over to change the ha'pennies
into silver – and the blonde is looking at him – waiting – but
he doesn't know what to say – she's just being polite – that's
what he tells himself – and she really is smashing – gorgeous
– he feels sick inside because there's no way she's going to
fancy him – and he realises 'Wet Dream' is playing in the
arcade – he bets he's going red – the girl blushes – says that's
Max Romeo – she knows her music – doesn't just dress the
part – and Terry nods – confused – he just doesn't have
the chat-up lines – he's fucking useless – a wanker – and
her friend returns – he can't say anything now – they wave
goodbye – walking out of the arcade – and he sees the
blonde glance back – that's the end of that – and he looks
at the machines and wonders why he wastes his money –
it's a game of chance – not like pool – that takes skill – and
he's broke and leaves – has to find the others – and he stands

opposite the Tube and looks at the pubs – The North Star on the Uxbridge Road – The Bridge House on the corner – and there's that Irish boozer towards the green – and he'll start in The North Star – he's been in there before and they've got a couple of pool tables – and he thinks of the blonde again and decides she is the best-looking girl he has ever set eyes on – she has it all – and he never said a word – he's a fucking joke – heads towards the pub – feels a tap on his shoulder and turns – sees the black-haired girl from the arcade – she pushes a piece of paper in his hand and says phone her up – for fuck's sake – and then she's running back to the bus stop – the two girls jumping on the back of a 65 – and he looks at the paper – reads the name April – followed by a number – and he carries on towards the pub – bouncing now – can't believe his luck – and Terry is still walking – he's had her number nearly a week now – it's in his pocket – right here – and he's written it down at home as well – just in case – and maybe he's left it too long – she won't remember him – maybe her mate was having him on – and he stands outside the phone box and the sharp little skinhead in his brain tells him to get on with it – so he dials the number and drops his coin in and April says it's a good job he called – she's going on holiday tomorrow with her mum and dad – a caravan in Selsey – and she'll see him next Saturday – can he get to Brentford station? – Terry says yes – he can find it – she's coming home in the morning – it's round the corner – there's a pause – she says she has to go – someone's at the front door – and he puts the phone down – presses his forehead against the glass – heat soaking into his skin – the sharp little skinhead in his brain telling him he's a lucky lad – a lucky boy.

Family Values

THE BOY PRESSED HIS head against the glass and peered into the darkness – eyes taking time to adjust – and he brushed condensation into his hair – stubble turning black – vision trailing the column of light cutting into the darkness from next door – and the further the beam reached – the more it faded – fanning out and forming a patch of blue mist – his brain clicking – connecting – neck snapping back as he rocked on his heels – a stabbing pain in his chest as a needle injected – as he tasted the terror of a grown man shocked by death – searching for words – voice croaking – this doesn't make sense – how did this happen? – yesterday we were walking in the sun – bouncing in the rain – everything was possible – yesterday I was a child – what is happening to me? – I don't understand this at all – and the boy was shaking – throat rattling – the voice vanished – an impression – he knew – but didn't have a clue what was coming – couldn't see what was happening right under his nose – wanted to run and hide from the shape moving – outside – in the dark – on the edge of the light – and it was a woman – somehow he knew it was a woman – a witch? – casting spells? – the boy bounced back – butted the glass – eyes searching hard – shifting to the fence – where the light was solid and bright – Bob and Molly stood there – horses sensed danger – before it happened – and they were calm – there couldn't be anything out there – he felt stupid – didn't know why he imagined this – trying to work out where it came from – he was a happy boy – took after his dad – and Lol knew he was safe – with his father – in this house – a Tony Hawks skater frozen on his screen – a cartoon boy who never bruised – kept floating in the air – feet stuck to his board – hovering – lit up by an artificial sun – and Lol pulled the curtains shut and sat on the edge of his bed – knew there was nothing to fear – nothing could be as bad as Mum dying – telling himself he was a lucky boy.

The most important thing is having a family that sticks together, people who look after each other never mind what happens, specially when you're young, or old, or sick, and not everyone has that, look at Kev the Kev, he has his mum, but that's all, no brothers, no sisters, never sees his dad, must wonder where he is, what he's doing, and his mum doesn't talk to his gran, so there's just the two of them in a house that doesn't even have proper heating, they've been burgled twice in four months, Kev sleeps with a knife under his pillow, his mum doesn't earn much working on the till, it can't be nice if your mum and dad hate each other, but it's worse for someone like Ian Stills, his dad used to hit his mum, least till Ian stabbed him with a fork, in the side, in the side of his head, and then he picked up a carving knife and his dad ran out of the house and they haven't seen him since, Ian wishes he killed him, bet he doesn't, not all of him anyway, and Mum and Dad loved each other and wanted to be together for ever, they weren't allowed, Dad says you have to think of the good things in life, you can't change the past, you have to forget it and move on, don't let it hurt you, smile and be strong, there's a lot to look forward to, the world is big and exciting, if Dad wasn't around he doesn't know what he would do, but he will always be here, he'll never go away, never die, like Mum, lightning never strikes the same place twice, that's what they say, and Lol has his sisters and Uncle Ray and all the rest of them, and he starts laughing, thinking of his dad and uncle and their friends, all those boys who'll never grow up.

Lol didn't know why he was laughing – guessed it was relief – knowing everything was fine – looking at his globe – lit up from the inside out – mountains and deserts and cities shades of brown – the sea blue – blue oceans – a patch of white burning below the surface – and it was like Lol was looking at the Earth from somewhere out in space – and he left the globe plugged in all night – turned it a little – imagined driving through the Kimberleys and down to the Great Bight – meteor sites in the Outback – sailing down the Amazon – climbing the Himalayas – singing with a band in Los Angeles – and he looked at Afghanistan and Iraq – couldn't imagine war in this sparkling world – these adventures were what sent him to sleep at night – and Joe Cole was standing above the globe – a football at his feet – the world at his feet – a Chelsea ball boy – next to an older poster of Zola – Lol's favourite player – just ahead of Joe – and JT – he slipped *American Idiot* into his CD player – sang along to 'Jesus Of Suburbia'– a long journey through the sprawl of Western civilisation – that line about being the son of rage and love – his cousin Chelsea said that was her dad – she was the daughter of rage and love – maybe she was right – Uncle Ray was different to Dad – maybe it was like LOVE AND HATE on Alan's knuckles – everyone called him Hawkins – he laughed again – being born into a skinhead family you didn't have much choice about how you grew up – the music you liked – he had been raised on his mum and dad's ska records – Uncle Ray's Oi – and Lol was the place where it all collided – and when the song was over he slipped in *Indestructible* – clicking through to 'Red Hot Moon'.

You can go where you want with this music, from Tropical London to the Ivory Coast, from Rancid into Transplants and Lars, going back to *American Idiot*, picking up the controls, and with Tony Hawks every kerb is calling, Duane Peters knows and he's no kid, playgrounds stretching out through warm streets, and even though you're moving forward you always end up in the same place, you're safe and free, riding ramps and flipping through empty loading bays, the factories deserted, machines asleep, traffic banned, and you move across car parks and glide into a subway, and when you crash you don't break any bones, don't bleed or die, no, it's a lush world, lined with palm trees, and the sun never ever stops shining, you're invincible, and that's the way to live, you love that line as well, the one where Billy Joe says his shadow is the only one that walks beside him, and that's true, for people on their own, and you aren't alone, and there's no shadows in this place, and you think about your cousin Chelsea, that's how she feels, she doesn't like her dad living away, wishes he would come home, not be angry all the time and get in fights, that's why Auntie Liz kicked him out, you think, and Chelsea asks what's wrong with these grown-ups, but you don't know, and this time it's not funny.

Lol was moving back and forward between bands – and his room began to shake – some heavy bass rising from the living room – Dad back from work – and the pub – blowing his CD away with forty-year-old vinyl – and it was Alfonso who had built the speakers – they were massive and filled two corners of the room – Lol recognised 'Pressure Drop' – knew the sound of The Maytals – had no choice – and in this house it was the son who asked the father to turn the music down – everything was back to front – his dad out late – coming in pissed – eating junk food – and the sunshine sounds of California had been swamped by the sunshine sounds of Jamaica – Zola flopping down – Blu-Tack shaken loose – Joe Cole grinning – and Lol paused his PlayStation – it was eight o'clock and with some drink inside him Dad would be thinking about an Indian – Lol suddenly hungry – hoping Dad had brought something home – and if he hadn't he'd soon be calling Chapatti Express – Lol's mouth watering now – remembering he'd had nothing to eat yet.

He goes in the bathroom and stands over the toilet, washes his hands and looks in the mirror. Uncle Ray says he looks like his mum, but really he's more like his dad, when he was young, hair cut short, the smile and extra-white teeth. Kev the Kev says he's a townie, a chav, with his Ben Sherman and Harrington jacket, the one with the Fred Perry logo, but Lol doesn't think about names, he listens to ska-punk, is a bit skater, a bit football. He doesn't care. He does his own thing. 'Skinhead Girl' is playing now and he brushes his teeth. Thinks of Mum. Dad always plays this one when he's had a drink. Lol stands on the landing and waits for the song to end. There's silence and he guesses Dad is sitting down, can smell curry and knows he's eating, the needle safe at the back of the record, the 45 spinning round and round – round and round – for ever. Terry and April – for ever together. That's what they wrote in shelters and on walls, at the back of buses, when graffiti was basic, about love and violence, before it moved on and became clever, full of colour and life. He goes downstairs, finds Dad in his chair, feet up, a tray on his lap.

Dad was home early – slurring and happy – like father like son – except Lol didn't drink – not much – not yet – but if he ended up the same way he'd be pleased enough – Dad never let him down – two unopened cartons and a paratha waiting in the kitchen – empties scattered along the counter – foil twisted and bent backwards – crushed doors and a dented roof – a shattered windscreen – and he ran a finger along the rim of something that burnt his mouth – a long streak of red sauce smearing the cardboard – and he thought of Mum – pushed at the image – trying hard – conjured up that Tony Hawks skater – a free spirit hitting concrete and springing back up – last night it was Chapatti Express – this was Taj food – they didn't deliver – Dad must've stopped on his way home – and Lol had been to The Taj enough times – for a sit-down – with Dad – and the owner – Harry – treated them like kings – came and sat with them when things were quiet – ordered three pints of Cobra – always said the same thing – that Lol was the spitting image of Terry when he was a boy – Dad and Harry went to school together – many years before – and Lol dropped rice on a plate – added his favourite – jalfrezi – grabbed a spoon and the paratha – went into the living room and sat down – Dad turning the volume on the TV down – Catherine Tate pulling faces in silence – asking Lol how he was – what he'd been doing – father and son tucking into their dinner.

Nutty Boys

RAY STOOD AT THE end of the bar and lifted a pint of Fosters to his mouth. The first drink of the night hadn't touched the sides, but he was savouring this one, gearing up for a session with Handsome, doing his best to ease the pressure in his head. It had been a hard week, but it had also been a good earner, Liz well pleased with the extra fifty he'd slipped her earlier. After three toasted–cheese sandwiches and four choco- late mini-rolls he sat on the couch and watched telly with his girls, one on each side, his arms around their shoulders.

They were growing up fast, Chelsea eleven and April nine, but he only saw babies, small bags of sugar and spice. Teenagers were skin and bone, even the porky ones, and he had to laugh when youths of eighteen or nineteen gave it the big one, knew that if he blew hard enough most would go flying. Despite all the shit they were fed through the TV, today's kids seemed more innocent than fifteen or twenty years back. They talked about binge drinking and high-street violence, but it had been worse when he was young. The problem now was drugs, easy credit and the endless gadgets, but he was doing what every father should, teaching his girls the value of money and the need for morals. It was up to every parent to educate their children. Show them right from wrong. The schools did their best, but they couldn't compete with big business and the media.

Liz brought Ray and the girls bowls of ice cream and disappeared upstairs, and he enjoyed the warmth of his house, vanilla melting in his mouth. Chelsea and April rested their heads on his chest, and he could smell their hair, which was clean and fresh and reminded him of coconuts. Liz was a good mum, who lived for her kids and just wanted her husband to calm down. She had changed. When he met her she was a spunky punk, but these days she didn't bother dressing up, didn't seem to have an opinion, happy to hide in her shell and guard the children. At least he was ten minutes down the road, and was getting on okay with Liz now they were living apart. The girls didn't say much about it, but it must have been having an effect.

If he thought about it too much it would do his head in, the best way to ease the tension a night on the piss. There was nobody better to do it with than the bloke next to him.

– I'm going to get fucking arseholed tonight, Handsome remarked.

– You do that every night. You'll get yourself nicked one morning and be out of a job.

– Don't care. Don't give a fuck.

– You will when you're signing on with the Kosovans and Albanians, rubbing shoulders with all those Somali muggers and Serbian pimps.

Handsome gulped half his pint.

– I'll get my share then, won't I? I've been paying taxes for near on twenty years and never claimed a penny, and these fucking asylum seekers turn up and are straight in, hand-outs for food, clothes, houses, drugs, everything, and then they invite their relatives and mates over. It's about time I had something back.

– What about the council house you grew up in, your school and health, all the rest of it? Ray laughed.

It was easy winding Handsome up.

– It's my fucking country. Now you've got these Russians running a slave trade in tarts, Afghans and fuck knows what else shipping in truckloads of smack, Snakeheads and their cockle-pickers. The Government doesn't do anything, sends them over to live with us, says the people over there won't fucking mind, they're just scum and all.

Handsome shook his head.

– No, mate. It's all wrong. Have a view about what you see in front of your eyes and they call you a racist.

Ray had no time for bullies, but knew there was truth in what the bloke was saying, that the establishment despised ordinary whites and couldn't wait to break up the UK, turn England into a European region. Ray was proud of Britain's tradition of tolerance, knew it was what made it so different to Europe.

– The EU's the real enemy.

Handsome sighed, realised he had walked into the trap.

– Yeah, I know.

Ray focused on the bored expression. The anger roared up inside him.

– No, you don't, that's the fucking problem. The EU has already raped your country and you're going on about some poor cunt who wants to clean your bogs and pick your cabbages.

– What about the drug dealers?

– Put them up against a wall and shoot them. Find the girl-traffickers and hang them. No problem. But this country has always taken in asylum seekers. That's what made us strong, not the East India Company or the slavers. You have to know your enemy.

– Nothing you can do about any of it, though. Not really.

Handsome frowned as he saw his friend's face twitch. Ray was a good friend, a diamond, but too serious.

– Come on, it's Friday, he said, trying to calm things down.

He wanted a drink, not another heavy discussion. Living with Ray wasn't easy. He could sympathise with Liz.

– Get some lager down your throat.

Ray nodded. People spent all their time moaning and groaning, going on and on, picking on the tabloid targets, lumping a girl raped in the Sudan with a gang of Arab pick-pockets, but were too lazy or gutless to challenge the people who were really fucking them over. Maybe they deserved what they got. Ray was tempted to give his friend a slap, knock some sense into him, but reasoned that he wouldn't have any mates left if he clumped every tosser he knew.

The door opened and Paul strolled in.

– Oi Oi, Handsome shouted. It's a rockabilly rebel.

Psychobilly Paul grinned as he came over.

– You're late, Ray remarked, inspecting his watch.

– Radiator went, didn't it? I was heating up in traffic and had to pull over and wait for the engine to cool down. Called Senior and he said park it out back and he'll have a look first thing. At least I made it without blowing up.

Ray remembered his gearbox, relieved it had settled down. Paul got the drinks in.

– Stop in any lay-bys today? Handsome asked.

Paul shrugged, trying to hide his embarrassment, wishing he'd kept his mouth shut.

– Brought your Viagra with you? Ray added, joining in.

Paul inspected a couple of women sitting nearby. Burberry handbags rested on a copper-topped table as they chain-smoked, reaching for silver bottles.

– I almost got caught, that's the worst thing. I'm sitting there and this van pulls in, full of kids. They're higher up than me and can see in the front seat of the car. Luckily I'd finished and managed to tuck it away in time.

Ray and Handsome shook their heads.

– I could be sitting in the cells now, branded a nonce, my life over.

– I hope Tel doesn't hear, Handsome remarked. He wouldn't like it. Bad for business. Don't blame him either.

Ray and Handsome finished their lager, reached for the fresh glasses.

– Terry not out tonight? Paul asked.

– Haven't spoken to him today, Ray replied. He usually starts early on a Friday.

– I saw him at the office, Paul said. You reckon he fancies Angie?

– Don't know. He hasn't gone out with anyone since my aunt died.

– That's a few years now.

– Nearly ten.

– Ten years? Fucking hell.

– It was just after his fortieth birthday. I still can't believe it.

– She was a lovely lady.

Ray recalled the accident. Him and Liz had rushed to the hospital when they got the call, but were too late. He would never forget Terry's face. A split second and everything changed for ever.

– She was that, Handsome agreed. You think life's good and out of nowhere it all goes tits-up. Terrible.

Ray didn't want to think about the accident, the funeral, any of that time.

– Come on, let's talk about something else.

– Sorry, mate. Handsome's face fell.

– Yeah, sorry Ray, Paul said, lowering his head.

There was a long pause.

Paul leant over.

– You see that bird over there?

– Which one?

Handsome turned and stared.

– Don't stare, you plum. The one with her hair pulled back. In the short white skirt?

– What about her?

– She's not wearing any pants.

Handsome nearly spilt his pint, but Paul was right. The girl began pulling at the leather when they kept looking over, and left shortly after, but she waved through the window as they disappeared into the night. Ray wondered how Paul knew.

– A lucky guess, was all he would say.

They were soon off themselves, heading towards the Wetherspoons. It was Ali G time at the other end of the high street, the local Muftis fighting the Kosovans and Albanians to a Daddy Yankee beat, the Pied Horse something out of the Congo. Ray liked Ali G, taking the piss out of white boys pretending to be black, Asians who thought they were from Compton. Funny thing was, Staines could be a dodgy place, as it was suburban, young, white and larey, and Ali G would have to watch himself. Ali C would be out and about as well, the difference between Comical and Chemical Ali. Ray didn't mind the Gs, those Asian lads made

68

him laugh, but the Ali Cunts were drug-dealing scum, selling to lost kids borrowing a rap patois cloned off the music channels, American businessmen telling them how to behave. There were too many white boys who didn't know their culture. Too many people conned by the corporate machine. He didn't care if it was a chavvie little herbert from Manor Park, Acton Town or Tower Hamlets, you had to respect your roots. That was the only way you could respect yourself. These wiggers and wankstas were a fucking disgrace. Let the TV decide things and you were fucked before you started.

Entering The Moon Over Water, Ray found the BB-Boys enjoying the special prices, clustered at the front by the windows, looking across the road at The Market Bar, where two boneheads in black flight-jackets stood talking to a gang of skinny girls. The BBs had been banned after Kev the Kev puked up, and they saw this as a result, part of the new breed who hated dance music, a nutty bunch of kids between ten and fifteen strong, ranging from fourteen to sixteen years old, a gaggle of brothers and cousins and mates of brothers and mates of mates. They usually knocked about in Uxbridge, but had come over to Slough for a special showing of *The Fast and the Furious*, wanting to see one of their favourite DVDs on the big screen. These boys didn't crave the expensive labels of the Stone Island chasers, the bullshit of the logo men, made their own look up, and there was some pikey in there with the skater, grunger, mosher, skin, townie, punk influences – a proper mash-up of M25, Outer London living.

The BB-Boys grinned when Ray nodded at Kev and some of Lol's other mates, names he forgot or didn't know, sipping their drinks and staying away from the bar, making their refreshment last. This new wave of kids pissed all over the acid-house rave brigade. Things were looking up. The Nineties had belonged to the children of the hippies, drugged-up flower-power babies charging top dollar for peace and love. The offspring of the skins and punks and football hooligans were claiming the new century.

– All right, Ray? Ian Stills asked, as the three men approached the bar.

Ian was one of three older youths branded The Young Offenders after getting themselves nicked for thieving sweets a few years back, and anyone who hung around with them was lumbered with the same tag. Ray towered above them and the boy went red. He was puzzled, then realised Ian was waiting for an answer.

– I'm good, Ian. How about you? Behaving yourself?

The boy swelled up, though Ray didn't notice. Ian and his pals, Matty and Darren, looked up to Ray, knew he was an old-school hooligan who had run riot back in the glory days. Ian was nineteen and football mad, knew his history, chuffed that Ray remembered his name. He was wearing a new badge, one with a Union Jack in the middle, Chelsea written above, England below.

– I'm good, thanks. Thanks, Ray.

– Nice badge, Ray said, patting him on the shoulder and nodding to the other Offenders, moving along the bar to where Handsome was buying the drinks.

Lifting more lager to his mouth, Ray scanned the pub, half-looking for the Table 29 crew, knowing they would be long gone. They'd been children during the war and had lived through the tough years when England was being rebuilt, but had also glimpsed a cooperative system, the blessings of state pensions, the NHS, a decent education system, periods of massive house-building, and even political parties with ideals. He looked at The Young Offenders and wondered what would be left when they retired. What about the BB-Boys? If things kept going the way they were, every social service would be privatised and the multinationals would have total control, every part of their lives run for profit. He worried for all these cranks, but most of all he worried for his daughters.

– Cheer up, Handsome said.

– I was just thinking.

– I told you before, it's bad for your health.

– Let's just have the one in here, Paul said. Get down and see the band.

The Rising Sun had a covers band playing. It was open late as well.

Ray finished his pint in two. Caught the barman's attention. Ian and his friends were waiting to be served.

– What do you want? Ray called over.

The Young Offenders jumped, moved along the bar.

– Lager?

– Three bottles of Becks, please.

– You want straws with that?

The Young Offenders laughed – nervously. Ray was a nutter. It was well known. He had hammers for fists and had stood up to a mob of Pakis single-handed when he was a boy, been beaten half to death, stabbed and still come back for more. Everyone called him Nutty Ray, but never to his face. They'd heard he did anyone who used that name. Bosh. Ian looked down at the steel-toecapped boots, which were a different league to today's trainers. He was a one-man killing machine.

– Three pints of lager, Ray insisted. Fosters okay?

They nodded. Ray didn't like men drinking bottles, specially when he was buying.

– I want to ask you three a question, he said, once he'd paid.

The Young Offenders waited, sipping their pints, moving Reeboks side to side, suddenly worried.

– I want you to answer me honestly. Don't worry that I might not agree with you, as I know you lot are a different generation.

The Young Offenders fretted. Maybe it was a trick question. Ian stood at the front. Darren pulled his baseball cap down, concentrating hard. Matty looked at the heavy man they called Handsome, saw the hard bone of his skull, a faded tear tattooed under his right eye, and then the other guy, with his hair shaved to the bone down the sides of his head, hair boxed flat on top, and finally Ray, his eyes blue and wide and staring, decided all three were headcases.

– Okay, Ian said.

– Do you lot think we should get rid of the pound and

bring in the Euro? You know, change our currency so it's the same as Europe?

The three boys were shaking their heads.

– What do we want the Euro for?

– We're not European, we're English.

– What did we fight the war for? Fucking German cunts.

Ray was pleased, turned towards Handsome with a meaningful look.

– What about the constitution?

The boys looked blank.

– Is that the one the Government says doesn't mean anything, but really it's getting us ready to become part of a single European nation?

Ian was a smart boy.

– That's the one.

– Don't really understand it, Ian continued, but I know it's part of a plan to take away our sovereignty. All you need is one politician to say what everyone thinks and take us out of Europe. If anyone did that, they'd win the next election.

Ray agreed, and his respect for Ian grew.

The boy reached in his pocket.

– We found this when we came in, he said, handing a sheet of paper to Ray.

Headed ONE BRAVE MAN, with a circle on the edge with TABLE 29 written inside, it read: WANTED, A BRITISH HERO, READY TO GO OUT WITH A BANG. Ray cracked up laughing, remembered the bloke he'd dropped off that morning, imagined the old boys sitting at their table drawing up a flyer, going across to the library and having it photocopied, handing them out around the pub. Ray shook with laughter.

– What does it mean? Darren asked at last.

– It means someone's got a sense of humour, Ray replied.

They drank and talked football for a while, Ray remembering how Ian had stabbed his old man, felt sorry for the boy, wanted to warn him off fighting at football, explain it was a waste of time, just ordinary people kicking fuck out of each other, but this wasn't the time or place, and Ian wouldn't listen. He looked over at the BB-Boys who were bundling outside, off to the pictures, and he wondered where Lol was, saw a figure jogging down the road and recognised Terry's boy, saw him grab the baseball cap off Kev's head, and they were all pushing each other and mucking about and crossing the road, sticking together like frogspawn, bumping into each other, having a laugh, innocent kids, and then they were out of sight.

Ray, Handsome and Paul left for The Rising Sun, The Young Offenders jumping in a cab, off to somewhere in Windsor. He saw the car pass, an Indian geezer behind the wheel, three scrotes in the back, and he should have handed them an Estuary card, watched the red lights dipping away, towards the M4.

It was a short walk to the next pub and they were waved inside by the bloke on the door, Ray leading the others down the side of the bar as the band chopped their way through 'That's Entertainment'. Ray had grown up hearing The Jam, a proper football band, and the song lifted him up. Paul Weller knew the score and had never sold out. He recognised faces, slapped some backs, stood nearby as Paul did the honours, saw Joe Martin, drinking with that pikey mate of his, Clem.

– Your uncle was in here earlier, Joe slurred.

He was pissed and Ray had to lean close to hear what he was saying, the singer moving into an Oasis song, doing a Liam Gallagher impression on stage, the only real differences his accent, age, voice, gut and bald head.

– What time was that? Ray asked.

– A few hours ago. He was with Hawkins.

Ray took a pint of Fosters from Paul.

– It's a shame Dave isn't around, Joe continued. Hawkins has got all this snide Lacoste in his lock-up and Dave would have helped him shift it no trouble. It's shit, though. Soulboy wear.

– Fucking ponce gear, Ray agreed.

Any self-respecting skin, herbert or punk would wear Fred Perry.

73

Ray didn't like Joe's mate Dave. He'd heard he was living in a caravan down by the coast, and thought it was a fucking good place for him as well. Joe stuck up for the bloke, but Ray couldn't see why. He was flash. Worse than that, he was off his rocker. He liked Joe, but that was the difference between a punk and a skin. Punks made allowances, tried to see the other point of view, while a skinhead stood firm, didn't budge an inch.

They stayed in the pub until closing, drinking faster, enjoying the noise and company, the band finishing with a mucky version of 'One Step Beyond' before everyone stumbled outside, Ray and Handsome waltzing slowly home, too pissed to think about food, remembering their psychobilly mate as they approached the flat, realising Paul had gone off with that bird without the panties. It was typical.

Ray turned the heater on in his room, feeling the cold, the emptiness, didn't worry about undressing as he climbed into bed. The walls glowed yellow from the street lights, but he couldn't be bothered closing the curtains. He could hold his drink, but was tired and glad it was Friday. The fan took its time, the motor soothing him as he pictured his house, wondering why he had ended up here, separated from his wife and daughters, and drunk, it all seemed so stupid, like nothing should be allowed to get in the way of family, and he knew it was a crime wasting this time, the sound of the heater charging his sleep, and he was half-dreaming, watching a toy car with a big yellow driver behind the wheel, his black mouth turned down and angry, and the car was moving around the room in a wide circle that soon became tighter and smaller, the driver swerving to avoid a red parrot and a tribe of Red Indians, banging into the skirting board, stopping dead, engine silent, a blonde doll sitting on the bonnet, flickering her huge painted eyelashes, forcing a big plastic smile across the driver's big plastic face.

BOSS SOUNDS

Flying the Flag

LEANING FORWARD, ELBOWS ON the bar, Terry watched as Buster poured the first pint, appreciating the way the London Pride built inside the glass, which was tilted at exactly the right angle, thereby avoiding a too-thick, frothy Northern head. Buster was a find, an Estuary driver with fifteen years of experience running pubs before he joined the firm, a mate of a mate from the Matthew Harding Upper Tier and a dead ringer for the legendary Buster Bloodvessel. While Terry wasn't keen on the muggier brand of bonehead, if a clean-shaved bonce was a response to natural hair loss, or a tribute to the legendary Gianluca Vialli, he wasn't going to complain. As far as the real Mr Bloodvessel went, well, the man could do no wrong in his eyes, and could piss in his pint whenever he wanted. Not that the Bad Manners general would want to, of course, as Bloodvessel was a gentleman and a scholar, a skinhead hero respected for his knowledge of ska and loved for his friendly English nature. The barman was honoured by the comparison.

With the London Pride waiting on the counter, Buster served himself, the two men raising and tapping their glasses together. The Estuary boss enjoyed the moment, filling his mouth and swallowing the Fuller's bitter, quickly nodding his approval.

– Perfect.

Buster had done the Union Jack Club proud, cleaned the pipes and ordered in London Pride, Fosters, Guinness and Strongbow as a start, hooking everything up and delivering a quality pint. He knew what he was doing. Terry was impressed.

– Not bad, Buster agreed. Not bad at all.

It was a month since Terry had walked in the place, and after another visit he'd made a decision. Angie tracked down the owner, a man who'd bought the premises from a developer eager to sell after Thatcher's boom turned to bust, having sat on the empty building for seven years. The current owner then inherited a farm and returned to Pakistan. He had never rented it out, his son living locally and happy to organise a cheap ten-year lease. He was keen to sell. The option was there.

Terry English was now the proud owner of his own club, with two top-notch pool tables, a good bar, and a half-decent pinball machine. The electricity had been connected and four electric heaters filled in for the broken radiators. It was early days, and there was a lot needed doing, but most of it was cosmetic. A good clean, some paint and a few minor improvements and it would be perfect. The Union Jack had a friendly feel and he wasn't going to change it, just spruce things up a little. As far as Estuary Cars went, there was a kitchen and storage area that was twice the size of the current office, and once that was cleared and done up the firm would move in. The rent was lower than the new quote on his old premises, so it was well worth the investment. All told, he'd had a result.

– The flag will be ready next week, Buster said. They've dry-cleaned it and someone is mending the rips.

– It's going to fill the alley. You won't be able to miss the place.

– Maybe we should raise it in the morning and take it down at night?

– We could hire a bugle boy.

– That's easy, pay Hawkins or Steve the Crisp. They could play the Last Post all night the amount of chang they get through.

The Estuary boys would have the office to rest up in between jobs, and the main part of the club to socialise in at night. Angie would keep the two separate. Terry didn't want his drivers pissed when they were working. He had plans. Moving the pool tables aside gave him a ready-made stage, and he imagined the bingo nights, birthday parties and wedding receptions that had taken place here over the years, pleased he was going to add another layer. He checked his watch. Couldn't wait for the jukebox to arrive. He emptied his glass.

– Come on, Terry said, grinning. I'm dying of thirst here.

Buster did the necessary.

– Welcome to the Union Jack Club. Good beer, good company. We'll have to buy you a wheelchair, like Peter Kay in *Phoenix Nights*.

They both liked that programme.

– We'll get Max and Paddy on the door.

– Ray and Handsome will be enough.

Buster started laughing.

– Remember that film? The one about the working-man's club in Liverpool? What was it called?

Terry shook his head, started to remember.

– The one with the blind boxer?

– That's it. The new manager comes in and they've double booked two mobs of pensioners. It's a Christmas party or something, and one lot's Protestant and the other's Catholic, and they've known each other for years, hate each other's guts, start raring up.

Terry smiled.

– *No Surrender*.

– That's it. Brilliant, wasn't it?

– Yeah, it was. *No Surrender*. Like this place. Someone shuts it down and now it's back.

Buster placed a pint of Strongbow on the bar.

– See what that one tastes like.

Terry took his time.

– Just as good, he said, grinning.

Terry ran his free hand along the bar, felt the perfect smoothness of the surface. It had taken a while to get rid of the dust, and then he'd bought some special polish and cleaned it right up. He saw a Polish soldier building it, a carpenter unable to return to his village thanks to Stalin, another wave of Poles arriving so many years later, looking for building work, slagged off in the press. Or maybe it was one of Slough's Irishmen who made the bar, fighting the Germans and later labelled with an IRA tag. Or a local man whose family went back centuries. They all drank in this place. It was the strength of the Union Jack. This bar was older than he was, and it wasn't going to tell him any secrets. The mirror had shone up nice as well, and he had ordered a fridge, bought a couple of boxes of pint glasses. He was having fun.

– The problem with these pubs trying to flog you over-priced food is they don't care about the beer, Buster said. The more you pay, the flatter it tastes.

– We want good quality and low prices, Terry observed.

– Seems the more you pay for a pint in some places, the worse it tastes. No pride, see. They're too bothered about making money on the food. All you need in a pub is crisps, peanuts and a big plate full of rolls. It's the beer that matters.

– And a pool table. You have to have a pool table.

Terry went over to the tables. Buster followed.

– You know what would be good, Terry mused.

– What's that?

– To put a show on.

– What, pole dancers and strippers?

– No, there's enough places you can go for that.

– You could get some of those Thai birds over. The ones Hawkins keeps going on about. Forget your Thai Kitchen, we'll have the Thai Kittens.

It wasn't what Terry had in mind.

– You know, firing ping-pong balls out of their fannies, Buster went on.

Terry shook his head.

– I was thinking of someone like Bernard Manning.

– What? Buster asked, surprised. You want Manning doing the splits, firing ping-pong balls out of his arse?

Terry sighed.

– Can't see that happening somehow, Buster continued.

You'd need footballs. Anyway, he's expensive. I heard nowadays he performs for the people who looked down their noses at him a few years back. Charges a fortune and takes them for a ride. That's what I heard, anyway.

– Good luck to him.

Maybe it wasn't such a good idea. It was getting complicated.

– You could put some music on, Buster said.

That wasn't a bad idea. Not bad at all. Angie was sorting out the drinks licence, so maybe he would talk to her about the music, see if they could get them both at the same time. But it was a lot to think about. The jukebox was enough for now. More than enough.

He placed the white ball on the table and sent it down. The triangle popped. Buster stepped up.

Terry looked around, admiring his work. He'd wiped the tables and hoovered the carpet a couple of times, used a mop on the bare floors, but knew the club needed a professional cleaner in. Some of the paintwork could do with touching up, but he wasn't going to change the colours or anything.

Buster potted a stripe, moved round the table.

Terry moved into the light coming through the top of the windows, didn't know whether to take the boards down or leave them up. He preferred things as they were. The boards made the Union Jack a secret hideaway, a civilised corner of the world, and he wondered if it even needed punters, but really it would only be the boys from the firm, and some of their women and mates. It would be okay. He liked company. He would make it members-only, maybe do some cards.

Buster missed his shot and Terry potted four balls in a row.

– That jukebox should have been here by now, Buster said.

Terry's mobile rang.

– You've got ESP.

– IPA more like.

A cheerful voice told Terry that his Rock-Ola had arrived.

He put his cue down and hurried to the main door, kicking a fag packet into the gutter as he stepped outside. The delivery van was waiting at the end of the alley, and he waved to the driver, who nodded and pulled forward, then carefully reversed towards him. Terry smiled at the cartoon quiff and brothel creepers on the side panels, thinking about Duke Reid and Prince Buster instead of Carl Perkins and Gene Vincent, the famous sound-clashes and battles for the best sounds, the biggest beer sales.

The driver turned off the engine and jumped out, a chirpy little geezer with a greased-back DA and a smell of Brylcreem, a big Irish lad coming round from the other side, fresh from the farms of Donegal.

– Mr English? the driver asked.

– That's me.

– I've got a jukebox for you, sir.

The back doors opened and there it sat, a reconditioned, vintage Rock-Ola. It was beautiful. It really was something special.

Buster came out and whistled, stood with Terry as the machine was unloaded, the Irish youth using the van's hydraulic platform and a trolley, bringing it inside and dropping it on the walkway, the four of them pushing the jukebox against the wall, at the far end of the bar, and it hovered same as a UFO in a Fifties sci-fi film, elevated and gleaming, plugged in with the electricity surging through its veins, pumping blood into its heart. Terry knew how to load the records, had written down the instructions when he went to the showroom, signed the delivery form.

– You two want a drink? Terry offered.

The youth nodded, but the driver shook his head.

– Thanks, but we've got to pick up an old Wurlitzer in Neasden.

He looked around, patted the Rock-Ola.

– You'll have fun with this. It's a classic.

– The Killers would sound good, the kid said.

– 'Brown Sugar', the driver insisted. 'Street-Fighting Man'. You've got to have some Rolling Stones on there.

– Nekromantix's 'Gargoyles Over Copenhagen', the boy added. If you can get it on a 45.

– Jerry Lee Lewis. Every Rock-Ola needs some Jerry Lee. He's the real Killer. Johnny Cash . . . Warren Smith . . . Carl Perkins. Lemmy doing 'Motorhead'.

Buster had finished pouring the pint of Guinness he'd started five minutes before, when he realised there was an Irishman on the premises. He handed it to the boy.

– What do you think?

The youth gulped a third of the glass, smiled and raised it in a toast.

– That is a fine pint. Thanks.

The driver was smiling, but keen to pick up the Wurlitzer.

– Go on, Terry said. Take the glass. Finish it in the van.

Terry stood outside as they pulled away, his arms folded, looking up and down the alley before going inside and locking the door. He opened the record box he'd brought in that morning and spilled singles along the bar. The Rock-Ola was burning stronger than the sheets of light coming in from outside, shifting the focal point of the club. It sat there glowing, waiting patiently. It was a flamboyant work of genius, dripping confidence, sizzling with the sheer joy of breathing, of having a strong heartbeat, the beat of the jitterbugging, twisting, rocking, skanking masses. It was America at its flashy best, refusing to apologise or bow down, the best side of the free world. It was well worth the money, Terry seeing the Teds in the pubs of his youth, decades of Teddy Boy 45s, the rock'n'roll singles everyone knew off by heart, the early mod records, the arrival of his own music, the story of his life scratched into the black vinyl, cutting across the grooves and making his mark, and now here he was, with his own jukebox. It was incredible. Hard to believe. It was like he had made it big. Estuary Cars was a living. This was more important.

He had come prepared, the middle of the 45s that needed it punched out at home, and he had given each one of them a spring-clean, written the names of the singers and songs on strips of card, suddenly unsure how to arrange them in the machine. He had forty singles with him, but there was room for plenty more. This was just a start, so he didn't bother about any sort of order, loaded them as they came into his hand. Once this was done, he went to the bar and collected another pint, returned to the jukebox and made his first selection. He stood back and waited for 'Skinhead Girl' to fall into place, smiling as the needle connected, and he could see April walking his way, a familiar flush of excitement lifting and filling him with the sort of innocent happiness only music, or a woman, could bring.

Class of '69 – Part 2

TERRY SITS ON A wall outside Brentford station – waiting for April – right leg stretched out in front of him as he admires his turn-ups – but mainly he's watching the ball of light bubbling inside the leather of his DM – he can feel the heat on his toes – and he's glad there's some shade – thorn bushes and wild grass filling the bank behind the wall – seeds and pollen hopping along warm air currents – scorching sunlight baking the tarmac slope running up past The King's Arms – the pub shut – figures moving behind frosted glass – and the station is deserted – he looks over – on the off chance – then back at his foot – he's given his boots an extra good polish – and he's wearing his Brutus – had his hair cut special – yesterday – by the fat sweaty barber round the corner from where he lives – pictures of DAs on the walls – the sweet smell of Brylcreem – and he's wearing braces – white Harrington folded on the wall – glances over the tracks – at the clock on the platform – and April should be here any minute – if she turns up – and he reaches for his jacket – brushes some pods off – picks one up and examines the seeds spilling out – slips off the wall and looks up the embankment – flicks the pod into the jungle – ambles down to the tracks and peers along the line towards Syon Park and Hounslow – stands on the edge of the platform – balancing – follows the embers running along the rail – a seam of cooling gold – quickly bored – walks back to the wall – kicks it a few times – imagines he's in The Shed putting the boot in – realises he's smudging the polish – lifts himself back up – pulls on his braces – shuts his eyes and wonders what it's like being an astronaut in outer space

– on your way to the moon – and he tries to imagine what they think seeing Earth down below – he hopes they make it – it's the sort of thing you could never imagine happening – not for real – and he stares at the road – looks up the slope – then over at the clock – and April is ten minutes late now – maybe he should stroll up on the bridge and have a look over the other side – but right here is where he's supposed to meet her – and he jumps down – bounces foot to foot – smiling – full of energy – Terry has energy to give away – and he's worried she's not going to come – he's so excited about seeing her his head burns – thinking he's missed out – and he looks at his DMs – loves these boots – kicks a small rock that flies across the road and bounces off the window of a Triumph – it makes a dirty great sound as well – he turns and looks around – grins and rubs the stubble on his head – glad nobody saw him – and he knows he's being stood up – that he is never going to see that girl again – feels sad – eyes running up the slope and there she is – right at the top – blonde hair shining in the sun – and April is swinging down the slope – sort of rolling her hips – he can feel it in his balls – and Symarip sing it right – she's wearing braces and blue jeans – and it's like a story out of a book – he's scared now – fucking right he'll have to be courageous – and she's getting nearer – he stands with his hands in his pockets – remembers his Harrington – picks it up and hangs it over his shoulder – and April is bigger – nearer – does what he expects – looks at him and smiles – and he can't help it – starts humming 'Skinhead Girl' – and she just strolls – reaches him – leans up – kisses Terry on the cheek – he almost jumps back – he can't believe it – and she turns and looks up the slope – he doesn't know what to say – she's bloody gorgeous – suddenly he feels very young – like she's smarter – more grown-up – but they must be the same age – more or less – he doesn't know what it is – and she stares at him and narrows her eyes – pausing – sort of weighing him up – and her eyes are big and blue and bursting – she reaches over and wipes his face – laughs – holds a pod in the flat

of her hand – and she decides come on – let's walk down
by the river – and they use the steps up the embankment
– turn to cross the bridge – she slips her arm through his
– he can feel her right tit rubbing his elbow – he hopes he
doesn't get a hard-on – and he doesn't feel nervous any
more – as they stroll along – and it feels good – being with
April like this – so he starts rabbiting away about anything
that jumps into his brain – and he makes her laugh – feels
her knocker firm on his arm – he can feel his cock moving
– tries to think of something else – and they stop outside
The Beehive – cross the road – April leading him through
a tangle of derelict buildings – to the river – and they find
a nice spot – sit down – gazing at the river below – dangling
their legs on the concrete bank – and he holds his right leg
over the water – sees the sun in his boot – April pointing
at Kew Gardens opposite – then Griffin Island – the old
docks of Brentford – tells Terry there's a griffin that lives in
one of the empty warehouses – that's what Brentford people
believe – a griffin is same as a dragon – and it must be an
old story because the football ground is called Griffin Park
– their house backs onto the ground – and she stands on
The Royal Oak with her dad and brothers – and there's a
Griffin beer as well – she flips her fringe back and puts a
hand above her eyes – protecting them from the sun – licks
her lips – and Terry could stay here for ever – sitting with
the dandelions – watching the river roll past – and he notices
different currents running at different speeds – one racing
down the middle of the river – others chugging slowly at
the edges – softly softly catchee monkey – his dad says that
– and Terry points at the fastest current – says it's like a
crowd surging forward – people flowing in the same direction – but moving at the speed that suits them – a few of
them pushing the opposite way – spinning sideways –
whirlpools that turn in on themselves – small pools out by
the shore – stuck with the rocks and driftwood – at low
tide – and April is smiling at him – looks at the water and
asks where he is in that river – he tells her he doesn't know
– reckons April is swinging down the high street – and she

laughs – reaches for her handbag and takes out a packet of fags – offers him one – he shakes his head – and she lights up and blows smoke towards the water – he watches it flatten out in a circle – a wobbling UFO coming in to land – and it bends in a breeze he can't feel – fades away – and April tells him about Selsey – the storm that rocked their caravan one night – she goes into her handbag again and brings out a stick of rock – a present from her holiday – a taste of the seaside – and Terry is pleased – it shows she's been thinking about him – and he opens it – they pass it back and forward – eat the whole stick sitting by the Thames – and when it's gone they stand up and walk back through more broken bricks – smashed windows and rotting roofs – warehouses waiting for demolition – and England is covered in rubble – it's the same in Slough – playgrounds for kids to explore – the crack of breaking glass chiming across the country – and when they reach the high street they cross London Road – sit in a cafe with a bun and a mug of tea each – talking in hushed voices as the cars and lorries clatter past – and there's a machine behind the counter that gurgles as it flushes out real coffee – the smell as strong as the Italian's accent – the man laughing with an old dear about the price of beans – the tables full – a hum of voices – and soon it's opening time – so they walk past The Beehive – the BR station – The King's Arms – to a pub April knows – Terry is big for age and always gets served round his way – but doesn't know about the boozers in Brentford – April is on the other side of him – rubbing against his arm – reads his mind and squeezes his hand – they cross the Great West Road and walk in The Globe – there's a few men already at the bar – one asking after her dad – and the landlord pours April a bottle of light ale – Terry a pint of London Pride – he likes the name and thinks he'll give it a try – they go and sit in a corner away from the bar – he sips his beer – likes the taste – and she tells him she's never been to Slough – Terry laughs and says she hasn't missed much – and she asks what he was doing in the amusement arcade – he was a long way from home – on his own – and he explains he was on his way back from Shepherd's Bush – that his mates were in the pub down the road – he stayed in the arcade because he wanted to win those ha'pennies – and she takes out her purse – hands him a ha'penny and says thanks very much – she always pays her debts – he looks at the coin in his hand – and she leans over and touches his fingers – asks what he sees – he shrugs – just a ha'penny – and she tells him to put his hands together – go on – palms open – and she pours all the coins in her purse into his hands – a small pile of ha'pennies – pennies – sixpences – a shilling – two two-bob bits – a half-crown – and she asks what does he see now – he shakes his head – she tells him to look at the heads of the kings and queens – go on – so he puts the coins on the table and spreads them out – turns them over so all the heads are showing – right back to Queen Victoria – and he nods and thinks – points out the different colours – puts a 1914 penny next to a new copper from 1967 – tells her imagine the people who have used these coins – see that 1914 penny – it could have been used by a child to buy sweets when it was freshly minted – then the same person spends it on a tin of tobacco fifty years later – or a soldier going off to the First World War spends it on a pint of bitter before he dies in the Somme – and his son is given the same penny now – in this pub – tonight – in his change – buys himself a pint of the same beer – and April is staring at him – smiling – same as when they were sitting by the river – like she's working him out – and she's going to hang on to some of these coins when the new money comes in – when the Conservatives make everyone turn decimal – and she asks him what's the point of that? – getting rid of all that history – and Terry doesn't know – it seems daft to him – the Government wants a hundred pennies to a pound – the same as in Europe – but he can't see why – it's still different money – it seems mad – and everyone is angry about it – he can see why – it's like wiping out the years since Queen Victoria – pretending the First World War didn't happen – the Depression and the Second World War – the hard times – all those things his old man talks about – trying to forget Britain won the wars and lost the peace – that's what his dad says – and those pennies and shillings are about the people who hold them more than it's about the kings and queens – it's like those people don't count for anything any more – and he finishes his drink and goes up for another round – brings a light ale bottle over and pours it in April's glass – does it wrong so the froth spills over the top – but she tells him never mind – don't worry – it's not important – she says there's a jukebox down the other end of the pub – so they take their drinks and go and stand in front of it – look through the singles – put a coin in and choose their records – Terry admiring the curve of April's tight-fitting jeans – specially when she leans forward – against the Rock-Ola – a lovely pair of knockers pushing against a red Fred Perry.

Razor Sharp

RAY SAT BOLT UPRIGHT, staring at the firmest pair of tits he had seen in a long time. He had no choice. They were right there in front of him, stretching a white Fred Perry, near enough poking him in the eye. Paul was right, Angie should have been a model, but instead of flashing her gash in Ibiza, splitting the beaver for a posh kid's zoom lens, she preferred shaving bonces down Slough way, choosing the mystique of the Estuary kitchen and its dapper patrons to those predictable posers over in the FrancoZone. Ray wondered if Angie noticed the effect she had on the drivers, and specially the older chaps who saw a classier, dressed-up version of their late-night satellite viewing. He doubted she cared one way or the other.

She looked a lot like that bird out of *Pulp Fiction*, kept in luxury by the big spade in the penthouse, the one who ran into Zed, the main difference being Angie could look after herself and didn't need a minder, and definitely not some greaseball disco-merchant like John Travolta, a smoothie with a ponytail and a thousand-dollar suit. Ray liked Tarantino's films, thought *Jackie Brown* stood out, but knew the skinhead world was ten times more surreal than anything him or David Lynch had come up with, a charged-up Technicolor drama that spanned decades and starred all sorts of eccentrics and players. The clippers moved to the side of his head and Angie followed, leaving Ray facing a bare wall.

The woman had been a hairdresser before joining the firm, and once a week she sorted out the Estuary barnets. It was cheaper than going to the barber, the scenery was better and she did a good job. Carol was on the phones,

Ray the first of fourteen drivers having their hair cut today, a list pinned to the noticeboard. Anyone who didn't turn up, or arrived late and missed their turn, still had to pay, and if they did it twice they were on a ban. Hawkins was the only one who'd mucked up so far, Terry forced to make a special appeal on his mate's behalf. Angie had a soft spot for her boss, but didn't make it easy, stuck Hawkins on probation, and he stood in front of her and took the telling-off, accepted a final warning, apologised, which surprised a lot of the lads who knew the man as an old-school thug. The rule was set.

Ray had never socialised with Angie, didn't know much about her to be honest, and was waiting for the right moment to talk seriously. She was a strange one, and he had to be careful, picked his moment once she was standing behind him. He couldn't concentrate with an eyeful of melon.

– It's my uncle's birthday soon, he began.
– He's going to be fifty.
The clippers buzzed softly. Ray laughed.
– He'll be collecting his pension soon.
– Fifty's not old, she snapped.
The clippers jolted, the sound closer, suddenly threatening.
She pulled his head back. He thought of Sweeney Todd and cut-throat razors, the weakness of his jugular, the pressure of the blood in thin veins, gulped and forced a smile she couldn't see. There was no need for her to get angry.
– I was thinking, why don't we have a party? You know, a surprise. He'd like that.
Angie continued shaving his head, the clippers mellowing out, and Ray could hear her brain clicking above the catlike purr, plastic guards protecting his scalp from steel claws. He was no good at organising things, but knew she could make the party happen, and fingers crossed she might even do most of the work.
– What do you think he'd like? she asked.
– A few beers and a curry, probably.
– He always does that. It has to be something special.
– I don't know.

92

– You must know what he likes.
– He loves the Full English.
Angie didn't laugh.
– Drinking, curries, the Full English, football. What else?
– He likes a game of pool, Ray ventured.
– What else?
Ray was going to say sex, but didn't think it would go down too well, and anyway, Terry hadn't been near a woman for years. Not since April died, probably, but it wasn't something you asked your uncle, Ray understanding that behind the front Terry was still in mourning. He didn't know if that was a good thing or not, but you couldn't stop loving someone just because they were dead. Maybe he should find himself a lady, maybe not. It was a difficult one.
– What else is there? he asked.
– Come on, you've known him all your life. You must have some idea.
– He loves his music. Things like that.
– I know, but what else?
He tried to think. His uncle was sociable, enjoyed being out and about, having a laugh. There was nothing wrong with being friendly. Fucking hell, Angie was a bit stern, cracking the whip and that.
– Why don't we invite everyone round his house? he suggested. He's got enough mates to fill the place up. Buy a load of cans, play his records, warm up a few sausage rolls, put out a plate of pork pies, some bowls of crisps and peanuts. Sort out a nice birthday cake. That would do the trick.
There was a long silence.
He could tell she wasn't impressed.
– It's not special, though, is it? Not really.
She finished Ray's number one and moved a towel over his skull, held a mirror in front of his face. He had to admit he was a good-looking geezer. The close shave did him proud, suited the shape of his head, which was strong and built with ancient Anglo-Saxon bone. He could understand women being impressed. He blew his reflection a kiss and winked, Angie raising her eyebrows and turning away.

He stood and stretched, rolled his shoulders and rubbed at his neck with the towel. Once he was dusted down, he passed his money over, plus a pound tip. He watched as Angie opened a shiny black handbag and took out a thick red purse, stashing the coins inside. She zipped the purse and snapped the bag's silver buckle shut, reached for the razor and began cleaning it with a brush.

– I'll have a think, she said. If we're going to give Terry a surprise, it has to be extra-special, something he's never going to forget.

Ray nodded.

– Thanks, Angie.

He reached for his flight-jacket, slipped it on and went into the office, stood facing Carol, pointing at his chest, showing he was ready for work. She passed him a piece of notepaper with a fare's details.

– Someone will be there in ten minutes, he heard her say as he left the building.

Ray took another, closer look at himself in the car mirror. Having his head shaved perked him up, and he was sure it was the same with the rest of the lads. He didn't understand Samson and those hippies and crusties, greboes lumbering around with gorse covering their faces and long mangrove roots hanging down their backs. He was open-minded, believed in democracy, each to their own, the freedom of the individual to express his or herself in whatever way they saw fit, that was only fair, but they were still dirty, smelly, skiving cunts. He beamed as he admired Angie's work. Hard as nails. It summed him up. Hard, but fair.

He started the engine and checked the address, recognised the street, paused, realised he knew the name as well. He hadn't seen Nick Wise for a long time. Maybe it wasn't the same bloke, but Nick had grown up in Eton Wick, where Ray was picking up. They had gone to school together in Slough, knocked about for a few years, though last time he saw Nick he was living in Bracknell. He tried to remember when that was, knew it would come back to him eventually.

Ray cut round the back and passed under the M4, put

his foot down and was soon entering Eton, the school towering up on either side, and he stopped at the lights, waited to turn right, saw the boys in their long black jackets, books tucked under their arms, and for a few seconds he envied their reading time, those ordered minds, the confidence that was drilled into them from an early age, and then the feeling was gone. They paid a high price. In one way he was stepping back in time, but really these boys were the future, and one of the kids he was looking at would probably be prime minister in twenty years, while the rest of them would be running private companies and government departments, deciding taxation, pensions and health-care investment. It was mental, specially with Eton being so near to Slough.

It was typical of the British. They were too polite to march down the road and wreck the gaff, didn't think it was right playing the numbers game. It was another example of the people's tolerance. Either that or they couldn't be bothered. Apathy and tolerance were good friends. He had loved The Jam as a boy, couldn't help singing the chorus of 'Eton Rifles'. But even though these kids had privileges, money and education and a head start which could set them up for life, he felt sorry for them. He didn't understand how anyone with a soul could send their child to a boarding school, dumping them with strangers. What sort of people did that?

True, it was probably a chain reaction, part of a family tradition, but that was no excuse. He didn't know if what they said about public schools and poofs was true, guessed it was a cheap insult, but he was thinking more of the fear a child must feel when they were sent away, the loneliness and killing of emotion, kids forced to grow up before their time. It was a wrong thing to do. He wasn't perfect, struggled to get by and was dossing in a mate's flat, but he didn't envy these people their lives. He wasn't the sort of bloke to hold a grudge either, believed you had to give everyone a chance, never mind where they started off. George Orwell went to Eton and he turned out okay, told the truth about

England, and about himself as well. Every single thing that happened to you had to have an effect, and this was why he would always believe in the welfare state and core socialist values.

Ray was soon approaching Eton Wick, which despite the name was a different world from Eton. He drove under the viaduct carrying the railway from Slough, the last stretch of the District Line a hundred years ago, before they cut the service, continued beneath the dual carriageway, flat fields on his left leading to the river, and he slowed down as a rabbit ran across the road, one of the biggest he'd ever seen, entered the village proper, tempted by the light inside The Shepherd's Hut, and he knew a few lads who lived down here, Chelsea boys who still travelled home and away. He had no problem finding the address.

The planes coming out of Heathrow echoed across the houses, riding low over the fields, and he knocked hard on the door of the house, smiled as Nick opened up. There was a pause as they stared at each other, the face opposite Ray puffy and red, a chubby scruff going to seed, a centre parting separating grey hair. The eyes were clear, and when the mouth moved Ray saw a gold tooth, remembered where they had last seen each other. He felt a bit awkward.

– Ray?

– Hello, Nick. How are you?

– Aren't you surprised? I am.

Ray laughed.

– I already had the name and address. What are you doing back over this way? I thought you were living in Bracknell.

– I moved back to look after my mum. The old man died and I broke up with the wife a few years back, so I was living on my own anyway.

– Sorry to hear about your dad.

Nick nodded, looked over his shoulder, then back at Ray.

– Hold on, I'll get my coat.

Ray waited, heard Nick talking to someone in the living room. He didn't know the woman who appeared, had never been round the house as a boy.

– Last time I saw you was in that pub at Wembley, in 1994, Nick said.

– The Cup Final, against Man United.

– Four-nil. What a day.

They walked to the car, Ray holding the back door open as Nick helped his mum inside.

– Where to? the driver asked, once they were on board.

Ray retraced his route, on his way to the hospital, thinking back.

– What was that pub called? Coming up from Wembley Central.

Nick laughed.

– Do you remember?

Ray nodded.

– You were with your uncle, some other blokes. I had my kids with me and those Mancs came round the corner and Chelsea steamed in, and I had a go at you after, about punching people in front of children. They were scared.

Ray felt bad, didn't need reminding, specially not in front of Mrs Wise. He'd been half-cut, but felt ashamed, subjecting children to something like that. It had been a long day, and Chelsea'd had a good mob out.

– Funny thing was, once we'd seen the game and gone home, the kids thought it was the best part of the day.

Nick laughed again.

– Nutty Ray. Remember?

Ray nodded, let off the hook. He wouldn't have a go at Nick about the nickname.

– Your boys must be grown up now.

– Nineteen and seventeen, and we had another. He's eight. The oldest one's in the Marines and the other lives in Reading, works for the council. They turned out well. All of them. Their mother, you never met her, she went off with a copper. Can you believe it?

Mrs Wise mumbled something, looking out of the window.

– I don't care any more, but it was a shock at the time. What about you, Ray?

– I've got two girls. They're perfect.

He didn't tell Nick about Liz kicking him out, and they passed stories back and forwards, like they knew each other well, though really they didn't.

They were quickly passing through Slough.

– Didn't we used to go in there? Nick asked, looking at The Rising Sun.

– I still do, Ray laughed.

They waited at the roundabout, continued when the lights changed.

Ray listened to Nick as he settled into a steady rhythm, switching to another frequency so he seemed to buzz, talking about his three years out of work, how he suffered from blackouts, bouts of depression, Prozac doing its job for a year, till it backfired and he was thinking about suicide, and he never went near pubs these days, just led a quiet life, a couple of cans and a takeaway for a treat, Sky films with Mum, and Ray glimpsed another face, a bloke in a pub he stopped off in when he was working nights at Heathrow, and he didn't know where that memory came from, didn't even remember his name, but it was someone Joe Martin knew, he ended up hanging himself, and the image vanished and he heard Nick stuttering for a few seconds, then buzzing again, lost in a world of cod and chips and pickled onions, a Friday-night ritual, and Ray wished he hadn't picked him up, snapped back to when they were at school, lighter on their toes, and he didn't have a clue what they thought in those days, how could you know the past honestly, and he felt he was different now, happier, wondered about Nick, couldn't see it, and yet, despite his rambling talk he seemed levelled out, and he was talking about his mum, turning to the lady next to him, and it was like he had a role again, someone who needed him, and Ray saw it clearly, knew enough people who never left home, men and women, children who were carers, and that was the reason for family, what tied you together, that unity and respect, something built into you, unless you had a bad time or an Eton background maybe, and he realised that Nick was moving forward. Things were better than they had been. That's all you could hope for. He didn't know what to say when Nick finished talking.

They pulled into the hospital car park and Ray stopped outside the main entrance. He opened the door for Mrs Wise. The two men shook hands.

– It's on me, Ray said, as Nick reached for his wallet.

Nick protested, but gave in. Nodded.

– Next time.

Mother and son walked slowly, gently swaying as they passed through the doors, and Ray sat for a moment feeling bad, but pleased they had each other. He hoped Nick would be okay.

An ambulance pulled up behind him and he moved out of the way, looping back towards the road, checked his mirror and spotted his uncle walking towards the entrance, a van stopping and blocking his view. He waited for it to move, turned in his seat. The automatic doors were opening and closing for all sorts of people, but there was no sign of Terry. A man with short hair and a black jacket stood nearby smoking a fag. Ray knew his eyes were playing tricks. Angie was on the radio, had a fare waiting outside The Green Man, and he called in fast, the pub a short five-minute drive away.

Trouble in the Town

THE MACHINE RATTLED AND rolled and roared with laughter as Terry prodded the cancel button, his coins long gone, sucked away and melted down. He had been falling for the same trick since he was a boy. He never learned. Him and millions of others. Even though he was parched, and craved that cold Sprite calling from the other side of the glass, he managed a smile. At least he wasn't on a packed King's Cross platform with two hundred Chelsea waiting for the Victoria Line up to Highbury & Islington, chasing a bar of chocolate and shaking the box as the train blew cool air along the tunnel, banging on the metal, hearing voices and turning to find Hawkins and a wall of grinning faces, every single one of them knowing how he felt.

At least there was nobody watching him here. Few people could know how he was feeling, either. Nobody saw him enter the hospital and nobody would see him leave. He didn't want a fuss, would handle his problems alone, walked back along the corridor to his chair, sat down and took out his mobile, started playing Space Impact. The game had come with the phone and it stopped him thinking. He tilted the screen so he could see better, the first phase set against a black background, where it was easy to lose yourself in the dark. He had to stay alert. Once he was safely through this section his attackers were clearer, and he started working with both hands, laying down crossfire, picking up extra lives as he moved forward, head lowered and determined, passing into new zones. He was doing well, dodging asteroids and giant lizards, ducking and diving as he headed for a new high score.

– Mr English.

Terry looked up at the nurse standing over him. He had the volume on his mobile turned off so didn't hear the explosion as he lost a life, glanced down and realised what had happened, wished he could keep playing and beat his previous best, fight his way deeper into outer space and wipe out every alien and demon sent to destroy him. He stood up and turned the phone off, shoved it in his jacket pocket.

– Here is your appointment card and some information on the tests we'll be carrying out, she said, friendly and efficient. And here is your medication, with the instructions inside, just as the doctor outlined.

Terry had no questions. He took the envelope and paper bag. The nurse smiled, turned and left. She moved easily, shoes skimming the floor, and by chance he found himself following her, walking in the same direction, and she glided along so smoothly he imagined her on an ice rink, April carrying their skates to Richmond on the bus, chopping out a trail her boyfriend couldn't follow, and he saw their son hanging around the local shops with his mates years later, one of the results of their chance meeting, heard the clank of skateboards as they moved from the pavement to the gutter, back and forward, battering the kerb, doing flips and, bashing heavy rubber wheels, over and over, until they got it right.

The nurse turned a corner and stopped suddenly, Terry nearly knocking into her as he skidded. He had never been any good on skates, but liked the cold atmosphere of the rink, the grace of the best skaters. He stayed by the side most of the time, April flashing past, blowing him kisses. She turned left and he went right, passing through clusters of spirits, the outlines of doctors, porters, patients, visitors, cleaners and volunteers, and lots more nurses, trolleys ferrying dehydrated bodies, tired faces hidden by oxygen masks, drips feeding glucose, blood-smudged dressings, tubes removing thick yellow piss, and when he reached the main entrance and went outside to the car park he didn't look back, drove away quickly, asking himself who was going to look after Laurel if he died.

The doctor's words replayed in his head – we are going to try another approach – we must stay positive – we must not give up – and yet they weren't certain what was wrong with him – Doctor Jones seemed puzzled – spoke about the tests to come – new medicine – stronger treatment – we have our suspicions.

The man's name was John Jones and Terry had found himself thinking of the Big Shot 45 as he sat in his office, mind hiding from the reality of what was going on. He was wondering what happened to Rudy Mills, wanted to call the doctor a son of a gun, laughing with fear, somewhere inside, and that cocky young skinhead had gone missing, handcuffed and led away. He placed Rudy in a sleepy village by the sea, a happy man in a rocking chair, sipping a cold beer, gazing across the Caribbean Sea while back in England grown boys trudged around in the rain and sleet, looking to shell out small fortunes on his old vinyl.

Terry drove along the main road, heading nowhere.

Laurel would have the rest of the family, but a boy needed his father to protect him and keep him out of trouble, to set an example. The shock would be too much. He had already lost his mum and it was a miracle he was so normal. It wasn't right if he lost his dad as well.

Terry wanted to get as far away from the hospital as he could. It was the place where the majority of people were born and most of them died, the true core of a community, and it was telling him to wake up and admit what was going on around him – the grubby arguments over money, the greed of men who had never learnt to share, the violence of the confused; and his conscience clouded as he saw himself as a youth in all his full-colour, present-tense glory, a youth in a gang of youths, a boot boy, realising the fear he must have spread, not admitting it at the time.

He thought of his parents, the carelessness of his youth, of a time when he thought nothing could touch him, that he would always be young and strong and in control, and he wished he could remember exactly what he had thought, but the words and events were blurred, so much of it hidden away. He saw a scared kid on the ground, felt the kickings dealt out by boys and men.

Terry didn't know why this was happening. He was a child, with so much to live for, everything possible. He wanted to run home and sit with his father. It didn't matter if they didn't talk. They could watch the television together.

The shock of April's accident was returning. He heard the crying of the emergency ward, was too late to even hold her hand as she passed away, and he tried to block the images out, felt dizzy, fought to control the steering wheel, and the pressure in his head and chest increased, smoke seeping into his lungs. He snapped himself forward ten years, knew Doctor Jones was a good man, shuffling sleek outlines of a bleached skull, moonbeam craters and empty caverns, more X-rays of Terry's chest and lungs. Doctor Jones narrowed his eyes and wondered.

Terry didn't want to go into work. Didn't want to be at home. Didn't know where to go or what to do. He could take the M4 down the Thames Corridor, beyond the satellites and out into the West Country where the land was old and quiet, out to the stone circles and burial mounds and sarsen avenues, but he found the countryside lonely, knew it was no escape. He headed for the club instead, parked at the end of the alley and ducked through the gate, was soon standing by the front door, running his hand over a stained-glass eagle carved into the entrance. His head was rushing as he built another story, identifying a Polish soldier unable to return home, forced out by the Germans, kept out by the Russians. He would have sat by this door worrying about his family, missing his parents, wife and children maybe, remembering dead brothers and tortured uncles. It was true what they said, that there was always someone worse off than you. He told himself he was lucky and began to calm down. This place was his sanctuary.

He plugged the jukebox in and watched it come alive, started with Prince Buster telling him that the court was in session, that Judge Dread was presiding, sitting in judgment, and he laughed, went over to the bar and poured himself a pint, learning from his barman and tilting the glass just right, watched the London Pride build up, took a gulp and carried it over to the pool tables, chose a cue and started playing, sent a spot and a stripe into separate pockets. He walked around and thumped the white. This wasn't his normal style, but it felt good.

Life's problems should have been settled over a game of pool. Stick Bush and Bin Laden on and see who came out on top. Jimmy Cliff strolled in the club and took the place of Prince Buster. He loved 'Johnny Too Bad', was sure he'd gone to the pictures to see *The Harder They Come* when it first came out, could remember April hiding her face when the rude boy cut up that bloke in the yard.

The single sparked confidence and the London Pride helped it grow, 'Johnny Too Bad' a song with an edge, the words and beat colliding. Terry felt strong again, the doctor's message softer, the hospital far away. Every skinhead knew what it was like to feel invincible, like nothing could touch him. It stayed with a man all his life, and was what set skin-heads apart from the masses. Terry was in control, knew he could beat his problems through sheer will-power, and he cleared the table fast, finished his pint and nodded his head, sang along with Laurel Aitken, moved his feet as he spelt out 'Jesse James', and he was going to ride again, the sun creating a mental spotlight effect. He was untouchable. Dodging bullets. Unseen and untouchable. Ready for another drink.

– Mr English.

He was fast, grabbed his glass before it dropped and smashed, searched the shadows by the back door, found a shape just inside, the outline of a woman. It was Angie from the office.

She moved out of the dark and into the light, walked towards him.

– How long have you been standing there? he asked, embarrassed.

– We're even, she laughed. Remember when you surprised me at work? I nearly wet myself. I came in right this second.

Terry felt stupid, but if he wanted to have a sing-song and shuffle his feet that was his choice This was the first time Angie had been in the club.

– I was passing and saw your car. I thought you'd be in here. You don't mind me having a look, do you?

– Course not.

– Are you okay? All alone in here.

– I'm fine, just came in to have a game of pool. Listen to a few records.

Angie glanced around. 'Spread Your Bed' jumped up.

– I knocked, but you didn't hear, so I came round the back. Like you did, when you discovered this place.

He would have to do something about that lock, but didn't mind Angie being here. Once it was a bit smarter the invitation would be open to all the boys, and the girls in the office as well. It wasn't ready yet, still needed a proper clean, and he was going to get some painting done as well. First impressions were important.

Angie had reached the jukebox and was looking at the cards he'd written out, running her fingers along the edge of the machine.

– It's lovely, she said.

Terry walked over, stood next to her.

– I haven't filled it up yet. I'm taking my time. Do you want a drink?

– Cider, please, if you've got it.

Angie followed him to the bar, pulled the one stool over and reached for the towel on the counter, gave it a good rub. Terry realised it hadn't been touched because none of the boys were going to use it, as it was thin and dainty, with red vinyl padding. If he clambered up the legs would probably snap. He looked at the stool properly for the first time, wondered who had brought it to the club. It was out of place.

Angie took her coat off and draped it over the end of the bar. She lifted herself up neatly, so her bum was on the edge of the stool, Terry noticing the skirt and fishnets, her fingers tapping on the counter, in time with The Versatiles.

–You sure cider's okay? We don't have any wine or anything like that.

Angie was looking around the room.

– I want cider, she said. I don't like wine.

– We've only got pints, Terry said, smiling.

– I don't drink halves, Angie replied, peering at him with a frown, which he thought was meant to be humorous, but as usual, wasn't quite sure.

She contined with her inspection as he did the honours, felt good behind the pumps, like he was a real publican. 'Johnny Too Bad' began again and he remembered he'd put it on twice.

– Did you ever see him? she asked.

Terry was concentrating on the cider.

– Who's that? he asked.

– Jimmy Cliff.

– Loads of times.

He knew Angie was in a scooter club, but didn't know how far into the scene she went. She seemed to know the songs played so far.

– When was the first time you saw him? she asked.

Terry was forced to think hard. He was useless with dates and places. Human memory didn't last long. He looked up, shut his eyes, trying to picture Jimmy Cliff on stage. He saw himself in that Brutus shirt he'd had as a kid. It was his pride and joy.

– Watch out, Angie laughed, cider spilling over the sides of the glass.

Terry wiped it and handed it over, nodded for her to go ahead. He busied himself with the London Pride.

– That tastes good, she said, obviously impressed.

He was pleased.

– It was the Caribbean Music Festival, I think. At Wembley. I was fifteen or thereabouts, 1969 maybe. There was Jimmy Cliff and Desmond Dekker. A band called The Mohawks. Pat Kelly and Max Romeo. But I'm not sure. It all blends together when you get to my age.

Right on cue Romeo started on 'Wet Dream.' Angie stared

at her boss, and he hoped she wasn't listening to the lyrics, but a big smile crossed her face and he realised she knew her rude reggae. This appealed to the bovver brigade. It was the sense of humour, the need to get your end away. She seemed to be fluttering her eyelids, but he knew he was imagining things.

– I went with Hawkins, I think. We called him Alan in those days. Do you know Alfonso?

Angie shook her head.

– Big black fella. Still lives local. He got into all that rasta reggae in the Seventies. Haile Selassie and Ethiopia.

Angie pulled a face.

– Don't get me wrong, that's fine for a black man, but it's not what I was interested in. We didn't want politics in our music, never mind black politics.

– I don't like that stuff either.

– Alfonso knows every reggae era, buys all that ragamuffin now, bashment, people like Elephant Man. You'd know him if you saw him. I think he went with us to Wembley. I can't remember. There was a load of us.

Angie lifted her glass and drank. She was relaxed, and he realised he had never seen her in a pub before. She hadn't even gone to the Christmas drink-up. It was a good job too, in the end, as she would probably have quit after that bundle on the high street. She had only been at Estuary a few months at the time.

– It must have been great seeing all of them on one bill, she said.

– Yeah, it was. There were others too. Suppose you took it in your stride. We must have been excited, but years later you realise you've seen those blokes in their prime. I still feel the same seeing Jimmy Cliff or Prince Buster today. Still can't believe they're right there in the flesh.

– I wish I'd been around then.

Terry shook his head.

– It doesn't matter what age you are, the music you listen to when you're in your teens shapes you. It's the same with my boy.

– Nothing touches skinhead reggae. I'd loved to have been there. I was born too late.

Terry smiled.

– Did you ever see Judge Dread? Angie asked.

Terry nodded. He loved Judge Dread, the king of rude reggae, starting off as a minder like that, for Prince Buster when he came to England, latching onto the song, adding his own seaside humour.

– You've got Prince Buster's Judge Dread album?

– Of course, he laughed.

Angie had a deeper appreciation of the original skinhead sound than he had thought. He was more and more impressed.

– I'd better get going, she said.

Terry realised she'd finished her drink.

– Have another, he said, taking her glass.

– No, I've got things to do.

– What time have you got to be at work?

– Another twenty minutes.

– Remember, this is your boss man speaking, Terry said, mimicking the voice of Roy Ellis.

– I'm looking forward to Symarip, she laughed. Thanks again for getting us the tickets.

He poured another pint of Strongbow, Angie slipping off the stool and going back over to the jukebox, and she sort of rolled her hips, the light playing on her black hair, and she turned and inspected the wall of photos, like it was a parade ground, which he supposed it was, in a way. She was in the light's full beam now, and her hair was blonde, bleached like his skull in the X-ray, but the record stopped, 'Skinhead Girl' started, and he could see her singing along, her hair black, as he knew it was, realising she loved this song as well.

He looked down, holding his glass under the tap.

– Can I have a go? Angie called over, and when he glanced up she was standing over the pool table he had been playing on.

Terry carried his pint over.

– Be my guest.

She arranged the balls and handed him a cue. He sipped his drink as she leant over the table, taking her time as she measured her shot, and he couldn't help noticing the swell of her breasts, where a couple of buttons had come undone. He looked away, back at the table, saw the white connect. He chalked his cue and potted three stripes in a row, remembered himself and missed the next one on purpose. Angie stepped forward, seemed unsure, made her decision and lined up a spot, tucked it away. It was a good shot. Terry could see the next one, and she chose it as well, put the ball in the pocket, but would struggle for a follow-up. She came round to his side of the table, but he couldn't see why, she had no chance, stretched forward with her bum in the air, and he remembered that time in the office, when she was leaning over the desk in her jeans, and he couldn't miss her skirt riding up, showing off the fishnets, a sliver of flesh appearing, and he turned his head, felt like a right old lech, glad Psychobilly Paul wasn't around.

The shot missed, but not by much.

– Unlucky, he said, and potted three more balls, couldn't get the fourth.

Angie missed her next shot and Terry finished the game off. He felt bad beating her, but it was difficult if you had to keep missing shots on purpose. She was good, though. He could see that. He collected the black and dropped it on the table with the white.

– I've got to go, she said, looking at her watch. Carol will be waiting for me.

– You sure? Another game?

– Honest, I'd love to, but I can't. You owe me one. I'll beat you next time. It usually takes me a couple of games to warm up.

She finished her drink and was off. He started potting balls again, staying with stripes till he missed a pocket, switching to spots and doing the same, clearing the table, forgetting about John Jones. The Rock-Ola was silent, but he wasn't bothered. He felt refreshed, would have to get cracking and fill it with singles before anyone slid in there

109

and took over. Buster had suggested a few songs, and Hawkins wanted to bring his old Slade singles in, if he could find them, while Ray said he was going to bring some Oi in, and Lol was talking about loads of music he'd never heard of, American punk bands. He wasn't going to have punk and Oi blaring out all day, though he wouldn't mind a bit of Slade. He didn't mind 'Harry May', as the lyrics had a special meaning, but that was all Ray was getting, and of course his nephew grinned and winked and his skull scrunched, and Terry knew it was stuck in Ray's mind now, a challenge that was going to start nagging at him. Everyone had an opinion. The delivery men had had their say and when Big Frank came down he'd probably want to add some polkas, Singer some sitar, while the boys with Irish in them would be piling in the marches, diddly-daddly and fuck knows what else. Terry wanted a skinhead jukebox, full of ska and blue beat. He had to stay firm. Angie was the first one not to ask if she could bring some records in, happy with what was already there.

He had a thought. Turned his mobile on. It vibrated in his hand.

– I am thirsty, the first text read.

He smiled. It was from Hawkins.

– Fancy a pint? said the second.

He'd also had a call.

– Where are you? Turn your phone on, you fat bastard. I'm in the pub, just ordered a nice pint of lager. It's nearly five. The pool table's empty, jukebox waiting. Give me a call, will you? And leave your fucking phone on.

Terry'd had a couple of pints and wouldn't mind another. He didn't fancy drinking alone. He pressed the right button and waited for his call to connect.

Class of '69 – Part 3

TERRY HEARS A KEY in the front door and knows it's his old man come home from work – Dad likes routine – doing certain things at certain times – but tonight he's late – for some reason – and he'll come through in a minute – after he's said hello to Mum – Terry in the living room having his tea – with his sister – cutting into a fish finger and adding a blob of peas – dipping it in ketchup – raising the fork to his mouth and stopping – a scream from the kitchen numbing his hand – ketchup dripping – splashing his boiled potatoes – crumbled starch – buttery blood – and the scream is smothered – a hand cupping a jaw – maybe – Terry points at his sister not to move – puts his knife and fork down and creeps into the hall – somehow knows to be quiet – finds a crack in the kitchen door and sees Dad's back – his head tilted at an angle – a towel pressed on his face – and Mum's hands are shaking as she tries to help – water crashing into the sink – a tuneless metal echo – there's water in Mum's eyes – tears – he thinks – and Dad turns and Terry sees the towel is soaked with blood – and it's down his shirt and trousers as well – a big red balloon popped and bubbling on the lino – Mum asking was it those boys from the cafe? – was it George? – was it? – Dad takes the towel away and his nose is swollen and black – lips a gooey purple batter – and he hunches over the sink and dribbles more blood – the water splashing – Mum reaching over and turning the tap so he can fill his hands from a trickle – and he pumps them up and down – cleaning his face – Mum rubbing his shoulders when he's done – the sink silent – Mum whispering so the children can't hear – Dad answering – those boys say they didn't steal the binoculars – it was my mistake leaving them in the car – you can't blame yourself – bloody little thugs – they get everything on a plate – they laughed and told me to fuck off pops – the one with Rooster on his jacket punched me so I hit him back – and then him and the other rockers all started in – had me down in the gutter – kicking me – you should get the law on them – they were angry I said they stole the binoculars – nobody wants to be called a thief – they bloody well took them don't you worry – I know they took them – I thought they did but I don't really know – do I? – they never had to do this – how many were there? – five? – six? – seven or eight – fucking bastards – never mind – never mind? – I've had worse – haven't I? – much worse that this – this is nothing – nothing at all – and Joan leans against George's chest and he wraps his arms around her – Terry watching the blood seep into his mother's yellow dress – sad as she doesn't often buy new clothes – and now it's ruined – and – he imagines Dad on his knees – being beaten up – and all the language Terry and his mates use – getting your head kicked in – getting a hiding – a pasting – being duffed up – bashed up – done over – it means something different suddenly – and he's shaking – this is wrong – all wrong – not his old man – and suddenly Mum is telling Dad he's a bloody fool – moving away from him – those yobs aren't going to admit it – you have to do something – and he shakes his head – what can I do? – they're out of control – life is too easy for them – anyway – it's my fault – no – I'll have to buy Bob a new pair – God knows where I'll find the money though – it's a shame they didn't steal the car instead – I'll have to dump it soon – how can you joke about it? – after what those hooligans have done – you work so hard – come on – let's forget it now – I don't want you to worry – I'll take care of everything – it's nothing – nothing? – stop saying nothing – George pulls Joan back to him – Terry walks off – angry at the rockers – sort of angry at his dad as well – goes back to the table and eats his fish fingers – peas – potatoes – tells his sister that Dad crept up on Mum and hugged her — smiles when the old man comes in and says hello — hurries upstairs — face clean — but turned away — Mum watching her children — searching — follows Dad up — Terry stuffing his food down — he can't wait to get out of the house — Alan asks what's wrong and Terry snaps back nothing — his brain full of Rooster and all sorts of faceless hairies — he wants to kick their heads in — do some damage — knows he wouldn't stand a chance — Dad tells him it's wrong to fight — important to stay out of trouble and make something of his life — this is a time of opportunity — things are different from the old days — people are more equal than ever before — he can find a decent job when he leaves school — if he works hard — in an office even — and Terry boots a Ford Popular — dents the door — feels bad and doesn't know why he did it — and Alan laughs and Terry turns and tells him to shut up — Alan's face drops — he doesn't say another word as they trudge through the streets of Slough — heading for the youth club — both boys with their hands in their pockets — heads down — in the vanishing warmth of early evening — DMs clumping on concrete — and Terry leans over the table and shuts out the world — knows he doesn't have to smash the white — loves the cracking sound of the balls connecting — but holds back — eases his cue forward — smiles as the black rolls towards the top left — and calmly disappears — he stands back — the noise and colour returning — voices darting around under 'Monkey Man' — blue and red and yellow checks — Alan and a couple of other boys watching the game — cherry-red patches of modern life — and Alfonso is next on — moves round the pockets collecting balls — sets them up — Alan sitting down on a chair and stretching his legs out — pulling on his braces — DMs on show — trying to catch the eye of a passing girl — and Alfonso breaks — Terry follows — pots four balls on the trot — he can probably clear the table if he wants — eases off and misses a shot — doesn't want to embarrass the bloke — he's not much cop — and maybe Alfonso guesses — mumbles thanks at the end — then louder says he's going to try and get some tickets for the festival at

Wembley – Prince Buster is headlining – he'll get them for Terry and Alan as well – if they want to go along – and that night Terry doesn't fall asleep till four in the morning – thinking about his dad – trying to work out why his old man wants to forget about what happened – and he knows Dad was in the war – a gunner in a Lancaster – shot down and taken prisoner – that's all he knows – Dad never talks about those things – it doesn't mean much to Terry – he never thinks of it as being real – he just sees his father as a quiet man – too quiet maybe – too decent – makes him half-believe what those rockers said – and he'll have to find the money to pay Bob back – they even broke the window of his car – an old banger as well – and Dad's belief in fair play has got him nowhere in life – working the hours he's told – money short – and he wishes Dad had hard mates – but there's only Bob and a few men in the pub – neighbours mainly – they're too old to do anything – and Terry is almost ashamed – ashamed? – doesn't know where this comes from – on his own Dad has no chance – what can anyone do on their own? – but he can't understand why Dad isn't raging – at least he could shout and swear – Terry feels like his house has been robbed – as if he's not safe any more – hears those greboes laughing – the sound high-pitched and birdlike as the sun rises and he finally falls asleep – hoping this doesn't mean Dad is a coward – and in the morning he asks Mum to iron his best shirt – she smiles and winks and asks if she's pretty – Terry nods – embarrassed – Dad and the rockers forgotten as his train arrives at Ealing Broadway – Mum and Dad telling him a porky – saying a rock broke the car window – cutting Dad's face – but April is the only thing on his mind now as he walks along the platform – excited – for a moment wondering if she'll turn up – but there she is waiting in the ticket hall – her hair so blonde it's almost white – and nothing else matters – he's clumsy as he approaches her – blue eyes making him lower his head – hands in pockets – she kisses him quick on the lips and turns – slides an arm through his – same as before – but the kiss is wet and she is really close this time – he has a hard-on as they walk down to the Uxbridge Road – and it's almost like she's rubbing against his arm – he knows she isn't doing it on purpose – but it feels like she is – he thinks of the showers at school – the boys laughing and calling him Chopper and Horse and Donkey Knob – he doesn't like it – feels awkward – manages to walk his erection off as they head towards the pictures – where Terry bounces down the aisle – air-cushioned soles meeting thick plush carpet – doesn't think about the back row – stops halfway – April following – she looks at him and frowns – sighs as they sit down – sharing her tub of ice cream as they watch the adverts – an Indian restaurant on Southall Broadway – leather chairs and lava lamps on Hanwell Broadway – and she leans against him when an information film tells them about steel production in Sheffield – he puts his right arm round her shoulders – and she smells good – lifts her face – mouth inches away – wants to have a snog – but Terry sees the older people sitting around them – stops – and anyway – the main feature is starting – and even though he's seen *A Space Odyssey* three times already he doesn't want to miss anything – it gets better every time – he loves the way it moves so slow – some people say it's boring – but he doesn't mind – likes the idea of Hal taking control – the mental sound of his metal voice – that whole idea of space and energy and time and everything – he really wants April to like *A Space Odyssey* as well – that's how things are going to be – in 2001 – a different sort of world – humans travelling across the universe – way beyond the moon – there won't be any wars then either – and he sits with his eyes fixed to the screen – April moving around – huffing and puffing – finally quiet as she falls under the Kubrick spell – resting her hand on his leg – Terry trying to concentrate on the film – finally she takes it away – and after – standing outside in the summer drizzle – they duck into a doorway – an army-surplus shop with its wire shutters down – boots and trousers stacked either side of the door – behind the glass – and April pushes up against Terry and kisses him – sticks her tongue in his mouth – and they are out of sight – more or less – and when she pulls away she asks him if he fancies her – and he says of course I do – wants to tell her she's beautiful – knows he'll sound like a right poof if he comes out with that one – instead moves forward and kisses her – an elderly couple stopping to look in the window – Terry and April walk back along the Uxbridge Road – and he wants to know if she liked the film – she smiles and nods – says it was a bit slow at first – but she wanted it to keep going – by the end – and the fumes from the traffic have been damped down by the rain – the exhaust of a passing double-decker filling his nostrils – and the rain stops and the sun lights them – so he feels great – the skinhead look sharp and full of colour – April the same – in her red Fred Perry and blue jeans – and he thinks what to do next – go to a pub up by Ealing Broadway – or back to the amusement arcade maybe – but he's going to have to walk her home eventually – can't leave her to get there on her own – they could have a drink in The Globe again – where they'll get served for sure – and they end up strolling towards Brentford – can't be bothered catching a bus – taking their time – April buying a box of matches on Northfields Avenue – tins piled high – Indian music behind the counter – and they pass a couple of Irish pubs built into shops – pass the Tube station and two more boozers – end up on Junction Road – the Griffin Park floodlights in the distance – and they're talking and laughing – two skinheads up ahead – coming their way – Terry trying to see if they're looking for aggro – reckons they're eighteen or nineteen – one calling out – hello April – and the two boys stand in the way – haven't seen you for a while April – where have you been hiding? – one of them has mutton chops – it's him does the talking – screwing Terry – looking him up and down – eyeing up April – who's your mate? – April stares – older than her years – he's my boyfriend – and Terry likes that – the skinheads nodding – Mutton Chops asking where you from mate? – Slough – and he laughs – you're full of wogs over there – fucking smelly Pakis – and April says they have to meet someone – Terry walking next to her – arms loose – glancing back – Mutton Chops points at him – then shouts I'll say hello to Dave for you April – give him your love – and he laughs some more – April turning right – left at the end of the street – soon they see the pub – push the door open and bundle inside – and when they've been served they stand against a wall – the pub busy early evening – The Who on the jukebox – all sorts of people drinking around them – an old geezer in a syrup telling April she's fucking beautiful – before staggering outside – and Terry asks who Dave is – April snaps a wally – a wanker – a mate of his went out with Cheryl – remember – Cheryl from the arcade – with the black hair – the four of them went to the pictures together – she's quick to tell Terry her and Dave never kissed – nothing like that – nothing ever happened – her and Cheryl made sure they didn't sit in the back – she laughs – looking at Terry in that funny way – she was never interested in Dave – Dave thought she was – but she wasn't – never – and because she doesn't want to know he's taken it all personal – Terry feels jealous – for no reason – hides it – and those two blokes we saw are his mates – they're always mouthing off – Paki-bashing and hippie-bashing – queer-rolling – bashing up anyone they don't like – but Terry isn't bothered – the drink goes down a treat – the pub busier than last time – Mick Jagger singing 'Street Fighting Man' – The Kinks following up with 'Waterloo Sunset' – and Terry notices four skinheads down the far end of the pub – everyone else older – herberts of every age out with their wives and girlfriends – and Terry and April are easy together – she wants to buy a round and Terry finally agrees – when it looks like she's getting narked – there's not a lot of birds who will put their hand in their pocket – but this is the Sixties – things are changing – April asking him what he's going to do when he leaves school – he says he doesn't know – shrugs – doesn't care – and she looks at him with this look from the pictures – same as when she met him last time – maybe she thinks he's thick – not going in the back row – or a wally like Dave – you must have an idea – haven't you thought about it? – she is

going to be a secretary – a typist can make good money
– she wants a decent job – there's opportunities out there –
it's different today for working people – and Terry nods and
smiles and drinks his beer – thinking it's just like listening
to his old man – rabbiting on about the future – a million
years from now – he has time to spare – there's no rush
– look at *A Space Odyssey* – see how life will be in 2001 –
he wouldn't mind the life of an astronaut – and he grins
and tells April he wants to be a spaceman – either that or
a cowboy – like John Wayne or Robert Mitchum – she
laughs – and every time he looks at her she's more beautiful – the bloke in the syrup wasn't scared to tell her – and
April keeps going – says you really make me laugh – but I
don't know why – and he takes it as a compliment – knows
she doesn't mean it in a bad way – at least – he hopes she
doesn't – and when she goes off to the bog he moves to
an empty space at the end of the bar – watches the men
on the pool table – the one in the black suit has been on
for ages – hair oiled back – and April returns and he follows
the game while they're talking – and finally there's no one
playing – the man in the old suit shouting won't anyone
play me – and April points at Terry – he's dying to play you
Uncle Pat – and he waves Terry over – tells him to rack up
– April sitting on a stool now – handbag on her lap – white
socks showing – loafers gleaming – Uncle Pat says I never
saw you there April darling – he buys them both a drink –
lets Terry break – has his turn and misses – Terry potting
three spots – just misses a fourth – and he does well – it
goes right to the black – Pat asking how old he is – Terry
looking at the bar – it's okay son – seventeen? – sixteen? –
fifteen – well – you're a handy player for fifteen – very
handy – where did you learn to play? – and Terry shrugs –
down the youth club – and Pat looks at his watch and says
you should keep practising son – try your luck in a proper
contest – I know of one coming up – and he ruffles April's
hair – whispers something – tells the barman to put any
drinks they want on his slate – shakes Terry's hand – half-
breaking a few bones – leaves the pub – and it's ten when

they follow — Terry walking April back to Griffin Park — he has to leave early so he can catch his train — and they stand against a wall — in the shadows — the floodlights in the ground silhouettes in the sky — tall the same as pine trees — but it smells more like beer and manure around here — and he props his hands on her hips and she leans close — kissing him — and she's worried he's going to miss his train — he watches her walk away — sees her safely indoors — starts running — down a long terrace — turns right and across the road — heading for the alley that runs behind some flats and down to the station — trips and goes flying — bangs his head — feels a thump in his back — looks up and sees three figures — one of the men putting the boot in — kicking him in the face — and he does his best to curl up — ears pounding — someone is calling him a cunt — and then all three of them are having a go — his fingers tingle where he's protecting his head — and finally he's pulled up — rocks back and leans on a wall — the light yellow behind Mutton Chops — who's laughing — his mate to the side — the third skinhead saying he's Dave — leaning forward and telling Terry next time he comes calling for April he's going to fucking kill him — and Terry is bruised but doesn't feel too bad — his strength comes back fast — he's a strong boy — and Dave says April's his girl-friend — so fuck off — and Terry hears his train coming along the track — pulls his head back and nuts Dave on the nose — the crack of bone same as the whack of a pool cue — and he's off and skipping down the steps — running along the alley with the train barrelling along on his right — he can see the light in the carriages — the outlines of passengers — and it's ahead of him now — stopping at the station — and he doesn't look back — has a head start he doesn't want to lose — bouncing off the railings — reaching the platform — doors opening and slamming closed — just makes it — a whistle blowing — Dave and the others arriving as the train starts to move away — and the guard shouts at them — Dave up by the window — nose red and bleeding — Terry gives him a wanker sign — tells the others you can fuck off and all — Terry English just wants an easy life — he never looks for trouble – doesn't see why people can't get on – and he doesn't care what that Dave says – he'll see April as much as he wants – she's his girlfriend – like she said – she's smashing – and as the train rolls along he starts to feel the kicks properly – thinks of Dad again – the blokes who attacked him – and he has two problems that need sorting out now – his head aching – skin swelling – and this is the first real kicking he's had – but he isn't going to cry about it – he's got more important things on his mind.

Cul-de-sac Blues

RAY PUT HIS FOOT down once he was back on the Bath Road, stammering through the trading-estate lights, slowing down and watching for speed cameras, the authorities robbing people like him blind with their endless fines. He reached Trade Sales, new-model automobiles filling the forecourt, and one day he was going to drive away in a fresh car, next to no miles on the clock and a three-year warranty in his pocket, no MOTs to worry about, cruising on smooth suspension, a slick gearbox that only needed the faintest touch. He'd driven his uncle's Merc a few times, and it was different class.

He turned right at the pub and drove along Tuns Lane, left towards Chalvey, down Church Street and past The Flags, stopped at the traffic lights and waited, glancing at the driver next to him, a bloke in bottle-top glasses, cheeks chipped out, either anorexic or narcotic. The hair was dirty, but it was the pale face that made an impression. This gent had been floating in the Thames for a week, with a bruised, blue gas glowing behind some seriously creamy skin. He had to be a drug addict, a horrible smack-injected junkie, the sort of lowlife scum who burgled houses and mugged old ladies, broke into cars and snatched radios and CD players, the petty-thieving rodents that made him sick. Even worse, he might be selling drugs on the side.

Like any skinhead, Ray hated thieves and spongers, never mind intravenous drug users. Maybe the man was on crack, sucking on a pipe or whatever it was the soppy cunts did, popping heroin into his knob and bollocks. He looked at the face when it turned towards him, smudged glasses blocking out the colour of the eyes. The junkie stared, but didn't see Ray, didn't notice his frown turn to a smile.

In many ways ecstasy was worse than smack. The whole dance-music world wound Ray up even more. What was the point of dancing to remixed disco and getting loved up when all around you your culture was being destroyed, rights people had fought and died for siphoned off and handed away. It was the oldest trick in the book. Sedate the population and give them a long line of credit, and nowadays the con was more sophisticated, hardware and software and endless updates and technological breakthroughs taking the place of food and shelter. The Nineties had to be the saddest decade in Britain's modern popular culture, but it wasn't a surprise, seeing as the acid-house, hippie revival belonged to the children of the hairies. But things changed. Ray was enjoying this new generation, the sons and daughters of his generation of skins, punks and herberts. The new century was shaping up. The youngsters he knew were more than familiar.

Ray was tempted to give the junkie in the next car a slap, but knew it wouldn't stop there, that he was talking about something much more serious, like dragging the morphine-riddled leech across the road and sticking the boot in – HARD. Eager toes itched inside his DMs, steel toecaps capable of inflicting twenty times the damage of a Reebok Classic. He would pay this Chemical Alf back for the misery he'd caused all those lost souls too trusting or thick to see what they were doing.

Ray realised he'd been raging since he arrived on the trading estate. This is what he did, went into one, and he had to calm down and leave the poor cunt alone. He didn't want to get nicked, for a start, and anyway, maybe the bloke was just short-sighted, suffering from an overactive thyroid, a touch of anaemia that was no fault of his own. You couldn't batter a man to a bloody pulp just because he was on the thin side and didn't have twenty-twenty vision. That would be unfair.

The lights turned and Ray continued, hurrying along the

high street and under the bridge, up the slope and across the junction, past the cemetery on his left, turning right. He found himself in a cul-de-sac, eased left, stopped and reversed right, braked and moved forward, parking in front of a crooked terrace. He felt boxed in, wanted the empty night-time streets, an open motorway, but had work to do, money to earn. He turned the engine off.

He heard the faint sound of music, remembered turning the CD player down earlier, when that idiot cut him up in Burnham, so he could have his say, and he increased the volume, found Combat 84 steaming through 'Trouble', a story of brothers fighting brothers, Chubby Chris's dog's-bollocks vocals delivering a message that showed the need for ordinary English lads to stick together. Ray agreed with Henderson's wise words, knew it was a crime so many of the boys spent their time rucking each other when there was an elite bunch of exploiters needing a size ten in the bollocks, plenty of arse-lickers begging for some righteous aggro. Problem was, the proles preferred lamping each other. It was easier that way. Less chance of a nicking. There were some proper wallies around as well, tarts who bullied and cheated their way through life, never thinking about anyone except themselves, a drain on society that deserved erasing. Ray was the first to admit he was no angel, but he had standards. He was more than a dead-end kid.

Despite 'Trouble's' message, he still got excited about the big Chelsea games, specially when it came to the likes of Tottenham. There would never be any unity as far as Spurs were concerned. He would never forget the Yids chanting 'Argentina' back in the Ardiles days, and it still made him angry how the England-haters further up the ladder had slagged off the army for caning the fascists and liberating the Falklands. It was the same with Afghanistan and Iraq today. He had to admit that Tottenham had a handy firm, but it wasn't something he was ever going to say out loud. Even thinking it made his fists tighten. The Tottenham match was coming up soon and he couldn't wait. He fucking hated them.

When the song finished, Gene Putney began gearing up for a dose of 'Chelsea Maniacs', but he paused the track, would save the All Stars essential for later. He opened his door, a rotten smell of cooked meat cutting through the air, like some crackhead was frying cat food in a pan thick with grease and ganja paste. He toppled out, a soft heap of muck bursting under his right DM, the familiar squash of fresh dog shit. He slammed the door shut and limped away, counting to thirty, tempted to drill a fist through one of the car windows, knew it wasn't the smartest move, that it would cost him the price of new glass and labour, bruised knuckles and maybe even stitches. There again, it would make him feel better.

If he could have conjured up a genie right now, his first wish would be for a mugger to stroll up counting the contents of an old dear's purse, the woman herself arriving and pointing a finger, the wanker responsible holding his hands out and flashing some steel, temporarily insane as he sneered Ray's way, hanging around when he should have been on his toes, asking Ray what he was going to do about this crime against society. There would be no chance of mistaken identity. No hoods and no confusion. He could batter the scum to a seed-splattered pulp and feel no remorse. It would also ease some of the tension he was feeling.

He noticed a terrier eyeballing him from across the street, somehow knew the mutt was innocent. This wasn't terrier shit. More like a fucking Rottweiler. Or one of those beasts you heard about in Cornwall, lurking out on the moors tearing up sheep, a monster only every seen by the local cider-drinker on his way home after a night on the scrumpy. But this was a concrete town and it was a concrete dog responsible. He was glad there were no people about, just that old codger floating along the pavement in a yellow space buggy, an NYC baseball cap sticking out from the hood of a lime-green raincoat.

The man might not be able to use his legs, and it was good the NHS had fixed him up with some wheels, but there was no need to turn him into a moving target. True, you'd never knock the geezer down in the dark, but the bright graffiti colours were asking for trouble, enough to stir up every piss-taker going.

Ray stood at the side of the road trying to clean his boot, using the kerb and the remains of a grass verge, but the grooves were too deep. He was struggling. Trust Doctor Marten. The best air-ware soles in the world were handy when you wanted to walk tall, but right now they were pissing him right off. He concentrated hard, helped by the soothing hum of the passing spaceship, a steady vibration, same as the relaxing throb of a razor on his head, and the buggy became a UFO, an alien crew going into shock as they scanned the streets of this strange new world.

He looked up and realised the driver had turned off his motor, was sitting there staring at him. First the terrier, now Captain Kirk. Ray was embarrassed and would've told anyone else to fuck off, but you couldn't go around slagging off cripples. You had to make allowances. He nodded and tried to smile, but the spaceman didn't move, an irritated expression wedged across his face.

Kirk lifted a hand and pointed. Ray turned, looked down the street, saw houses, cars, grass, clouds. He shrugged his shoulders.

– The puddle, the Captain snapped, waving a finger.

Ray saw a small pothole filled with dirty water.

– Use the puddle, he continued, as if he was talking to an idiot.

Ray went over and dipped his boot in the water, moved it around so the mixture swirled, flashes of grey darting through a brown stew, as if it was full of tadpoles. The puddle was doing the trick though, and he looked at the elderly space cadet, noticed an air rifle wedged next to his seat, imagined a couple of Ali Cs giving him grief, running home with pellets in their arse. He grinned at the image.

– Twig, the man commanded, pointing at the gutter.

Ray went over and picked up a thin piece of wood, knew what was expected, the twig perfect for cutting into the grooves. His boot was soon clean.

– Lucky it wasn't fox shit, Kirk concluded, turning a key and pulling away, quickly hitting Warp Factor Five.

Ray watched the bloke speed off, wondering how he'd lost the use of his legs, what he did with his days, specially during the darkest months when the clouds sunk down and smothered the streets, swamping the drains with a gluey rain, soaking sensitive souls and drowning the more thoughtful in depression. He remembered his manners and called out thanks, but there was no reply.

Ray sighed and walked up to the house, pressed the bell. He tried again, a woman opening the door, a towel stacked on her head and a thin dressing gown covering her body. She jammed a hand over her mouth.

– I said half-eleven, she said, looking at a clock in the hall.

– I was told to come straight here.

– I'll only be a minute. I'm almost ready.

First the dog shit, now a fare who was going to take half an hour doing her lipstick.

– I can't hang around, he said. I'll tell them to send another car at half past.

– I won't be long. Honest. I don't want to miss my train. I can't miss my train. You're only fifteen minutes early.

She left him standing on the doorstep, hurried through a glass door into the living room.

– Wait in here for a minute, she called back.

It was fucking typical. He was too soft, sighed, wiped his feet on the mat and followed her inside.

– Come on, sit down. I promise I'll be quick. I leave everything late. It's the story of my life, but I'm sure I said half past.

She thought hard.

– Maybe I didn't. I'm not sure. I'm sorry.

Ray sat in a chair, leant forward and scanned the room quickly, his eyes immediately drawn to the sideboard and a framed photograph of a young solidier, a vase of red roses next to him. His heart jumped.

– That's my son Stuart, she explained. He's serving in Iraq. He's due home in a month.

She raised a hand to her mouth.

– A lad he knew was blown up last month.

Ray nodded. Didn't know what to say. He was glad Stuart was alive.

She had already passed back through the living room and he could hear her running up the stairs, hurrying to get ready. She could take as long as she wanted. He leant his head back in the chair and closed his eyes. She wasn't much older than him. Fucking typical, as well, getting wound up. Her son was serving in Iraq and he was worried about waiting a few minutes for her to put her knickers on.

There was something wrong in him that he couldn't explain, something that was mucking up his life. He noticed other pictures, different stages in the boy's life, photographs of what he imagined were a brother and sister, the woman's husband, grandparents and a black cat. Every family had its story.

He thought about his own family, knew his big mistake was that fight over in West Drayton. He was lucky he hadn't been nicked, really. It wasn't his fault, but Liz wouldn't listen, his clothes covered in blood as she called him a nutter, even though most of it was from his nose, and he didn't like that, being told he was a nut job. She started up again, shouting he couldn't stay angry all his life, but Ray couldn't see that having an opinion was wrong, and what was he supposed to do when someone started having a go at him and his mates?

Five minutes later the woman reappeared, dressed and ready to go, hair damp and messy. She had an energy that he liked, the ability to forgive and forget, he could see that clear as day and yet he didn't even know her. He was falling over himself to be polite, but there wasn't much he could say or do. He opened the door, closed it gently, made a couple of cheerful comments, but while she was friendly when she answered, he could see she didn't want to chat. She was messing about in her handbag, looking at the streets outside suddenly, then brushing her hair straight, really pulling at the tangle. She saw him glancing in the mirror and smiled back.

– I worry about him every second he's away, you know.

Ray couldn't imagine what it must be like. If one of his kids was in a war like that, he knew it would be murder. If they never came back, well, he couldn't think what he would do. It would be the end of everything.

He pulled up outside the station, was out in a flash, opening her door and telling her not to bother about the fare, but she was a proud lady, was having none of it, smiled again and walked towards the ticket hall. He sat back in the car and waited a few minutes before calling in.

He thought about the coming summer, if he would be allowed to go on holiday with Liz and the girls. Chelsea and April wouldn't mind, but he didn't know about the wife. They had a laugh when they were away. There was never any aggro. He supposed Liz was just worn out before her time, and yet it wasn't her fault. It was the grind of everyday life, of raising a family, and he hadn't made things any easier. If she wouldn't let him go with them on holiday he'd take the girls away on his own. But he had to get back to work. Angie had a job for him over in Colnbrook. He started the engine and indicated left, reached down and put his music back on, turning the volume up as loud as it would go.

Running Riot in '81

FOR RAY, BEING A skinhead is all about the stripped-down sound and pumped-up lyrics of Oi, it's about having a say and having a laugh, standing tall and standing proud, and he is fifteen years old and six foot tall, growing fast, the green flight-jacket he wears his pride and joy, specially now Mum has sewn on the Union Jack patch, and his roots are in Sham 69 and the hooligan anthems 'Borstal Breakout' and 'Angels With Dirty Faces', the *Tell Us The Truth* and *That's Life* albums, and Jimmy Pursey is a punk and a herbert but more than anything he's the leader of the Sham army, a mental mob of skins who don't give a fuck and hate trendy lefties and rich students and the rubbish who spend all their time slagging off England and Britain, slagging off anyone with some pride and self-respect, and Ray loves the hard skinhead look, the shaved head and Doctor Marten boots, Fred Perry and faded Levis, because it's honest and up front and in your face, and with a skinhead you know what you get, no con and no lies, and Ray knows about the aggro at Sham and 2-Tone gigs, and when Pursey starts pushing some new bands he discovers The Cockney Rejects and Angelic Upstarts, and the Rejects are East End herberts, the Upstarts Geordie miners, and like Sham they're proud to be British but don't like the NF, say British soldiers died fighting fascism, and the Rejects and Upstarts are real punk, street punk, and he's listening to the likes of the 4-Skins, The Last Resort, Blitz, The Business, Infa-Riot, and reading *Sounds* and learning from the godfather of Oi, Garry Bushell, the only writer worth reading, and Ray is discovering older bands like Cock Sparrer and Menace, it doesn't matter if you're a skinhead, punk, herbert, rockabilly or psychobilly, with Oi they're all connected in a funny sort of way, part of a family, street rock'n'roll for yobs and tearaways, rebel music, but Ray knows what he likes, Oi is the real skinhead music, white music for white kids like him and his mates, harder than the lighter 2-Tone beat, talking about the things that matter, and Ray loves being a skin, it's a smart look, a lot of other kids are scruffs, and everyone hates this mainstream synthe-siser shit, the boring beat of the disco elite, and they're teenagers, innocents, angels with clean faces, and it's Independence Day 1981 and Ray is going over to Southall to see the 4-Skins, Last Resort and Business play at the Hamborough Tavern, a lot of the Oi bands he likes come from the East End or down in South London, and living in Slough he isn't going over to the Bridge House in Canning Town, it's all West Ham over there, for a start, and how is he supposed to get home after, and there's football connected with Oi, that's a shame, he can understand a punch-up at a match, but not when you go and see a band, so Southall is a chance for the boys in West London to see these bands, and it's a ten-minute train ride from Slough, there's five of them making the trip, and coming out of the station they're the only white faces, there's more Indians here than in Slough, and it's a fair old hike to the pub so they hop on a bus to the Broadway, jump off and begin walking along the Uxbridge Road, one of the boys, Nicky Wise, his dad's drawn them a map so they know where they're going, and a police car shoots past, siren blaring, and Ray and the others see a big gang of locals looking over at them, and one of them's carrying a long stick, Nick reckons it's a sword, and Ray can see a knife, and it's dawned on him that skin-heads are supposed to hate immigrants and maybe these Indians believe what they read in the papers, perhaps they don't know what Oi and street punk is all about, and he's heard plenty of people moaning about how the wogs and jungle bunnies are taking over, but none of the skins he knows are interested in party politics, and anyway, his uncle was one of the original skins and all he ever listens to is reggae, and boot-boy bands with hair over their ears like Slade, so it doesn't make sense, and another siren screams and a police van flashes past, and suddenly Southall seems a long way from home, they're still the only white faces on the high street, Ray notices older locals watching them as well, it's like they're in another country, and he's scared, can see they're going to get their heads kicked in as the mob starts across the road, and it's bad enough the numbers, but seeing them tooled-up, that's no good, and one throws a bottle and Ray and the others freeze, the first Paki over calls him a fucking white cunt and punches Ray in the face, but it doesn't hurt much, he punches the bloke back, blood spurting out of his nose, and suddenly they're all bundling in on him, Ray's at the front, the rest of the boys aren't as big so he knows he has to stand up and be counted, and they're punching and kicking him, somehow Ray stays on his feet, fights back, most of them are his size or smaller, even the older ones, and he smacks two more in the face, and it's like he's in Calcutta or Bombay, in one of those films on the telly where the savages are after the white man and they're going to chop him up if they can just get him on the ground, and he keeps thinking about the knife, doesn't want to die, but he's angry he's being attacked for being white, on the streets of his own country, the mob is shouting and screaming, and Ray isn't going to give up, he's English and proud, has his back against the wall and feels the blows on his face and body, and the other boys with him are doing their best but they're not as strong, and they're young, like him, and Nick goes down, Ray turns and boots the wog who's trying to kick him in the head, and his DMs are having an effect, these Indians are wearing shoes and plimsolls, his DMs are a secret weapon, he's a skinhead and they're just a bunch of cowards, and his heart swells with pride, he's enjoying it suddenly, the odds stacked against him but he doesn't care, this is his fucking country and he can walk where he wants, dressed how he wants, he's done nothing wrong, and the stick swings against his shoulder, just missing his head, rises up in the air again, and Ray puts his nut down and charges into the crowd, arms spinning like wind-mills, he's taking them all on, isn't going to run away, not even if there was somewhere to run, and he's doing well, but eventually the mob pull him to the floor, hitting him with the stick and kicking him, but it doesn't hurt as much as he thought it would, they're too wound up, and he's in front of a grocer's and these oranges are falling down and bouncing against his hands, which are wrapped around his head, and he looks up and sees the flash of the blade, knows he is going to get badly hurt, trying to get back on his feet, and the blows stop and he hears an older voice telling the mob to clear off and let the boy stand up, bloody hooligans, leave the child alone, have you no shame, so many attacking so few, and when Ray sits up his attackers have scattered, there's only one of them left, the bloke with the knife, he's standing in the middle of the road and Ray sees the hate in his face, sheer twisted rage, and the man saving him is the shopkeeper selling oranges, and other men have come over and some try to grab the boy with the knife, but he dodges them and runs off along the Uxbridge Road, one of the older Indians picking up an orange and throwing it after him, like he's a cricketer out on the boundary, and Ray hears the hiss of one of those Tests from India when they show it on the telly, the buzzing is in his ears, inside his head, and the shopkeeper is steadying Ray, who's wobbly on his feet, his mates around him asking if he's okay, and Ray says fine, but he feels numb, and Nick is saying I can't believe you took them all on like that, you steamed into them single-handed, you're a nutter, Ray, a fucking nutter, and he's proud he stood up for himself and the rest of the boys, and the man wants to know if he needs an ambulance, no thanks, he isn't bleeding, at least he hasn't been stabbed, and once his head clears he'll be as good as new, and some of the men walk them down the Uxbridge Road, say there's going to be trouble tonight, for Asian people a skinhead means the National Front, racists who attack innocent people in the street, and Ray replies we've only come to see the bands, thinks about what he sees in the paper, the way skins are written about, his head is starting to hurt, and he's angry as they walk past shops and cafes, police vans passing fast, and up ahead he can see the pub and hundreds of locals are hanging around, and this lot are older, youths and men, and there are coppers between the pub and this other mob, and the shopkeeper and his mates see them to safety, and they're ushered in by some big skins standing at the door, patted on the back, and at last Ray and the others are safe, glad they're with their own people, it's a good feeling, and they buy five pints of lager at the bar and drink them fast, the Hamborough filling up, and there's stories of machetes and swords, petrol bombs stocked up, and there are all sorts in the pub, maybe half are skins, and there's herberts and punks and some women as well, music lovers, and The Last Resort have brought two coaches over, and there are proper geezers from East London and a lot of West London lads as well, and someone says the Old Bill have closed the area off, whites aren't being allowed near Southall now, news is spreading, but once the music starts Ray forgets about the aggro on the high street and the siege building up outside, these are bands he really wants to see, and when the last one is on stage, the 4-Skins, the windows start smashing, and the harder lads want to go outside and get stuck in, they've had enough of this, others trying to calm things down, and then Ray and his lot are outside in the night, bricks shattering on the road, petrol bombs exploding, and the police are fighting a fucking huge mob of Indians, holding them back, there's skins who want to steam the Pakis but there's no real chance, the police and whites are pushed down the road by the numbers, a van on fire and run into the pub, the Hamborough Tavern burning, coppers cracking heads and nicking people, and Ray and Nick and the others stick together, everyone shunted away from Southall by the Old Bill, taken towards Hayes and Harlington, and from there they catch a train back to Slough easy enough, and as they walk out of Slough station it's good to be home, and none of them have a clue what's going to happen next, and over the coming months Oi is attacked from all sides and loses gigs and the street bands suffer and it's all on the back of a load of media lies, and while Ray is angry at the unfairness and feels sorry for people he respects, and the rightwing press dig up the cover of the *Strength Through Oi* album, the cover shot turns out to be a British Movement skin, and the trendy left backs up their cousins on the right, and everyone slates Oi, the 4-Skins release their 'One Law For Them' single and everything they say is right, Ray more and more angry about the lies being told, and repeated, and the year passes and the Cockney Rejects release *The Power And The Glory*, and Ray loves this LP, specially the title track, and it's true, the only pride that working people have left is for the part they played in the war, because beating the Germans and smashing Hitler and Mussolini is the one thing even the rich cunts can't take away from the masses, and there are more riots after Southall, and Maggie Thatcher is running riot herself, unemployment is soaring, and the Angelic Upstarts release their *Two Million Voices* LP, another classic, and Southall is the start of Ray's adult life, part of his education, the reason he becomes known as Ray The Nutter, Nutty Ray, that geezer Oi: The Nutter, the headcase who took on fifty tooled-up Pakis single-handed and ran them all over the shop, and if Terry English became a skinhead in the Summer of Love, then for Ray it's more like the Summer of Hate, and it's a long old summer, one that's going to last for the next three years.

The Thinkers

LOL SAT IN MCDONALD'S counting his chips, measuring the different lengths, Kev The Kev next to him, chewing on a straw as they waited for Matt to come and sit down, and he was taking his time, late as usual, carrying a Big Mac bundle over from the counter, the sun flickering through the clouds and lighting up the front windows for a couple of seconds, summer only a few months away, the boys couldn't wait, they had plans, and Lol flexed his arms, strong from using his dumbbells, and they sort of just went along with things normally, but today there was something important needed doing, and Matt sat down and opened his carton, running a finger over the surface first, flipping the lid and reaching inside, mayonnaise and ketchup dripping against the foam, raising the burger towards his mouth, munching, and Kev put a mangled straw back in his Coke, sucking icy liquid into his mouth, Lol biting into a chip, the bright colours shining, cheap and cheerful, meat and potato filling them up, the food of the people, the three boys happy in their little corner of America, Uxbridge town centre bothered outside, drizzle falling on cars and buses, rainbows forming inside McDonald's, digits popping across happy tills, paper hats and striped liquorice suits for the boys and girls serving, a smell of gherkin and mustard, everything lodged inside Lol's head. They needed a name for their band.

– What about The Thinkers?
– The Tinkers?
– Thinkers.
– The Pikeys?
– The Thinkers.

– It sounds like Tinkers.

– They burnt an old man out of his house last year, down by the garage.

– Not The Tinkers. The Thinkers. Tinkers don't think.

– Only about themselves. Take what they want and don't care about anyone else.

– The Thinkers. We're the boys who think.

– You don't.

– He does. All he thinks about is food.

– Girls more like.

– Better than thinking about boys.

– Harsh.

– Fuck off, gay boy.

– Who you calling gay boy?

– What about The Gay Boys?

– Dufus!

– Gay. Shit.

– The Shit Boys?

– We want to sound good, not like a load of batty boys.

– The Shitters?

– The Thinkers is okay.

– What about The Drinkers?

– You puked up after one bottle.

– That was well funny.

– We're banned now.

– So what. That place is shit.

– The Pukers?

– There was something wrong with my drink.

– Like it had alcohol in it.

– Someone must've spiked it.

– Dufus!

– What about Love And Hate?

– Love And Hate?

– Yeah. Or Rage And Love.

– They're both good.

– My dad's mate . . .

Lol was going to say Uncle Hawk, as that's what Dad called Hawkins when his son was around, seeing as when he was a kid Lol couldn't say the whole thing and called him Uncle Hawk. Or Hawk. Like a big bird, except Hawkins wasn't like a bird, with the size of him and his short white hair.

– . . . my dad's mate Hawkins. He's got Love And Hate tattooed on his knuckles.

– Why change it to Rage And Love?

– It's a line from 'Jesus Of Suburbia'.

– Rage And Love?

– Rage And Love. It's like Love And Hate.

– Your dad's mate Hawkins, his name's Alan Bentley, isn't it?

– Alan, yeah.

– My mum says he's been in prison.

– Probably. They all call him Hawkins.

– I thought his name was Bentley.

– It's someone in a book they read when they were young.

– You read it?

– No, it was when my dad and Hawkins were our age, or a bit older maybe. I don't know.

– They were skinheads, weren't they?

– Still are. My mum was as well. Dad's got lots of photos from when they were young. Never looks at them though.

– Mum hasn't got any photos left. My dad chucked them in the bin and she didn't know he did it till after the dustman came.

– Why'd he do that?

– Because he's a wanker. Maybe your dad and Hawkins could find him and beat the fuck out of him.

– You want them to beat up your dad?

– I hate him.

– You can't hate your own dad, Kev. Not that much, anyway. My dad's not like that. I mean, he's not a nutter.

– All skinheads are nutters.

– Hawkins isn't either. Not really.

– How do you know what they were like? Your Uncle Ray's a nutter.

137

– He's all right.

– My mum says he's a nutter.

– How does she know?

– Don't know. That's what she told me.

– Uncle Ray's okay.

The band sat back and concentrated on their food, watching five girls walk in and line up, studying the menu on their own little catwalk, the boys grinning seeing that two of the girls had low-cut jeans and silver studs in their belly buttons, and Kev started laughing and lowered his head when the girls looked over, and then Lol and Matt began laughing and they all sat with their heads down, doing their best to hide it, watching as the girls ordered and flicked their dyed hair out of their eyes, waited for their food, the boys nudging each other and kicking Reeboks and Quiksilver under the chairs.

– We should have special names.

– What do you mean?

– Like Hawkins.

– We haven't got a name for the band yet.

– You're already Kev The Kev. Lol's not his real name either.

– Sounds like a chat-room perv.

– Lol's short for Laurel. Mum and Dad called me after Laurel Aitken, the godfather of ska. Laurel George Skinner. George is after my grandad.

– Not surprised you prefer Lol.

– I don't like Kev The Kev.

– Why?

– I'm a skater, like you.

– I like skate-punk, but wouldn't dress like a punk. I like everything. I don't call myself anything.

– What about Sexy Kev?

– Sexy Kev?

– Dufus!

– Just Dufus?

– Killer Kev? The human drum machine.

– Killer Kev's okay.

– Kev The Kev. Drum head.

– All right, then, Lol The Skin.

– I don't care.

– What about you, Matt?

– Matt's good enough.

Lol shook his head. This was going nowhere.

– Come on, what are we going to call the band? Haven't you two got any ideas?

– What about The Dufus Brothers?

– We're not brothers.

– What, you mean we're all dufuses?

– If we start taking the piss out of ourselves, everyone else will as well.

– Yeah, that'll look good when we're on TV. Here's Green Day, Sum 41 and The Dufus Brothers.

– Lol Dufus.

– And his brothers Kevin The Dufus Kev.

– Matt Dufus.

There was a long pause.

– Dead Americans? It's a song off that Lars Frederiksen album.

– Dead Englishmen?

– Dead English.

– That's not bad. Dead English.

– You know what my Uncle Ray calls us. Not just us three, but everyone we go around with.

– What?

– The Dufus Brothers?

– The BB-Boys.

– What does that mean?

– Don't know, he won't tell me. He laughs and says we're the BB-Boys.

– Big Bad Boys?

– Bad Breath Boys?

– Dufus!

– You see on the news, those kids called themselves the Burger Massive. They raped a girl in London.

– Duhhh. Good name. Why don't they call themselves

the McDonald's Mafia. Or the Next No Marks? Or the Tesco Terrors?

– American Idiots?

– English Idiots?

Kev ripped into his straw, splitting the plastic.

– I saw your cousin the other day. Chelsea. She had that American Idiot sweatshirt on, with the hand grenade.

– She never takes it off.

– She was down near school, by the supermarket. She was with Ian's little sister. What's her name? Tanya?

– I didn't know she was mates with her.

– Yeah, don't know what she was doing there. That Tanya buys drugs off these rude boys who sell them in the car park. You think your cousin's buying stuff off Pakis?

– No, not Chelsea.

– If Ian knew he'd kill them. If he knew someone was selling drugs to his sister. She's only twelve.

– You should tell him.

– Not me. Why don't you?

– Chelsea was probably just buying some food. What do you want to go and spy on them for?

– I wasn't spying. I was going in to buy a magazine.

– What? The Dufus Express?

– Come on. We're supposed to be thinking of a name for the band.

– What about something like The Streets? He's all right. He's not rock, but he's okay.

– The Townie Twins?

– There's three of us.

– The Twin Townies?

– Three of us, Dufus.

– The Thinking Three?

– What about something from a song. Those other ones sounded good. Rage And Love.

– The Slim Shadies?

– You can be N&N.

– Dufus!

– The Chemical Romantics?

140

– The Wicked Boys?

Lol drifted off, had finished eating and screwed his wrappers into a ball, sat back and looked around, glancing at the girls with their pierced belly buttons and low-cut jeans, his Uncle Ray telling him they looked like cleaned-up hippies, and he felt pretty good about life, just hanging about with his mates, he preferred it over here in Uxbridge, it was nearer his house than Slough, and Queensmere wasn't much, not compared to Chimes and the older Chequers, and it was easier to get down here, there was more to do and there were more white kids like him and his friends, they were safer as well, didn't have to think about those Paki rude boys so much, and he watched Kev and how he wobbled his head around, full of electricity, and he was funny, just the way he creased his face, pulled his hat back off his head and scratched at his eyebrows, and Matt was big and quiet, he was learning the bass, reckoned Slash was the best guitarist in the world, and maybe he was, maybe not, Lol didn't mind old bands like Nirvana and Guns N' Roses, preferred Sum 41 and Bowling For Soup, things like that, and really Matt should've been the big drummer and Kev the smaller guitarist, but Kev wanted a proper kit, was hoping his mum would get him a job at the shop where she worked, and he was going to try and get Lol one as well, and Lol smiled, felt happy and content.

– Have you asked your dad about going round your place to rehearse?

– He won't mind.

– You've got a big enough house.

– Don't want a couple of lodgers, do you? I could fix my mum up with your dad.

– He's too busy for all that.

– You think he can give us jobs when we leave school?

– You've got to dress a certain way, but it's not much different to how a lot of people dress normally.

– He's mad, your dad. Wish mine was like that. All he does is work and sit in front of the telly. Never goes out or anything.

– You have to have short hair and a Ben Sherman.

– We've got short hair.

– Kev's okay, but yours is a bit long.

– What else?

– Don't know. They all look the same. It's like an army when you see a load of them together.

– What else do you have to do?

– Pass your driving test. Buy a car. Get a radio fitted and then Dad gives you a job.

– How do I get a car?

– Duhhh, Dufus. Work. Borrow the money. What do you think?

– What sort of car?

– Four doors, not too old probably, unless you know Dad and then it doesn't matter too much. He's got these rules, but he doesn't keep them. He thinks he does, but he bends them all the time. You just get set up and work as many hours as you want.

– Your dad owns Estuary Cars, so we should be all right.

– He worked for them first, then bought the company, but he doesn't take anyone. Angie does most of the work. I don't know what Dad does really.

– Who's Angie?

– The woman who works there. Carol works there as well. She's Stacey's mum.

– I know her. I thought she was a prostitute.

– What, Stacey's mum?

– Yeah, after her husband died.

– I don't think so.

– That's what someone said.

– You wouldn't like someone saying that about your mum.

– No, I wouldn't. I'd fucking kill them.

– A woman down our way does that. Then her daughter drove her sports car through a pub window when she was pissed.

– She should get a job with Dad.

– She didn't even have a job. You're right, you can get a car easy.

142

– You have to have a four-door to work at Estuary Cars.
– Mum's down to move. There's some new houses near you. We might have a place there. I hope so. It's all pikeys down the other end now.

Lol looked at the band.

– Come on, what are we going to call ourselves? It's got to be something that's to do with us.

– We don't do anything, just sit around.

– The Do Nothings?

– That's no good. I'm going to get another drink.

Matt walked back up to the counter, and Lol looked over at the window, into the road outside, his head drifting as he thought of those Love and Hate tattoos on an old man's knuckles, and the more he thought about it Lol guessed those two words really did sum up his dad and uncle, and Chelsea was right, rage and love was like hate and love, and he wasn't sure if rage meant the same thing as hate, he would have to think about the difference, if there was one, picking up a chip and smirking, flicking it at Kev The Kev, who grinned and sucked Coke into his straw, lifted it and squirted it at Lol, missing, and he didn't want his new Fred Perry stained, didn't say anything, let things settle down again, the boys laughing, without a care in the world.

Night Shift

RAY PREFERRED DRIVING DURING the day, but didn't mind a Wednesday or Thursday night, once or twice a week, seeing as the roads were quiet and the money good. It wasn't much fun ferrying piss-heads around, but it wasn't like they worried him, just got on his nerves after a while, talking bollocks and repeating themselves, but things usually evened out, with plenty of sober citizens preferring a minicab to a late-night bus stop. He was easy on the drunks, put up with them, but as someone who looked after his car, cleaned it inside and out every week, really made the effort and went down the garage to use the industrial hoover, he had a rule that any man who was sick in the cab got a slap. And by a slap he meant a hiding. No fucking about. Pure fist and boot. As far as the fanny went, well, there wasn't much he could do, just pull over and let the little darlings spew their souls into the gutter. You couldn't slap a bird, and you couldn't leave her on the side of the road either, an easy target for some nonce to kidnap and rape. The girls could take a few liberties, but the boys had to behave. One of Tel's golden rules said don't batter the customers, which was fair enough, but Ray had his own regulations when it came to puke. So far nobody had tested him, but he knew it was only a matter of time.

He stopped outside number 47, noticed the walls were pebble-dashed, the window frames and gate flaking paint, wood splintered. He preferred his house bricks out on display, not smeared with gravel, and he pictured his own home, the yellow segments neatly lined up, cement crisp inside thousands of individual blocks. He saw Liz sitting on the couch watching TV, the remote on her lap, his daughters tucked up in bed, safe and warm, smiling and happy in their dreams, everything in its right place, clean and tidy and protected.

The front door opened and closed before he could walk up and ring the bell, a tall woman hobbling down the path, doing her best to balance on high heels. Miss Rowlands bent her way into the back seat, straightened up, her head nearly touching the roof, keen to get over to The Cosmopolitan.

– Can you pick my friends up on the way? she asked. I told the woman when I phoned.

Ray could see that Miss Rowlands was nothing special to look at, but good luck to her, she'd made the effort and done herself up, the plastic red coat matching thick glossy lipstick, mouth pouting out of proportion to a skinny face, glistening as street lights passed orange smears across the surface. The Cosmopolitan was over towards Maidenhead, one of those glitzy clubs that pretended they were upmarket, but was really the usual suburban dump full of small-time posers and overpriced drinks.

– I heard Stomper 98 are playing down there tonight, he said, trying some humour. And Garry Lammin is DJ-ing.

Miss Rowlands smiled, but didn't really hear, didn't have a clue what he was on about, more interested in giving him directions.

Ray tried a couple more one-liners, some trusty Oi Oi patter, but she preferred her view of familiar streets, a ragged knot of junctions and curves, semis and terraces, flats and garages and a whizzing crank on a skateboard, a pair of Hickmott goggles wedged into his eye sockets. Ray respected her privacy and shut up, knew there wasn't much a fare could do once they were stuck inside a cab, forced to either agree with the wheelman's wisdom or pass back short answers and hope that he got the message. Even so, Ray felt as if he didn't matter, was turning invisible, but wasn't the sort of bloke to go all moody on her. He reached for the CD player and flicked through to 'Disco Girls' by The Business. He was professional and kept the volume down, but just loud enough for some subliminal *Brave New World* suggestion.

Miss Rowlands seemed happy, flickering around inside her head, the same as him and every other person alive. Maybe she was shy, or nervous, sitting in a car with a man she didn't know. There was some proper pond life out there, scum who pretended they were minicab drivers and attacked women. He hated thinking that a stranger could look at him and worry he was a nonce.

They reached a row of flats and he watched her peg it up the path, realised she wasn't wearing her heels, turned and found them propped neatly on her handbag, side by side, so they didn't leave a mark on the seat. He was impressed, by her good manners and the fact she knew she could trust him. He turned the CD off, let the radio rise up, dodging the lecturers and social advisers, the cartoon ghetto-chat of the urban pirates, settling on a yachtsman talking about sharks and a storm, the seasickness and loneliness he felt as he crossed the Atlantic single-handed, how there came a time when he was sure he was going to die. His biggest fear was that his body would never be found, that he would melt away and disappear in the ocean. He didn't want to become a man without a body. He wanted to be found.

A door blew open and three figures glided down the path, an explosion of perfume perking Ray up, Miss Rowlands squeezing in the back seat with a chubby doris, her face powdered matt white, the real beauty sitting next to him in the front, a leopard-skin jacket over a silver miniskirt, tanned belly with a silver plug, and he thought of the Belly Button Boys but wasn't laughing, bare legs stretching into tiny, straps-only shoes. He wouldn't say no, if she was offering, but he was just the driver, her chauffeur for twenty minutes. She was near enough thirty, bubbling away, and with her short peroxide blonde hair Ray could almost persuade himself she was a punk. She was on her way to a local version of the big EuroTrash clubs in the West End, minus the tourists and students and grade-one wankers. He thought of George Orwell again, the power of the proles, their energy sapped by the glitzy disco ball and some fizzy technology. He wondered how many people who melted their brains watching Big

Brother on the box realised where the term came from, how many had ever heard of *Nineteen Eighty-Four*. It was another way of ruining something important, changing the meaning.

He breathed deep and concentrated on the road, the hard black asphalt of so many dead navvies, those soft brown thighs a distraction he resisted, worming his way out onto the A4, conscious of a jerky gear change, the women nattering away and not noticing, Miss Rowlands and Fatty calling the doll next to him Yvonne.

– You busy tonight? Yvonne asked.

Ray nodded, eyes on the broken white line.

– Everyone's out having fun and I'm working. Can't complain, though. Got to make a living.

– Poor thing, she laughed

– It's Thursday night, the best night of the week, Miss Rowlands said, finding her voice.

She was coming alive, and Ray reasoned she was shy, her confidence back now she had her mates along to help out. It was strength in numbers.

– It's only the best night because of what happened last week, Yvonne teased.

The girls roared.

– Shut up, bitch.

Ray could guess what Randy Rowlands had been up to.

They were laughing away, Randy pushing Yvonne, who leant over the seat and pushed her back, Fatty sitting still, trying to act dignified, waiting for her friends to finish, and when they settled down their whispered words mingled with the voices on the radio, Ray drifting off and thinking about Liz, how she looked like Beki Bondage when they first met, and that had been his chat-up line. It wasn't the greatest opener in the world, but it worked. It was a good time, and Liz was tasty, didn't worry about anything, but she changed once the girls were born. She had really dressed the part as well, and women dressed pretty dull now, unless they were off somewhere special like these three, to a venue where they were locked in and out of sight. These were conservative times. Liz had moved with them.

– Can we book a cab for later? Yvonne asked, when they were near The Cosmopolitan. One o'clock okay?

– You get all the Paki cabs hanging around, with the drivers staring at your tits, Fatty said. The old men are okay, but some of the younger ones are dodgy.

– I'll radio it in. If I'm free, I'll do it myself.

– It'd be better if you picked us up. We know you, don't we, and you know us, so nobody will steal our ride and we won't end up with a rapist.

He could see the logic.

– One on the dot. I can't hang around. You'll have to be there waiting.

The girls started talking faster as they approached the club, becoming more and more excited, and Ray was sure they were on drugs, frowned, thought of Randy's shoes propped on her handbag and didn't care. They were soma pawns, dressed by corporations and fed by gangsters, programmed to work and breed and consume, encouraged to have fun, to laugh and spend and dance to a digital beat, and the fact they stayed warm and human showed the strength of their souls. Yvonne dipped into her purse, paid and gave him a two-pound tip, which was generous, and she smiled and followed her pals to the door where four bouncers waited, dripping steroids, one plum with his arms folded, leering as he inspected the new arrivals, posing in his headset and mouthpiece like a giant fucking puppet. The girls didn't look back as they filed inside.

Ray checked right, Carol sending him over to The Earl Of Cornwall, and he turned the radio off, rode in silence, wishing he hadn't promised to pick them up. He wasn't certain he'd have work till one, but worse was the way they forgot him as soon as they were out of the car. He was a mug. Charmed by a smile and a flash of bare flesh. They would leave early, or late, blag a lift or jump in another cab. Either that or some greaseball's new motor. But a promise was a promise, and there would be plenty of other punters outside. He thought about Yvonne, knew he was going to have to shag something soon. Liz was a no-go zone, and he was only human. He had to move on, accept that she just didn't want him. This thought made him more fed up, and he played the memory again, how they met by chance, and it was the same with most people, these connections happening at night, in the electric glow of semi-darkness, in pubs and clubs and music venues and people's houses. Now he was the invisible man, ferrying lovers around, a shape in the front of a car, their drink and drugs blurring his features.

He entered the pub car park and a man and woman stepped forward, waving him over, spare arms wrapped around each other's waists. They stumbled forward in a pissed-up three-legged race, went into slow motion, then reverse as they staggered backwards, like they were going to topple over. The sweet smell of Yvonne, Fatty and Miss Rowlands was replaced by a different sort of scent, the sour mash of Jack Daniels and Sam Smith's. They stumbled against the side of the car and tugged the back door open, tumbled inside, pulling it shut with a burst of slurred chanting. They were laughing. He didn't mind happy drunks. They were old enough to hold their drink, and must have started early. They wouldn't see sixty again, the woman coated in chunky jewellery, her lipstick perfect, new jeans under an old jacket, and even though she was paralytic he could see she wasn't in bad nick, keeping her dignity after a long session. The man with her was rougher-looking, his face creased and eyes swimming. Ray wondered if they were married, how long they'd known each other, how long they'd stay together.

Driving towards Langley, he made a few enquiries, but couldn't work out what they were saying. They were more interested in each other, the bloke leaning his head down as the woman whispered in their own private language. The radio muttered inside the dashboard, and he couldn't make any sense of the debate, intellectuals discussing various forms of Islam and how it was up to the white English to accept these new customs and beliefs. It was shit. These drunks made more sense. He focused on the traffic, the boy racers and superstore families, excited couples, Muslims who didn't care

149

about all that fundamentalism, just wanted the special-offer sofa from DFS. Lights were blinking up ahead, indicating left and right, roadwork cones cutting across the painted lines, and he really wished he was at home, with his wife and daughters, wished he was different. Ray crossed a junction and found himself on an empty stretch of road.

Stopping outside the address Carol had supplied, Ray turned to his passengers and found them sound asleep. The man's head was resting on the woman's shoulder, and her face was tilted back. He didn't like to wake them up, got out and opened the door, tried shaking the man. He stirred, said something about a late train, and nodded off. Ray tried again, pulled the bloke over and found his hand was stuck in the woman's, and she was moving now, and when he had them out in the evening air the man handed over a tenner, told Ray to keep the change. It was a big tip, too big, and he returned two pounds, watched them sleepwalk to a house, climbed back in his car and waited, making sure they got inside. They were having trouble with the key, and he saw Yvonne and Randy and Fatty in thirty years, if they were lucky, struggling with a Yale lock, protecting a small house in a small street, the same as Ray and Liz. Neither of those drunks would remember him in the morning.

He became less moody as he moved people around, between houses, a Methodist church and a Chinese buffet, time passing, and he stopped at a garage and bought a carton of coffee and a sandwich to keep himself going, felt better, dipped in and out of radio conversations, watching the pedestrians who were out and about, passing cars and faces. It had turned into an easy shift.

Shortly after ten he picked three blokes up from the Marriott. They were suited and booted, pissed and charlied-up, on some sort of training course, their heads full of internet porn and expense-account treats. Ray passed under the M4 and took the older parallel road towards Windsor. They were cocky, the one next to him telling the wankers in the back that he could buy anything he wanted, that every woman had her price. Ray tried to ignore the drone, a fudge-packet in the back going on about shaving some geezer's pubic hair during a war-games weekend. This sounded like poof behaviour to Ray, but he guessed these corporate cocksuckers had different standards, preferred one of their managers and a Crunchie bar to some honest slap and tickle with a woman. They spoke well, but he guessed it was put on, that they were Northern, maybe Scottish, Irish even. He didn't care. They believed in elites and wanted to get in there with the big boys, but Ray knew they had no chance. Their scratching, grabbing natures gave them away. They were rootless, floating around, willing to say anything that would earn them a pat on the back from their bosses. They were the enemy within.

Minicabbing was an education, and that was one of the things he enjoyed about the work. It was a chance to meet the sort of people you would never see in everyday life.

His passengers were excited, working themselves up now, effing and blinding like Ray wasn't there, but he was more interested in their matching barnets, fluffy hair riding the top of their heads the same as fins. It was a ponce look, dunce-like, gelled and dyed and flicked. He narrowed his eyes, realised they were finheads. Reptiles. Cold-blooded parasites. Dollar signs in blank eyes. Mind you, he was being a bit unfair on the old iguanas and geckos, all those snakes demonised by the Bible, serpents who only steamed in when they were defending the parish, the harmless sea turtles who lived for hundreds of years and remembered Captain Cook. He didn't know what went on inside the mind of a tortoise or an alligator, so couldn't judge them, but he had these three wankers sussed. Skinny money-lenders in expensive clobber. Cunts. All he needed was an excuse.

– I thought all the drivers round here were Pakis, the finhead next to him said. You're not a Paki in disguise are you, mate?

Ray turned his head and stared. Usually a firm glance was enough, but these three didn't seem to understand.

– I hate the smelly bastards. You're not a Stani pretending to be a white man? Slough's like fucking Calcutta. Two days here is enough for anyone.

– What was that poem? his friend laughed. Something about dropping bombs on Slough.

Ray treated people as they treated him. He showed respect and expected it in return. He knew lads who had marched with the NF in the old days, men who voted BNP, and living in a democracy he believed everyone should be allowed their views, but he didn't appreciate strangers ramming their opinions at him as if they knew him. He would listen to a person's ideas, try and work out why he held them, but what did these three clowns know?

Scum came in all shapes, colours and sizes, and he had decided his passengers were scum. They were disrespectful. He didn't like these people.

– Doesn't say a lot, does he, a voice barked from the back.

Ray imagined a sneer, but didn't catch it in the mirror. Someone lit a fag without asking, flicked ash towards the wanker in the front, and this floated past his scaly body and landed on the dashboard. Smoke filled the car, ruining the lingering scent of Yvonne and her pals. Ray imagined a clearing. Fresh air and privacy, dew washing the soles of his DMs. He smiled.

– Fuck off, the slag next to him whined, leaning back over the seat and slapping at one of his chums.

– Wanker. Fuck off.

Ray didn't appreciate the fag ash on the dashboard. He worked hard and this car was his livelihood. They had spoken to him, but didn't see his face. He passed a woman driving alone. His passengers shouted and banged on the glass, licking their lips the same as a nonce outside a primary school. She was frightened.

Ray thought about his kids asleep at home, sheltered from the world. It was a shame they had to grow up.

Half a mile further on he pulled down the slip road he had in mind, long grass and a bank of rubble separating it from the bypass. He stopped and turned off the engine, leant down and tapped a button, turned the volume up loud. He left the cab and stood in the semi-darkness, headlights firing beams into the bushes, sucked the smoke-free air into his lungs. 'Romper Stomper' off the first Transplants album rose up, joining with the analogue thud of the motorway. His favourite tracks were 'We Trusted You' and 'Weigh On My Mind', but he had decided on this song, as there was little that needed saying. He preferred more of an instrumental.

He glanced at his passengers. They saw him clearly now.

He opened the back door and dragged the nearest bloke out, punched him a couple of times, then stuck the boot in, the power of the music driving him on. All it needed was some good manners. It wasn't a lot to ask. It didn't matter if he was a solicitor or a bog-cleaner, a man's job was important. Flicking ash around was a challenge. The same went for the swearing and the Paki comments, slagging off his home and shouting at that poor woman. He had accepted their invitation and could feel his head clicking, the kicks harder, brain about to shut down, and he pulled himself back, realised what he was doing, set a limit, left the man semi-conscious, reached into the car and pumped buttons, 'Liquidator' taking over. This was the only ska record he really loved, and while it was urgent in its way, it was also mellow, hit the right channel. He had to watch himself, didn't want to stray towards ultraviolence, Ray The Nutter land, which was easily done. He didn't want to maim or kill anyone.

The second back-seat bandit refused to come out to play, so Ray was forced to bang his head on the door as he dragged him half out of the cab, bringing a hand down in a chopping motion, like he was Bruce Lee giving it some of the old kung-fu treatment, at least until the bloke let go of the frame. He hauled him to his feet and punched him twice, kicking him up the arse when he fell to his knees, sending him rolling into a ditch full of brambles and beer cans. The front-seat fare was out of the car and begging, so Ray used his head, nutted him on his chang-snorting, Pinocchio-like hooter. This was a slap, nothing more, and he didn't give it the full John Terry treatment, didn't want to hospitalise these people, remembering his responsibilities to the firm. They were lucky, though the sobbing did irritate him, stuck in his ear for a while after he had driven off, 'Liquidator' filling his mind with warm thoughts. He would save 'Romper Stomper' for later. That song would mean he was well and truly off the lead.

The rest of the evening passed smoothly. Ray felt more relaxed and had eased some of the tension he had been feeling. He worked until half-twelve, before heading back down the Bath Road. He wasn't going to leave those girls stranded, specially not with so many sleazy finheads on the loose. He laughed as he drove. The trading estate was deserted and he slowed right down near Trade Sales, ignored the EU flags on the plates and gave the new models a good look. This time of night was perfect, as things were generally quiet and dying down.

– I knew you'd come back, Yvonne shouted, as he pulled up.

– Usually the drivers forget, Fatty sighed. It can be a nightmare getting home sometimes.

– Where's your mate? Ray asked.

They laughed that way birds did, when something sexual was going on, coy and cocky at the same time, and he imagined Randy getting a length off some silky wannabe dago. Up to her, of course. It made no difference to him. They were soon on the move, the two ladies with their heads together, whispering away, and he didn't try to listen in, was looking forward to finishing for the night. A police car flashed towards him and he checked his speed, watched it whizz past and quickly shrink in size.

– You know Handsome, don't you? Fatty asked.

Ray looked in the mirror, both his fares sitting in the back.

– I'm staying with him. Keeping an eye on the bloke.

– Handsome! Yvonne said, in a deep voice.

It had been his friend's catch phrase a few years back.

– I used to go out with him, she continued.

Ray looked at her, but couldn't place the face.

– You're Nutty Ray, aren't you? Ray The Nutter?

He didn't appreciate her memory.

– Nobody calls me that now.

– Handsome doesn't say Handsome, either.

That was true. He wondered why.

– How is he?

– Brand new. He's got a wife and six kids and he's given up drinking.

– He's been busy, then. When I saw him four months ago he was still single, could hardly drink he was so pissed.

– It's only me living there.

– Mrs Raymond Handsome.

Cheeky mare.

– Something like that.

– Ask him to give me a call, will you. Tell him Annie asked after him. He should have my number. I gave it to him when I saw him. It was a few years ago when we were going out.

Ray reached in the side pocket and found his phone, scrolled down to Handsome's number and pressed the button.

– What do you want? his friend asked. I was asleep. Dreamt I was shagging Billy Piper up against a phone box.

– The Tardis?

– No, that one across from KFC.

– Here, Ray said, handing the phone to Annie. Have a word with him yourself.

She screamed and flopped back, but grabbed the phone all the same. Yvonne slapped Ray on the back of the shoulder, but not hard. He switched off, didn't want to earwig their conversation, thought about the Tottenham game in a couple of weeks, wondering what sort of mob they'd bring down. He always looked forward to Tottenham.

Annie handed him the phone.

– Ray? Bring her round, mate. Now you've woken me up.

– You want to go see him? he asked Annie.

She seemed keen, and he was happy to oblige. Yvonne moved into the front when he dropped her off. Handsome waved from the front door.

– Who's this? Yvonne asked, listening to the CD.

Ray turned it up.

– The Templars. From New York.

– You ever been to New York? she asked.

– No, but there's a bloke I know, he goes over, brings back bags of iPods, a few laptops, those Timberland working boots you see. It's cheap. The Yanks know how to do things. See, they're old English, more British in some ways than we are. They still rate the individual, believe in themselves.

– I'd like to go to New York.

Yvonne smiled and looked out the window.

– Punk's too noisy for me.

– It's Oi, skinhead music. There's a difference.

– I don't like angry music.

She began rabbiting about some dance band, then about how you could get two drinks for one at The Cosmopolitan, even though it was a bit upmarket, and he stopped listening, would be dropping her off soon, wanted to get home.

– I live with my mum, she said, as he was slowing down. Why don't you drop me off round the back, by the garages.

She squeezed his arm. He was visible all right.

– You've got big muscles, she laughed, putting on a funny voice.

He knew he was in.

He did as she said, stopped and turned the engine off, Yvonne running her hand down his leg and rubbing his groin. Ray caught sight of himself in the mirror, the strong head and cropped hair and was pleased his night's work was done. Yvonne slid back in her seat and lifted her feet in the air, slipped a white G-string off and popped it in her handbag, climbing into the back seat.

The skinhead considered his uncle's golden rules – short hair, decent clobber, no beating fares to a pulp in slip roads and no shagging the customers. He felt his defences weaken and hauled his tired frame out of the cab, went round and sat in the back with Yvonne, her spangly dress glittering white and silver stars, millions of dreams sparkling in the darkness. He closed the door, reasoning that he couldn't be expected to maintain his standards twenty-four hours a day, seven days a week. Even a dedicated Estuary professional deserved some rest and relaxation.

STREET PUNK

A Handy Little Firm

IT WAS THE SAME with any firm. There was always a core that could be relied on to do the business, home or away, year after year, never mind the odds. Terry only had to look back over forty years of football to see the truth in this, recognising the faces who kept turning out across the decades, come rain or shine, and it took all sorts – smilers, brooders, nutters. Younger lads emerged and kept the numbers up, learnt lessons and maintained the firm's standing as it slowly mutated and adapted, and some of these boys stuck with it, while others moved on, found other things to do, the core adjusting to different eras, adapting to new customs, winning and losing all sorts of battles along the way. He chanted WE ARE THE FAMOUS, THE FAMOUS CHELSEA in his head, a wide smile filling his face.

Looking at the boys making themselves busy around him, he knew he'd chosen the right people for the job. It was Thursday morning and in two days Chelsea were at home to Tottenham, a fixture that most of those here would be attending, and Terry still got excited about his football, the build-up starting already, expectation rising, and it was all about the game these days, the spectacle and the sportsmanship. First he had to get through today and Friday. He wanted the club painted by tonight, with everything finished, as tomorrow he had an appointment at the hospital. He wasn't looking forward to it, the doctor warning him that the treatment was going to make him feel rough.

It was nearly twelve and he scanned the room, started laughing. He leant forward and laughed harder.

– What's the matter? Ray asked, frowning as he paused, roller pressed against the wall.

Hawkins was looking around, wondering what the joke was, ready to join in when he worked it out.

Lol shifted from foot to foot, playing chords in his head, watching his father and smiling, not paying much attention, a small brush light with paint.

– What a sight, Terry said. What a picture.

Ray didn't get it right away, but he did know that he felt like a right plum, the overalls he was wearing too small, specially when it came to the legs, which stopped halfway up his calves. He was wearing an old pair of Doc Martens, split along the insteps, boots that had been left unpolished for years, kept for odd jobs around the house. The overalls were white and sprinkled with red paint, left over from a job a decade before probably, a polka-dot effect he didn't appreciate, the material crusty or starched, he wasn't sure which.

He glanced at the others – Ian Stills and Big Frank working on the ceiling, Lol and Kev taking their time cutting in, Buster fannying around by the bar, Hawkins on the walls – knew they were no smarter, Terry in a blue boiler suit directing operations, like he was a fucking general or something, the dodgy threads coming from down the back of Hawkins's lock-up, stuck behind the snide sports shirts and twenty years of Arthur Daley rubbish collection.

– Dear oh dear, Terry continued. What a mob.

Ray saw what he was on about. It was like *A Clockwork Orange* meets *Teletubbies*. All they needed was the bowlers and cricket boxes, a bunker built into the turf. He grinned, glad he wasn't painting the outside, stuck up a ladder. Hawkins laughed and continued, Kev pushing Lol, who made a face, telling him not to muck about. It was good money, a hundred pounds for a day's work, and Dad had let his mate come along as a favour, once he'd persuaded him the boy was capable of using a paint brush.

Terry didn't want any slacking. This wasn't football. It wasn't a social. The bar was definitely closed. He'd spent extra on the best paint available, believed in the one-coat promise on the tins, needed the walls, ceiling and wood-work done today. He had enough bodies, so there was no excuse. Ray had visited the paper bank, while Angie'd spent a week gathering old sheets and rags together, Terry and Buster coming in last night, covering anything that couldn't be moved. He was worried about the jukebox, Buster the bar, and those areas had been painted first, both men keeping an eye out for slack work.

– You're like a couple of old women, Hawkins remarked.

The pool tables needed watching, but the surfaces were protected by wooden boards, some pink sheets enough to cover the legs, a massive piece of plastic moving along the carpet as Ian and Frank worked overhead.

Terry had been around with a screwdriver and taken the photos down, drew a plan showing where each one belonged, insisting the holes weren't filled in with blobs of paint. He had made sure the colours matched, didn't want to change the decoration, just freshen things up. Angie had suggested it first, Buster and Ray agreeing with her. He was wary, but could see the logic. It wasn't like he was gutting the place, only livening it up a little.

– You'll have to open the windows, Terry said, first thing, as the tins were popping and the paint was being stirred. We'll all be gassed otherwise. And Ian reckons the paint-work will end up patchy without proper light.

Terry didn't know this Ian kid, but had been told he worked as a painter and decorator, had done some work for Ray, reasoned that it made sense to have a professional along. Mind you, he'd imagined the bloke was older, but Ian turned up with his own overalls and some decent tips, seemed to know his stuff. He hadn't been in the Union Jack Club before and was impressed, asking the sort of questions that made Terry warm to him. He was showing Laurel and Kevin what to do, and Terry was pleased that his son had come in, accepted the chance to work, the money he was paying a tidy sum for lads their age.

– It'll make the smell go quicker as well, Ian pointed out.

Terry knew they were right, but wanted to keep the club as shut away as possible, wondered if opening the windows would allow something to escape, but bowed to the inevitable, could close them once the job was done.

Ray and Frank took down the highest boards, the narrow shaft of light he liked so much broadening out and filling half the Union Jack Club, but he made them leave the wood below, and this meant there were plenty of dark corners, lots of shadow. He blinked as his eyes adjusted, fresh air following as two windows were opened, and he remembered the musty smell he'd noticed first time he walked in, realised he'd become used to it, and the clean air took over, put him on edge for a while, made him wonder if he was making a mistake. He imagined spirits leaving, the atmosphere evaporating, told himself he was being stupid. That had been three hours ago. Now he was fine. The Union Jack Club was more alive. Decorating it was a good idea. Later they would close the windows, but he wouldn't replace the boards. Nobody could see in from the street.

– You got any more of that coffee? Frank called over.

He was trying to get it delivered, but Buster wasn't a waiter, standing behind the bar, blowing on his own chunky mug, filter machine bubbling away. He had a sound knowledge of quality beans, wasn't afraid to splash out on the better blends, loved his Blue Mountain. He had bought something cheaper today, seeing as they were dealing in numbers, but it was still good stuff.

Working in a pub, you needed something to keep you off the drink during the day, and the caffeine made sure he stayed on his toes. He kept the jug topped up and had biscuits ready, knew they'd get more work done if everyone was happy. The smell of coffee brewing was enough to cheer most people up. Mind you, he didn't know if it had done much good yesterday with the man who'd come to look at the club, the gent responsible for supplying a drinks licence.

Robert Marston was young and nervous, seemed more worried about the name of the place than anything else. Buster had shown him around, and he'd cheered up a bit, but then

Terry announced he wanted to put on 'proper skinhead music' as well and the bloke froze. When he was leaving, he brought up the flag hanging in the alley, said it was insensitive, that it should be taken down. Buster didn't know what to make of it, was worried that they were missing something.

This story was just filtering into the ranks, Buster opening his mouth, Frank realising he wasn't getting waiter service, coming over for his coffee.

– Might have to turn this place into a Starbucks, the barman announced.

Terry wished he hadn't made his comment about the scruffy appearance of the troops, Ray and Hawkins following Frank, now they'd stopped working, maybe thinking they deserved a break.

Buster explained Marston's visit.

– Thing is, Ray said, annoyed, stirring milk into his mug, a bureaucrat like that can really fuck things up. Look at the courts, a bank, any government office. Look at the EU.

Ian joined them. Only Laurel and Kevin were still working. Terry looked at his watch. He wanted the job done today. Tomorrow was no good. He watched the boys standing around the bar, which was still covered by sheets, the ceiling above dry. The radio was talking somewhere, nobody listening.

– It's a fucking liberty if he doesn't give you a licence because of the flag, Frank said. He can't do that. He can't refuse. Fucking hell, I used to come in here when I was a boy. I remember this place. If the blokes then didn't mind, why should he? Who the fuck is this Marston, anyway?

Terry stepped forward. Buster was blowing things up out of proportion. The kid had made a couple of remarks, which, while he found them a bit odd, didn't mean much. If there was a problem, he would try and explain things better.

– He never said he wouldn't. It'll be all right. He didn't understand what skinhead music is.

– It's Oi, Ray said.

– It's ska, and that's what I meant. If he knocks us back, I'll appeal, but it'll be fine. You'll see.

Marston was a different sort, university-educated, probably

been on all sorts of courses about the empire and slavery. The Union Jack said something else to Marston, was about imperialism and right-wing politics, while for the lads here it was more important, part of their identity, didn't carry the same meaning. It depended how you looked at things, that was all.

– The Union Jack is being phased out, Ray said. These kids now, they know the Cross of St George more than they do the Union Jack. It's one of the EU's plans. Break up the UK and make England a region in the United States of Europe. If they can break up the UK, get rid of the symbol, they're halfway there. It's fucking obvious.

There was a pause, Terry looking at his watch again.

– What you want to do is kidnap the cunt, Hawkins announced. Pick him up off the street and take him to the lock-up. You've been there, haven't you, Tel?

Terry nodded. So had Ray and Frank. They all knew the place, didn't feel right when the door was closed behind them. It was more than the usual lock-up. Like a bunker. Some blokes reached middle age and rented themselves a nice allotment, started double-digging in the spring, raising runner beans and rhubarb and all the rest of it in the summer, brewing up and staring at the sprouts in winter, but Alan preferred a garage with no windows, a bulb and an ultra-comfortable chair. Fuck knows what he did in there, reckoned he just liked having his own place away from the wife. Somewhere he could sit and be alone.

– We tie him up and take him to the lock-up, right, maybe use some handcuffs so it seems more planned. Maybe put a hood over his head once he's in the van, so he can't recognise us.

– Sounds a bit gay to me, Ian laughed.

Hawkins stared at the kid.

– Yeah, nonce-like, Ray said, backing Ian up. We're not fucking Spurs, Alan. Not a nonce firm.

The boy lowered his head.

– No, you don't get it, Hawkins continued, smiling now. See, this bloke has to think we're someone else.

– Who? Ray asked.

– I don't know. Anyone.

– What, like Julian Clary and Boy George?

The others laughed, but Hawkins looked serious.

– He has to think we're organised, with a bit of clout behind us.

– Tell you what, Ray thought out loud. We'll say we're Combat 18. The cunt will love that. It'll be something to tell his mates.

– That sounds good. Those trendy council fuckers love it, don't they.

Terry thought of *Skinheads And Swastikas*. He was going to have a look at it soon, seeing as Angie kept asking him what he thought, seeing as she'd gone to the trouble of recording it for him. Hawkins could have been writing a scene for the documentary.

– We take him to the lock-up, Hawkins continued, maybe drive him around for a while first, so he's disorientated. I'll print a poster off the internet, get some TERROR MACHINE shirts made-up, proper C18 skull and all that. He'll fucking shit himself.

– Then what? Ian asked.

Hawkins leant over, grinning.

– Then I'll do his kneecaps, cut his fucking throat.

There was some laughter, but mainly silence.

– Say he goes to the police? Terry asked. You going to kill him?

He had a point.

– You can't be doing that, Terry continued. You're talking bollocks. He just understands things different. It's university teaching. I'll talk to him if I have to, explain things properly.

– All a cunt like that sees is a bonehead, Hawkins said. No offence, Tel.

– Right, listen. Terry was stern now. No lock-ups, no kidnapping, and I'm not paying you lot to sit around talking all day.

Terry looked at his friend and knew he was joking –

hoped he was joking. There was the odd time when some threatening behaviour was needed, but this wasn't one of them. He clapped his hands, urged the boys back to work, would get down the chip shop in a while and sort out some food. He didn't want them strolling off down the pub, and he wasn't serving drink here. They had to be at their best.

He looked at Ray, who was pointing at his head and then Hawkins, the lock-up man busy with his roller, soaking it in paint, searching for his place on the wall. Terry saw his nephew's face change as he turned towards the radio, listening to the news that two British soldiers had been blown up by a roadside bomb in Iraq, and he seemed worried, then relieved when they were identified as coming from Lancashire, and finally guilty. Terry didn't know what it meant, didn't try to find out. He had other things to think about, like making sure the decorating was finished today, and his hospital appointment tomorrow. He checked around the club and was pleased to see everyone was back working, putting their backs into it as well, Laurel and his friend Kevin concentrating hard, earning their money like the rest of them. That made him proud.

Running Riot in '82

THE VICAR STRUGGLES TO sum up the short life of a British soldier who has died fighting for freedom in the Falklands, his fingers scuttling along the edge of the pulpit as the boy's family crouch at the front of the church, trying to understand this message of forgiveness. There's no flag-draped coffin for Mrs Fisher to touch, no charred torso shrouded inside, just the picture she's had specially framed, sitting on a table near the altar. The service will end soon and Barry Fisher will never be forgotten — until his parents pass on and his brothers and sisters follow and the photo is discovered in a drawer, the frame broken, glass cracked, a young voice asking who is he, who is that boy, who is it? Barry's story will be forgotten and his memorial washed clean, the same as all the others. His sacrifice will mean nothing, but right now this service is the most important thing in the world.

Ray sits at the back of the church, honouring a neighbour, someone he hardly knew, but it's the principle that brings him here, a chance to show his respect for the family and the man's sacrifice. He believes in the war, and means no harm, but even though he tries to concentrate on the vicar's words, tries to picture the young squaddie, he can't help remembering another funeral, not so long ago, and how it wasn't until afterwards he found out that when his grandad was shot down in France, during the Second World War, the Vichy French handed him over to the Germans, the SS torturing Gunner George so bad he nearly died. Ray knows this by chance, overhearing two of George's mates talking, asking and learning some of the details. He must never tell his mum or uncle or aunt. His grandfather didn't want his children upset. Ray promises the older men, who feel guilty he's found out, as if they've let their friend down. They leave soon after.

Ray offers his condolences outside the church, avoids the drink at the house, walks home and changes into his work clothes, steel toecaps and a donkey jacket, drives to Heathrow with the hymns from the service playing in his head. 'Jerusalem' is the people's favourite, Billy Blake piling into industrialisation and exploitation, proud of his country and its people. It's a song that stirs up his pride, stirs up anger at the scum slating England over the Falklands, all those Union Jack haters who think it's fine for a dictator to steal someone else's land. The trendy lefties whine that the Falklands is full of sheep, say it's windswept, spouting any excuse that comes into their soppy heads, and he wants to ask one of these wankers if the Spanish in Argentina should fuck off as well, let the Indians have their land back, how a Red can prefer a bunch of fascists to a democratic task force, but he never meets these people. Never gets a sniff.

In at work and out on the airport perimeter, Ray begs the drill off Sean, has a go at the concrete they're breaking up, body pogoing with the bounce of the machine, arms quickly aching. He doesn't mind. Labouring keeps him fit, and being a fully fledged skin it pays to have a bit of muscle. There's enough people around who want to kick his head in for the length of his hair, the colour of his skin. He doesn't give a fuck. He'll fight them all. Doesn't care about the planes crashing over his head either, the non-stop hum of lorries and buses on the trunk road a nagging treble beneath the steady booming of jet engines. His head is banging and the ache in his arms grows, hurts his anger so he starts thinking about this punk bird he's knocking off instead, sees her this morning before the funeral, record player spinning Roi Pearce street punk as he pokes her, and she's a right little raver, a proper music lover, appreciates the sweetness of those Last Resort vocals.

The drill kicks back mule-style, reminding him to concentrate on what he's doing, the ache in his arms switching to a sharp pain, but he's knows he's lucky compared to Barry Fisher, that Fisher will never love a girl again. When he's had enough Sean takes over, Ray walking to the truck that's just arrived, unloading bags of sand and gravel. He sees the men around him and wonders if he'll be doing this when he's forty years old. They're tough characters. He wouldn't want to pick a fight with Sean or Michael O'Driscoll or John Brady, none of these Paddies from Slough and Hounslow, their faces chapped red and cracked blue, the Guinness and Murphies breaking too many blood vessels, and they never slack off, keep the pace up, day and night, hearts trotting to their own rhythm. He looks at his life and the work he's doing, getting by, knows it's nothing compared to what those soldiers are doing in the Falklands. There's no glory here. None of the horror either.

That night Ray's whole body is sore, his brain numb. He sits in the bath and rubs at the scum coating his skin, the distortion in his ears slowly fading. He tries to hear the thump of an Argentine shell, the dull pain Barry Fisher might have felt, but he can't get close. What did Grandad George feel? What did he think? It makes him sick, thinking of those German perverts who tortured his grandfather. Seeing the way people behave and treat each other makes him want to give up, and he sinks under the water, imagines Fisher's body sinking into the ocean, his arms and legs flapping, waving to the empty sky and disappearing light. It's a scene from *Jaws*. Pathetic film imagery. It's all a load of old bollocks.

He has the house to himself, empties the water and rinses the tub out, feels the grease and smells the petrol fumes, scrubs harder, fills it again and climbs back in, soaks for half an hour in his mum's best bubble bath. Twice he nearly nods off, but once he's dry and reaching for his blue Fred Perry, pulling on his jeans and DMs, this rush of energy arrives from nowhere and he's raring to go. He eats a thick Cheddar and Branston Pickle sandwich and drinks a bottle of milk, calls a cab and slips his flight-jacket on, rides with a middle-aged Sikh to The General Elliott in Uxbridge, thirsty now, gagging for a drink. The radio plays a speech by Winston

Churchill, part of a programme explaining the build-up to D-Day. Ray adds a pound to the fare and hurries into the pub, his uncle and aunt at the bar. He reaches for his money, but Terry has already bought him a pint of Fosters, seeing his nephew arrive through the window. Auntie April runs a hand over Ray's head and announces what a good-looking boy he is turning into, and he's embarrassed, looks at the carpet, knows his face is turning red as some of the locals turn and smile.

He feels like a kid suddenly, his size and strength evaporating so he's just a big puddle of life that doesn't know which way to run, and Terry has been on his back recently, telling him to keep out of trouble and behave himself. His uncle knows how to calm things down, a voice of reason among the men he drinks with, blokes like Hawkins who's due out of prison, someone who'll be dead before he's thirty, kicked to death or shot in the head. Ray admires a nutter the same as any other likely lad, just as long as he's at arm's length, prefers his uncle's kinder ways, and he'll have to be on his best behaviour tonight, Terry helping him out last week, handing out a right bollocking once they were out of the pub and on their way home. Thing is, Ray doesn't see he did anything wrong. He pays attention to Terry, tries to listen, the best he can, but there's so much nonsense whizzing around in his head that sometimes it's hard to concentrate. His attention wanders. He forgets lessons.

Ray's in this pub in Camden Town, having a drink before they go and see Madness, and there's this tub of lard holding court, one of a mob of Arsenal skins, and this bloke is telling a joke about drowning Argies, and the thing is, Ray doesn't like that sort of humour, is picky about what he finds funny. The man's a bubble, and he's going on and on, and Ray's wondering who the fuck are Arsenal anyway? Terry rates them from the old days, and he knows they have a decent white firm, and some tooled-up blacks, but who's this fat fucker mouthing off? The bonehead spies Ray's look, asks him what's the matter, is he a Red or a Commie, and the younger man answers no, he's a patriotic socialist, fast, just like that, Tommy Cooper style, knows this is going to upset the fat cunt, that people confuse nationalism and patriotism, don't expect to sees patriotism connected with socialism. The cocky grin turns into a sneer, a Clock End tart playing to the crowd.

Ray doesn't like people who sneer. His old man used to sneer, before he fucked off. His dad's a wanker and Ray's going to change his name one day to Ray English, take his mum's side, and anyway, Terry's more of a father to him. Tel's everything rolled into one, and he wouldn't mind being like his uncle, standing at the bar loved by all those around him, but it hasn't worked out that way, at least not yet, though being Ray The Nutter earns him some sort of respect. Being a nutter isn't bad. Except it's not true.

He doesn't think about much now, his brain sort of shuts down and he goes into remote control, this anger coming from nowhere with a big shot of energy, and he doesn't count the odds, just flares up and piles in, punching the goon in the face with his right, knocking through his lager with a left, back with the right so the bonehead slides into the glasses on the bar, and Madness are on the jukebox, Ray loves the music-hall flavour, nutty beats and a dose of sadness, he sees it in Terry, who reminds him of Suggs sometimes, the expression and that, and Madness talk about London and England, about Ray and Terry and all the rest of the boys. It's a different beat to Oi, another approach, but part of the same world. Woody keeps the beat going, Ray surprised the fat boy's mates don't take advantage, and his respect for Arsenal is raised up as they play it fair and square, they can see he's a nutter, a kid who doesn't give a toss, maybe think their friend is out of order. Ray's built like a brick shithouse, a psycho who steamed a tribe of Pakis single-handed, word spreads, it's a small world, he was slashed across the stomach with a sword but kept on rucking and ran the wogs back down the Uxbridge Road. He ended up with fifty stitches. That's Oi The Nutter. That skin over there. He's Chelsea – barmy – off his fucking head.

Southall never happened the way they say, but nobody

listens to Ray when he tries to explain, so at first the Arsenal boys hold back, and if he stops with the fat geezer he'll be okay, it's a fair enough fight, no harm done, but he's lost the plot and kicks the man a few times, he only has four blokes backing him up, sees Nick legging it out of the pub door, that makes three, another Arsenal lad stepping in front of his knocked-out mate saying he's had enough, and Ray punches him in the face and starts on the rest of them, and he's gone too far, taking liberties now with skins who've played the white man, and they've had enough of this wanker and pile in, and he's on the back foot right away, boxed into a corner, ready to go down as Terry and an older crew arrive with Nick, quickly clearing the pub, one of his uncle's mates, a bloke he doesn't know from Adam, pulling him to his feet, and they leave sharpish, before the Old Bill arrive, and that night, when they're nearly home, after seeing Madness, Terry gives him a proper telling-off, once they're on their own, asking him what the fucking hell he's playing at, what the fuck does he think he's doing?

Ray glances around The General Elliott, remembers sitting outside this same pub when he was younger, Mum and Auntie April nattering away, him with his lemonade and crisps. He's changed since then. Wishes he was a kid again. They were outside by the canal, at one of the tables, and inside he could see his uncle playing pool. He goes in and stands nearby, watching Terry with his shoulder-length hair and worn-down denim jacket, Ray no more than eight or nine years old. This is the heyday of Noddy Holder and Slade, Sweet and Mud, Alvin Stardust and David Essex, Gary Glitter and Roxy Music. Terry might have been out of his suedehead phase and into the scruffy boot-boy look, but he still sticks Desmond Dekker on the jukebox, the blokes with him singing the chorus, and years later Ray's having fun with his uncle, the skinhead revival in full flow, punk opening the door again, and he's having a laugh at the older man's expense, remembering the length of that Seventies barnet, the width of those Seventies flares. There's no excuse. Terry nods and smiles, calls Ray a bloody punk rocker, but can't hide the truth, that punk has done him a favour, helped the old firm out.

His uncle has always treated him right. Ray still appreciates his strength, but sees another side now he's older, admires Terry's easygoing nature. He drinks his Fosters and realises how much his uncle looks like George English, someone who knew all about his mission but pleaded ignorance, kept his mouth shut, finally dumped in a POW camp where British prisoners nursed him, an American doctor saving his life. George never said a lot in peacetime either, a serious man who believed in the system, and the happiest Ray ever saw his grandad was when Terry gave him a pair of binoculars as a birthday present, a year or so before he died, and they were good quality as well, professional standard, George hugging his son and shocking everyone, this hard-working, hard-up, dignified man who was proud he sat at a desk half the day, someone who dressed as neat as possible, wore a shirt and tie, keen on the details. Ray wishes Grandad George had lived longer. He was too young when the old man died, never thought to ask questions, knows he has lost out on a chunk of his history.

Ray's going to stay for an hour then walk over to The White Horse. There's been some aggro with a bunch of South Ruislip soulboys and three carloads of skins are heading over to sort them out. Terry leans close as Ray's getting ready to leave, tells him to remember what he said, that getting in fights isn't clever, that it's a mug's game and he doesn't want to end up in trouble with the law, stuck in Borstal, breaking his mum's heart, worse than that, ending up hurt and damaged for the rest of his life. Ray smiles and tries to listen, and Terry asks him to stay, to hear what he's saying, and there's an edge to his voice, April placing a fresh pint in front of Ray, and he can't leave a full glass, he tells them about Fisher's funeral, mentions his grandad, Terry softer, mumbling something about George and a load of greasers, how when he was a kid this cocky little skinhead he used to be imagined his dad was scared of fighting back, and he's older and wiser, wants to pass on what he's learnt.

Terry looks so sad Ray wishes he could tell him how George was the bravest of the brave, but he's promised to keep quiet, and he wants to get off now, go and kick fuck out of those soulboys, pay them back for Fisher and the England-haters and Terry English and Grandad George, Terry leaning over and changing the subject, making him laugh, making it impossible to walk away.

The Famous CFC

THE PUB WAS PACKED ten minutes after it opened, Ray standing in the front bar, near the doors, in case Tottenham turned up, and he was pacing himself, a long day ahead, nursing a bottle of Carlsberg. Gary and Paul stood next to him, doing the same, The Young Offenders holding pint glasses, looking confused. The District Line down from Paddington was quiet, a squad of Chelsea on their way up through High Street Ken, a bloke from Harrow certain the Yids were drinking on the Edgware Road. A couple of Sands End herberts swore Tottenham would be in The Ship on Jews Row, over the other side of Wandsworth Bridge, but they'd tried that route before, would come in a different way. Tottenham were early risers, liked their bagels freshly baked, and Chelsea were in The Black Bull, Imperial, Jolly Malster, but with so many pubs around the ground, so much transport into the area, it was impossible to cover every angle. Rumours started with the first alarm clock sounding, and would last all day, mobiles the biggest stirrers around, and while Ray knew most of the stories were bollocks, football was all about expectation.

The Premiership was money-mad and had little to do with real football, the spectacle ruined by businessmen and New Fans, but a few fixtures still had some flavour. Tottenham and West Ham were the home games that mattered for Ray and the boys he knew, while Man United and Arsenal were interesting for sporting reasons. He was a fundamentalist and preferred watching Chelsea in the pub, with a drink in his hand, surrounded by good people. The big European nights and some Cup games drew him into Stamford Bridge, but the atmosphere was poor, too many loyal supporters forced out by the silly prices and endless regulations. The glory hunters, yuppies and tour groups made him sick, and he wasn't going to sit with a bunch of tossers, would only attend if he had a ticket for the Matthew Harding Stand. He had suggested some yuppie-bashing, but nobody was interested, and it pissed him off when they looked at him funny. It was fine fighting other mobs, clumping your own kind, but a no-no slapping the knobs who walked in your stands and took your seats and stole your fucking club. Mind you, his uncle hadn't turned up, was sick again, and Hawkins had passed on his season, so this was one game Ray would be attending. He tried calling Terry, but there was no answer. He would be gutted, missing one of the biggest games of the year.

Hawkins and his mates had come up in Bob The Builder's van, and were already milling around outside when Ray arrived, the doorman nodding new arrivals in, pointing out that it was nice to be nice. He was right as well, Ray knew that, but today was different. Plenty of faces had come out of the woodwork for a rivalry that went back to the 1967 FA Cup Final and Chelsea steaming the Park Lane End not long after. Terry and Hawkins had been there that day, and Hawkins never tired of telling the story, those listening forgetting that they were skinny schoolboys and not the heavy-weights of today. Nearly forty years after Chelsea went in the Park Lane, the journalists who wrote the sensationalist articles about the skinhead menace and demanded the return of flogging had vanished, but plenty of those young lads were still in the pubs around Chelsea, some with tickets, others turning out for a drink and the chance of a row. They were older, and after a couple of pints not much wiser, but out and about, drinking and laughing and dabbling in all sorts. For Ray and Terry English and Hawkins and thousands like them, being a skinhead was more than a youth fashion. It was a way of life. England belonged to the grown-up skins, mods, punks, herberts and hooligans of the Seventies and Eighties. They had cash in their pockets and had shaped the new generation.

Tottenham had been lively for a good few years now and some people rated them the top mob in London, the view at Chelsea being they only wanted to know when the odds were stacked in their favour, the older chaps regarding them as scum. Ray hated the Yids, like everyone else, their only real rivals in his mind Leicester and the Merseyside slashers. Tottenham had youth, and good numbers, but Ray put this down to their lack of success and tickets being easily had. Nothing else made sense. Why would anyone support Spurs? Whatever was said, the game was still the focus of the day out, and Chelsea had suffered most from the Premiership effect. Even so, plenty of youngsters had come through the ranks on the back of the Zola side and Chelsea were still the pride of London on and off the pitch.

Hawkins, Buster and Big Frank squeezed through the crush, Steve The Crisp crunching along behind them, spotting Hammerhead and comparing flavours. Ray nodded to blokes he had seen age over decades, and while the great days of the past would never be matched, it was the here and now that mattered. The majority of men in the pub were thirty-plus, with plenty in their forties and some in their fifties, a lot of them drinking from bottles, which he felt showed maturity, the knowledge that draught lager meant volume which meant a need to piss, which was a problem when you were looking for a punch-up. The Gianluca was flowing, big men with shaved skulls disappearing into the bogs, coming back out with creaking jaws and a thirst, but apart from the chang little had changed. Maybe things just slowly mutated, so you didn't notice, like the EU. It was hard thinking back and focusing on details. When he first started going to football there were only a handful of mobs around who could boast the sort of age group with him now, and they were from traditional dock areas such as West Ham, Millwall and the North-East, areas built on heavy industry, where the local mobs already existed in close-knit communities, long before the teenage rampage roared out of the suburbs. He remembered a day in Rotherham when the miners got the hump. It was men against boys. He didn't like thinking about that, had plenty of better memories to concentrate on. Now all the big firms had experience and muscle.

– All right, Ray? Tommy Johnson asked, passing back from the toilets, his mate Mark behind him.

– Not bad. Good turnout.

– The Yids are mobbed up at Euston, Old Bill all over them.

– That's what they reckon, Mark laughed.

They continued over to where Harris, Brighty and that psycho Facelift waited. Harris stared through the window, and while most people mellowed, calmed down, he just became meaner. The jolt in his features shifted Ray's glance to the street and a police van unloading uniforms. A cameraman was busy fiddling with buttons, ready to record the grown-up stars of the BBC news and those old VCR recordings, the true stars of CCTV, the daddies of the DVD age. Ray knew it was inevitable, that Fulham Old Bill would be all over them, but he still loved days like this, and despite his hatred of Tottenham he knew they would be on their way, that they would do their best to oblige. He smiled, thinking back to the glory days, home and away, before the clampdown, those trips out of London in the Eighties when Chelsea were taking five, six, seven thousand everywhere they went.

The famous Chelsea boys are running riot in '83, and despite their reputation the local coppers haven't twigged the thirty Londoners in the home enclosure, Ray watching as Harris filters down the terrace, the rest of the lads following, the crowd surging forward as Joey Jones comes over to pick the ball up for a throw-in, Mickey Thomas calling for it down the left wing, Johnny B waiting further back in midfield, and the puddings around Ray are screaming at Joey calling him a cockney bastard, never mind he's a Taff, typical thick Northerners, and Thomas controls the ball and knocks it to Speedie, Kerry ahead of him and on the run, the centre half cutting the pass out, hoofing it upfield to where Joe

McLaughlin steams in and heads it out to the right wing, Pat Nevin flicking the ball past a defender, a clogger who clatters into Pat and sends the wee man flying across the churned-up, muddy grass. The ref blows his whistle and Nevin gets up, rubbing his shin. Ray switches back to the terrace and the column that's stopped and is firming up in in the middle of the dodgy Pringles and wedges and too-tight strides, and it's not going to take these divs long to work things out, seeing as these Londoners look so different, bollocks to all that latter-day soulboy look, this mob is proper, half the Chelsea in green flight-jackets, a few with cropped hair, a couple of psychobillies, the rest herberts and scruffy street-fighters, and Harris has got his Lonsdale shirt on under his jacket, you can't get more blatant than that, but it's more like the genes that make Chelsea a cut above these mugs, the bone and skin and eyes, a touch of class, a Southern tribe in a Northern wilderness, and the pie-munching, spiv-tashed heads of the whippet-shaggers are turning to a ripple in the crowd in front of Harris, and it's the same as a stone dropping in a pond, the energy spreading its nervous-ness across a wet film of faces, rocky fists breaking the calm, turning ripples into waves, more eyes straining to see what's going on, and Ray is the youngest bloke with Harris and Billy Bright and the rest of them, but big enough and strong enough and nutty enough to have a go, against the odds, and suddenly it's gone mental and he's piling in with the rest of the boys and anyone in the way is getting whacked, that's how it is at football, if you're the right age and in the right place, but the wankers mouthing off don't want to know now, scrambling to get out of the way, Chelsea's repu-tation causing panic, they're the biggest hooligan club in the land, travel everywhere, home and away, and do it in style, in numbers as well, but Ray knows that if he gets knocked down then the shitters will be back and some of the first to kick lumps out of him, so he doesn't care who he smacks, you have to give it to them before they give it to you, it's as simple as that, and the bottle-merchants have given Chelsea the edge, the game Northerners battling to get through the cry-babies and do the cockney bastards, and Ray is bouncing and whizzing in his brain as Chelsea bundle down the terrace, pushed forward in the crush, by the swell of bodies coming from behind them, a wave running back from the shore, and the blokes above are punching and kicking the cockneys, Harris headbutting a massive pigeon-fancier with bird-shit tints in his hair, feathers stuck in his zip, and Chelsea are down by the wall now, at the front of the terrace, next to the pitch, squeezed by the weight of the crowd, punches connecting with Ray's head, and there's thousands of the gits trying to do them, and the coppers have run over and some are on the terrace, using their truncheons on both sides, creating a gap, more police above on the touchline, Chelsea being pushed and pulled onto the pitch as a surge from the home fans pushes through the Old Bill, another fist catching Ray in the mouth, his nose stinging, a copper belting him with his truncheon, forcing him to climb on the pitch where he moves his hand from his nose and swallows blood, fingers soaked, and Chelsea are all together and laughing at the goons going mad in the paddock, Ray looking into the sea of red faces shouting and pointing and trying to get at them, he can't believe they've fought through all that lot, fucking hell, and he feels the blood in the back of his throat and an eye closing up, but he's giving them the wanker sign and reckons he's ten foot tall, telling them they're all fucking mouth, all fucking mouth, you fucking cunts, a copper raising his stick, telling him to shut up, his eyes bulging and cheeks red, Harris leading them down the side of the pitch towards the away end, and the boys in the home seats are trying to jump down into the next enclosure, legging it along the front of their stand, and there's another Chelsea mob in the seats, separated by rows of police, and they're clambering down the aisle, but they're separated by two sets of railings, a horse trotting along the side of the pitch as the ref blows his whistle and the players move towards the other side, and there's a fence across the away end, and that's where most of the Chelsea are standing, and they're trying to pull it down, kicking at the stanchions, and Harris and Bright start running down the side of the pitch suddenly, before the horse reaches them, telling the others to come on, and they jump into another paddock that's half-empty but could let them into the home seats, if they can break through the gate, but they're forced straight back out by more Old Bill, and the coppers are doing their nut, there's nothing Harris and the boys can do, surrounded by Old Bill and knocked towards the away end, and Ray is walking with the big boys, feels fucking brilliant, swelled up with pride as they amble and strut and milk the limelight, that's the business, going in against the odds and smashing fuck out of those Northern wankers, and he's floating as they reach the entrance the stewards have opened, and the Chelsea on the away terrace are clapping them all the way, the roar of LOYAL SUPPORTERS, LOYAL SUPPORTERS filling his head, another roar making their heads snap towards the pitch, where the game has restarted, the ball launching towards the Chelsea goal, the Chelsea end, Colin Pates moving forward, timing his jump, watching it all the way.

John Terry rose above Robbie Keane and knocked the ball forward to Super Frank, and Lampard was moving quick and thinking fast, gliding over the smooth surface, threading it through to Robben, who was off and running, excitement racing out of the Matthew Harding Stand and along the sides of the ground, colliding in the new Shed End. Lol was on his feet with everyone else, and Robben just sort of went through the middle of people like it didn't matter if they were there or not, and while Zola was as skilful, he had a different style, was slower-moving, more of a craftsman, and he was still Lol's favourite player, but Robben and Joe Cole were special in this team, along with JT of course, and Lol had been going to Stamford Bridge since the glory days of the Nineties, raised on the best Chelsea team ever, managed by Luca Vialli, sitting in a corner in The White Hart or Jolly Maltster or Cock before kick-off with Dad, Uncle Ray, Dad's mates, fed on crisps and Coke and peanuts, a burger outside the ground if he was still hungry, that or a hot dog, and he had been raised on Zola and Dennis Wise and Super Dan Petrescu and Gus, and Vialli was the leader, he should have been manager for longer, and those players were brilliant, that's what Chelsea were all about, attacking football, Dad said Peter Osgood was the greatest-ever Chelsea player, and he'd been told about Alan Hudson and Charlie Cooke as well, Uncle Ray going on about Pat Nevin and the great Eddie Niedzwiecki, and someone called Doug Rougvie, but Robben was running at three defenders now and gliding past the first, then past Ledley King, near the Spurs penalty area, the last player didn't know what to do, whether to try and push him wide, jump in, bring him down, and everyone was shouting go on, fucking skin him, go on, skin the cunt, and Robben cut inside, shifted left, the defender on his arse, and the shot was low and hard and beat Paul Robinson but just missed the far post, the Upper Tier raising their hands towards their heads, faces towards the sky, finally clapping the effort and skill, and the magic of the beautiful game.

Lol stayed on his feet and sang 'Carefree' with the rest of the Matthew Harding, and Hawkins and Buster were on his right, Dad's seat still empty, Frank and the others on his left. Dad had flu, looked terrible in his dressing gown, had told him to pass his season on to Ray. Bob The Builder had given him a lift up, and while Hawkins took the ticket to the pub he walked down to the fanzine stall opposite the Tube, talked to some kids he knew, hung around and watched people arriving, stopping to buy programmes and badges and T-shirts at the other stalls, listening to the street traders, enjoying the build-up. He went in the ground early, sat in his seat reading *cfcuk*, the best Chelsea fanzine going. None of his mates could afford to go to Chelsea, or if they did it was a one-off, with their dads for a birthday or special game. Hawkins said he had passed Dad's ticket to Ray, but he still hadn't come in.

The game drifted, Chelsea passing the ball smoothly, Tottenham digging in. His attention wandered to his mobile, and he checked his messages, a text from Kev saying he was down the shops with his mum and was bored, that she was trying to decide on what toilet paper to buy. Lol laughed out loud. He saw his friend pushing a trolley, weighed down with plastic bags and waiting for a bus, felt sorry for Kev, without a dad, but at least his father was alive, and then Lol envied Kev, who still had a mum to go shopping with, and he pushed a key to escape. The screen hummed, shades of blue and red, cartoon characters moving in jerky steps, bleeping, and he turned his phone off, looked towards the floodlights which seemed brighter, and he liked it best when the darkness arrived, thought of the Zola days a few years back when everything looked so much bigger. Maybe that's what happened. Things shrank as you grew. His memories of his mother had shrunk as well, were merged in with her photos, and he couldn't remember her voice, just carried the feel of her inside, a smell and an impression.

Winter and football belonged together. It was different when the World Cup was on, the England players sweating and moving slowly, everyone turning into a football fan suddenly. He had been to Wycombe and Brentford a few times, liked the smaller grounds because you could stand up and move around, and it was cheaper and he could go with his mates. The best time going to Chelsea was when it got dark really early. That and the night games. He liked coming up with his dad in the car in the evening, just the two of them in the warm, and they laughed, playing music, part of the procession along the Chiswick Flyover, down Fulham Palace Road, a tunnel of lights and advertisements, pavements crowded with people. This was the time when they talked. Not really serious, but more serious than normal. Dad was always positive. Nothing bothered him. Sometimes they stopped in Earl's Court on the way back, a stand-up kebab house that sold good Indian food, and they stood at the counter and ate a curry and chapattis and samosas, sipped on Coke and Pepsi before continuing. If there wasn't a lot of traffic and they were really hungry they'd go to Harry's back home and sit down for a feast. The away games were Dad's time with his friends. Lol didn't mind, had plenty of other things to do. But he missed Dad not sitting next to him, Lol standing up with the rest of the Matthew Harding, his father would be red-faced like Hawkins and Frank and Buster and the rest of them, mist in their eyes, singing, THE SHED LOOKED UP AND SAW A GREAT STAR, SCORING GOALS PAST PAT JENNINGS FROM NEAR AND AFAR, AND CHELSEA WON, AS WE ALL KNEW THEY WOULD, AND THE STAR OF THAT GREAT TEAM WAS PETER OSGOOD, OSGOOD, OSGOOD, OSGOOD, OSGOOD, BORN IS THE KING OF STAMFORD BRIDGE.

Ray walks along the back of the terrace and spots his uncle standing with Hawkins and Johnny Crane. Terry looks at his nephew and shakes his head, touches the blood on his jacket, hands him a hanky and tells him to wipe his face. Hawkins is laughing and this annoys Ray for some reason, but he doesn't say anything. This is Gate 13 on the road, full of beer and burgers, old North Stand and Shed boy puffing on a fag, and Ray shrugs, says it's not his fault, will claim anything that comes into his head, awkward in front of family. He stands with Terry and the older men for the rest of the second half, sees Harris down near the fence, wonders whether to catch the train to London with him or take the coach back to Slough with his uncle. The coach is stopping in Northampton, and it's a good laugh down there, going round the pubs, leaving at closing time, but he knows there's the chance of a punch-up with Harris and Billy and the rest of that lot. He thinks back a few months to a row with some West Ham at King's Cross, the big bloke with the flat nose and scarred mouth who traded punches with him for a full minute outside a bookshop selling anarchist pamphlets, a dark side-street near the streetwalkers and drug dealers, the sound of sirens breaking things up, the police out in force as usual. The train means getting over to Paddington and catching a late service home, while the coach will drop him off near enough outside his house, a door-to-door service. You could get to any football ground in England from Slough. Thing is, he doesn't want Terry on his back all night, telling him to stay out of trouble. He doesn't need another bloody lecture.

The Shed surges forward and Terry's chest heaves as the Class of '69 shout abuse at Martin Chivers, the packed skinhead ranks giving the Spurs forward the sort of verbal he deserves, and the Chelsea boot boys breathe in deep, haul themselves back, shaved heads packing the terrace, thousands of teenagers squashed in under the old greyhound roof, and somehow they raise their hands in the air and clap three times after chanting CHELSEA, do this four times, straining to see Eddie McCreadie bring the ball out of defence, and Eddie plays it long down the left wing towards Peter Houseman, and he takes on Joe Kinnear on the outside, Nobby Houseman the boy from Battersea with the clever left foot, a fine crosser of the ball, a cultured footballer according to Terry's dad George, and Kinnear times his tackle and knocks the ball towards the West Stand, onto the running track, and the Harringtons and Crombies and denim jackets in The Shed are crushed tighter, police in the aisles pointing at boys, shouting at them to stop shoving, a big sergeant leaning in and shouting at a black kid, trying to reach the boy's head with his truncheon, and The Shed starts up, WHO'S THAT CUNT IN THE BIG BLUE HAT, DO-DA, DO-DA, WHO'S THAT CUNT IN THE BIG BLUE HAT, DO-DA, DO-DA-DAY, and everyone laughs and grins, The Shed is calm for a few seconds, waiting for the coppers to move in, a line of ten helmets ducking under the barrier and forcing their way into the crowd, heading towards a load of older boys in the middle, they like coming in and grabbing people, chucking them out, but can hardly move, pushing harder, and when they've got further in everyone raises their legs in time and tumbles forward, bouncing the coppers down the terrace and splitting them up as they sing, KNEES UP MOTHER BROWN, KNEES UP MOTHER BROWN, UNDER THE TABLE YOU MUST GO, E-I E-I E-I-O, AND IF I CATCH YOU BENDING, I'LL SAW YOUR LEGS RIGHT OFF, KNEES

UP KNEES UP, GOT TO GET A BREEZE UP, KNEES UP MOTHER BROWN, and the boys at the front of the section, above the walkway, are squeezed on the iron poles but somehow it never hurts too much, barriers strategically placed up above, breaking up the weight, and The Shed flows back again with, OH MY, WHAT A ROTTEN SONG, WHAT A ROTTEN SONG, WHAT A ROTTEN SONG, OH MY, WHAT A ROTTEN SONG, WHAT A ROTTEN SINGER TOO-OO, and the roar of CHELSEA, CHELSEA, CHELSEA sees the police trying to get back to the aisle, angry and tugging a couple of the nearest kids with them, one copper has lost his helmet and it's being lobbed around The Shed, and there's a surge towards the police and one of the skinheads gets free, and the police are wound up, can't do anything much, left with one poor sod who's done nothing, just some pushing and shoving like everyone else, and Terry wonders why they bother, there's plenty of worse things happen at football, and none of it compares to what goes on in life outside, just wait till after the game, then there'll be some trouble, and that kid is being led up the gangway and round the walkway at the back of The Shed, and he'll be kicked out and told to fuck off home for no good reason, a waste of entrance money, and The Shed pauses and looks for the ball, Charlie Cooke knocking it inside to John Hollins, who's moving towards the halfway line, and they can hear the Spurs fans singing their GLORY GLORY song, up the other end in the North Stand, and The Shed crashes forward again answering with, YOU'RE GOING TO GET YOUR FUCKING HEADS KICKED IN, YOU'RE GOING TO GET YOUR FUCKING HEADS KICKED IN, and Spurs are probably doing wanker signs, but they're a long way away and it's hard to see properly, and those North London skinheads will be ready for a bundle after, no doubt about that, and being in The Shed like this Terry is in his own blue-and-white heaven, feeling smart in his blue Harrington, DMs polished up, hair cut after school on Thursday, his scarf tied round his wrist, and thousands of Chelsea hooligans are clapping in perfect time and chanting

CHELSEA, and Ron Harris has the ball now, taking his time ... IF YOU'RE FEELING TIRED AND WEARY, AND YOU'VE GOT A JEW BOY'S NOSE, YOU'LL GET YOUR FUCKING HEAD KICKED IN, IF YOU WALK DOWN THE FULHAM ROAD, YOU WALK INTO THE RISING SUN, YOU'LL HEAR A MIGHTY NOISE, FUCK OFF YOU TOTTENHAM BASTARDS, WE ARE THE CHELSEA BOYS ... passing it neatly back to Peter Bonetti ... NOW BIG JIM IS A FAIRY, BUT HE'S GOT A HEART OF GOLD, HE HASN'T HAD A FORESKIN, SINCE HE WAS ONE DAY OLD, HE WALKS INTO THE PARK LANE END, AND ALL THE JEW BOYS WAIL, BIG JIM IS OUR LEADER, THE KING OF ISRAEL ... and The Cat picks the ball up and looks towards Ossie up front, coming into his own half searching for the ball ... AS I WALK THROUGH THE CITY, WHERE THE GIRLS ARE SO PRETTY, I FIRST SET MY EYES ON SWEET MOLLY MALONE, AS SHE WHEELS HER WHEELBARROW, THROUGH THE STREETS BROAD AND NARROW, SINGING ... and The Shed claps out the rhythm ... CHELSEA ... Peter Osgood has the ball in midfield, and is turning a couple of Spurs players, neatly laying the ball off. Terry loves Ossie. He represents everything that's flamboyant about Chelsea, a big skilful centre-forward who likes a drink and, better still, comes from Windsor, a couple of miles from Slough. Ossie is the King of Stamford Bridge. He has it all. He's one of the boys ... MY OLD MAN, SAID BE A CHELSEA FAN, AND DON'T DILLY DALLY ON THE WAY, WE TOOK THE TOTTENHAM IN HALF A MINUTE, WE TOOK THE NORTH BANK AND ALL THAT'S IN IT, WITH HATCHETS AND HAMMERS, CARVING KNIVES AND SPANNERS, WE SHOWED THOSE TOTTENHAM BASTARDS HOW TO FIGHT ... and Ossie might enjoy a pint, but he can play football like nobody else, and he's picking up speed, beating Alan Mullery, moving forward, towards the Tottenham goal.

★   ★   ★

187

Lol saw Ian Stills coming down the row, everyone standing to let him through, and Ian nodded at the younger boy, sat down in Dad's seat, said Ray had let him have the ticket, seeing as he was staying in the pub, drinking, with other plans. Ian was all right and Lol looked up to him a bit, seeing as he was a few years older, and he knew he was a good fighter, had a reputation for being fair about things. He wasn't a bully like some kids who were hard, and he'd helped Kev out once when he was having his mobile nicked again by Pakis, over at the skate park in Slough this time. Kev had been put in hospital six months before by rude boys who could have been the same Pakis even, but that was somewhere else, near Montem, and Ian had turned up with his mates and seen what was going on and they sorted out the Pakis. He was no wigger, either. Ian sat down excited, head moving side to side, buzzing now he was inside the ground, rolling his shoulders around, eyes bright and eager, and he had the rest of the day and his whole life ahead of him, waiting to be lived, face burning with his love for Chelsea FC, reaching in his pocket and texting his mates outside, telling them he was in safely and in the Upper Tier with a good mob of Chelsea.

Ray stood leaning against the bar, watching the game on a plasma screen. He was back on pints, fucked off with bottles. The jokes were rolling, rumours speeding up. It was halfway through the second half and Harris was sober and on his mobile, in touch with the Yids, and they would leave before the end, try and have it with Tottenham away from the ground, jump on the District Line and get out of Fulham. The police van was still parked outside, Old Bill sitting in the back, camera on standby.

The final whistle goes and The Shed tumbles down the main stairway leading out of the ground, turns right opposite The Rising Sun, spreading and filling the Fulham Road, an army of shaved heads and cherry-red Doctor Martens joined by more Shed boys coming out of the Bovril Gate, everyone slowing as they reach The Britannia, the road blocked as thousands of Chelsea boot boys wait for Spurs to come out of the North Stand, and there's the sound of police dogs barking their heads off, Terry can't see them, but knows they're up ahead, and Spurs will be coming along below the back of the West Stand, and there's police lined up across the exit, he can see their helmets above the heads of the crowd, and there's coppers coming over and shouting clear off home, go on, clear off, and Terry and Alan move round and stand next to the pub, behind older and bigger boys, and they can hear the muffled sound of Spurs singing, a horse lumbering towards the Chelsea mob, the rider shouting and leaning down and pointing at individuals, and the horse splits the crowd as it keeps going, and another two horses follow, but more and more Chelsea are coming down from The Shed pushing those at the front forward, and there's a crush as they pull back from the Alsatians, and Terry can see them through a gap, jaws chewing and flashing teeth, more like bears than fucking dogs, and the police are letting them into the mob, holding on tight, and everyone in the way moves sideways to avoid the horses, but the mob keeps growing, swollen and swelling up, the police raising their truncheons, the air tight as if the oxygen is being battered flat, and people are shouting, swearing, and it's like a crowd of onlookers around a road accident, boys pretending they're just having a glance at the scenery, a scared sort of excitement freezes Terry's brain, the noise of Spurs singing louder, and the coppers are nervous, realising nobody is moving on, one of the horses trotting faster, chasing some Chelsea into Britannia Road, Alsatians moving others towards the flats, and the skinheads pressed against the front of the pub don't budge, seven or eight of them in the doorway, the pub locked and dark, and the mob is like liquid, moves back as a horse rears up, front legs dancing in the air same as a boxer's fists, and its panic spreads into the crowd, Terry's heard stories about people kicked by horses, ending up brain-damaged or dead, those hooves are worse than a sledgehammer, and they crash on the street with the clatter of old iron, and everyone backs off, nobody wants to be crushed to death, have the arse bitten out of their Sta-Press, and some of the older lads in Union shirts and braces are telling everyone to stick together, Spurs will be out in a minute, we're going to do them, kick their fucking heads in, and Terry is worried, crushed in with a big mob of angry skinheads, threatened by horses and dogs and the police, and Spurs are going to be outside any second and there's going to be a massive bundle, but more than anything he's excited, he's with his mates and they're Chelsea, that's what it's about, being part of The Shed, and there's a gap in the street that's full of more police, people jumping up and down now, he's doing the same, can see helmets coming out from the North Stand, and they're followed by shaved heads and Spurs scarves, and the roar from the Chelsea mob makes his skin burn like he's hearing 'Liquidator' on the tannoy and everyone pushes forward, shouting and swearing, but they can't get past the horses, Terry sees the riders bringing their sticks down, the sound of the dogs under the shouting, the gap in the road smaller, but the two sides are being kept apart by the police, and they are belting Chelsea with their sticks, and the Spurs mob are pushing down towards Fulham Broadway and Chelsea outflank the coppers and Spurs are out of their escort and both sides are beyond the police further down the road and fighting each other now, and Terry and Alan can see the fists flying, constables catching up, stuck in the middle, cracking heads, and Terry thinks he's going to piss himself, and the horses move back between the two sides, everyone bouncing around trying to have another go, and then they're running towards the station, for a few seconds nobody knowing who's who, the fighting spilling across the road sideways and suddenly Terry and Alan are near the front with the Chelsea boys who are kicking at some Spurs skin-heads, one of them going down, and the boot goes in, Spurs forced back, the whack of cherry-red Doctor Martens in the Yiddo's back and face, Terry glimpsing the fear in his eyes as he covers his head with his hands and curls up, and Terry feels the reality of violence rising in a wave of sickness, a shocked nausea, glad when two coppers break it up, another policeman pulling the boy to his feet and helping him away.

Moonstomping

TERRY COULDN'T WORK OUT what was real, was struggling to sort out the confusion filling his head, knew he had to keep moving, the streets around him soaked in moonlight, and he was a happy boy in boots and braces, a kid in white trousers and blue jacket, moving like a gunslinger in a Western, mixing swagger and conscience, and all around him silver sparks danced, electricity skidding across millions of black slates, and he was heading towards an arcade, a place where a new breed of spirits spent their time surfing concrete, bouncing in and out of the gutter, the kids there sliding away when they saw him approach, a middle-aged man carrying a shotgun, showing off a false mask of confidence.

His son was with that gang of boys and he wanted to tell him to be careful, that the world was a dangerous place, tried to walk faster, hurrying through curved terraces tunnelling into a misty future, the windows holding his reflection too long, refusing to let him speed up, and looking into the glass he saw April walking next to him, tugging at his sleeve, pulling him back, and he felt the swagger drain away, replaced by sadness as his shoulders sagged, realising that he could only ever see her as a reflection, her words a whisper, touch so faint he would never be sure if it was true, and he saw her pressing into the glass, which stretched as if it was a plastic wrapping, her fingers trying to tear a way through, trying to reach out to him. He didn't want to leave her behind, but knew that if he didn't keep moving he would explode and drown in his own blood. The houses suddenly stopped and were replaced by rubble, a mass of burnt-out bomb damage. He continued alone.

Laurel and his friends had left a stream of impressions behind, a trail of faces and events that he passed through and immediately knew. This clean new world he'd seen advertised so often wasn't much different to the old one. It was full of parallels and versions, feelings chopped up and sampled, a show of love and respect. It was as clear as day. He must be on his way home. He was relieved.

He heard thunder. It was angry, made him jump in the air, and he found himself hovering like he was a spaceman, realised it wasn't thunder but a shotgun blast, a single barrel unloading in the distance. He was shocked to see himself down below, on his bed, in his house, wrapped in a blanket, teeth chattering, body covered with sweat, features blurring as a big buttery head melted into a stack of pillows. He could smell the sweat soaking his sheets, a sour smell of fear and failure. The side effects of his hospital appointment should have been over by now.

The second shotgun barrel burst and he dropped back into the street, heard the roar of a crowd in a football ground, moved on.

He walked through more terraces, more hidden souls, was soon facing a dead end. He couldn't see where his son could have gone. He turned and looked back, saw lock-ups and allotments on a hill high above the houses, a row of arcades and takeaways. Thousands of light bulbs flickered, but he saw no people. Even the glass was empty. The town was deserted. He smiled. It was no real surprise. It was obvious what had happened. He felt wise. Everyone had gone to the moon. His excitement caused tremors, bile rising from his belly, pushing into his throat, only easing when he tilted his head back and stared into the sky, at his ceiling, felt the warmth of the moon's rays on his face, the medicine in his system sinking back down into his gut.

An alleyway opened and he hurried towards it, found it cool and heavy with shadow, hands slapping him on the back, foreign words mingling with English, and he glimpsed the brilliant colours of the Union Jack covering a wall, smelt fresh paint, came into the open again, back into the moonlight, realised he was facing his childhood home. His younger sister was looking out of a window. She waved, jumping up and down, tapping on the glass. He couldn't see her face, realised it couldn't be her, as she was somewhere else. He wondered who the girl could be. She was small, young, blonde. He saw his mum and dad in the kitchen, talking quietly, hugging each other and laughing, reaching for plates of food, moving out of sight, off to sit down and eat. He smiled, felt so happy, wanted to go in and join them, talk freely, all the mysteries and secrets of the past obvious and unimportant now, but he knew he couldn't enter, not yet, wasn't sure what he should do, could only wait in the street, realised George would be out in a minute.

He was a child on a space odyssey, a youth in an amusement arcade, a father looking at his life and not wanting to die, a surge of determination forcing the nausea further down as the moon thickened, turning red and bending out of shape, pulsing in time with his heartbeat. He wished he had a pair of binoculars. Wished he could dive into one of those craters and see what was going on below the surface.

Terry English is going to the moon one day – in twenty or thirty years – when rocket travel is the same as catching a bus – it won't be long now – this is the Space Age – anything is possible – Neil Armstrong taking a massive moon-stomp for mankind – Buzz Aldrin dancing in heaven – and Terry is proud as punch – everyone is so proud – it doesn't matter if it's Americans or Russians up there – they are men – Dad shakes his head – leans in towards the telly – inspecting the fuzzy white rocks and silver ridges – Terry seeing moon spirits in the distortion – souls coming out of their craters to watch the aliens – and his old man leans back and smiles – ear to ear – this moon landing is breaking a barrier – things will never be the same again – there will be no mass destruction – no atom bombs dropped – no more wars – Dad hates war – tries to do the right thing – believes in rules – common decency – the evil riding around inside human beings – and while some of the changes taking place surprise him – and there are things that make him angry –

he's pleased that life is much easier – doesn't even mind hippies – their love and peace talk – their drugs and rock music – these are the good times – after the First World War – the Depression – the Second World War – the years of post-victory hardship – and he wants his son to realise how lucky he is – and George knows that reaching the moon is a miracle – only worried that the astronauts have a long journey home – he will be relieved when they land safely – that's the main thing – getting home after a mission – and he wishes he could talk to his son – tell him how he feels – but he can't find the words – doesn't know the words.

Terry's a boy running down the Fulham Road with hundreds of other boys and they're throwing punches and sticking the boot in, a youth in claret and blue hitting the road, Shed boys swarming over him, older West Ham punching their way into the mob and pulling the kid to his feet . . .

He's on the Underground and the coppers don't like The Shed's 'Knees-Up Mother Brown' rocking the carriage, thump the nearest skinheads with their truncheons, pull Terry off and bundle him over to the steps, give him a clip round the ear and a knee in the goolies. They laugh and he knows he is going to puke up . . .

He's walking the streets of Slough, ten youths enjoying the sun, out on the prowl, swaggering along, looking for trouble, the bigger lads up front spotting an Indian boy coming the other way. They cross the road. Terry is further back, talking to Alan, sees a friend from school, feels sick, has to make a decision quick, if he's one of the mob or the boy's mate, doesn't know if he can be both . . .

Terry was older, standing outside The Moon Over Water, a brassy Victorian boozer with carved windows and patches of stained glass, ornate letters trimmed with white light, silver threads running around blue panels, and he was holding a pair of binoculars to his eyes, feeling the rubber in his sockets, staring hard at the moon, following long creases that could be dry river-beds, canals maybe, bending past craters where meteors had crashed and burned. He focused on a

Lancaster silhouetted against the moon, stretched to see the gunner's face, saw a leather jacket and goggles, knew it was Dad coming back from a raid over Germany, long ago, before he was born, before he was even a twinkle. They were relying on the moon to reflect the sun and show them the way home. He heard men praying, silently, to themselves, and God.

Terry was nearly fifty, sitting in the Union Jack Club, the bar lined with nurses and the porter who pushed him in his wheelchair yesterday, the one they called Boxer. Female faces flickered in a wartime newsreel. He saw nurses with April in Emergency. His old man dying slowly in a hospital bed. The oxygen mask telling him he was back in the RAF. He mumbled about fire and ice, frost on the wings, burning men and torturers in leather coats. He was delirious. Terry watched the West Indian and Pakistani and Irish nurses helping these old English people, knocked out a big-mouth at football who kept moaning about immigrants.

Terry blinked and the Union Jack Club was lined with men his own age. They were the sons of heroes. The sons of their fathers. He saw grandsons as well. They didn't have the same realisations as the older men, but listened to what was said, seemed to be learning. He looked at the wall and saw a photo of a classic Chelsea team, Ron Harris smiling the best he could, a ball on his knee. Paddy Mulligan's sideburns made him laugh and he started humming 'Carefree', switched to the original words from 'Lord Of The Dance'.

The radio kept him up to date on the game he was missing – John Terry beat Martin Chivers in the air . . . Alan Hudson played the ball to Garry Stanley, who knocked it on for Micky Fillery to find Ruud Gullit . . . Joe Cole was chipping the ball forward for Ossie to bury in the back of the net. He thought of Joe, but saw Charlie Cooke. Players came and went, but the club lived on. Terry was at Old Trafford, standing on the Stretford End in 1970, Peter Bonetti hobbling on one leg, Chopper lifting the FA Cup into the air thanks to David Webb's winner. He was in Stockholm in 1998, shaking Ossie's hand in the street after Zola's goal, going over to Ron and doing the same. He was at Bolton in 2005, as Chelsea won the Premiership with two Frank Lampard goals, had grown up and seen his club win the league.

Terry felt happy, wanted to stay in the Union Jack Club for ever. Past, present and future merged there. Everything seemed straightforward. But no, life wasn't simple. He'd always wanted it to be, but it never was, however hard he tried, conning himself everything was fine when it wasn't. There were problems he'd dealt with, problems that he was facing, problems looming. His confusion returned, the same images playing again, and he tried to understand what he had done to deserve this, what he had done wrong, knew he would have to walk the streets again, try and find his way, work things out, see where he took the wrong turning. Thing was, he was tired and didn't know if he could be bothered. He sat up in his bed and reached for the bucket, found it just in time.

London Pride

THE TOTTENHAM WAS A decent pub, never mind the name, with high ceilings and ornate fittings, full of the brassy flavour that had made London such a warm city before gentrification arrived. Ray had already been up to King's Cross for some traditional entertainment, the robocops out in force, preventing a clash with Spurs. Some of the boys walked back down to Euston and ended up chasing a no-mark Northern firm into the back streets around Somers Town, the police busy along the Marylebone Road, epileptic lights blaring on one of the busiest hooligan highways in the capital. Sirens were the best soundtrack going, the hardest techno for the hardest faces, Ray and those with him worried about being boxed in as more Old Bill arrived, these mechanised peelers forcing them away from the station, two cameramen recording faces for their database, a roar sounding as more Chelsea arrived off the Tube. He hung about for a while, left when the others decided to double back to Victoria.

The rumours were still flying around . . . Tottenham's young golems sharing a shandy in The Duke Of York . . . the dwarves from Salford chewing prawn sarnies in The Shakespeare . . . the Inter-City Hobbits plotted up in The Raving Iron, over the river in Vauxhall. He couldn't help smiling as that last one had the ring of truth about it – those fucking hobbits would drink anywhere. There were plenty of possibles, mobiles mugging away, but he couldn't be bothered traipsing across London, doubted anything was going to occur. He was bored, wanted a drink and some music, soon marching down Tottenham Court Road, passing windows stacked with gadgets, an icy wind of debt riding the glass walls, forcing his hands deep into the pockets of his flight-jacket. He winced at the shoppers and tourists wrapped in plastic, pleased he wasn't one of these specky cunts holding hands with the girlfriend, nagged to death by the missus, relieved he still spent his Saturdays watching football – even if it was usually on a pub screen.

Paul and Joe were in The Tottenham waiting, drinks resting on a ledge, relaxed and sinking into the evening session. Ray ordered a pint off a Polish bird, one of the many beautiful women who'd come to England from Eastern Europe and livened the place up. She was fucking gorgeous, laughing as she poured his lager, and he could see her with her legs wrapped round his back, pants in his pocket as he welcomed her to the promised land. Poles, Russians, Latvians. He loved them all. They fitted in, appreciated England's liberal ways, unlike some countries he could mention. He thought of that documentary on the telly, CCTV following Albanian women robbing handbags outside on Oxford Street, five Algerian youths half-inching phones, just to show their thanks to the English for offering them a better life. His eyes narrowed. He'd love to catch one of the snidey little cunts in the act. He drank a third of his pint and felt good. Spurs were forgotten. It didn't mean much now. Not with a cold pint of lager in his right hand and the bellow of a busy Saturday night around him.

They had two pints in The Tottenham, then walked the short distance to Denmark Street, passing through rows of guitars and amps and songbooks full of lyrics and chords and the thoughts of Mick Jagger, Johnny Rotten, Kurt Cobain, Pete Doherty. The Twelve-Bar was at the far end, the home of London Callin', the best night in London, a mix of punk, rockabilly, Oi – anything the governor fancied.

Barnet ran London Callin' and was well known over at Chelsea, stood near the door beaming his Strummer-like smile. He had a long music pedigree, had helped maintain the football link after the arrival of the trendier independents and the student brigade. London Callin' pulled in a collection of herberts, punks, skins and assorted rock'n'rollers, with some properly dolled-up punk and rockabilly sorts supplying the eye-tremblers. After a brief chat, Ray followed Paul and Joe through to the bar, waited for his lager, continuing into the room where the bands performed, DJ Dong rounding off the first part of his set, moving from Wizzard's 'See My Baby Jive' straight into 'Zorch Men' by The Meteors.

Dong was famous for his fanzine activities, and feared for the size of his wanger, hardly shy about using it on any stray that crossed his path. The story doing the rounds was that he'd recently split some stunning Bolton beaver over the bonnet of Sam Allardyce's motor, but like the golem rumours, Ray was sceptical. It was grim up North, and shagging some tart in the Reebok car park would be a chilling business. Allardyce might have been labelled Big Sam, but Ray doubted he could compete with Dong, and the girls *were* drawn to the shaven-headed man from South London, seemed to trust him with their lives.

First on stage were Viva Las Vegas. Barnet fronted the band, the former Gundog drummer Tariq keeping the beat. Ray was a big fan of both Gundog and Argy Bargy, the two best Oi bands of more recent years. Viva Las Vegas played Elvis songs, but with a punk delivery. It was a perfect blend, and it was true what Joe always said, that Presley was a punk rocker. Ray could see the link between the different strands – traditional British music moving to America with the settlers, given a lift by the class freedoms of the New World, mutating into bluegrass and hillbilly, the new production techniques and dynamic approach of their descendants turning it into rockabilly and rock'n'roll and putting it on wax, the originators in Britain sucking it back across the pond, the Teds forming a cult around the music, England reinventing the sound, firing it back with the Stones and originating another tribe in the mods, the open-mindedness of the Anglo-Saxon tribe nibbling at the meat of boogie-woogie, rhythm and blues, reggae, and then rock and the boot-boy sound became punk, the chain mutating fast, back into 2-Tone, Oi sticking the boot in and cutting out the wankers who were synthesising punk, and the US picked up on Oi and cobbled it together with ska, sent it back again so a bloke his age could hear Rancid, Die Hunns, Social Distortion and all the rest of them and love the music. His daughters were living a version of his own experience, minus the aggro.

Ray thought all this as he stood in the crowd, marvelling at how good a drink and live music could make him feel, matching the sneers of Elvis and Rotten. They said time was a cycle, and that was an easy way of explaining things. The fundamentals of life were repeated, and he could see the way this knowledge was manipulated, speeded up and slowed down with some clever propaganda. He heard Harry Champion's vocals on 'Any Old Iron', so much like 'Anarchy In The UK', saw the blondie thread of Dietrich, West, Monroe, Madonna. Computer games replayed the heroism of soldiers, sailors, airmen. He looked at the heads around him, the range of ages, the mix of styles which he had to admit hadn't always been possible when he was younger. It was silly, skinheads and punks fighting each other, punks and mods fighting, mods and rockers fighting. There was always someone fighting. He counted himself one of the worst offenders.

They went back to the bar once Viva Las Vegas were finished, the sound of Cock Sparrer's 'Runnin' Riot' booming, Joe mumbling something about vinyl as he took the cider Ray handed him and disappeared towards Charlie Harper, Paul busy chatting up some rockabilly bird, winking as he took his Guinness and turned his back. Ray thought that was charming, raised his eyes to the battered televisions high up on the walls, screens passing on fuzzy images of the empty room next door, Dong on the edge of the picture laughing with a chubby girl. Menace would be on soon and the place was busy. Ray had nothing but respect for Menace, Cock Sparrer and even The Cockney Rejects, despite their ICF links. When it came to music, he'd always seen the bigger picture. It was impossible fighting a bloke who turned up to see the same band, just for the sake of it, and he had been like that all his life. Oi and punk were supposed to bring the proles together, not cause more divisions.

He took his money and moved out of the way so others could reach the bar, squeezed against a pillar where he leant back and drank his lager, scanning the faces.

– ''Cos I can't stand the peace and quiet, all I want is a running riot,' he sang, joining in the chorus with Colin and the boys.

He turned his head and saw a punk bird at the bar, ten-pound note in the air, waiting for some service, smiling back.

– Oi Oi, Ray called, grinning, having a laugh.

She kept a straight face.

– All right? he tried instead.

– I am fine, thank you. I prefer 'England Belongs To Me'.

It was another Cock Sparrer classic, and he loved the B-side, 'Argy Bargy', as well. She doubled her sex appeal with those words.

She was foreign, maybe Swiss or German. It was in the bones. The eyes. The way she stood and moved. Too many English people slouched, heads down, forced to bow by centuries of bullying by posh cunts – Romans, Normans and their yuppie descendants. Maybe she was Scandinavian. Ray noted the badge she was wearing, Bombshell Rocks, the clear skin and blue eyes, glad she wasn't a china doll done up in designer clothes. She had the rough edge he preferred. For her part, she was well impressed by the strength of the skinhead towering over her.

– Is this good? she asked, pointing at the Fosters, then switching her attention to Stella.

Ray indicated the Fosters.

– Stella's a Belgian beer, or French maybe. Same difference, anyway. Fosters is English. You're better off with that.

– I thought it was Australian.

– Again, no difference. English crooks living it up in the sun.

She laughed and he wanted to unbutton his flies and introduce her to Eric The Red, that old Norse god of love and hate. Good manners stopped him.

– Red Stripe is Jamaican, I think, but it's Commonwealth, an offshoot of the Anglo-Saxon elite – Britain, Australia,

New Zealand, America, Canada, Scandinavia. There's plenty of Viking genes floating around in there as well.

She nodded, didn't have a clue what Ray was on about. Neither did he. She had to be Scandinavian. His guess was a Finn or a Swede. It must be hard for her learning to live with the fucking Euro. He pointed at the tenner.

– Good British currency. This is an EU-free zone.

Paul had just moved back to the bar and turned away as he earwigged his friend's mention of the EU, put his hands over his ears. Ray was uncomfortable with the reaction, didn't want his mate to think he didn't have any chat-up lines.

– No. Norway is EU-free. Britain is not. Why did you British give up so easily? Why don't you fight back?

Ray was ashamed of his country's capitulation, but respected Norway's common sense. Along with the Swiss, Norway had refused to bow down to the fascist axis, and their economies hadn't collapsed as threatened. They were doing very nicely, in fact. He thought of Ted Heath and his anger returned.

The Norwegian was leaning forward and ordering, Ray studying her fine lines, the swell of her tits under a Warriors shirt, a short vinyl skirt and heels, but he couldn't concentrate on sex, the image of Ted Heath stuck in his brain. He had been reading a lot about Heath recently, the events leading up to Britain's entry into the Common Market, couldn't believe the Tories had handed over so much, couldn't believe how they had surrendered fishing rights like that. The Norwegians had a near miss, looking to enter at the same time but telling Germany and France and the rest of them to fuck off. Nobody had ever been held to account. Nobody with power was ever held to account.

The Norwegian paid for her lager and turned to face Ray, had a sip and looked up at the English skinhead.

– So, why did you let your government betray the people? she asked.

– I was a kid.

– It was a stupid thing to do. The English won the war

and are famous for their bravery, but their rulers act like cowards.

– I know. I can't work it out.

She was thirty or thereabouts, and seemed to be on her own.

– It is like a very bad film, she remarked, mouth open, lips shining.

She was right.

– A black comedy starring John Cleese and Mr Bean, he said.

– Mr Bean?

How did you explain a funny-looking geezer who never said anything, just mumbled and moved his eyebrows around. It wasn't funny. He didn't think so, anyway, but it would fit in with the betrayal of British fishing rights. Blackadder was a lot better.

– John Cleese will do.

She laughed and moved away from the bar. She was fucking beautiful, had a brain as well, an original opinion that was hard to find. People were starting to move and Ray told her they should as well, if she wanted to see the band, as they'd be on in a minute. She followed him and they stood at the back of the small room, over by the wall. It was dark and sweaty and cramped, the perfect place for live music. He preferred small clubs where it was all about the energy of the band. It was like being on a football terrace in a way, before they ruined things with seats. He wanted people like him to plug in and have their say, their words expressing ideas he felt himself. Music gave him a sense of belonging he didn't find anywhere else.

He glanced to his right and saw Dong looking back, his eyes narrowed. Ray was glad he was between the DJ and the Norwegian, who had a smile on her face, eyes fixed straight ahead. He felt her brush against him and knew he was in. There was no doubt about it, no doubt at all.

Club Ska Classics

THE CLOCK BY THE bed told Terry it was seven-fifteen. His neck was stiff, body caked in powder, the room musty with the sweat and worry of a sick man. He saw himself as a giant gecko, slow-moving and dazzled by sunlight, lifted by the idea of an iguana shedding its skin on the National Geographic Channel, getting itself ready for a new season. He pushed himself off the mattress, legs heavy as he went and opened a window, cold air freezing the muck on his face, shocking him awake, forcing his lungs to breathe deep on the oxygen, until he found a rhythm. He was out of his fever and looking at another sort of sky, burial mounds of low cloud highlighted by a shut-out moon. He saw a woman in the field, squinted and coughed, knew the mirage was a leftover from his dreams.

Bob and Molly stood by the shed, noses to the ground, sniffing dock leaves and clumps of grass. He shivered, but kept the window open, finally shutting it when he felt stronger, hurried to the bathroom for a shower and a shave. He might have missed seeing Chelsea play Tottenham, but he wasn't going to miss Symarip at Club Ska. No chance.

An hour later he was parked outside The Rayners. He had time, walked up to the Indian cafe on the corner, across from the Zarathustran temple, sat on a stool by the window and ate a spicy curry and chapattis, turned his mobile on and heard 'Blue Is The Colour', messages flowing in like Joe Cole on a run through the Fulham defence. He didn't have a chance to read them, saw Hawkins and Buster coming out of Rayners Lane Tube, tried to will Alan to look his way, the big lump turning and shouting back at Johnny Crane and some Chelsea lads from Greenford. Terry let them go, decided to finish his food in peace, kept eating while he looked at his messages – three from Hawkins taking the Michael, two from Ray asking if he was okay, one from his son saying he would be home late as he was going round Kev's house. There were a few others, sent this morning, blokes asking what pub he was drinking in.

Once he was done he headed for The Rayners, paid at the side door and walked into Club Ska, entered a collision of music and characters, shook hands and swapped hellos, Dennis Alcapone busy melting valves. This was where he belonged. Out and about, with good people, not stuck indoors like an invalid, worrying about things. The room was busy with skinheads and ska-lovers, people from the local area and further out, Chelsea mingling with plenty of QPR and West Ham, smaller groups from all over. There was always a good atmosphere at Club Ska. He loved the place. Everyone was welcome. And they'd put on some serious legends here over the last few years, with the likes of Prince Buster and Laurel Aitken gracing the stage. Symarip were right up there with the best of them. They were true skinhead legends.

He couldn't see Hawkins or Buster, so went straight to the bar, a big reggae collector he knew standing in front of him, Will turning and adding a pint of bitter to his round, handing it to Terry. Like Tel, he loved his vinyl, knew it pissed all over CDs and MP3s, but neither of them were in the league of Geno Blue and Duke Dale, the DJs who ran Club Ska. They were walking encyclopaedias when it came to musicians, studios, producers, labels, releases, versions.

– I heard Hawkins was over in Thailand, working as a pole dancer, Will said when they had stepped away from the counter.

Bernard Manning flashed across Terry's mind.

– He's back now, he said.

– Fat Harry bumped into him in Bangkok.

– Harry's living in Thailand now, is he?

– Last couple of years. Says he misses the cold.

They talked for a while, Alfonso joining them, and Terry gave it ten minutes, made his excuses and went and stood on the edge of the dance floor, where he could hear the music better, The Aggrovators moving into The Skatalites as he settled down and soaked up the power of some serious sound-system speakers, seven-inch vinyl raised to another level. It was a different class to what he could hear at home, and he loved to stand in the shadows and feel the records run across his skin, didn't want to be making conversation right now. Every cell in his body came alive and it was going to be a good night, his worries meaning he appreciated every second. There were some decent-looking women out, shuffling and singing, and he felt good himself, smart in a brown tonic suit, checked blue-and-white Ben Sherman, brown loafers. Skinheads scrubbed up well. It was in their blood to hate dirt and failure, reject weakness. It was right what he'd thought earlier. Skinheads were maintaining the standards set by their fathers, men who understood the importance of staying clean and looking your best, the need for an ordinary lad to try his hardest in life. Skinheads were an example of Britain at its finest.

He was happy, sensed April next to him, smelt her perfume and heard her whisper, felt her touch his fingers and squeeze his hand. They were kids at Burtons in Uxbridge, feeling the boards bounce as hundreds of youths danced across the sprung floor, a special venue for them and thousands of other kids from West London. Terry had asked April to marry him at Burtons, blurting it out like a pillock, then shouting to make himself heard another three times. She seemed to understand at last, wrapped her arms around his neck and hugged him tight, but later he started wondering if her tears really meant yes, had to make sure outside the chippie, down by The Regal, when they were on their own. When his mates found out they used to shout GONE FOR A BURTON every time they saw him, at least till after the wedding. Burtons was long gone, the shop and dance hall knocked down to make way for the precinct, but he remembered it like it was yesterday. And April was still there by his side, like she promised.

– You made it, then? Hawkins said, appearing from the back of the hall.

– Just about. It was a bad day.

– You sure you haven't got Aids or something?

– It's just a bug.

Hawkins didn't look convinced, though it could have been Terry's imagination, but that was as far as it went, his friend saying nothing more, talking about the game instead, who he'd bumped into, the turnout, and the Estuary general listened, knew this was right, that each man should be given room to deal with his problems and keep his secrets. He wondered if those twilight streets of spirits and gunslingers existed in everyone's head. It must be the drugs opening it up, and while he was interested in the pictures now, the hidden meanings, he didn't like the loss of control.

Maybe deep down Hawkins knew the truth, that Terry was a sick man. He brushed this thought away, went back to the music, the positive beat that lifted his mood and kept a smile on his face. He couldn't live without this music.

– We were stuck on the fucking District Line for half an hour after the game. Got as far as Acton Town and had to get off, wait there for another forty minutes. I was pissing myself.

– Leaves on the track.

– Driver fancied a tea break.

– Did you see Laurel?

– Yeah. He got a lift back with Bob The Builder.

– Ray? Did you give him my season?

– I gave it to him, but he never came in the ground. Passed it on to one of those Young Offenders. Ian the painter.

Terry nodded. It was up to Ray if he couldn't be bothered.

– You want another one? Hawkins asked, pointing at his pint.

– No, I've got the car. I'll make this last.

Hawkins left and Terry focused on the stage where the DJs were busy with their Vestax turntables, moving into 'Loch Ness Monster' by the great Laurel Aitken, trading under the name King Horror. Terry concentrated on Geno, knew what was coming next, saw the man's face contort as he went into a frenzy, mimicked the talk-over, screaming LOCH NESS MONSTER.

He smiled. It was a fine effort.

– Hello, Tel. Haven't seen you for a while. Good result today.

Dave was a massive geezer from Dagenham, his busted nose and scarred face the leftovers of too many street fights. These weren't the free-for-alls everyone loved, where one mob was quickly on their toes and injuries were mainly to pride, but more like twenty-a-side set-tos where neither side ran, just fought till they were broken up or too tired to go on. Dave was a decent bloke, clever with computers and programming, someone Terry had known for years through the ska scene.

– I missed it. Been a bit under the weather lately and spent the whole day laid up in bed.

– You wouldn't miss tonight, though, would you? he said, and grinned.

– Must be joking. If I couldn't walk I'd have come by ambulance, had them bring me in on a stretcher.

The West Ham man laughed, spinning round and eyeing a couple of women nearby.

– Couple of crackers, those two.

Terry could only see the back of them, but the one with black hair who was dancing by her handbag stood out. If he was younger he wouldn't say no, but he was still married, and anyway, why would a young bird be interested in an old geezer like him, someone pushing fifty? He hadn't been with a woman since April died, his natural modesty combining with years of mourning, the sad part of his life he kept buried. He remembered April naked sometimes, got a hard-on seeing the good times, but it wasn't right thinking about sex with a dead woman, someone whose ashes he'd scattered himself, in the river near the Brentford docks, across from the place she called Griffin Island.

– I'm going to the bar, Dave said. You want a drink?

Terry repeated his driving excuse, and while he liked a pint, he couldn't risk his licence, and anyway, he didn't want to get pissed, even if he could. Not after the day he'd had. 'Reggae Fever' played and he had a fever all right, was still charged up by the things he had seen and thought, didn't need a replay, specially not out in public. He looked at the lights behind the stage, small balls of electricity, artificial moons from his moonstomped streets.

– Hello, Terry, he heard April sing.

He looked at the skinhead girl facing him, felt a rush of excitement in his groin, her black hair cut just how he liked it, and it took him a second or so before he realised it was Angie from work, dressed up sharper than ever, extra badges pinned next to a familiar 69 button. She was one of the birds Dave had pointed out, the one he'd fancied. He looked over and Carol waved back.

– Hello, she echoed.

– You made it, then? he said, recovering fast.

– I wouldn't have missed Symarip.

She was stunning and he felt awkward, eyeing her like that, hoped she wouldn't pick up on his surprise, the attraction he'd felt. Angie leant in close, trying to make herself heard above the music, brushing his neck and arm, looking round as Geno took the microphone and introduced the band. Angie stood next to him cheering and shouting, the bar emptying as everyone piled in.

Terry watched from his place near the mixing desk. Angie leant over a couple of times to say how brilliant they were, squeezing his arm, then disappeared into the mass of bodies for the last few songs. There was a good exchange between the band and the crowd, who eventually spilled onto the stage, a real outpouring of respect from the skinhead ranks. Everything was shut out as he listened to Symarip. He was floating in the music, heat rising from the crowd, spotlights catching heads and bodies, lighting up the brass. 'Skinhead Moonstomp' was a true anthem and was lapped up. He clapped with the rest of them, tired as if he had been performing, Angie coming back out of the crowd, her face covered in sweat, Fred Perry wet and sticking. She was laughing and different to how he saw her at work, drink loosening her up, and it was obvious she loved the cult more than he'd realised. Gradually people began to leave, and he shook a few hands on his way out, offering the girls a lift back, seeing as they'd come by taxi and Tube.

He stood outside in the car park talking to Hawkins and Buster while Angie and Carol used the Ladies, his mates getting a ride with a couple of blokes from Bristol, Terry banging on the roof as they pulled away. There were a handful of classic scooters in the car park, and these started moving off, a few people left now, hanging about to talk. It was hard to believe, so many people gathering in one location, coming together and then fading away. Soon the place would be deserted. All that was left was the memory.

The girls were taking ages and he was cold, started walking towards the car, reckoned he would wait for them there. He heard his name called out, turned and found Carol swaying, drunk and slurring her words, Angie in a sheepskin, helping her cousin along. They eased Carol into the back seat, Angie shutting the door and climbing in the front.

– She'll be okay, Angie said. She's been on the vodka.
– Go on . . . Carol giggled.
– Had four pints of cider first.
– Go on. Give him a kiss.

Angie turned like lightning and leant into the back seat, hissed some words he couldn't hear. Poor Angie. She didn't need that, being embarrassed by her cousin, in front of her boss. He reached towards the music.

He drove up the hill and along the high street, stopping for lights and roadworks, working his way back towards the Western Avenue.

– That was the best night out I've had for years, Angie said, breaking the silence. They were brilliant. I can't believe I've seen Symarip.

Terry glanced sideways. She had a badge with a Union Jack next to the others, right by her 69 button, BRITISH MAID scrawled through the middle. She saw him looking.

– That's a new one, he said.

– I'm British made and a British maid, she laughed.

– Waiting for Mr Right to come along, Carol screamed.

Terry knew Carol had been through a lot, guessed she didn't get out much, and you couldn't blame someone for having too much to drink. He'd done it enough times. Made a habit of it, if he was honest.

– I told you, Angie warned. Yes, I'm waiting for Mr Right.

Once they were on the Western Avenue it was an easy drive home. The needle was nudging sixty as he rejoined the fresh tarmac, temperature perfect, hundreds of songs waiting for a tap of his finger. Angie leant down and turned the volume up, the car vibrating to the sound of 'Fatty Fatty' as he cut through a long sprawl of housing, the Clancy Eccles vocals making him smile. He held his speed at seventy, the Merc smooth luxury, and it was mental how life could change. He was the same boy who used to wander the streets in the cold, hanging around for buses and bunking rattlers, counting every penny. Trouble stood on every corner, back when there was no CCTV and no will to stamp it out. He saw the punch-ups and kickings, more than schoolboy bundles, the sort of violence that would be cracked down on today. Ray was right saying they'd grown up surrounded by anger left over from the war, but he couldn't remember noticing it at the time. He wasn't an aggro merchant or anything like that, but fitting in was important, and he must have done things that were wrong.

He thought about the Paki-bashing in his dream, couldn't remember what had happened. If there was a judgement day there would be no hiding – everyone would be held to account for their sins.

He wished he could talk to his mum and dad, as a grown man. He respected their silence now, the secrets they kept, the way his old man wanted him to do well. He was the same with Lol. His parents had struggled to make ends meet, believed in hard work and wanted to better themselves. They didn't envy others, couldn't handle scroungers. It was important to be respectable in those days. Now people thought

acting thick or selfish gave them credibility, seemed proud
to claim they were poor. It was hippie thinking. His father
would have topped himself rather than admit he was hard-
up. He realised they had never lost their pride. He was
pleased. They never whined, even when they were sick, or
in mourning, or dying. He saw his mum in her normal
chair, him with a takeaway, a carton of her favourite sweet-
and-sour in with the noodles and water chestnuts. She was
staring at the wall above the television. He turned it off.
Couldn't remember what she'd been watching. Dad was
already gone, his picture in line with her open eyes. He
cried like a fucking baby. If he was on his own maybe he
would cry now.

Terry switched lanes to overtake a slow-moving, swerving
Escort full of goths, moved out of the darkness at the same
time, wished he wasn't thinking about these sad things. It
was the treatment. He moved back into the middle lane,
turned his head when Angie lowered the volume again,
offering him a piece of her Kit Kat.

– Don't worry, it hasn't melted, she said. I won't get it
on the seats.

– I've had all sorts in here, when Lol's been with me.
Indian, Chinese, kebabs, chips. Usually we stop somewhere,
Earl's Court after football, but it's hard not to take a snack
along for afters.

– It looks spotless in here to me.

– I use that place on the Slough Road. Twelve pounds
and they clean it inside and out, give it back like it's brand
new.

– You should have told me about Club Ska before.

– I thought you were more interested in 2-Tone, the
newer bands around today.

– I like that stuff, but the originals are special. Why settle
for second best when you can have the original?

– That's true enough.

– I've always been like that. Music matures with age, don't
you think? It sounds better all the time. At least ska and blue
beat does.

– I think so, but everyone reckons the records they listen to first, when they're a teenager, are the best around. It's natural, I suppose.

– Maturity is attractive. I've always liked older men.

The clouds had blown away and moonlight flooded his steering wheel, lit up the dashboard. His hands were holograms, fingers silver screws, nuts replacing knuckles, thumbs fitted with washers, currents moving along brittle veins, copper wires floating in the mist of his lit-up skin. He was something out of *A Clockwork Orange*, a machine man, though the rape in the film had ruined it for him, along with some of the ultraviolence, specially when they battered the drunk Paddy down in the subway. He was certain that subway was in Slough as well, by the bus station, and that made if seem worse somehow, more real and everyday. Ray was clever, thought things through better than he ever did, had pointed out how films like that always had to have a nasty edge.

– What do you think of *A Clockwork Orange*? he asked.

– The film or the book?

Angie seemed thrown by the question.

– The film. I couldn't read the book. Couldn't understand the made-up language and couldn't be bothered flicking to the back all the time to see what the words meant.

– The film's okay. I can imagine you out with your droogs, when you were younger.

– They weren't skinheads. Boot boys in bowlers, smoothies gone mad maybe, but they were nothing like us.

– You're a droog with a couple of devotchkas in his car.

He reckoned Angie was a bit pissed as well. She kept looking at him funny. He hoped she wasn't going to throw up. He remembered ferrying drunks around when he was driving for a living. A sick passenger wasn't much fun.

– Who's first? he asked.

Carol giggled in the back. He didn't know why.

– Carol's nearest, Angie said quickly.

– I know the way.

Angie turned to look at Carol as she started to say something. It was the same with all families, good friends as well.

People got on each others' nerves after a while, specially if they were close, but it didn't mean anything.

He was soon waiting outside Carol's flat, Angie helping her indoors, taking her time coming out again. He wondered what she was doing, turned the engine off and sat in silence, ears buzzing from the band. The street lights burned softly. He was tired. Happy, but tired.

The car door opened and a flood of perfume rolled in, Angie's coat off and in her hand. He hadn't noticed how strong her scent was before, turned the ignition on and continued. He needed directions to Angie's, as he'd never been there before, but it didn't take too long. He was soon stopping outside a small block of flats, turned and saw her looking at him, eyes wider than usual. The buttons on her shirt had come undone and he tried not to look at the swell of her breasts under the material. There was something different about her, but he didn't know what. He remembered looking at her at Club Ska, before he realised it was Angie, and he felt awkward remembering the attraction. He blocked it out, didn't need his mind playing more tricks on him. He'd had enough of that for one day.

– Would you like to come in for a coffee? she asked.

Terry thought about it, but he was knackered, and if he drank coffee now his brain would probably shoot off into orbit, like earlier when he was stuck in bed all day. He had to get home and go to sleep.

– No, I won't. Thanks, though. This is where you live, then?

He looked at the block.

– I've got my own place. Why don't you come in for a cup of coffee? I can make some sandwiches if you're hungry. I'm starving. I'll play some records. You'll be impressed with what I've got. You don't want to fall asleep driving.

He was tempted, and he was hungry suddenly, but it wouldn't be right. She was only being polite. Probably praying that he said no. Wanting the fat bastard to piss off and leave her in peace.

– No, thanks. I have to get home. Make sure Lol's in.

215

Angie sighed and he didn't blame her, could see she was tired as well. She hesitated, fiddling with her handbag, touched his arm quickly.

– Thanks for the lift. I'll see you on Monday.

He watched her walk slowly away, waited to make sure she got in safely. She turned at the door and waved, stood still so he wondered if she'd lost her key or something. She was wiping at her eyes, a flake of loose mascara probably, finally turned and was gone. Terry saw a light come on, knew she was okay, put the car in gear and pulled away, the moon hard in the sky, lighting his hands as he drove in silence through the deserted, sleeping streets.

DOUBLE BARREL

Long Shots

THREE WEEKS AFTER THE Symarip show, Terry found out
that Roy was selling Bob and Molly. He was stunned as he
listened to Roy explaining how the field had been sold, the
new owner turning up and telling him he wanted the horses
shifted by the time he came back from a trip abroad, in
three weeks. If they weren't gone he said he'd have them
shot, and the man was in his thirties, lippy, a cocky git done
up in a designer suit and gangster shades. The land was part
of a house sale over near Gerrards Cross, and as it couldn't
be built on it didn't have much value, the bloke doing it
out of spite. Twenty years ago Roy would have knocked the
gorger out and strolled the horses to another plot, but there
was nowhere near, the good fields fenced in or used, waste-
land open and unsafe. Roy couldn't afford any trouble. He
was moving into a new flat after years on the waiting list,
and the housing association didn't need problem tenants. He
felt old and weak. There were places he knew in Burnham,
but he couldn't get there twice a day, needed somewhere
local. He'd bought the horses at Southall Market to sell on,
but had become attached. They got him out of bed in the
morning.

He'd put the word out and a family ten miles out was
interested in Molly, through a mate who was putting a new
roof on their garage, while another friend said he'd take Bob
as a favour. Pretty Molly would have her own paddock, a
toy for the children to ride, but the parents weren't interested in the bigger, older, rougher-looking Bob. His new
home would be smaller, and he'd be sharing it with a ton
of scrap. It was under the Heathrow flight path as well. His

life was going to be noisy and dirty, and Roy knew Molly would be unhappy as well. She was good-looking, but clever and thoughtful, didn't trade on her appearance. It was a terrible pity to split them up. He couldn't sleep thinking about it, knew they'd pine for each other, maybe die from broken hearts. His voice crackled as he stood on the edge of the field, talking to Terry, a fire spluttering in the rain.

– I'll keep asking around. Maybe something better will turn up. What else can I do?

The field was heavy with mist, the horses lost in the haze, Terry's shock turning to anger. The grass crunched under his feet as he stepped side to side.

– What's his name? he asked.

– Slater. Robert Slater.

Terry didn't recognise it, clicked into gear, would think about this later. He had something he had to deal with first, walked back to the house, turned at the door and saw Roy over by the shed, noticed how he seemed smaller, bent forward and frail, as if his lungs had been deflated. Even the strongest men faded, lost their health and their nerve, finally the will to live. Roy had spent his life travelling, stopping here every year when he was younger to pick apples and cherries and strawberries, had mates who could back him up in a pub fight, but this was a different story. He had the flat to think about, the safety of the horses, and was dealing with a man who maybe had connections. He could be a soppy bastard who didn't know the score, thought money could let him off anything, a grass who'd be on the phone to the law as soon as he saw five gypsies coming up his path. There was no way of knowing. Not yet, anyway.

Back indoors, Terry flicked through a box of 45s, the design of Gas, Horse, Banana labels lifting him. He selected 'Long Shot Kicked De Bucket' by The Pioneers, sat down and leant his head back, closed his eyes, listening to the story or a racehorse, saw the men who lived in the bookie's he occasionally used, knew his future was hanging in the balance the same as Bob and Molly, that the odds would be clearer in an hour.

He was riding a fast horse across open land, through a Utah landscape he had seen in so many Westerns. This was where decent men were rewarded with a happy ending, where good intentions made up for honest mistakes, the land open and free with plenty of space for everyone to come and set up a homestead, and while he knew the truth was different, that they never showed the scalping of the Indians, the skinning of the buffalos, this mythical world telling thousands of boys that they could be invincible. It was a promised land of clear skies and clean sunlight, where a single punch meant a man dozed with a smile on his face, one shot sending him into a relaxing sleep. There was no blood or guts. Horses were the symbols of this freedom. These were the dreams of boys his age. He felt the same way about space travel and astronauts.

His treatment was releasing things he had spent his whole life blocking out, and he didn't want this side effect, preferred life out on the range, where the deer and the antelope played, jolted awake when he heard his pulse skipping, realised it was the needle on his record player tapping against the label. He lifted the single off and checked his watch, saw he had to get a move on, left the house and drove to the hospital.

He sat in front of Doctor Jones. There was a pause.

– I'm afraid we're not getting the results we had hoped for.

Terry was stuck in an echo chamber. Kind words followed, but they were distorted, phrases broken apart and bouncing back on themselves. He was a mash of battered bones and creaky joints, weaker than the nuts and bolts that held his car together, his system poisoned. The noise flattened out, the doctor's sentences lost in the buzz of mechanical bees, and yet he could understand the sense of what he was being told, that they weren't giving up hope, even though they weren't certain what was wrong with him, could only make educated guesses, and act accordingly. It would be hard. The side effects were going to be more extreme. They were doing their best.

– Do you have any questions that you'd like to ask?

He pulled himself together, lifted and shook his head.

There was a chance he would live, but he knew he was going to die.

Terry stood up and thanked Doctor Jones, talked to the nurse outside, walked from the hospital and sat in his car. He stayed there for ten minutes. He didn't see his surroundings, heard no sound. He couldn't leave his son on his own. It wasn't fair. Fifteen years old and an orphan. What about his daughters? His unborn grandchildren? He thought of the horses in the field, the home he'd worked so hard to buy. He couldn't help smiling as he remembered how he found the deposit for their first place together, the flat over the joke shop. It all went back to a game of pool. April's Uncle Pat was responsible. Good old Pat.

The flat was a real little love nest, record player spinning, him and April laughing and dancing and talking. She used to buy him presents down in the shop. A fake chewing-gum packet that snapped his fingers like a mousetrap was the one that stuck in his mind. The flat gave them a start, and they moved from there to a terrace when the children began arriving, then took out a second mortgage, bought the cab firm, finally made a go of it, eventually moved to the semi. The money from the flat helped them, but really it went back to that game of pool, a knock-on effect from the first ball.

He heard a siren on the main road, started his engine and moved away, the ambulance racing along outside the hospital, turning towards A&E as he left the car park. He didn't know where he was going, took out his mobile and called Angie at the office to check everything was okay. She sounded worried, asked if he was sick again, and he said no, he just fancied a day off, had a thought, the tough little skinhead in his brain asking her if she could find the address of a Robert Slater. Terry had seen her do this before, on the computer, putting names and addresses together, from a postcode usually, and while he didn't have a clue how it worked, he knew she had the knack of tracking people down. He pulled into an overgrown bus stop and turned the engine off.

– He lives over near Gerrards Cross. Stoke Poges, maybe. Somewhere round there.

– Give me a minute, Angie replied.

Uncle Pat was a diamond, same as her old man John, but it was Pat who pushed the pool, started Terry playing competitively, in the clubs and pubs of West London, for a fiver or a tenner, which was good money for someone his age. It was Pat who took him up to Hanwell to play McNeill. This game had an edge, a local affair, but with no bad feeling attached. There was some serious money riding on the result, a private competition between Pat and McNeill's manager. Terry was a lot younger than McNeill, an intense man of thirty who ran on the Guinness lined up along the bar as he potted ball after ball. Terry had been to the Hanwell pool hall once before, with Pat and John, seen the bloke in action, wasn't bothered about the money but felt honoured he was sharing the table with a legend.

– I've got two R. Slaters here.

– Hold on, I'll find a pen.

He reached into the glove compartment, took out a pencil and scribbled the addresses down on his map book.

– Thanks.

– When will I see you? she asked.

– I'll be in tomorrow, he white-lied, knowing he would be at the hospital. He would call in sick first thing.

– Thanks again.

He studied his map and started towards the nearest Slater, turning round and continuing across the roundabout, doing a right and following the winding road, was soon among trees and hedges, moving into a small council estate, guessing this wasn't the right Slater. He pulled up outside a pebble-dashed semi, saw an elderly man mending a bike in his front garden. He didn't need to ask if his name was Robert, continued through Fulmer and across the motorway, in moneyed territory now. It was another world away from the likes of Slough and Uxbridge and the outer suburbs, yet only a short journey by car, and he turned left, followed wide roads through scattered houses, a mixture of newish and older detached homes, each with its own design. The streets were deserted, with no people or parked cars to be seen, the tarmac plush and new, reminding him of a luxury carpet.

He found the house he wanted and stopped outside. It was a monster, but obviously empty, the curtains drawn and no cars in the drive. Terry knew this already, wondered how he could get past the gate and entryphone to speak to Slater when he returned. It was clear he didn't need the sort of money Terry could offer for the field, but he usually found people were friendly enough if you approached them in the right way. He was sure he could persuade Slater to leave the horses be. He didn't imagine him as a *Lock Stock* villain, more like a wide-boy estate agent who'd done well and let success go to his head. He would tread gently, only worried that he would be in no fit state in a couple of weeks' time. If he was on the way out, so were Bob and Molly. Their futures were tied in together.

He sat for a while, taking in the avenues and clipped hedges, the gravel curves and stone of the driveways, the subtle security cameras. There were tall trees among the houses, their branches stretching out above the roofs, and he saw colour in Slater's garden, red berries and yellow buds, a statue of a Greek god just beyond the railings. He was in one of those Hollywood neighbourhoods he'd seen on the telly, a district where producers and directors lived, considered how hard he'd worked for his place, the small returns that mounted up the more hours you did, and yet it would fit into most of the garages here. He wasn't bothered, at the same time couldn't see how people ended up so rich. City bonuses were something he heard about but couldn't get his head around. He felt lonely just sitting here, couldn't see himself being happy hidden away from the world, guessed you probably got used to it after a while. He had done well, for his background, but this was another league, a merging of lump-sum scams and trust-fund investments, inherited wealth rubbing against tax dodgers, drug dealers, property shifters. It was another way of thinking.

Pat had come up to him in a pub, The Globe or Lord Nelson probably, though it could have been The Griffin or Beehive or Brewery Tap, and he could see the man standing there smiling, sitting down and broaching the idea of playing for cash. Terry laughed, but April told him off, said it was important to grab any chance that came along. She was right as well. His memories were jumbled up, but he'd played in Brentford, Ealing and Acton mainly, Houslow once or twice, Greenford against a Chinaman with one eye, and they went up to North London another time, to Kentish Town, and there was a punch-up there, he laughed, had forgotten about that, though it didn't involve them personally. He was young and Pat looked after him, didn't keep him hanging around after he'd finished, not till he was a bit older. He played in Hayes a lot as well. Richmond once with some drummer from Eel Pie Island. He was about seventeen or eighteen by then.

The McNeill match was clear, though, and he saw them pulling up in Pat's motor, with John and another bloke, a bruiser in a sheepskin, walking into the social club, a young lad with his skinhead style lost in the scruff of the boot-boy era, pool cue in his bag, and he was surprised so many people were milling around, the colours of the fruit machines the same as flash bulbs, Pat and John shaking hands with McNeill and his mate, who managed him, a chubby geezer in a snazzy Crombie. To his credit, McNeill didn't look down at him for being so young, came over and had a chat, said he'd heard Terry was a decent player, didn't give him any grief or seem bothered about his age. Looking back, it must have been hard for McNeill, being beaten by a kid. And he was beaten all right. It was tight at first, but Terry's brain clicked in and playing against quality meant he raised his standard, edged in front and stayed there with a game to spare. McNeill came over and shook his hand, told him well done and good luck, that he was a *great* player, then returned to the bar. There were no bad feelings and they stayed for a few hours drinking. Terry wondered how much Pat and John made, but it didn't matter, they were fair men, true to their word and giving him a hundred quid. He passed twenty to his mum and opened a building society account with the rest. A hundred pounds was a lot of money in those days.

Really, it was peanuts compared to the money the people round here were used to, even back in the early Seventies. For Terry, though, it was his lucky break. He guessed these kids selling drugs felt the same. It was easy money. He did okay over the next six months or so, playing smaller games, and then it sort of fizzled out. He was pleased in a way, preferred playing for fun. He knew the value of saving from his old man and he put the win to good use. The McNeill money was definitely their start in life.

He wondered what had happened to McNeill. He would be in his early seventies now, maybe in the same club, or drinking in one of the pubs around the Broadway. Pat was still living in Brentford and so was Mary, April's mum, though John passed away shortly after his daughter. He hadn't seen them for a good six months, felt bad suddenly. He had let that part of his life drift, though his daughters went and saw their gran regular. There was no excuse, except recently it had made him sad. He didn't know why now.

Terry started the engine and went back to Slough, parked around the corner from the Union Jack, walked to the nearest chip shop and ordered off the Polish kid behind the counter, watched as he reached for the cod, asked him to make sure it was a big piece, reminding him he wanted a large portion of chips when he started shovelling them onto the paper, finally adding a tub of curry sauce to the order. Terry slipped along the alley and went in the club, turned the lights on. It was looking better all the time and felt like home, lived in and used but fresh as well, scrubbed and painted, private but with more light, the laughter of the Estuary boys beginning to merge with the laughter of the past.

He went over and poured himself a pint of lager, fancied something cold and fizzy, glad Ray wasn't around to take the piss. He had plans, but they were on hold till he knew what was going on with his health, and the worst thing was he had no control over what would happen, and yet in here he felt revived, as if the only result would be another twenty or thirty or forty years of life.

Terry sat down at his usual table and opened the fish and chips, wet heat rising into his eyes, and he thought of the jukebox, went and made his selections, starting with Dandy Livingstone and the lovely Hortense Ellis, ate his chips with his fingers, couldn't be bothered finding a fork. He was all alone in his own little corner of heaven. He laughed at the thought. Finished and screwed up the paper. Leant forward onto the table and rested his forehead on his folded arms. He dreamt that an old Pole in a Crombie came and sat next to him. They drank coffee and toasted the beauty of life, smoked fat cigars, eventually strolled over to one of the pool tables and played for ten hours straight, the score evening up as they went along, so in the end there was no winner and, more important, no loser.

Court in Session

HE KEPT QUIET, DIDN'T moan or look for sympathy, needed to get well and continue with his life, keep an eye on his daughters, look after his son, and there was nobody at home to help, Laurel didn't know what was going on, didn't have a clue, he was busy with his guitar, lost in PlayStation world, mobile texts, MSN, propped in front of *Scuzz* and *Kerrang*. This suited Terry. He didn't want his boy worrying. It was a father's job to appear strong, to keep his fears to himself, shut out the past and make sure the future was bright, it was all part of being a role model, and still nobody outside of the hospital knew he was sick, the nurse Ruby and the porter Boxer helping him into a wheelchair, pushing him through swing doors and along a short corridor to a quiet corner of a dozing room, a ward for day patients, and he stood up on his own, ever so slowly, wobbling a bit, eased himself onto a bed where he could close his eyes and ride out the fever, recover enough to drive home on his own, and he curled up tight, pulled the sheets around his body, felt the crisp material on his bare arms, for a split second imagined the flag from the club, hoped the big buttery head welded to his shoulders wasn't going to melt and spoil things, it would be a shame if he stained the pillow cases, it would mean more work for the laundry, and he could hear the whirring of machines in the distance, washing and rinsing and destroying germs and pollution and clouds of poison.

Hooks rattled as a curtain was drawn around him, and he opened his eyes, was in his own box room, the walls patterned cloth, hanging from silver tracks, a chipped white ceiling above, nothing complicated, the ache in his body hardening, and he could feel milk swilling in his belly, custard and cream mixed in with orange or lemon juice, rotten grapefruit and pineapple, but he was talking rubbish, hadn't drunk anything except water for ages, like the doctor told him, but he felt seasick, he was leaning over the side of a ferry, the edge of a rowing boat, there were faces in a flushing toilet full of purple bleach, snakebite-sick at a party, and he was seeing his son and daughters and his sisters and his nephew as a youth and himself as a boy and he was thinking about two horses grazing in a field, how they were going to be split up like April and him, and that stirred up his anger again, no, it wasn't right, a ghost stepping through a cut in time and ripping the horses, it was a case for the Witchfinder General, or Judge Jeffreys, tough on crime and tough on the causes of crime, because it was an evil spirit that killed April, made her car skid, burst a tyre, there was nobody he could see to blame, and he shivered and his teeth chattered, the devices planted in his mind leaking hundreds of nagging doubts and bitter stories, and it was rising like the sickness it was, telling him he was nothing much, nothing decent, in fact, he was nothing at all. Didn't he know that?

The machine had done its work, tried its best, but it had also weakened his defences, he knew the doctors were honest men, they had to be cruel to be kind, it was the same when he was drilling with the TA, there were always side effects, but with this the leftovers could be physical, could be mental, both ways he was left wide open, on the ground and on his own, it was worse than last time, there were no streets to wander through, no moon or lights to guide him home, he was all alone, stunned and too tired to fight back, was being kicked along a pavement into his own private horrorshow, a series of subway beatings and public-house glassings, pool cues used as maiming weapons, a world where droogs raped devotchkas, the world of *Skinheads & Swastikas*, his eyes held open forcing him to viddy the horror, like Alex, and he saw April broken and dead, saw his old man frail and rambling, Mum wide-eyed and silent, memories he had turned into secrets, which he kept from himself, there was no room for a pint, some stodge to warm his soul, no music or laughter or innocent mistakes, only the accusations stuck inside, in his subconscious, and they were strong, constant, built up over decades of abuse, conditioning clicking into place, so the court said the cocky skinhead in his brain wasn't some cheeky little geezer talking Dodger-speak, no, Judge Jeffreys was presiding and knew Terry English was a vicious thug who hurt defenceless pensioners and immigrants, a racist bully with a swastika tattooed on his forehead, a lowlife who stole from his mum's purse and pushed his father down the stairs, called a war hero a coward, raped girls in back alleys and boys in his borstal shower block, yes, he was the face in *American History X* and *Romper Stomper* and *Skinhead*, he was the thick fat man in hundreds of dramas and sitcoms and documentaries and cheap undercover TV movies.

Terry was sitting at the pictures with his mum, and up there on the silver screen he saw his old man high above France, lit up by a full moon, so he could have been starring in *The Dambusters*, the moon lighting the dams down below, but he knew somehow his dad's story would never be told, there was something his son had missed, and it was all very different now, an age of plenty, good times and lazy times, and he was in the Estuary office with the woman who worked the phones, he had a huge plastic knob, like Alex in *A Clockwork Orange*, and Angie was lifting her skirt and bending forward, wiggling her bum in the air, Judge Dread was singing along to Beethoven's Big 9th on the radio, she was ready and willing as the skinhead general stepped forward, but he turned away, made himself see April, didn't know how he could think of pushing her away, into the past, blocking her out when he knew she was watching from the other side, through a thin layer of film, his mum and dad behind her, holding hands, free from war and killing and debt, they were standing near the bed now, he could see three shadows, tried to sit up but didn't have the strength, closed his eyes, and they had old coppers in their palms, ready to place over his sockets, and he leant towards the bucket the nurse had left him, just in case, the sick spilling out of his raw throat, a rusty pipe chugging and vibrating along his system, and when he fell back on the pillow again he smelt the vomit of a boy throwing up on a dance floor, the laughter of his pals, good-natured stuff, that's what he thought, at the time, that's what he used to think, anyway.

He sank into the mattress, slime covering his mouth, wished he could stop the hurt banging inside his muscles, the ache in his heart, and it was like that feeling he had when he watched too much telly, it was the same but a hundred times stronger, and he saw him and his mate Joe Hawkins on the television screen, in Slough with *The Office* credits running, Ricky Gervais slapped in the air by some of the boys, for laughing at their town in interviews, and Harry was on the ground and they were crowding round and laughing as they kicked him, the boy crying, curled up, and Terry prayed it wasn't like that, but he was a skinhead, Judge Jeffreys shouted, and skinheads were bullies, rapists, Nazis, and Terry hoped his memory was true and that he was right and the outsiders were wrong, that he told the other lads Harry was his friend so they left him alone, and he had to remember what happened, if he did the right thing, but there were other times, other accusations crowding in, and he didn't want all this, couldn't shut down, his mind racing so he couldn't stop the torture, all he wanted to do was lose coins in an amusement arcade with April Showers, he wanted them to be young again with all their lives to look forward to, sitting by the river in Brentford, standing on a dance floor in Uxbridge, working and laughing together in Slough, moving between the two towns, holding hands as their children were born, the normal lives of normal people, but he could see this bent figure scattering ashes in the Thames, from the bank where they used to sit, and he was alone and standing on the edge of another dance floor, wanted to be with her, his brain burning, he was in the water, spinning in a circle, pulled down, good memories drowning, he couldn't remember the past, not really, nobody could, that's what the professionals were for, to tell people about their own lives, explain what had happened and where they fitted into society, and he was a white man and a skin-head and had done terrible things, that was obvious, he was conning himself with ideas of honesty and decency, had to accept the professionals were right, that he was no more than an extra in *Skinheads & Swastikas*, and he nodded sadly, saw there was no point arguing, that he had to accept he was a liar, accept there was no real future, that he deserved his punishment, and for the first time since the months after he lost April he wished he was dead.

Liquidator AKA

RAY'S HEAD VIBRATED TO the sound of 'Liquidator', the Harry Johnson classic echoing under the roof of the Matthew Harding Stand, that Winston Wright organ doing his nut in as it rocked The Shed, generations of Chelsea boys clapping in time, and he was rolling over and opening his eyes, didn't feel too bad, which was a result, seeing how much he'd drunk last night. He had been dreaming of that Norwegian bird he'd met a few weeks back, forgetting how she'd disappeared when he went for a piss, and he didn't have a clue why, had ended up drinking late and went for a chow mein in Chinatown, taking a minicab home, sitting in the front with a driver from the Sudan, Paul and Joe asleep in the back, hearing about a dead wife and a missing daughter, the man struggling to stay sane, his surviving son a reason not to kill himself. Ray's world was work, drink, football. He was naive, didn't have a clue about real suffering. Last night had been less complicated. Strictly lager.

Yesterday had been his best days for months. When everything went smoothly, minicabbing was one of the best jobs going. Life was sweet. His fares were decent human beings, people who fancied a chat and had something interesting to say and, even better, were looking to travel a distance. He was out on the open road, the pick of the bunch a run down to Wokingham, the traffic moving and light. It was a good earner, with a generous ten-pound tip added, thanks to a toy salesman called Baz. The bloke was a crank, but in the best possible way, a nutty professor with a photographic memory and a deep love of tin soldiers. He was carrying samples, hanging over the front seat and showing off infantry and cavalry, pointing out the fine detail and paintwork options. He was anti-war and had been on marches against the violence in Iraq and Afghanistan, but didn't think toy soldiers did any harm. It was a release for children and no different to the games they played on their computers.

Baz was following on from a girl training to be a nun. Ray had picked her up from a house in George Green, took her over to Ascot. He enjoyed listening as she spoke about God and Jesus and Saint John the Baptist, how she was going to help others, travel to Africa or South America. She could talk as well, but he hadn't wanted the journey to end. She knew her stuff, went on about whales and the planet, stuff he agreed with but never thought of in a religious sense. She was a frail little thing and needed protecting, guessed the Church would take care of her, and he couldn't decide whether being a nun was a good or a bad thing, but respected her dignity and determination.

He had the weekend off but hadn't seen Liz and the girls last night, celebrating his good mood and healthy takings with an early drink in the Union Jack with his uncle, Hawkins, Buster and Big Frank, continuing with Paul, Handsome and some other lads, a session that went the distance, polished off with a kebab and chips. His head started to hurt, thinking about the lager and meat, the onions and wax peppers, the grease on his chips. He couldn't remember coming in.

'Liquidator' kept playing, on and on, across the decades, growing louder and stronger, getting on his nerves.

Liz was calling his mobile. The last thing he needed was an ear-bashing. He answered anyway.

– You better get round here, she shouted.

– What's the matter?

– Just get round here and talk to Chelsea. She had two fucking ecstasy pills in her purse.

Ray was out of bed and dressed inside two minutes. He brushed his teeth and had a piss, grabbed a carton of milk from the fridge and drank it as he hurried out of the flat. He climbed in his car and started the engine, music blaring as Gundog delivered 'In The Eyes Of A Jury'. He turned it off. His daughters didn't take drugs. There was some mistake. He thought about this for a moment. Someone must have sold them to Chelsea. Drug dealers were pond life, and should be taken out and shot. Specially the ones selling ecstasy to girls of eleven. Specially the scum selling it to his fucking daughter. Ray tried first gear and the cunt wouldn't connect. He banged the stick, smashed his fist into the dashboard and cracked the glass over his speedometer, chose second, heard the engine gasp as he pulled away, slowly picking up speed. Once he was moving he crashed a red light and raced down the main road towards his house. It was early and there was no traffic. The sun was a hard ball of aggravation and he finished the milk, tossed the empty in the back seat. His thinking was drawing in, tightening up, anger focused. Ray knew what had to be done.

He was soon pulling up outside the house, walking up the path and passing through an open door, Liz flat against the wall. He went in the living room. Chelsea was sitting on the couch eating a boiled egg, the plate balanced on her knees, and she looked at him sheepish as she dipped toast in the yoke. She obviously didn't know what she was doing, and yet, with all the shit they put on the telly about poofs and drugs and everything else, you'd think the kid would have an inkling. His daughter didn't fear him, and she had no need to either, as he had never raised his voice or hand to either of his children. Liz dealt with the discipline. He sat down and his wife went off to make him a cup of coffee. The TV was playing, but nobody was watching the grey bureaucrat lecturing the world, and he could hear more bullshit in the distance, more fucking lies, more fucking corruption. He was tempted to stick a DM through the screen, but stayed in control, didn't want Chelsea to think he was angry with her. He found the remote and turned it off.

– So, he said at last, what's this about some pills?

– They're E and they make you feel happy. I didn't know it was wrong.

Ray chewed his lip.

– Where did you get them, darling?

– Why do you want to know?

Ray wanted to know because as soon as he found out who was selling drugs to his eleven-year-old daughter he was going to hunt the cunt down and fucking kill him. His fists swelled and he could feel the pressure in his head, plates shifting ready for an eruption. His brain was boiling up, but somehow he stayed calm, the goal of finding the scum responsible doing the trick.

– I just want to have a word with whoever sold them to you. You see, those pills are very dangerous.

– Are you going to tell them off?

Ray smiled. He wasn't sure. He might just move straight to the corporal punishment. He saw himself being caned when he was at school, the head delivering a load of verbal, always bringing his haircut into the lecture, telling him he was a nasty little skinhead, and that skinheads were thugs and guttersnipes. The man knew nothing. There were some decent teachers, but the head wasn't one of them. Ray just laughed in his face. It was the cane that hurt, not the words. Mind you, he could understand the temptation to explain things first, but would these drug dealers hang around to listen? He wasn't sure. He would have to play it by ear.

– Those pills can kill you, he explained. They make your head go all funny and you think things are real when they're not, and if you're drugged bad people can hurt you and you can't fight back. They can do evil things to you. It could be rat poison or some other bad stuff in those pills.

Chelsea pulled a face.

– What, like bogeys?

– I suppose so.

– I thought they made you feel happy.

– You're happy already, aren't you?

Chelsea nodded, but didn't look sure, and he guessed she was happy, but he should really be living here in his own home, keeping an eye on his girls, and yet he was only down the road, and him and Liz weren't arguing or anything.

– So where did you get them?

– Promise you won't be angry?

– I'm not angry at you. Honest. There's bogeys in them, don't forget. Big, thick, green, crusty bogies.

Chelsea looked angry.

– There's these boys that sell them in the car park, down near my school. You know, next to the supermarket.

Ray knew the place.

– What are their names?

– The one who sells the pills is called Ali. He's older, and there's two others who are always with him. You'd better tell them the Es have got rat poison in them so they don't hurt anyone, and tell them off about the bogeys as well.

– I will, don't you worry. What do they look like?

– Don't know. I can't remember.

– Have they got a car?

– I don't know what sort it is.

He frowned, thinking.

– Can you remember the colour?

– It's blue. Ali's got his own number plate, but I never spoke to him.

They shouldn't be too hard to find. Three ethnics in a blue car with a personalised number plate. This was going to be easy, and Saturday morning was as good a time as any to track the vermin down.

Ray didn't use weapons, but had carried a sawn-off pool cue for a while in the cab, started leaving it at home when Terry warned his drivers about being stopped by the police and caught tooled-up. The Old Bill would nick them and it wouldn't look good on Estuary Cars. Ray believed in the old standards. Fist and boot was the only way. As a young man he had hated those soulboys, Scousers and blacks who carried knives, and while every cult had their scum element, he sincerely believed that real skinheads fought like men. But he might need the cue, seeing as these were different times, so he went into the cupboard by the stairs and dug it out.

He was soon plotted up in the car park, settled down

with a perfect view of the entrance. It was a big place, but he was in a good position, resisted the temptation to listen to some classic street punk. He wanted to stay in control, knew the music would only stir him up. Skinhead music was fighting music. He had to bide his time and felt like an undercover copper, waiting for the crooks to arrive, the only differences being he was on his tod and didn't have a gun. He liked that geezer out of *The Shield*. The bonehead who bent the rules. Vic Mackey, that was his name, and while he didn't agree with Vic and The Strike Team when it came to nicking drugs off the dealers and selling them on, he couldn't help admiring their approach when dealing with lowlife. That other bloke was a bit of a plum, the one always fucking up their plans, the Spanish geezer, but Vic was sweet. Ray smiled, thinking of the LA skinhead steaming into the Mexican and black and Russian gangs, something the censors hadn't been able to cut out. Not like *American History X*. What a load of bollocks that ended up as, and after a decent start as well. Like every patriot had to be either a Nazi or a shirt-lifter.

The supermarket opened and people began arriving. It was soon busy. He watched the new arrivals. A hangover started to set in and he was hungry, looked at his watch. It was ten. Ali and his mates weren't going to turn up early, so he had time, locked his car and went inside, took a basket and filled it with a couple of papers, a cold bottle of Lucozade, a carton of orange juice, a big bag of tortilla chips, a couple of Scotch eggs from the cold counter, a bag of jam dough- nuts. He was fucking starving now, the tills moving fast. He looked around the car park when he was back outside, still couldn't see Ali and the Cs, sat in his car and got stuck in.

Ray ate his food and drank the Lucozade, read his papers, amazed at the things people got up to once they were rich and famous. Last week's roasting story was carried on, and it was bang out of order what some of those footballers did in their spare time. If he was a manager and his players were behaving like that he'd sack them. Each girl was someone's daughter. Some might have been slags, star-struck and thick as shit, but the players were older and should know better. The clubs did fuck all. Money was all that mattered. There were people with zero morals living the high life and he blamed tossers like Ali E for doing what the politicians wanted, promoting soma and a dazed acceptance of everything they were told. The world was full of cunts. He sat back and waited, wound up and itching to get started, slipped the *Viking* album by Lars Frederiksen into his CD player.

It was after twelve when Ray spotted the E-males. There were three of them and as expected they were pure Ali C, every one of them a chemical cunt. He remembered a documentary on Chemical Ali, how the Iraqis had attacked the Marsh Arabs and drained their water, gassed the Kurds and killed women and children along with the men, and now he had mutated and his rabid spawn was swilling around Slough, destroying lives. Ray's plan was to wait for the dealers to leave the car park and follow them home, sort them out away from the shoppers and the car park's CCTV. The problem with this was that, although logical and sensible, he couldn't wait that long. He was seething. At this exact moment he had to admit his nutty side was on top. He waited three minutes. Left his door unlocked. Didn't bother taking the cue.

There was a small hedge next to the Ali Mobile and he noticed how one of the youths had broken it, red berries squashed under white trainers. The biggest one he took for Ali, a man in his early twenties, the two wankers with him a year or two younger. He played black-ghetto bollocks on his stereo, the tinny whine of today's drug dealers and muggers, the nation's wiggers and wangstas, a fashion notion that they were poor and downtrodden. Their rebellion was fresh out of the global market, second-hand shit. Three onto one made these boys fair game, and he wouldn't be surprised if they were tooled-up. He didn't give a fuck. Fist and boot was what counted. Traditional skinhead standards applied.

He caught the gaze of one of the younger ones, the youth sneering, then looking away when he saw the slow smile crossing Ray's face, realising the danger in the shaven-headed, green-jacketed, black-booted giant approaching. Criminals meant nothing to Ray. He had no respect for people obsessed with wealth and possessions, men who hurt others for profit, no time for inflated egos and that old respect chestnut. These people might be vicious, handy with a knife or gun, but essentially they were ponces. He was going to enjoy this.

– Which one of you is Ali? he asked, once he was standing opposite, arms loose at his sides, a bulldog raring to shake off his lead.

The youths were nervous, but Ali saw a deal.

– I'm Ali. What do you want? Crack, charlie, acid, E?

Ray's fist connected with the jaw and the strength of his punch sent Ali flying over the bonnet of his car and into the hedge. He tried to lift himself up, but fell back down, his mates snapping awake.

C's sidekick pulled a knife.

– Come on, Ali, let's see what you can do, Ray laughed.

The bloke was shitting it as Ray closed in, while his mate had picked up a rock from the flower bed and was trying to move behind him. C2 slashed and missed, and Ray grabbed his arm, bent it back so the youth screamed same as a girl, kept going until the blade fell and bounced along the ground. C2 felt the pressure on his arm ease, saw a square skull pulling back, ready to strike. There was a moment of calm as the Anglo-Saxon mouthed strange words, and then Ray nutted him, C2 sagging to the floor.

– Come on, you fucking white trash.

Ray turned and dodged right, the rock missing and smacking into C1, who was trying to climb to his feet.

Ray planted a Doctor Marten between the racist's legs. C3 sunk to his knees and Ray pushed him over with the famous air-ware sole. He stuck the boot in – HARD – before turning to C1, who was on his feet, swaying as he tried to find his balance. The skinhead was zooming in.

– Sell drugs to my fucking daughter, would you, you fucking slag? I'll fucking kill you.

C1 was on his toes, Ray walking fast as he followed him. The bloke was younger, but still unsteady, panicking as he bounced off a wall, running behind the bins beyond the car wash, boxing himself in. Ray was no sadist, and would only do what had to be done, but allowed himself time to catch his breath.

– She's eleven years old. She's a child and you sell her drugs? You want to put that shit in my girl's brain? Turn her into a fucking tart? That's my daughter, you fucking cunt.

C1 was confused. He was also a big boy, but no match for the skinhead. Ray worked fast, inside a minute dragging the battered drug pedlar back to his car so he could be with his friends. On the way he lifted him upright and wiped his face in one of the revolving brushes of the car wash. The problem with England was that the people were too easy-going, let the piss-takers get away with murder.

He dumped Ali and strode back to his car, saw people watching, attracted by the shouting, reached for his cue, shoved it inside his jacket. He was far enough from the shops to be able to carry out his work unhindered, returned to the blue Renault and smashed the windows before denting the bodywork. The cue snapped and he swore, threw it into the distance. Some watered-down rap was moaning about bitches and whores and a need to make more money and hang out with a load of bent-looking geezers in string vests. Ray ripped the unit out and smashed it on the concrete, picked up C2's knife and ran it around the lining of each tyre, stood back and admired his craftwork. He lobbed the weapon into the nearest hedge, saw C2 move and try to stand up, went over to the manky cunt and rolled him onto his back.

The youth stared at the sky, sunlight blocked out by a Viking lookalike, but instead of long blond locks the warrior's head was shaved near to the bone, the Nordic eyes emotion-less, cold and hard and unforgiving. C2 had seen a programme on the telly where white supremacists in America worshipped pagan gods, the likes of Odin and Thor, and he noticed that this man's fists were hammers, fists he had seen in comics, next to posters of Judge Dredd in that shop on the high street. Ali's head ached and the digital rhythm inside his ribs

jumped as the warrior leant in close and said something
about E and Europe, a British nation that would never fucking
surrender. C2 didn't understand. He was scared, the skinhead asking if he knew what the E did, something about
soma and hippies, and he said yes, and sorry, but he'd meant
no harm. The man's smile was pure evil and Ali realised he
was at the mercy of a nutter off that *Skinheads & Swastikas*
programme. He was going to die, pissed his strides and
fainted.

Ray felt good as he drove away. The Old Bill would be
on the scene soon and some busybody would have written
down his number plate, and maybe he would even be on
camera. He hoped so, as it would show the knife being
pulled, and anyway, the police would probably find the drugs.
He might get off. He'd always been lucky when it came to
the law, had been clumped a few times with truncheons but
only ever convicted of a single threatening-behaviour at
football, way back in the Eighties. It was incredible, really,
but they never seemed too keen on nicking him.

Five minutes later he was being pulled over. The police
were only doing their job, out of their cars fast, hesitating
when he stood in front of them in the street, wary of coming
too close, pepper spray ready and truncheons drawn. The
younger ones were the most nervous and he found this
surprising. An older officer stepped forward and Ray went
quietly, cuffed and led to the back of a car. He had done
the right thing by his daughter and he didn't care what
anyone said or did.

At the station he was put in the cells, then charged with
three counts of aggravated assault, each one deemed racial.

– What do you mean, racial? he asked.

– They said you called them Pakis and black bastards.

The sergeant referred to his notes, while two PCs grinned.

– What, and you believe them?

The sergeant smiled.

– That's what they say. Between you and me, I think you
did a good job on them. They're known drug dealers, scum,
but we have to charge you, and as for the race angle, well,

that's political. If they make the accusation we have to treat it seriously. There's a special law now, you see.

Ray shook his head, remembered the 4-Skins single 'One Law For Them' after Southall. Nothing changed. The world was mad. He thought of something.

– Is that a European law?

– I don't think so. It's one they thought up themselves.

– Thing is, I never said it. I'll hold my hands up to the assault, but I never called them Pakis or black bastards. That's the truth.

– I bet you thought it, though, said one of the PCs.

Ray couldn't remember if he had thought it or not, but the thing was, he hadn't said it, and even if he had said it, what difference did it make? When you were in a fight you said and were called all sorts of things. That was life. Had he thought it? No. He didn't think so. He realised that they were talking about thought crime, just as Orwell predicted. It was the next step on from *Brave New World*, soma–ecstasy and the digital beat of the capitalist trance machine.

– Get yourself a good brief, that's my advice, the sergeant said. Why did you do it? You weren't buying off them. Was it a vigilante attack?

– I've got my reasons, Ray replied.

That was all he was going to say.

One of the coppers told him there was no CCTV in that corner of the car park, so it was down to the accusations made against him. He supposed it made sense, selling drugs beyond the cameras.

When Ray was bailed he returned to the flat, had a hot bath and changed his clothes, pleased that Handsome wasn't around. He stopped by his uncle's on the way to the house, but Terry wasn't in. April hugged him when he arrived, and he picked her up and kissed her forehead, Chelsea hanging back, waltzing over when he smiled and pulled a face. She seemed relieved. The girls drifted into the living room and he talked to Liz in the kitchen, told her he had sorted things out, without going into any details, and she seemed tired, a few seconds of silence hanging between them, her right hand raising towards his face, stopping and falling away. She turned to the sink, said she'd do him some pizza and chips, that he should go and sit in the living room with the girls.

Cartoon animals chased each other across the TV screen, feeling no pain as they battered each other with hammers and planks of wood, laughing as they were blown up and flattened by bulldozers. When April went into the kitchen for a drink Chelsea whispered that she was sorry about the Es, and anyway, she probably wasn't even going to try them. Ray understood that children made mistakes, but adults should know better. She was growing up fast and he squeezed her shoulder, reminded her that she had to stay away from drugs, that they would wreck her brain and turn her into someone who couldn't think for herself. She mustn't forget what they had inside them either.

– No, I won't forget the bogeys.

Ray licked his lips and Chelsea pulled a face, shook her head when he offered her a bite of his pizza. April returned and sat on the other side of him, leant her blonde head against his side as he ate.

Running Riot in '84

RAY'S WORKING NIGHTS IN the summer of 1984, warm graveyard shifts that slide into hazy sunrises, the temperature increasing as he knocks off and heads home, a faint breeze on his arm where the Granada churns the air, resting on the door frame like a Ted in a Zodiac, and he's tired, but in a good way, sort of mellow, which is unusual for him, and during the night he sits in a hut on the edge of the airport, behind wire fences and a metal barrier, in front of low-lying offices, windows white and sparkling when there's a full moon, the roads softened by yellow street lights, X-rays catching stray cats and a giant fox, a soft hum or generators the only sound, and Ray's world is peaceful and quiet while during the day England riots and burns, politicians and the trade unions at war, and he is outside it all, segregated from the nine-to-five, watching for intruders, night-prowlers and the sort of villains who aren't interested in the typewriters and filing cabinets of the offices, men who prefer gold bullion and precious stones, looking towards the cargo holds over the other side of the airport, really he's more concerned with drunks and vandals, except there's few of those on the Heathrow perimeter, or maybe IRA bombers, but it's an easy job, nothing ever happens, the money better than when he was sweating his bollocks off labouring, he can swap his shifts around as well, which is handy, he's happy being away from the noise of the runway, the stink of fuel, the dirt and itching of jet engines, the novelty of his first full-time job long gone, and how those navvies do it he doesn't know, they keep slogging away, year after year, he'll respect those men for the rest of his life, but this new job suits him fine, specially when he can work till ten, drive home on quiet roads, enjoy an early pint and some food in a nearly empty pub, then when he gets in at half-twelve or so he's ready for bed, sleeps till seven, has time to watch a bit of telly, lift some weights, he's drinking less, this new world is a relaxing place, the morning pubs used by a different tribe, men on nights like him, Post Office workers, the self-employed and unemployed, the unemployable, the hard up and the well off, every one of them with a different approach to life, but mainly the change gives him the chance to calm down, to think straight, means he can move at his own speed, isn't knackered every second, his mind is clearer than it's ever been, with easy work and less drink, and it's funny because it is 1984 and this year is supposed to be different, the build-up went on for ages, the title of George Orwell's novel taking on a meaning of its own, it's like the end of the world has arrived, and despite the talk on the telly and in the papers nobody says much about the actual book, and the one thing Ray finds hard about his new job is that it gets boring with nothing to do, so he decides to see what the fuss is about, buys *Nineteen Eighty-Four* and starts reading it one night, can't put it down, finishes it in two goes, his brain racing with excitement, it reminds him of when he heard his first Oi records, the book connects, like his own ideas are woven into the sentences, and he's never read much, only papers really, books at school, but he can't stop thinking about Big Brother and thought crime and the power of the proles, because it makes perfect sense, and while he can't imagine a place where there is that much surveillance, or where a man can be persecuted for what he thinks but never says, he knows Big Brother is the face of a dictatorship, something that can never be hidden or trivialised, and he goes back to the beginning, reads the book again, slower this time, taking more in, and as soon as he finishes *Nineteen Eighty-Four* he wants to read other novels, and it's like a whole new world is opening up, he knows it links up with Oi, in a way, the real skinhead approach, because street punk has told him it's okay to be proud, not to back down

246

for an easier life, that he can stand apart and ignore the political parties, that there's something beyond the machine, power in numbers, that he's allowed to think for himself, to refuse bribery, to be proud of his Englishness and his culture, and all the pretence and bullshit is shaved away, right back to the bone, he juts out his jaw and clenches his fists and isn't going to let the intellectuals or money-grabbers or fake patriots take his flag away from him, that's how he feels, and it is all there in Orwell's writing, Ray doesn't care that the man went to Eton, doesn't believe in judging someone on their background, doesn't believe in class, he wonders how many of the lyric writers he respects have read George Orwell, guesses a fair few, and Orwell and *Nineteen Eighty-Four* are right there in the heart of the country, Ray's playing catch-up now, goes straight into *Animal Farm*, feels sorry for the horses, specially Boxer, hates the pigs, reads Orwell's essays, which match what he's seen in the fiction, finds these titles listed in his copy of *Nineteen Eighty-Four*, reads *Coming Up For Air* and *Burmese Days*, doesn't know what other authors he can try, so one day after work he sits in his car outside Slough Library, picks up his courage and walks in, needs some advice, finds a woman who works there, middle-aged and thoughtful, she listens, writes out some names, and he joins the library, feels strange with all these people sitting at tables studying for certificates and whatever, but he takes the woman's advice and thanks her, moves into Aldous Huxley's *Brave New World*, and again he's hooked, sees how a dictatorship wants the family destroyed so it has complete control, how free sex can be manipulated, reads about soma and fun and how bribery keeps people quiet, those in power free to do what they want, good citizens created in test tubes, programmed to accept their lot, sense-pleasure the new truth, and he can't see it happening in his lifetime, not with the way people argue and fight today, but it could happen in the future, in fifty or sixty years maybe, that has to be the aim of the men behind the scenes, and he is reading every night – *Fahrenheit 451* by Ray Bradbury, *Cancer Ward* by Alexander Solzhenitsyn, *The Loneliness Of The Long-Distance*

Runner by Alan Sillitoe, *The Aerodrome* by Rex Warner, *The Outsider* by Albert Camus – the list grows and books take over from music, because while there's a few bands still doing the business, Oi has been battered and bruised and forced underground by a combination of media-class Tories and Lefties, replaced by the easier indie of the student brigade, Northern bands he can't relate to, and sitting in his hut reading about the burning of books, the Borstal kid who refuses to surrender and loses a race to beat the system, the man accused of killing an Arab but hanged for his attitude, well, he wants to tell someone what he's found, share his discovery, and one day he leaves work and goes into Southall, thinking back three years and remembering how he felt like an outsider, and he could have blamed every Paki going for what happened to him, but something stopped, controlled the anger he felt, and now he feels nothing, they have a view of what a skinhead is, and they've taken some kickings over the years, been bullied, can dish it out as well, knows it's mainly Hindus and Sikhs over here, not real Pakis as in Muslims, and he still feels like an outsider even though he's in his car, early enough for most of the shops to be shut, the pavements quiet, grocers starting to set up, and he doesn't really hold it against those boys, knows they're mugs like anyone else, going on appearances and the colour of his skin, a race attack on a handful of white boys, there's skinheads who are cunts, of course there are, but the skins he knows are decent people, honest people, and it's the same anywhere, if you're a different colour living in a white town there's going to be a lot of paranoia, he can't see it ever changing, everyone needs their identity, he thinks about Hate Week in *Nineteen Eighty-Four*, it's not advertised that way but it's going on right now with the football mobs rucking each other, bashing up their own kind while there's a massive strike going on and a war between capital and labour, and the Lefties are bashing the whites, telling the native English they've got no culture, winding them up, it's fucking mental really, the proles fighting among themselves, like Orwell says, and maybe they should all get together and smash up the

Left and Right, do the dogma cunts on big salaries, the journalists and television controllers, but it will never happen, he can't see it occuring, can't see thought crime happening either, not in England – how can they know what you're fucking thinking? – guessing isn't knowing, that's Nazi and Commie behaviour, and he leaves Southall and is soon in Slough, stops in a pub he uses, it's been open half an hour and there's a few men in sitting at tables with their drinks and papers, he orders a pint of lager and a Ploughman's, sees this bloke Smiles at a table, knows his face, picked him up a week ago hitching back from the airport as well, and there's something not right about him, but not like he's a real loony or anything, Smiles is all right, spotted *Fahrenheit 451* in Ray's car, asked him what it was about and listened when Ray told him, he's older, a punk rocker in his tastes, big into The Clash and The Ruts, they compare Orwell and Joe Strummer, and now he's inviting Ray to sit down, and they have a good talk about music and books and heaven and hell, Ray has his Ploughman's and another pint, buys Smiles a drink, there's something extra-sad about him today, it's the same with a lot of these people who grin and joke around, it's how they block the reality out, pretending everything's sweet when it's really sour, but he's going on the name, couldn't say Smiles was happy-go-lucky, there again, he hardly knows him, can't ask or anything like that, and Ray yawns and shakes the man's hand, drives home, flops down on his bed, he's calming down by the week, but is full of another sort of energy, he can feel it inside, maybe this is what happens when you get older, and he might be drinking with a different sort of nutter in these daytime pubs, the thinking man's nutters, but he doesn't want to be called a nutter any more, it means different things to different people, hates it that people see him as someone who steams in and hurts people for fun, and it's true he likes a row, gets wound up, but he knows it's not healthy, maybe Uncle Terry is getting through to him, thanks to his new job, and he lies on his bed for a while, warm and content, can't help looking over at *Saturday Night And Sunday Morning*, another novel from Alan Sillitoe, reaches over and flicks the pages, smells the paper and ink, knows he should save it for tonight, read it right through when he's not tired, and he remembers his last visit to the library, how he's a regular, calls the librarian by her first name, and the books he's reading are confirming things he knows, deep down inside him, and this is his education, he's moving along nicely, his need for physical work put into his weight training, he has an easy job with better money, and best of all he's really using his brain, keeping his mind active so he doesn't go mad about things like he did before, and he has to admit, if he's honest, that he's never felt better in his life.

Son of Your Father

HE ACCELERATED AND LEFT the skate park behind, clipping pavements and barriers as he flew across smooth tarmac, knocking a tramp high into the air, the ragged figure lost in a glow of red advertising, hanging for a second before falling back to the ground, his gleaming shopping trolley bouncing into a digital display selling glucose and carbonated cocaine, the tramp immediately back on his feet, he didn't feel a thing, and Lol's exhaust fumes floated spirit-like under a column of alien-necked lights, ET electrics inside skinny silver tubes, and the night was sultry and humid, an artificial moon glowing from a ball of graphics, and it was always night-time in these streets, when Lol drove his car fast, wax dripping from coconut palms and forming puddles, roadworks blocking turn-offs, the steady beat of punk and hardcore and hip hop competing with the roar of his customised engine, controls vibrating through his hands as he sank into an underpass, accelerated, quickly coming up out of the dip, reaching a flat strip of black road that led out onto the M25 where he could put his foot down properly, score clicking clock-like, numbers snapping out seconds and minutes, whole lifespans, and everything was speeding up, turning faster and more furious, and yet he was careful with the bends, at least at first, didn't want to lose time, he was saving his nitro for later, keeping something in reserve, the bypass a blur of streamlined concrete, a new America of UK satellites, and he was surfing the rhythm of his life, it was one short game, repeated over and over, sadness washed out, he was thinking of skateboard moves, in this car he was safer and more comfortable, knew he could never be bruised or cut open, there were no A&E units or prowling ambulances in this world, there was no need, and he was moving faster, taking killer bends at full speed now, skinning walls, oil spilling as flames flashed behind him, he didn't have to worry about the screech of tyres, his crying engine, these sounds were stuck in his brain, he had been here thousands of times before, smashing fences and flipping across ramps, colours blending, and he felt the thrill of being indestructible, rolling with Rancid and 50 Cent, 'American Guns' by Transplants, and he imagined a fit girl sitting next to him covering her eyes, the lines in the road broken, turning solid, he didn't care about scores, just wanted to keep moving, in a straight line.

That last dose of treatment was the worst yet and it was taking Terry a long time to sort himself out. He stared at the ceiling. Wasn't going into work today. Could hear Laurel moving around, off school again, and he couldn't remember having so many holidays when he was a kid, wondered if it was good thing, if his son was learning as much as he should be. This weekend Terry would be fifty years old and he couldn't see himself making it to fifty-one.

Terry was a teenager hearing his dad screaming in the darkness. Terror rippled across his skin, then and now, his mum hushing her husband, singing a lullaby softly under her breath, and he could make out whispers far away in another reality, never knew what she was saying, what his dad answered, and didn't want to know either. He couldn't understand what was wrong with his father, why he had so many nightmares. There was a time once when he heard him crying. He felt ashamed. His dad shouldn't cry.

Things were different between Laurel and him. He hoped so anyway. His old man was never a big one for talking, but looking back maybe he was just unsure what to say, unable to find the words, holding his tongue, like Terry did now. It dawned on Terry that maybe Dad was protecting him from something, but he couldn't think what, and yet the idea lingered. He probably couldn't see what was going on in his own house, the same as Laurel, but was sure that he had sensed something, was too busy to follow it up, out and about with his mates, lost in his own little game. Terry liked to think his dad would've been proud of him. He laughed. He was fifty and fucked. Heard Laurel on the landing, pretended he was asleep, didn't want to talk to him at the moment.

Lol was thirsty and hungry and on his way to the kitchen, stopped and opened Dad's door, the window open, curtains closed, listened to his breath disappearing, waited for it to return. It was after nine, but he wasn't going to wake him up. He was either drunk or tired out, didn't have much energy lately with his flu and that. Lol went downstairs and poured lemonade in a glass, added blocks of ice, grabbed a load of chocolate biscuits and went back upstairs, stood at the window in his room, munching away. Bob and Molly were in the sun, the field white with frost, and he wondered how bad they felt the cold, could see their breath hovering. He felt angry thinking how Roy was being forced to move them, maybe split them up, all because some rich cunt had bought the land. It wasn't fair. Yet somehow he knew it wouldn't happen. His dad would sort it out. Dad always knew what to do. He had thought about finding out where the man lived, Kev The Kev saying they should hire Ian to go round and threaten him, tell him if he didn't leave those horses alone he would get himself hurt, but Lol couldn't see this working somehow. Dad would think of a better way.

He wondered if he should sort out some decorations for his dad's birthday, knew he had a big enough surprise coming on Saturday night. For the first time in years he saw how empty the house was, started thinking about his mum and what life would be like if she'd lived, but he blocked it out quick, was young when it happened and didn't have too many clear memories, just impressions, a presence, a smell and touch that faded, then returned, things he'd been told. He had to be strong, like Dad said that time, when they spoke seriously. He didn't say a lot, at least not important stuff, but when he did Dad was usually right. Lol was glad he was like that, wouldn't want a gay sort of dad who talked about things for hours and made him feel embarrassed. He turned away from the window and went back to his console, waited for the game to load, finished the biscuits, Bob and Molly firm in his mind. The heat was increasing, in the radiators and in his controls.

Terry stood under the hot water and took his time washing. He dried himself off and looked at his face in the mirror, knew he should have a shave but was tired, thought of George's soldier values and got to work with a razor. It was funny thinking that the day you came into the world was the most important day of your life, yet you couldn't remember a thing about it, didn't know what your mum was thinking, what she said, how your old man felt. He went back to the birth of his own children, knew exactly what was happening in his head, guessed you were gentler with girls, treated them different, saw Laurel wrapped in a blanket, his nose squashed up like a boxer. The picture was clear. His father must have felt the same when his children were born. Now Laurel was almost a man, would leave like the others soon, and the house would be well and truly empty. He would meet a girl and settle down, and that was how it should be. He would have kids of his own and live his life and if he was lucky he would turn fifty and stare in the mirror and know a bit more about his father, appreciate how his old man had tried to set an example.

Terry loved all his children the same, but was pleased he had a son. It was nature, passing your genes on, and something extra, as he wanted Laurel to be like him, on the inside at least, and better in the way he acted, the things he did with his time. He didn't want him taking chances or misbehaving, like so many boys did. Terry had done his best, put a roof over his children's heads, food on the table, watched out for them, and April and him had nothing when they started, nobody to help them, just worked hard and did without. Pride was inside you, couldn't be bought, beyond money, and he was glad he had something to leave his children when he died. Ray and Terry's sisters were also looked after.

He could see his father buried in his face. It was the illness putting sadness into his expression. He had the same haunted look. That's what it was. His dad was haunted. He remembered when the Apollo 11 mission reached the moon, the joy squeezing out, a childish excitement when they saw those flickering images on the television. He smiled, thinking back.

Not long after the moon landing Dad knocked on the door of his room, told Terry to come with him. They left the house and walked through the night-time streets, and he asked where they were going, Dad smiling and telling him to wait and see, and even though Terry thought he was grown-up he was still a kid, and chuffed by the attention, pleased to walk anywhere his dad said. He felt safe, sensed his dad's strength, knew nobody would have a go at them, and he snuck a look at the rigid head and straight back, the power of the jaw and focused eyes, and it all came back to him in a rush of memory, a heavy tide of emotion.

They went to Salt Park, walked into the middle of the grass where a cricket pitch had been marked out. It was late, but the sky was clear away from the street and house lights. Dad pulled out a pair of binoculars he said he'd borrowed from someone at work, and they were heavy, smelt of metal and rubber, obviously expensive, the sort a general would use. And they took turns looking at the moon, Dad showing him how to focus the lenses and explaining that when he was in the RAF a full moon meant more flak, a better chance of being hit, but it also meant they could see their targets. There were pros and cons in everything, but he always saw the moon as his friend, able to guide a man home when he was far away, wandering and lost. It had a pull on the mind. People used to worship the moon. In the POW camp he looked at it and knew his family could see the same thing back in England, that Terry's mum looked as well. It was something they'd agreed on. The war was a strange time. Nobody knew how long they had, specially not an airman. The moon was reassuring, when he was a prisoner. His voice sounded different. He frowned and remembered himself, asked Terry if he could see the craters. And he could. It was magic. They were sharp, the light intense, a reflection of a sun that was blocked out and hidden away, and he felt part of a very special universe, knew at the time he would never forget being in Salt Park with his dad. And he never had.

They stood in the field for ages, not saying much, just looking out across space, and when they finally left the park and were walking home his father put his hand on his shoulder and told him he was a good boy. That's what he had said. A good boy. His heart swelled with pride.

Terry saw the bones under his skin, the ridges and craters of his skull, where his hair would have fallen out if he hadn't been clever and shaved it right down, a few people making remarks, Ray specially, frowning, and he knew things were going to get worse, that he would end up a walking corpse. He had seen it happen before. He was a rock of a man with a pair of child's eyes staring out. They were still clear. He was a man with a rock on his head. A rockhead, bonehead, skullhead. Soon he would be a butterhead. The poison was right there in the middle of the rock, and he couldn't even see it, the doctors not certain it was really there. His enemy was inside him, gnawing away, the cocky little skinhead who used to run the show knocked out. He punched the mirror and broke the glass.

His hand was bleeding and he ripped off some bog roll, watched as the blood seeped through. He wrapped a towel around the wound, waited to see what happened, and it started to change colour, slowly at first, turning red, more blood dripping on the floor. He sat on the end of the bath and held the towel tight, pushed hard. He was a silly sod. What was the point of that? He leant over the toilet and puked up.

The boy heard his dad being sick and shook his head. Dad must have been out last night, drinking too much as usual, and that was how he lived, coming in with takeaways and leaving cartons sitting around, dishes unwashed, hanging around in pubs and playing pool during the day when he should be working, playing his music too loud and spending a fortune on records, buying replacements for the singles he's fed into that jukebox in the Union Jack Club, setting up his own corner where he could drink London Pride and pot the black for hours on end. He laughed. Dad would never change and he would never grow up. Lol was the sensible one in this house. At least his father wasn't bringing girls home, or on drugs, or in trouble with the police. He thought again, something nagging in his head, turned the volume down and listened to the silence, worried suddenly, heard a cough and relaxed. It could be flu, of course, that bug he couldn't seem to shake. If he'd been out drinking there would have been empty curry cartons downstairs, a couple of dishes waiting for Lol. He never forgot his son. Lol would go and see how he was, after he finished this next game.

Class of '69 – Part 5

TERRY HAS TWO PROBLEMS that need sorting out – and when he tells Alan what's happened to his old man – his friend does his nut – effing and blinding and telling the rest of the lads down the club – and they crowd round – want to find the rockers and do them – fucking grease – robbing Tel's dad like that – thieving the binoculars – taking liberties – and while he's glad of the support – he can't help wondering what a bunch of kids can do against grown men – rockers are famous for using axes and bike chains – everyone knows that – but Alan tells him there's strength in numbers – if they all stick together they'll be okay – it's the law of the jungle – skinheads might be young but they hunt in packs – and the boys rant and rave and finally calm down a bit – start playing pool – smacking the balls – Alan swearing he's going to help Terry – they leave it like that – and the next day these older skinheads – blokes who drink in the same pub – hear what's happened – and one of them – Jefferson – he collars Terry and tells him he knows George – see – he's a war hero – their old men are mates – went to school together – George was shot down over Germany – ended up in a prisoner-of-war camp – had no fucking choice did he? – but he never surrendered – never gave the game away – Jefferson tells Terry his dad's as tough as they come – but what could he do? – outnumbered like that – by those fucking rockers – and Terry can't help wondering if Jefferson knows something he doesn't – but what? – it doesn't make sense – maybe he could tell him why Dad isn't angry – just accepts what's happened – isn't doing anything about it – no – Terry can't ask – can't say this to anyone – he's angry he even thinks it – angry it's true – Dad won't fight back – and this Jefferson tells him skinheads have to stick together – specially if they're Chelsea and drink in the same fucking boozer – he laughs – a hard man – Terry nods – keeps quiet about April and Dave in Brentford and all that bother – doesn't tell anyone – not even Alan – that's one problem he has to sort out for himself – he isn't going to keep away from April – no chance – Dave is bigger – handy with his fists – and boots – has his mates – Terry needs to even the odds up – he could challenge him to a game of pool – like in a Western he saw where the gunslinger wins his blonde in a game of cards – he can carry his cue over in his football bag – that's an idea – but Dave would have to agree to play him first – it *might* work – with Rooster though – and his pals – well – he isn't thinking about playing pool with that cunt – he can't sort out the grease on his jack – doesn't need to either – Jefferson telling him the rockers use Mick's Cafe down near The Three Tons – they have a fry-up every Saturday morning – a sort of tradition – habit – Jefferson knows those fucking leather boys – so it's eleven o'clock – Saturday morning – Terry arrives outside The Swan – along from the cafe – and he can't believe it – a mob of skinheads is waiting – must be at least fifty lads – talk about mob-handed – a smart parade of braces and Doc Martens – and soon as he arrives they start off down the A4 – quickly reach the crossroads – Terry and Alan are up the front – with Jefferson and his brothers – one of them has a cosh tucked inside his cardigan – takes it out and slaps it in the palm of his free hand – Terry realises people are going to get hurt – for the first time in his life he doesn't care – he's thinking about the binoculars – the broken window – most of all he's thinking about his dad – bleeding over the sink – punched and kicked – down in the gutter – his bloody nose rubbed in the dirt – and the mob spills across the road and stops the traffic – they're climbing over railings – walking fast along the parade of shops – towards the cafe – a line of bikes outside – the first one up a Norton – and Terry smells bacon frying – his mouth watering – a rocker spots them and hurries to the cafe door – a brick beating him to it – cracking the window – poor old Mick – and there's rockers spilling outside now – cocky bastards – smelly cunts – hesitating when they see how many skinheads are coming their way – there's maybe twenty grease – they're older but the numbers are against them – they don't run – they're ready for a punch-up – and there's a stand-off for a few seconds – everyone shouting – and then the two sides are fighting – Jefferson pointing at a bloke with a bruised face – shouting that's Rooster – and they bundle through and jump him and he goes down – Terry kicking the bloke as hard as he can – in the face – the back when he curls up – paying him back for his old man – and there's five or six skinheads sticking the boot in – Terry best of all – and Rooster's rocker mates – who try and help – they get it as well – they must be the ones who helped Rooster rob Dad – Terry puts the boot into a couple of them as well – and when the rockers have either run off – or had enough – six of them spark out on the pavement – Terry stands and look down at Rooster – shouts at the half-conscious man – that's for George English – you fucking cunt – boots him again – this time in his belly – follows the rest of the mob back over the main road – dodging people who've come to see what's going on – and the skinheads are running back past The Swan now – towards the centre of Slough – before the police arrive – they'll be here soon enough – some Nosy Parker has probably been on the blower already – they split up – Terry and Alan jumping on a bus – it's going their way – climb the stairs and sit at the front – watch a police van speed past – light flashing – bell ringing – and when Terry gets in – his mum makes him a couple of fish-paste sandwiches – he sits in the living room munching away – watching the telly – an hour later hears a knock on the door – Mum will answer it – she comes in – looking worried – Dad behind her – he seems okay – and Terry's heart jumps – he can't believe it – there's two coppers with them – how do they know those rockers getting bashed up has anything to do with him? – he was one face – fucking hell – his old man's going to go spare – Mum asking Terry to leave the room – they need some privacy – and he walks out with his head down – pretends to go upstairs – creeps back – listens at the door – and he'll be off in a minute – he's not hanging around – but the police are more interested in Dad – for some reason – asking him questions – about a firearm – two firearms – ask if he threatened a youth – waited for him in the street near his home – pointed a shotgun in his back – made him walk into a derelict house – kneel on the ground – put a revolver to his head – cocked it – threatened to blow his brains out – made him piss himself – one of the coppers laughs – Terry watching through a crack – they haven't shut the door properly – sees a flicker on his father's face – hears the denial – carefully chosen words – the police continue – say the youth has marks to his face – bruising – a broken nose – it could have been caused by a fist – or the butt of a gun maybe – the officers say the youth is known to them – a bloody layabout – a thug – they stand – the men shake hands – Dad seems to know one of them – the copper calls him George – Terry hurries upstairs – stands on the landing – hears the door shut – and there's some whispering between his mum and dad – silence – rustling – he thinks they're kissing – shouldn't listen – Mum tells Dad she loves him – goes in the kitchen – starts singing – and the back door opens and Terry runs to his room – stands by the window – he can see Dad in the garden – going in the shed – he's moving around inside – doing something – then Dad leaves – the binoculars in his right hand – he walks through the house – Terry can hear him talking to Mum – and he leaves – Terry looks out of a window at the front of the house – sees a bag under his dad's arm – his father walking down the street – Terry waits – till it's safe to look in the shed – Mum washing clothes in the sink – covered in suds – he closes the door behind him – starts searching – doesn't know what for – the binoculars have already gone – and he finds a bundle – frowns when he sees what's inside – he is shocked – shakes his head – and that night he can't sleep – thinks about what he's found – realises now that Dad is a man of action – he hasn't made a song and dance about things – has done what needed to be done – on his own – and Terry feels ashamed for doubting him – and the next morning he arrives in Brentford – leaves the station and walks to Dave's house – finds a place nearby – a boarded-up yard – the fence kicked in around the side – it's nice and private – reaches in his kit bag – takes out the sawn-off shotgun he found in the shed – hidden in an old drawer – under some wooden planks – and there was a Luger as well – he can't use that – it might be special – taken off someone Dad killed – a souvenir from a prison guard – who knows – what if something goes wrong – and he loses it – has to dump it – the shotgun is good enough – wrapped now in the towel he takes to school – when he plays football – he takes it out – loads it carefully – with the shells he found in a smaller box – his hands are shaking – he's scared – can't help it – knows he's doing the right thing – nervous but excited as well – he is going to do this – he won't back out – puts the gun back in the bag – leaves it unzipped – the shot gun is on top of the towel – easy to reach – starts walking – fear vanishing as he steps out of the yard – with a shooter he can do anything he wants – doesn't have to be scared of anyone – nobody's going to fuck him about when he's pointing two barrels at their kneecaps – that cunt Dave will have to beg – never mind leave him and April alone – he's angry again – taking the piss like that – and Terry is the hardest man in the world knocking on this front door – ready to force Dave back into the hall if he's on his own – or over to the yard if he's not – either way he's going to pay – and when Terry's anger comes – it's like a dam exploding – the pressure builds up – held back – and he's ready – but a man answers the door – puffing on a fag – looks Terry up and down – answers Dave's not living here any more – he's moved in with that new bird of his – he's only been with her a week – the bloody idiot – the man stares at the youth in front of him – the bag he's carrying – Terry hopes he can't see the gun – do you know her, son?

– they call her Twiggy – she looks like the model – he's living with her in Acton – good riddance as well – Terry laughs – they both laugh – and five minutes later Terry's in a phone box – talking to April – meets her outside The Beehive – and they walk down to the river – sit on the bank looking over at Griffin Island – in the same place as last time – watching the way the current switches around – moving forward and sideways – back in on itself – they can't see what's going on under the surface – can only guess – and there's places where the water swirls and sinks – pulling at itself almost – and April leans her head on his shoulder – everything is perfect – till she asks him what's in the bag – just my Harrington – I had to drop some clothes off for my mum before I caught the train – he doesn't want to lie – but more than that – he doesn't want her worrying – the gun is wrapped up in the towel – he's taken the shells out – he'll put it back in the shed tonight – and he sort of wishes Dave had been in – he owes him – but it's better this way – he won't have the police on him for a start – and anyway – he's got what he wanted – wonders if he could have pulled the trigger – if it was needed – but he'll never know – thinks he could have shot Dave in the leg – if he lost his temper – went mad – he doesn't like to think about it – he's got a lot to lose – if he had nothing to lose maybe it would be different – but it doesn't matter – it's not really his style – it's a one-off – and he's sitting in the sun with his girlfriend – watching the river – April telling him that's their lives down there – he doesn't know about that – but he doesn't have a care in the world – feels relieved – and happy – knows nothing can stop them being together now.

Blood and Honour

HE HAD DONE HIS best, tried to live an honest life, but it wasn't allowed. Like everyone else, Ray had been labelled, and it had nothing to with Southall either. There was a time when he was clear in his thinking, *Nineteen Eighty-Four* and *Brave New World* changing his direction, a working-man's revelation. Now drug dealers sold soma to his babies and thought crime was more important than rough justice. If he went to prison, what would be waiting for him when he came out? Chelsea and April would be further away than ever. They wouldn't forget him exactly, but it wouldn't be the same when he returned. The system demanded total surrender, even this fake-liberal version he was living in, and the pressure had spread into his own home, infected his wife. It was divide-and-rule tactics, with ordinary people doing the dirty work, the fat fuckers in control rubbing their hands. Liz had bottled out and let it happen.

He thought of Arthur Seaton in *Saturday Night And Sunday Morning*, how The Arctic Monkeys had picked up so many years after the novel was published on his refusal to be labelled. Arthur insisted that whatever people said he was, that's what he wasn't. The same rules applied today. Ray was labelled by know-nothing no-marks, seen as a nutter and a neo-Nazi and a nasty bit of work. The working man had no chance, specially if he was white and said what he thought. It was so long since he'd read those books. Maybe he should have another look. They marked a good time in his life, when he was thinking straight, met Liz and settled down, was focused, had children, felt easy in himself, in control. Things had mucked up in the last couple of years and he didn't know why, didn't think he was in the wrong, and definitely didn't regret giving the Ali Cs a kicking.

The main road was busy and he was happy to turn off it, the traffic lighter on the estate, and he couldn't help wondering what the world would be like without cars, how you had a bike when you were a kid and then it became childish to ride it, so you put it away, went out and bought a car instead, revved the engine and rode the clutch, left half your tyres on the tarmac, forked out for road tax, insurance, MOTs, repairs, petrol and the all rest of it, paying more and more every year. They painted patterns on the streets and put up endless signs, added cameras, fined you for straying into their yellow boxes, for doing a few miles more than their speed limits. One day the oil would run out and people wouldn't move around so much, would start working near where they lived again. The same things would get done, but life would be easier, more localised, more interesting. Mind you, without cars he would be out of a job. He'd have to find something else. Maybe he could retrain when he was inside.

He was appearing at the magistrate's court next week and expected his case to be referred to the Crown Court, his brief warning him that a jail term was likely on the assault charges, which Ray admitted, but refused to explain, and that the racial element would ensure it was for at least a couple of years. These charges he denied and was deter- mined to fight, not because he cared about being labelled a racist by wankers he didn't know or respect, but because they were untrue. He was trying to stay calm, but it was hard. He was numb, not sure what he should be doing, could only keep working and do his best to put it out of his mind.

– It's the third on the right, his fare announced, a timid middle-aged man in thick glasses. Thanks.

If the oil ran out, they wouldn't bother with electric cars. Not the mob running the West World. There was no money there, not in the long term. They could have everyone driving around on batteries now if they wanted. He would do some- thing a lot different than driving. Mind you, if he could go back to when he was sixteen he would do it differently anyway.

If he was starting out now he'd learn a trade, train up for something rather than drift along, or better still, find a job he was interested in. There again, when he was leaving school apprenticeships were hard to find, and there was plenty of unskilled manual work about, at least in the South, and the money wasn't bad, if you were living at home and only bothered about paying for your social life. Football, drink, music were what mattered. Things were easier today, but there were new pressures as well, and there wasn't the physical work, immigrants and East Europeans undercutting English lads, affecting the building trade as well, putting firms out of business and causing a lot of bad feeling.

Lol was a good boy, had a quiet determination about him, was keen on his music and had formed a band, said he wanted to make a living out of it, and Ray laughed, loved his Oi but had never thought about doing something for himself. He wouldn't made a wage out it, that's for sure, the honest views of street punk banned and demonised. Angry young white boys weren't allowed to say what they felt. He wondered what Lol's band were called, who wrote the lyrics and what they were about.

– It's the house at the end, his fare cooed. Thanks.

He would never have thought it possible to make a record, despite the punk DIY ethics he'd heard so much about, wouldn't have known where to start, but now with Cubase and computers and Logic and the internet anyone could get in there and have a go.

– This'll do. Thanks.

The man stood by his door and paid, and Ray saw him properly for the first time, as more than a pair of glasses. He was very polite, gave him a pound tip. Ray usually noticed his fares. It was the best part of the job, viewing new faces, wondering about a passenger's life, having a chat when they were in the mood. He had concentrated on the goggles, missed the personality. He watched the man walk away, heard Section 5 playing, realised he had turned the volume down out of respect for his fare. He felt better.

266

He reached for his mobile and punched a number in his phone book.

– Where are you? Hawkins asked.

– Just dropped off, I'll be there in ten minutes.

He called in and told Angie he was taking a break. She didn't seem well pleased, as things were busy and she needed her drivers working. He told her he was picking up something for Saturday and she was friendly. Ray turned the radio off and retraced his route, was soon back on the main road, slowing down for the traffic lights. He turned the music off as well, wasn't in the mood. He moved his head and saw a blonde smiling back, and she looked familiar, with her suntan and glamour-model hair, but he couldn't place her, thought about that fare he'd serviced, felt guilty, tried to remember her name. Yvonne. That was it. He had taken her number, but never called. He looked away, continued when the lights changed, was soon winding his way towards Hawkins. He saw his car parked in with some back-street garages, that Yvonne sort sitting on his lap. Poor old Liz.

He took the main road, which was clear in the other direction, was soon picking his way through the dozing streets of another estate, passed pensioners and skiving schoolkids, a woman with a pushchair, heading towards the Hawkins HQ. He'd been there twice before, with his uncle, and on the outside it didn't seem the best location to be storing goods, but Hawkins wasn't the sort of bloke to rob, and he'd made it secure, invested in some serious locks. The kids knew him and had the message reinforced when he found some plum trying to break in. He gave the boy a clip round the ear, found out who he was and where he lived, promised him that if anything happened from now on he'd hold him personally responsible. Hawkins did spot checks and the local urchins were happy to keep away.

Turning into the garages, he saw the man himself up ahead, standing in the middle of the potholed oblong, arms folded, doors on either side, a breeze-block wall at the far end with SKINHEAD NATION painted in black old-firm letters. Ray smiled, recalling the title of the George Marshall book, the work the man had done for the cause, didn't need to guess who was responsible. He had always been wary of Hawkins, specially when he was younger, but had known him since he was a boy so had learnt to live with his presence. He had a hard side, which he kept away from Terry. Everyone was the same, Ray guessed. Different faces for different individuals. Everyone wanted to be liked and needed to fit in somewhere.

– You found it? Hawkins said, when Ray had stopped and lowered the window. You haven't been to see me for a long time.

It sounded like an accusation.

– Park up the end, by the wall.

Ray was tempted to salute, but did as he was told, locked up and walked back over. Hawkins had some sort of remote control in his pocket and pressed a button. The door lifted and they went inside.

He had moved things around since last time, improved the decor as well, one wall lined with boxes and a clothes rack for his Thai imports, Stone Island and Lacoste for the mugs, Ben Sherman and Fred Perry for the boys, ten boxes of Timberlands he'd brought back from New York, stacks of DVDs, more boxes filled with dusty videos, Mr Motivator and Jane Fonda rubbing shoulders, and looking into the tunnel further in it seemed as if the place had expanded.

– You had an extension built? Ray asked.

– I'm going to buy the garage next door, Hawkins said, taking the joke seriously. Put a wall behind the door and knock a hole through from in here. It's getting a bit crowded these days.

He was a proper Arthur Daley when it came to hoarding, but minus the trilby and patter. Del Boy without the flat cap and three-wheeler and thick brother. It took Ray's eyes a while to absorb everything – blue and red bathroom tiles, tins of paint, a couple of broken Hoovers. He jumped as something moved, realised he was looking towards a huge mirror.

Hawkins had two fridges and ten plastic chairs, had inherited a lot of the junk from Joe Martin's mate Dave, the loony who'd fucked off to the coast.

– Come on, sit down, Hawkins said. Relax.

Ray saw a second chair, a twin of the one he remembered, a luxury item that must have cost a few hundred quid. He did as he was told, Hawkins reaching for a blue flask, poured some funny-smelling coffee into a Jog On mug, passing it over. Frank Harper's face stared at Ray, threatening to put him off his beverage.

– I had some sandwiches the wife made, but I've eaten them. Ham and cheese, with sliced tomatoes. She puts pepper in there as well. Spices it up.

Hawkins moved to his chair, sank into the leather, reached down the side and pulled a lever, a footrest raising up. He sipped his coffee.

– I like to get out of the house when I'm not working. My wife's a lovely lady, but never stops talking. Drives me fucking mad after a while.

Ray nodded. Liz was quiet. He wished she had more to say for herself. But every man needed a hideaway. Terry was big into the Union Jack, though it was a bit different, seeing as it was a club. There again, he was taking his time sharing it, moving slowly, hogging the jukebox. This place was different. Hawkins was king, and at ease, but it made Ray nervous. He didn't know why. They sat in silence. There was no noise. He wondered if you could hear a man scream from outside.

– So, Hawkins said. What are we going to do about these drug dealers?

– Not much I can do.

– You remember what I said?

He didn't know what Hawkins meant.

– When I was talking about that bloke from the council. Pick him up off the street and bring him here.

– Terry's dealing with that.

– Fair enough. Maybe that was a bit extreme. But what about the wogs?

– How do you mean?

– Bring them here, or the main one anyway. Give him a

kicking, tie him up, add some Combat 18 posters, and I can get a Terror Machine T-shirt. Shit them right up. They won't say anything then, the fucking grasses.

– You serious?

– Do I look like I'm joking? Hawkins said, narrowing his eyes.

– So they try and make out it was a racial attack and I turn around and try and stop them by pretending I'm Combat 18.

– That's about it. But they won't know it's you, will they? Balaclavas. Hoods. We play the cunts at their own game.

– So I'm doing what the courts tell me. I become what they say I am.

– You are, mate. There's no fucking escape.

Ray thought about this. He had no qualms about doing those drug dealers again, but had already taught them a lesson they would never forget. Maybe it was something to think about, tracking the big cunt down, but he didn't know what was going on out there, doubted Ali C would be sitting around waiting for the thing to escalate. For all Ray knew, they might be planning a reprisal themselves. There again, they wouldn't have grassed if they were going to sort it out themselves.

– No, it's not my style.

– What is your style, then?

Ray sat forward.

– I'm in enough trouble as it is.

– I'm disappointed, Hawkins said.

– How's that? Ray bristled.

– Thought you'd have a bit more in you. Sure, you done the Pakis, but now they're trying to send you to prison.

– It'll only make things worse. Ray was angry now. If they've grassed once, they'll do it again. I don't care about those cunts. I've already dealt with them and it might make things worse. I'm thinking about my kids, Liz, the house. If it was only me I'd do them, wouldn't bother about lock-ups and posters and all that bollocks. I can sort them out myself.

Hawkins thought about this for a minute.

– Maybe you're right. But think about it, will you? Terry's going to be upset about this when he finds out. He might seem like a soft touch, but he isn't. Not when it comes to the crunch. You don't know what he'll do. Could be better if we sort it out first.

They both sat back, stared at the wall, drank their coffee. The longer Ray was in the lock-up, the smaller the place felt. He had been in police cells, but they were lighter and the air moved around, imagined a prison cell would be a lot different. Hawkins had been inside. Maybe that was why he was trying to help him out. He didn't have to, as they weren't close. Ray wondered what Hawkins meant, talking about Terry like that. The air was heavy, needed the door left open for a few hours. He felt nervous, wanted to get away, reached in his pocket and turned his phone on, without Hawkins seeing. It played 'Liquidator' and he took it out.

– Didn't know you could get a signal in here.

– What do you mean? Hawkins asked, laughing. Of course you can get a fucking signal.

It was the office. He answered.

– Are you coming back to work soon? Angie asked.

– Any second, Ray said, relieved for an excuse to leave.

– I've got a Mrs Pepper wants taking from Langley to West Drayton. Her and a friend.

Ray remembered the parrot, the vicious beak inches from the back of his head, those eyes watching him in the mirror, the mind-reading and heavy discipline.

– She asked specially for you, Angie said.

She laughed.

– Asked for the big driver with the mad blue eyes. Said her friend Peter took a shine to you. Said he usually makes a mess when he travels in a car. Does that make sense to you?

– I'll get her, Ray replied.

He stood up and the door began to open.

– I won't come over, Hawkins said, peering outside, looking left and right. Bring the car over, will you.

Ray obeyed, parked as near as he could, popped the boot, went inside, right down the back of the garage, the two men carrying boxes of salt-and-vinegar, cheese-and-onion and ready-salted crisps out, filling the back up.

– I'll drop them off when Terry's not around, Ray said. Buster will let me in.

He shook Hawkins's hand, thanked him, meant it as well, now the door was open and he was in the fresh air.

– Don't forget what I said, Hawkins snapped, eager to close the garage door again.

Ray drove over to Langley, wondering if the nutter's plan would work, and if it meant he stayed out of prison he would be a mug not to give it a go. Maybe that was all that did work, threats and the ability to back them up with force and a power structure, and he only had to look at the Yanks steaming into Afghanistan and Iraq, see how they'd caned the Taliban and spanked Saddam Hussein. The other side was that the problem didn't disappear, and often escalated.

He passed the bus station, dodged a coach that didn't indicate, gave the driver a wanker sign, continued over the roundabouts, turning left eventually, reached another round-about and could see the pub up ahead, the bench where Mrs Pepper sat, surprised by the bright colours of Peter, the parrot out of his cage and refusing to hide under his poncho.

Ray turned right and circled round, saw the bird look his way, was sure it had sensed his arrival, thought he noticed a faint sneer, knew it was his imagination, felt strangely proud that the bird hadn't pissed or pooed in his car, that he had been asked for specially, and he entered the car park by the shops, pulled in opposite the Peppers. He saw a gang of teenagers nearby staring, one of them pulling a face and flapping his arms, and Peter didn't fuck about, took three fast steps along the back of the seat, beak raised, the kids screaming and legging it, Ray impressed with the parrot's direct approach, which seemed more effective than the Dispersal Order the Old Bill had served on the area.

Skinheads a Bash Them

THE UNION JACK CLUB was heaving and the bar staff were struggling to cope with the crush of thirsty drinkers, Buster keeping his staff on their toes, sweat staining his Ben Sherman as he poured, Carol and her friend Tanya in blue Fred Perrys, white piping creasing the collars. The pool tables had been covered and moved back against a wall, a makeshift stage set up in their place, the club's flag brought inside and hung on the wall behind the turntables where Geno Blue and Duke Dale were busy bringing Club Ska to the heart of Slough. Terry watched as some of the younger Chelsea arrived, fresh from a row with Luton at Warren Street, the Young Offenders at the front, working their way towards the bar, ordering fifteen pints of lager. Terry saw his nephew Ray noting their choice of drink, mouthing the words GOOD BOYS to Ian when he turned his way. He thought about telling Ray that lager was a girl's drink, that proper men drank bitter, or light ale, or Guinness – anything but that European piss-water – but decided to let it go.

Terry knew he was dying, but at least he was going out in style. It was as if he was attending the drink-up after his own funeral, except people could see him and have a chat, weren't glum or anything. It was a nice send-off and he had to savour every second. The side effects of the drugs he'd been taking and the after-effects of his treatment had stirred up a lot of memories he'd buried years before. Many of the faces involved were flashing in front of his eyes, but in real life. He stopped thinking about funerals and send-offs and all the rest of it, concentrating on the moment, the music pounding from the speakers, and he'd twigged early, knew a surprise was coming, assumed it would be a party at the house.

As soon as Laurel dropped out of football and Ray took his season, swore he would make an appearance inside the ground, for the visit of Newcastle, his suspicions were confirmed. When Ray suggested stopping by the club on the way back from Chelsea, after a drink in The Cock on North End Road and a ruby at Paddington, he figured it was another delaying tactic, that the sausage rolls and sandwiches weren't ready. It was obvious what was going on and he played along, Hawkins and Buster shooting off after the game, Terry mucking them about, saying it was his birthday, weren't they going to have a pint with him, finally letting them leave, never expecting anything like this. He couldn't believe how much trouble they'd gone to, the amount of people who'd turned out. It was incredible really.

He watched Hawkins leaving the bar, three pint glasses in his hands, thought back to when they were boys at the youth club, sipping tea and munching biscuits, how he'd looked up to the West Indian singers, learnt about the music, and he tried to remember what the place was like inside, the colour of the walls and the smell of the air, and it came back to him, slowly at first, an artist's impression, then more clearly, a sparse little hall with metal or wooden chairs, rickety tables, a dartboard and the pool table, a sink and kettle in a small kitchen. He saw Christmas tree lights and a record player, speakers and a crackling microphone, chairs arranged close to the longest wall, tables folded up, and the picture was sharp suddenly, and looking at the bloke Hawkins was handing one of the glasses to, he frowned, clicked, couldn't believe it, hurried over and shook the hand of Rob The Mod. Their faces cracked and Terry couldn't stop shaking his head.

Rob had the same haircut and looked great, like Ronnie Wood, told Terry he was living in Basingstoke, had heard about tonight through a mate at his scooter club, recognised the name, got in touch with Alan and decided to come and say hello. It must've been thirty years since they'd seen each other, and Terry was pleased to see he was as smart as ever, smarter probably, and they talked for ages, shared their stories, Rob handing Terry a card with his address and number, a line drawing of a man and his records, Terry glancing over and seeing his son and his mates by the jukebox, peering into the machine, and it was an incredible feeling, to see so many friends and family in one place, everyone together. He could almost drift away in his sleep tonight, if it wasn't for his children.

The Union Jack would survive. If people understood that the red, white and blue was about having a drink and a laugh, about sticking together and not letting the outsiders divide you, it would fly in the alleyway outside come rain or shine. It was the young who would have to keep the club going, eventually, and he had confidence in the nation's youth, didn't believe the shit written about them in the papers, had heard it all before. His daughters passed and he introduced them to Rob, the man who had educated him about music and, really, had influenced his life. They were bubbly and funny and just like their mum, knew about the classic records and performers – like Lol, they'd had no choice. April wasn't here tonight. He couldn't feel or smell or hear or sense her. She was somewhere else. If there was an after-life he would see her then, and he felt as if a cloud was passing, moving on and fading away. Angie came and stood nearby, Frank handed over a pint and Steve offered him a bowl of crisps, one of many he'd noticed placed around the club. He hoped they wouldn't end up trodden into the carpet. He finished his drink and Angie reached for his empty, Terry moving onto Frank's glass.

Ray slapped Terry on the back, and they joked and wound each other up like a couple of kids, and even though Ray was going to prison, for a couple of hours he wasn't going to think about it, just be with his uncle and the boys. The drug-dealing scum had got what they deserved, and if he saw them again, maybe they'd get some more. Next time, there'd be no more Mr Nice Guy. He started laughing. That was his problem. He was too easygoing. And Terry looked at his nephew and was pleased he was so happy. He worried about Ray, wanted to tell him he was dying, ask his advice on how he should break the news to the children, but now wasn't the right time. It was strange how things changed, because he felt great, couldn't believe he was near the end of his life.

Ray glanced across the room and noticed a fit-looking bird, and she was walking his way, a Beki Bondage sex machine. He couldn't help himself, loved punk birds, thought of the Norwegian who'd done a runner at London Callin', the girls he'd known in the past, proper sorts who'd livened up the likes of The Electric Ballroom and The Clarendon. He thought about Liz and smiled, saw her when they were younger, and she had been something special, really made the effort. Sex in stilettos. He'd had to tell her about his nicking, how he'd done the Ali Cs, been accused of all sorts. She sat there in their bedroom, the door closed, wide-eyed at first, saying nothing, her head lowered so she was staring at the carpet, and finally she stood up and came over, sat on his knee and wrapped her arms around his neck, kissed him on the mouth, the best kiss he'd ever tasted. They had slept together and it was as if something had sparked inside her. She promised to visit him in prison, wherever he was sent, glad he'd battered those fucking drug dealers, and afterwards, dressed and sitting downstairs, she was hesitant, holding back. He didn't know what would happen next, but sensed it was a one-off.

This woman coming his way had something about her, was different from the others in the room, and he followed her as she moved through the crowd, easing past the admiring glances of the skinheads filling the place, the pockets of scruffs and herberts, Handsome and their sleazy psychobilly mate Paul who licked his lips, and he saw females frowning, not appreciating the competition. The way she moved reminded him of Liz, ten or fifteen years ago, and his balls jumped as he realised it *was* Liz. It was mental. She might be thirty-four, with two kids under her belt, but she was fit and looking like the girl he married. She'd thrown away the tracksuit and housewife leisure-wear, returned to the essentials of peroxide hair, PVC skirt and fishnets. He saw Joe in his Demolition Dancing T-shirt, doing a double take and almost drooling as he watched her pass by. She came and stood next to Ray, didn't say a word, reached for his pint and took a gulp, handed it back, lowered her hand and, unseen in the crowd, gave his nuts a healthy squeeze.

'Liquidator' filled the club, the trance-like energy and terrace-culture relevance of the song bringing the generations together, tightening a tribe that had to stay united against its enemies. Terry smiled at his youth and April and married life and middle age, knew life didn't stop until the rude boy with the scythe came and tapped you on the shoulder, till his pork-pie hat stretched to a topper, and he was going to make every single breath count. He was happy. The Union Jack Club was up and running, a place where the firm could socialise, and others would come along, word would spread, and he wondered what the Pole thought, sitting in the shadows with his coffee and cigar, a glass of vodka or pint of bitter, and he wondered how many spirits were with them at this moment, and he would be with the ghosts soon, sitting at a table earwigging conversations, maybe joining in the talk that went on in the subconscious of the living.

Ray remembered the kicking in Southall and the drug dealers decades later, and he had defended himself, been labelled a nutter, and he would have to serve his time, fight to stay positive, keep out of trouble, and Liz had offered him a lifeline, his arm around her waist, but he knew the drink was making things look better than they were, that it was going to be tough, but even so, he would have time on his hands, wouldn't be working or out drinking, and he would definitely go back to the first serious fiction he'd read, excited when he thought about rereading Orwell and Huxley and Sillitoe, like maybe he needed ideas and suggestions more than pages of facts . . . and Terry saw the crowd, skinheads from the ages of fifty down to their teens, fathers and sons and wives and girlfriends, people from football and music, black faces in with the white, Oi The Sikh, the scooter boys who gave April her escort to the cremation . . . and Lol looked at the LOVE and HATE tattoos on the knuckles of Hawkins, told Angie that summed his dad and Ray up . . . Dad was LOVE and Ray was HATE . . . and she listened, shook her head, said no, explained that skins were more than an easy slogan . . . Ray wasn't about hate, as he didn't sneer or hurt people without a reason, he was just angry, the same as a lot of other people, but more extreme, and honest, and she laughed, paused . . . said his dad had passion, and that was better than love, stronger . . . he had a passion for life, and Lol nodded his head, not sure if she was right.

She was still thinking, looked away, turned her head back.

Angie told him that maybe Ray was angry because he loved life, and maybe his dad was passionate because he was angry, asking if that made sense? They were two sides of the same coin. You couldn't have one without the other. She looked at him and smiled. Perhaps you're a bit of both? She laughed and patted him on the arm and Lol blushed as electricity raced along her fingers and through long painted nails. Angie was beautiful. It was obvious she was in love with his dad, everyone could see it, everyone except Dad, and he would never realise either, and if he did find out he wouldn't do anything about it, which was a shame. Lol missed his mum, but she was dead and never coming back. He didn't think Dad should be on his own for ever. He had another twenty or thirty or forty years ahead of him, and he looked at Dad and saw his smile widening as some familiar faces from Brentford appeared, Kev The Kev and his mates further on, waving and calling him over.

Out and About

IT WAS THE TUESDAY after his birthday and Terry English had a busy afternoon ahead. He had two problems and had to step forward and sort them out. First thing Monday morning he'd put in a couple of phone calls, doing his best to smooth the way. The first approach went as he'd feared, the expression 'you must be fucking joking' sticking in his mind. It was a shame. He kept replaying the voice in his head, and the more he listened the more angry he became. He would have to make sure he stayed in control. He had an objective. Even so, he was encouraged. Big mouths didn't make the bravest men. The second call was much more friendly, as expected, and he'd gone into the details, explained the situation, the cause and what was true and what was a lie, hoped he'd left nothing out, had been on the phone for over twenty minutes, the two men ending the call on the same terms as when it began. Even so, this second meet was the one that worried him the most.

Three o'clock would always be kick-off time in Terry's world, and he left the house with fifteen minutes to spare. He was dressed smartly, as if attending a business meeting – white Ben Sherman, black loafers, his favourite Crombie, a coat that carried shades of the legendary London villains. He smiled at his reflection, split by the crack in the mirror, enjoyed this element in the traditional skinhead look, and it was something he had appreciated from when he was a kid, the dodgy geezers in Shepherd's Bush and Brentford, pilgrimages over to the old East End, stories boys heard about the Krays and Richardsons. He wouldn't want to be compared to one of today's cinema crooks, where grown men hugged each other like Sicilian mobsters. He knew the connection went back further, into the Thirties and Forties, but didn't understand this new wave of English actors hugging each other. The originals were Sicilians and Italians, and it was in their culture to hug each other. If Hawkins or Buster tried that on, they'd end up with a thick ear.

It was a sign of the times, respecting people who hurt others for money, blokes without morals who didn't care about the results of their actions, just as long as they had that latest fashion accessory. Their admirers were as bad. It was pathetic. He had no time for the gangster industry, agreed with Ray sorting those drug dealers out, wished he'd known so he could have helped. They were scum and deserved a kicking, Ray telling him what had happened on the Sunday night, when they went in to tidy the club up.

They were playing pool, Lol doing a final hoover, Buster and Angie drying the last glasses, Hawkins nowhere to be seen, the Union Jack back to its best. He wasn't shocked, could only promise to look after Liz and the kids if Ray went to prison. He couldn't tell him about his own troubles, that he might not have long left. Ray didn't need to worry about money, as Terry would cover everything, and he could pay him back one day, if he wanted. Terry was embarrassed by his nephew's thanks, would check his will meantime, make sure Ray was looked after properly. He turned back to the table, potted a couple of balls, took his time lining up the shots. The Hoover faded into the background and he was in his own world, an idea firm by the time he potted the black. He didn't say anything to his nephew. Didn't want to raise his hopes.

Dead on three Terry pressed the buzzer on the entry-phone and waited. The machine snapped and hummed and he announced a special delivery from Japan, a package that needed the signature of a Robert Slater. There was arrogance in the voice that told him to leave it in the letter box, Terry politely explaining that the parcel was urgent and its contents valuable, and that his company had been specifically hired to deliver the item by hand. He couldn't leave it without a signature and proof of identity. It was more than his job was worth. There was a brief pause, no more words, the hum cut off and the gate slowly opening, black bars moving towards a bank of exotic plants, their long light-green leaves lined with slashes of gold.

Terry listened to the crunch of gravel under his tyres, a sound he found relaxing, but he couldn't pretend he wasn't nervous. That was all it was – nerves. He wasn't scared or in two minds about what needed doing. He thought of his old man, how he didn't rant or rave when something bad happened, didn't threaten or even criticise. He was a man of action and did what was needed. People who didn't know him might have seen his mild manner as a sign of weakness, but his son learnt the truth. His father had an inner strength Terry could never touch, but he felt he'd inherited some of his determination, stopped outside the house, checked his mirror and was pleased to see that the gate had been left open. There were cameras on the front of the building, but he didn't care, expected a place this size to be well protected.

He turned the engine off and walked quickly, with his head down, to the front door, which was open and showing a man in his mid-thirties. He was Terry's height, but lighter and fitter, with black hair and a pink face. Terry was giving away fifteen years and guessed it could be close in a fist fight, but he wasn't bothered or taking any chances, carried a cardboard box, saw Slater's eyes move towards it, noticed the chain around his neck, trying to see what sort of man he was dealing with, couldn't work him out, and the box was long and open and he reached in and pulled out a plum.

He pointed the shotgun at Slater's head, moving forward and pressing the barrels between his eyes, so he could feel the cold reality of what was happening.

The weak needed to even the odds up occasionally. George knew the score. No point fucking about. War was about winning, not the taking part. It wasn't a game of football, some honourable contest. It was butchery. When Terry was fifteen and facing bigger and older boys, he wanted a result, nothing else. The young needed to even things up a bit as well, specially with that bloke trying to nick April off him. Funny, he couldn't even remember his name, and it had come to nothing in the end, but he was never going to end up on the losing side. Now he was fifty years old and carrying a shooter, like Harry May, because you reached a time when you were up against fitter and younger men so, again, he needed some insurance. Slater was another bully and this thing was important. There was only going to be one winner. He had no qualms.

The man's arms were out by his sides as he tried to pacify the stranger, inching backwards as Terry motioned with quick nods, turning round when he was told, hands in the air now like something out a war film.

Terry saw his old man on French soil with rifles pointed at him, didn't know what happened after that, and he must have been terrified, thought he was going to be executed, buried in a ditch, but instead they sent him to a prison camp where he was with other Englishmen, but he remembered Dad screaming in the darkness, wondered if it was for his burnt mates, didn't know if the bomber had crash-landed, if that was even possible, or whether Dad had baled out, if he was wounded, maybe the Germans shot some of his friends in front of him, and Dad had been haunted by his experience, the same as Terry was haunted by April's crash. There were times when these horrors pressed in, burst through and caused chaos.

Terry and Slater were standing in the middle of a big white room, large photographs of skyscrapers and sunny beaches dotted around the walls, pictures that looked expensive and impersonal and meaningless. There was a chance someone else would be in the house, but Terry didn't think so. Angie told him the electoral register showed Slater living alone and there was only one car in the drive. It was the single thing that would make him back off. He was determined. He was also reckless, taking a chance, but didn't see it that way, just didn't care. He had nothing to lose, and if things went pear-shaped, at least he'd tried. He was holding himself together, but his anger was on the verge of breaking out. He told Slater to kneel down, which he did. Terry hit him between the shoulder blades with the butt, shouted at him to stay still, stood to the man's right and pressed the barrels to his temple.

Slater's arse went and he started begging that he didn't want to die, that Terry should take anything he wanted. He was no player, just another chancer.

The field wasn't worth a lot and Terry wasn't looking to con anyone, and none of this was necessary. The problem could have been sorted out with a sit-down, some dialogue, the same as with Marston, the bloke dishing out drink and music licences, someone who didn't understand what the Union Jack Club was about, the essence of skinhead music. He had taken Angie and gone and seen him, explained things. Marston was fine. It was just different worlds. Problems were best sorted out over a pint, or a mug of hot tea, like men. But this cunt in front of him – bullying an old man like Roy – trying to break the horses up – just because Roy and the animals couldn't defend themselves – because they were bottom of Slater's bloody totem pole.

He cracked the bloke in the face with the shotgun, kicked him a few times, the wanker sprawling across his plush white carpet, blood from his nose staining it with a splash of red, and the skinhead stood over Slater, and he could have been an estate agent or City boy or small-time criminal, there was no difference. He definitely wasn't a proper villain, which was a relief. Terry explained what he wanted and what would happen if he didn't get it, the choices Slater had to make. Then he walked out of the house.

He drove away casually, even though he was tempted to put his foot down. In the house he had been fine, but now he could feel his heart pounding, his hands wet with sweat. He wiped them on a hanky, but didn't stop, was soon through the acres of detached houses and patches of old woodland, following a lane and returning to more built-up areas, the traffic returning and thickening as he was sucked back into the commotion of Slough. He stopped at a red light and his breathing was easier, heart quieter, hands dry, an Estuary driver passing the other way, though he couldn't see who it was, the light changing so he could continue and turn right, pulling over and parking in front of a parade of shops.

His phone vibrated in his pocket. It was Hawkins. He read the text.

– I am thirsty!

He turned it off.

He sat in the Merc for half an hour, killing time, and he had no rush of confusion, none of the worries he had been experiencing, was happy to wait, watching the people pass by, a fair few disappearing into a Polish bakery, attracted by the neat red-and-white sign over the door. There was Polish food for sale in the windows, posters for Polish techno on a nearby lamp-post, Polish men and women munching cakes near his car. A second wave of Poles had definitely arrived in Slough. He wondered what the Polish spirits in the Union Jack Club thought, if Big Frank had a view, if any of the new arrivals were related to the war generation and, most importantly, if they knew their history.

Would he have done the nasty if Slater had fought back? He was sure he had it in him. It was nice to be nice, but sometimes you had to make a stand. Slater could grass him up to the Old Bill, and if he did Terry didn't have a leg to stand on, but he had sworn that if this happened Slater would be dead inside a week. It was all about front, the hard-man image, the other person's expectations. Terry English looked the part, and as every skinhead knew, appearance was important. He would buy the field at a fair price or Slater would end up shot. His first problem had either been sorted out, or was about to escalate.

He moved on and was soon parking outside The Taj, two doors down from Chapatti Express, part of the Harry Ram empire. It was only half past five, early yet, and the restaurant wouldn't pick up for a while. In fact, it was empty when he walked in, except for two waiters and Harry sitting at the back, in one of the booths Terry liked, a bottle of Jack Daniels on the table in front of him. They shook hands and one of the waiters brought over a pint of lager. He preferred Carlsberg, which had been the traditional curry-house beverage when he was growing up, but couldn't blame the boys peddling this Cobra. It was fine. He wasn't a lager man, but once he was in a curry house didn't consider anything else. Mind you, he wasn't worried about the lager in his glass, and specially not the make, as he had more important things on his mind.

Terry had explained the basics over the phone – that his nephew Ray had been arrested; what he had been charged with; what he admitted; the name of the leader of the three boys who had made statements against him; the reason Ray had attacked them in the first place; the age of his daughter.

Harry knew everyone, was Slough born and bred. He also knew the name of the man selling drugs. He had said he would make a couple of calls.

– Do you remember when we were boys? Harry asked.

Terry nodded. They'd gone to school together, played football in the playground from the age of eleven. They lived different lives when they were in their mid-teens and older, came from different cultures, but said hello whenever they saw each other, and Terry had been coming in this place for well over a quarter of a century, their friendship lasting the years in a specific location. Post-war England was a different time, and if you were a Pakistani or a Bangladeshi boy he knew it could be hard, that some of those lads had had the shit kicked out of them. The Asians ran areas now, and there were bullies in their ranks as well, rude boys who racially abused and attacked whites, threatened to stab them up for no good reason, and while it was sad, the truth was most people didn't behave that way, just got on with each other and their lives. That was the Slough he knew.

– I remember walking home and a gang of whites with a black lad was going to kick my head in, calling me a smelly Paki.

Terry felt his half-dreams, his doubts and guilt.

– It's hard to go against your own people, but you did it, Harry said. Do you remember? You stopped them.

The pictures came into focus, but they were vague. He was pleased he had behaved properly.

– It meant more to me than to you, Harry said, laughing, but you could have easily turned away, not run to catch up, backed off when that boy argued and pushed you, but you told him to fuck off, pushed him back, said that I was your mate. You could have lost your friends, been beaten up as well, anything. The rest nodded and walked on, as if nothing had happened.

Terry knew what Harry was like, that he was quickly sidetracked, went off into different stories, making a joke of things. It was the English way. But he was being direct, to the point.

– Drugs are no good. The boy you told me about, I know his family. I spoke to his uncle. He knows it is the truth about the drugs. The boy has been caught before, by his father. He will withdraw his statement and so will the others. He has shamed his family. It is done now.

It seemed too simple. It couldn't be this easy, surely. Terry had expected to have to persuade Harry that everything he said was right, maybe meet someone else, offer money even, and if that failed, he would track the youth down and try and do the job himself. It couldn't be this simple. And yet it was.

– Thanks, Terry began. Thanks . . . I owe you one.

– No, you don't owe me anything, Harry said, reaching for the menu. Let's not talk of this again. I'm hungry.

His eyes were looking at the menu and Terry understood, knew how he felt, but he had done him a big favour. Terry raised his pint and drank a mouthful, a plate of poppadoms appearing from nowhere, a tray of pickles following. He was a bitter drinker, but this lager tasted like heaven. He was suddenly very hungry, lifted the menu up and inspected the contents, even though he already knew what he was going to order.

Splash Down

Two weeks later Terry was turning suedehead. His hair was back with a vengeance and he felt stronger than he had done for years, the drizzle coating his head so he imagined he was halfway to an Afro. He ran a hand over his bonce and skimmed the water away, a stray current running down his face, making him blink as it shunted sideways and rested in the corner of his eye, an inky prison tattoo bursting with the sort of joy only a reprieved man can feel. He stood with his right hand out, Bob and Molly lifting sugar lumps from his palm. The field was his and the horses were safe. They could live out the rest of their days together in peace.

It was a perfect Sunday morning, bright and crisp and fresh and quiet. He looked over the field and the air was clear and cool. He gulped it down, knew it was going to be a good day. He was a lucky man, John Jones swearing a human being's will to live could conquer anything, that doctors could only scratch the surface of the physical. He remained puzzled. They had tried different approaches, never been certain what was wrong. Something had clicked and the clouds had passed.

Terry went back indoors and made himself a cup of tea, two pieces of toast, loading them up with strawberry jam, the seedless variety, ran through the football scores in the paper, read every match report before skimming a Kate Moss story. It was nine when he heard Lol moving around upstairs, gave the boy a shout and went in the kitchen, raided the fridge and stuck some sausages under the grill, chopped up a carton of mushrooms, added oil to the frying pan, waited till it was spitting and dropped in four rashers of bacon and the mushrooms. Moving faster than Jaimie Oliver on a baked-bean vindaloo, he popped four slices of bread in the toaster and a tin of tomatoes in a small pan, grabbed a plate and lined it up on the table with knife, fork, salt, pepper, ketchup, brown sauce and the remains of a Chapatti Express tub of lime pickle. He was a blur as he moved the sausages, bacon, mushrooms and tomatoes to the plate, cracked a couple of eggs in the still-hot frying pan, thereby saving on washing up, positioned two slices of toast, added the fried eggs once they were ready, and carried it over to the table. Laurel arrived on cue and sat down, dived into the Full English.

– Your toast will be ready in a second, Terry said, buttering the two remaining slices.

– Thanks, Dad, I'm starving. You not having any?

– I'm going round your Auntie Liz's for dinner. She invited you as well, but I told her you were busy.

Lol cut into his bacon and eggs, added brown sauce. His dad might have been king of the takeaways, the sort of man who struggled to make a cheese sandwich, but when it came to a fry-up he was the master. He seemed a lot happier recently, like he used to be, so maybe turning fifty had been harder than he said. He still didn't act his age, and Lol hoped that when *he* was fifty he would be the same, and he was looking forward to a good practice session, Dad trusting him with the keys to the club, The Thinkers picking him up, Matt's big brother Jack driving. He was going to make the most of the place while he could, as it wouldn't be long before the firm moved in and they started opening for the Sunday session.

– She's making Yorkshire pudding, his dad added, talking to himself.

Terry washed the dishes and went upstairs, made his bed and brushed his teeth, left at half-eleven, couldn't resist, tapped in 'Judge Dread Dances The Pardon'. First stop was Ray's house, and as soon as he pulled up the front door opened, his nephew marching down the path, April riding up on her bike, Terry lowering the window so she could lean in to give him a kiss on the cheek, Chelsea jumping off the wall where she was sitting, talking to some other girls, coming over and saying hello.

– I'm gagging for a pint, Ray announced, once he was in the passenger seat.

– You and me both.

They were soon sitting outside The General Elliott, waiting for the doors to open, the first ones in, ordering and settling down by the window, with a view of the canal outside, thirsty men following them in. London Pride and Fosters sat between Terry and Ray, two packets of peanuts spilling over the table. They took their time, enjoying the slow pace of a Sunday pint, the reward every working man deserved at the end of a long hard week.

– What time are we leaving on Tuesday? Ray asked.

– One o'clock. Terminal One. I'll sort out a couple of cabs.

– We got tickets?

– Everything's sorted out. Five-star hotel as well.

Chelsea were playing in Italy. The European games were a long way from the Second Division days, and specially the years between Eddie McCreadie leaving and the arrival of John Neal. Grim football, but a good laugh off the pitch. Dark nights in northern streets had been replaced by the glitz of Europe. Ray preferred the likes of Scandinavia, Holland, Belgium, down into Germany, the beer cheap in Poland and Russia. He wasn't so keen on Portugal, Spain, France, Italy. Turkey and Greece were even worse. But Milan and a visit to the San Siro couldn't be turned down. All the boys were going – Terry, Ray, Handsome, Pychobilly Paul, Buster, Hawkins, Frank, the Young Offenders, some of the other Estuary lads.

– We should've gone down in a convoy. Estuary Cars on tour.

– It's a long old hike to Italy. Don't want the motors smashed up.

– Yeah, those fucking Eyeties love a defenceless target. Picking off people on their own and stabbing them. Fucking scum.

– What about Luca and Franco and Bobby Di Matteo?

– True, they're gentlemen, and I don't think of the Italians in the same way since they came over, but those ultras, or whatever they call themselves, they're fucking wankers.

Terry was thinking.

– We should do it for a laugh one day. Next time we play in Holland or Belgium.

– You only need to take four or five cars. Ten cars would handle everyone on the books.

– It would mean a dip in business.

– Four cars means sixteen of us. That'll do. Book a hotel with a car park, keep them off the street.

Everyone wanted to have a go at the famous Chelsea hooligans and there were plenty of people ready to oblige. If Chelsea had been in Europe back in the Eighties it would have been mental, but Ray had to admit things could still be pretty naughty, even if the numbers were usually heavily stacked agains the Pride of London.

– Liz give you the okay? Terry smirked. You've only been back a week.

– I don't need permission, Ray laughed. I do what I want.

He raised his glass and felt the lager flow through him. He was reading *Brave New World* again, having already dealt with *Nineteen Eighty-Four*. It was odd, but he was picking up a lot more in the novels, and even though the predictions of Orwell and Huxley had come true, he felt their messages were more important than ever. They couldn't be described as fantasy any more. He compared soma and ecstasy, test-tube babies and mass abortion, the abolition of parenthood and the rise of one-parent families, mindless dances and today's dance music, thought crime and political correctness, Big Brother and *Big Brother*, the erasing of attachment and the destruction of personal responsibility.

– She was fine about it, he admitted. Said I should go while I still can. Jose could leave and Roman sell up and we'll be looking forward to Rotherham Away. Mind you, I preferred those days. Never got too upset if we won or lost.

– Easy, Terry warned.

– There were games I hoped we'd lose so there'd be a riot.

– That's terrible.

Ray shook his head. He was a lot different these days. And his uncle had given him a second chance, sorting things out with Harry, getting the accusations and charges dropped.

Terry was pleased Ray was back home with his family, keeping his head down and staying out of trouble, hoped it would last. His nephew had to hold his tongue sometimes, chew his lip if need be, but couldn't change his feelings, his manner or beliefs. Liz was more like her old self, and he saw her sitting in this pub years ago, and she had been a punk rocker with plenty to say, a pint of cider in her hand. Her and Ray had argued, kissed and made up. People were made different. He had to laugh, Handsome pleased to see the back of Ray, telling Terry that the bloke had been driving him mad. No offence intended.

– Hair's a bit long, Ray remarked. You going for the finhead look?

– I'm getting it cut, don't worry. Can't go to football like this, can I?

Ray emptied his glass and Terry followed his example. He watched his nephew walk over to the bar, leaning down so that his eyes were level with the barmaid, standing with his neck pushed forward, the same as when he was a boy, questioning everything. Even as a kid he'd had the same nervous energy, used to get angry when something was unfair, and there was a lot of unfairness in the world. In another situation Ray could have been an inventor or a philosopher, but most people didn't have the confidence or push or chance. Even so, life was sweet.

Terry was going to concentrate on the Union Jack Club, get it running properly. There was potential there, for a proper drinking club and a pool hall, and music was a possibility. Slough had been crying out for a decent venue ever since he could remember. A regular ska night was a must. It was a fresh challenge. More than anything, it would be a laugh.

When they went back to the house Liz did them proud, and sitting down for Sunday dinner with Ray and his family Terry remembered the good times with April, when his own girls were growing up and Laurel was small, passing the gravy around, his favourite the Yorkshires, and they'd had their problems along the way but his children had turned out great. Ray and Liz were both making an effort and Chelsea and April were obviously happy to have their dad home. It was a fine Sunday roast, up there with the Full English and his Chapatti Express deliveries.

When Terry left it was after five, the Nutter Family sitting in front of the television, watching *Lady and the Tramp*, and he drove along listening to 'Skinhead Girl', feeling full and content.

The sun was sinking, but it was still sunny and the sky remained clear. Summer wasn't far away and he was glad. Three nights ago April had come to him in his sleep, yet it was much more than a dream, more real than everyday life. He was walking down a long empty street, avoiding the reflections in the windows, eyes straight ahead, water filling the gutters lining the rooftops above. He saw traffic lights and was soon at a crossroads, glanced right and saw a coach approaching. He looked in at the people sitting by the windows and saw April at the back, and suddenly the world was electric and sparks were flying off the roofs, everything in colour for a few seconds as she smiled and blew him a kiss, the coach passing and shrinking and vanishing. She was leaving him again and he knew that she wanted him to enjoy his life while he could, had returned to help him move on. Before he knew it they would be together again. He woke with water covering his face, tears soaking his pillow. He felt sad lying in his bed, but gradually he began to feel happy.

He ran a hand over his hair, after all these years unable to get used to anything over a Number 2. It was really bothering him, now it had grown back, not exactly hippie style but pushing smoothie. He pulled up outside Angie's flat and went up to her front door. She'd said half-five and he was five minutes early, didn't think she would mind. He pressed the buzzer three times before she opened the door. She looked at her watch and smiled.

– Hello, she said, standing aside so he could enter. You're early.

The television was on in the front room, the volume turned down. 'Jay Moon Walk' was playing. He noted the turntable, the spinning 45.

– Do you want a drink? You like London Pride, don't you?

– Tea will do me, ta.

– Go on, I bought a couple of bottles for you.

– Well, seeing as you went to the trouble.

She went in the kitchen and Terry glanced around the room. She had done it up nicely and he was impressed to see framed photos of Desmond Dekker and Prince Buster and Laurel Aitken, each one dedicated and signed. He jumped when he spotted Judge Dread, the king of rude reggae. It was another one that was dedicated, this time TO THE BEAUTIFUL ANGIE. He smiled, saw a picture of her when she was younger, early twenties maybe, sitting on the back of a scooter, arms around the waist of boy in a flight-jacket. He wondered if she'd been married, or was engaged now, had a boyfriend maybe, but didn't like to ask. She was a fine-looking woman and if he was younger, well, who knows what might have happened. But she could have any man she wanted and was never going to be interested in the likes of him.

– Do you want a sandwich? she asked, coming back into the room.

– No, it's all right.

She held out a glass and a bottle, which he took.

– Crisps, peanuts, a biscuit?

– No thanks, I had dinner round Ray's house. He's back with Liz.

Angie opened a bag and took out her clippers. The room was full of memorabilia and he realised he knew very little about his employee, that her love of ska and the skinhead world was deeper than he'd thought. She positioned a chair in the middle of the room and patted it, and he took his coat off, sat down. She wrapped a towel around his neck.

– I'm looking forward to this, he said.

Angie started at the back, working her way around his right side, was soon standing in front of him, her breasts inches from his face. He did his best to think of something else, tried the ugly mug of his old mate Hawkins, as that was enough to make anyone feel sick, saw a craggy geezer sitting at a bar, only problem being that it was in Thailand, baseball cap pulled down against the sun seeping in from outdoors, a girl in a skimpy leotard rubbing his leg. That wasn't working. He thought of Buster pouring a pint, taking his time, Terry lifting it and walking over to the Union Jack tables, his pool cue sending the white down the table, smashing into the black, and Angie moved nearer, clippers gliding across his skull. It was no use. There was a lot of pressure in his groin and he was going red, tried to focus on a pile of 45s, flicking through Big Shot, Joe and Bamboo labels, the scratched memories of a boy looking at the moon, wondering if one day he would walk on its surface, some day in the future when rocket travel was the same as catching a bus, when there were no more wars and no more poverty, like the politicians promised, a day when he could just bounce along and play with gravity, a spaceman who would live for ever, medicine curing every disease ever invented, a grown man doing his skinhead moonstomp. He had lowered his eyes, admired Angie's hips, heard the sound of her voice above the razor, half-listening, answering, mind elsewhere, going through the Full English routine, adding some bubble and squeak, a nice mix of cold potatoes and cabbage and sprouts, moved towards his jukebox, shuffling vinyl, saw Angie leaning over the machine, checking his selections – in a black skirt and stockings.

Terry was a big man with many passions. Angie stopped to adjust the razor. He raised his head, saw the faces of Laurel and Desmond Dekker and Prince Buster, the turntable spinning, needle silent, stuck in a groove at the back of the record. A radio was on in the kitchen, voices playing in the background.

– They keep getting clogged up, Angie said, pulling at the flex and moving behind him.

He was glad of a breather. If she glanced down she wouldn't have been able to miss the bulge in his Levis. Maybe she'd noticed already, but he didn't think so. He heard a radio far away in the distance, talking about oil and death squads and fundamentalism. He switched off, looked at the pattern in Angie's couch, followed the ridges and tried to imagine a freezing Scottish mountain range, wind and sleet slashing at granite, ice packing his ears and mouth and balls. It was working. He was her boss. He didn't want her thinking he was a pervert.

– Come on, Angie coaxed. Chin up.

His eyes nearly popped. Several buttons were loose on her shirt and he couldn't miss the healthy swell of her breasts, the frilly black lace of a low-cut bra adding to her cleavage. He wasn't thinking about his barnet, closed his eyes, could feel her hands stroking his head, gently moving over the stubble, down to his temples. The ice in his jeans melted.

– You're an original, Mr English. An original.

It didn't make any sense, but he had to admit that maybe she really did fancy him after all. He could be wrong, but he didn't think so.

– Pure class. One hundred per cent skinhead.

Angie eased his head forward so it rested on her breasts, rolling her fingernails over the back of his skull and down his neck, tracing lines that oozed knowledge and wisdom, massaging his shoulders, finally easing the Estuary general upright and reaching for the front of his Levis. She smiled as he lifted his head, her lips inches from his mouth, carefully easing his belt loose. She jumped back, glanced down and opened her eyes wide, smiled a cheeky smile, began whistling 'Big Nine' by Judge Dread. Terry loved Judge Dread, the king of rude reggae, but he wasn't thinking about the Brixton bouncer right now. She pressed her lips to his mouth and any lingering sadness drained into his subconscious, where it belonged. He heard the radio talking about torture and murder and drugs and a bomb somewhere, but he wasn't really listening. He had more important things on his mind.